D0184286

RITA BRADSHAW

# *Beyond the Veil of Tears*

MACMILLAN

First published 2014 by Macmillan
an imprint of Pan Macmillan, a division of Macmillan Publishers Limited
Pan Macmillan, 20 New Wharf Road, London N1 9RR
Basingstoke and Oxford
Associated companies throughout the world
www.panmacmillan.com

ISBN 978-0-230-76621-1



1 3 5 7 9 8 6 4 2

A CIP catalogue record for this book is available from the British Library.

Typeset by Ellipsis Digital Limited, Glasgow
Printed and bound by CPI Group (UK) Ltd, Croydon, CR0 4YY

For my wonderful grandchildren –
Sam and Connor, Georgia and Emily, and Reece.

I pray for you always, precious ones, and hope life
will hold God's blessing and joy in abundance and great
happiness. May you always have the courage to stand up
for what you believe is right, and the strength to
be yourselves in this fast-changing world.

You are the future, my darlings, and I love you more
than words can say.

While researching this book I soon discovered how little I knew about 'Lunacy, Liberty and the Mad-Doctors in Victorian England'.

I drew material from many sources, but special thanks must go to Cara Sunderland, MA, Museum Curator of the Fieldhead Hospital in West Yorkshire, and to Dr Michael Finn, Post-Doctoral Research Fellow, School of Philosophy, Religion and History of Science, University of Leeds. As always, huge thanks to my lovely husband, Clive, for gathering reams from the Internet, too!

Books that deserve a mention for their wonderful content are: *Inconvenient People* by Sarah Wise, and *Stanley Royd Hospital, Wakefield, One Hundred And Fifty Years: A History* by A.L. Ashworth, AHA.

# *Author's Note*

I had absolutely no idea of the horrors of the old lunatic asylums until a sentence or two on a news programme set me thinking. The result was the idea behind this story, and a personal journey for me, into a world that was both disturbing and harrowing.

Before the nineteenth century, and in the absence of any curative treatment, public and professional attitudes veered towards the opinion that mental illness was somehow the fault of the individual – a spiritual weakness. Sometimes the manifestations of this disease were attributed to evil demons that had possessed the soul, and the cruel punishments that were inflicted on some unfortunates are among the worst records of man's inhumanity towards his fellow beings.

In Britain, apart from private madhouses – many of sinister repute – little existed beside Bethlem Royal Hospital in London, known as Bedlam. This grim institution became a macabre tourist attraction where, for the fee of one penny, genteel society could mock the strange and terrible antics of the inhabitants and watch them being bled or beaten.

In 1774 Parliament passed an Act for the regulation of private madhouses, and a further Act in 1808 – the County Asylums Act – legislated that counties should establish institutions for the care of pauper lunatics. However, it was customary for mechanical restraints to be used, such as straitjackets, muzzles to prevent patients biting, and chains and iron manacles to prevent them harming themselves and others, along with purgings, bleedings, beatings and sometimes starvation; and each ward held the dreaded padded cell.

These sprawling institutions were often self-contained, isolated villages in their own right, cut off from the outside world and cloaked in dark mystery to outsiders. And their remote locations tended to make visiting the patients difficult, particularly for the poor.

One of the most horrific aspects that has come to light in recent years is that 30 per cent of the asylum population was unjustly incarcerated, without crime or due cause, often by members of their own family who had 'inconvenient' relatives, wives or husbands they wished to get rid of. These patients could be imprisoned for months, for years and sometimes even for life, amid those who were genuinely insane.

By the middle of the 1800s restraint was beginning to be questioned by more enlightened and humane doctors as a form of treatment, but the fact that the Lunacy Act of 1890 provided for the use, under 'careful medical supervision', of both mechanical restraint and seclusion speaks volumes.

As the century neared its close, campaigners for the improved property rights of married women – and for the greater freedom of women in general – seized the lunacy–liberty issue and rolled it into a larger battle. But the twentieth century saw the 'new' cure of electric-shock treatment come to the fore (although electric eels and electric fish had been used by people in ancient times to treat mental illness). ECT, or electroconvulsive therapy, sent patients into violent convulsions worthy of a medieval torture chamber, often destroying the memory, and so the fight for the rights of the mentally ill can have been said to have merely taken a sideways jump, rather than being advanced.

By the 1960s there was growing disquiet about ECT and lobotomy (surgical severing of connections in the frontal lobe of the brain). And with new scanning devices in the 1970s and 1980s, such as the CT (computerized tomography) scanner and MRI (magnetic resonance imaging), and more effective drugs in the 1990s, the twenty-first century has seen the treatment of the mentally ill change once again.

However, the million-dollar question still remains: do we really have any idea of what we do, when we interfere with a human being's most sensitive and complex organ – the brain? It's a sobering thought.

# *Contents*

# *Preface*

It was the smell that brought her to herself, a nauseating odour that the stronger stench of bleach and disinfectant couldn't quite mask. She began to struggle again as they half-walked, half-carried her along the green-tiled, stone-floored corridor, desperately trying to rise above the deadening stupor that had resulted from the injection administered some time before in the carriage, when she wouldn't stop fighting.

*How could this be happening to her? How could she have been manhandled out of her own home in broad daylight?*

She was still weak from the complications that had followed in the wake of the miscarriage, but fear poured strength into her limbs. She kicked out wildly, and one of the men dragging her growled a curse as her shoe made sharp contact with his shinbone. They came to a brown-painted door and the same man knocked twice. Although her body was aching and bruised from the fight she had put up when they had come for her, and she felt sick and dizzy, she continued to twist and wrestle against the hard hands, and screamed with all her might.

The door was opened by a stout woman in a grey dress and a starched white apron and cap. For a moment she felt a flood of relief at the sight of one of her own sex. Surely this woman would listen to her? She wasn't mad – they would see that and understand this was a terrible mistake.

'You've got yourselves a right handful with this 'un,' the man she'd kicked muttered morosely to another woman sitting behind a large polished walnut desk. As she rose to her feet and stared disapprovingly, he added, 'Carryin' on somethin' wicked, she's been. I'm black an' blue.'

The woman ignored him. Looking over his shoulder to the third man who had been following in their wake, she said, 'What medication have you administered, Dr Owen?'

'She's been on bromide and ergot for the last weeks, but I had to administer morphia on the way here, such was her agitation. I dare not give more for some hours, Matron.'

The matron nodded, then inclined her head at the other two burly uniformed females in the room, who stepped forward and relieved the men of their prisoner. Their grip was every bit as powerful as that of their male counterparts.

Granite-faced, the matron said coldly, 'Do you understand why you are here? The court has issued a lunacy order, on the grounds that you are of unsound mind following a recent malady. If you do not cooperate, my staff will be forced to use the necessary restraints to prevent injury to yourself or other persons, and that will not be pleasant.'

*They weren't going to help her.* She stared into the gimlet eyes, and a terror that eclipsed her previous fear caused her ears to ring. She may well have lost her reason in the minutes that followed, because she couldn't remember much of what happened, only that she fought until they thrust her into the padded cell. A number of women held her down and stripped her to her shift and drawers, before pulling a rough linen frock over her head and strapping her into a straitjacket – the white, stained, leather-covered walls and the floor packed with straw deadening any sound.

And then they left her to the hell that had opened and engulfed her.

# PART ONE

## *A Lamb to the Slaughter*

## 1890

# *Chapter One*

Angeline Stewart stood in the swirling snowflakes that the bitter north-east wind was sending into a frenzied dance, but her velvet-brown eyes did not see what they were looking at. The bleak churchyard, the black-clothed figures of the other mourners and Reverend Turner standing at the head of the double grave had faded away. In their place were her beloved mother and father, as they had looked that last evening. It had only been a severe head-cold that had prevented her from accompanying them to the theatre, otherwise she, too, would most likely have been killed in the accident that ensued after they left the Avenue Theatre and Opera House in the midst of one of the worst snow blizzards Sunderland had experienced in years. The overturned coach had been found early the next morning after their housekeeper, Mrs Lee, who was also the coachman's wife, had instigated a search after they'd failed to return. Her parents and the coachman were dead, pinned beneath the badly smashed coach. It had veered off the road and down an embankment, and the two horses had been so badly injured that they had been shot at the scene.

Angeline brushed a strand of burnished brown hair from her cheek and took a deep breath against the picture that her mind conjured up. She hadn't been allowed to see her parents after the accident. Her Uncle Hector, her father's brother, had forbidden it after he had identified the bodies. He said she must remember them as they had been. He wasn't to know that her imagination presented her with horrors probably far worse than the reality, images that caused her to lay awake most nights muffling her sobs.

'All right, m'dear?'

Her uncle squeezing her arm brought her back to the present, the moment before Reverend Turner beckoned them forward so that she could drop the two long-stemmed red roses she was holding on top of the oak coffins that had been lowered into the earth. Red roses had been her dear mama's favourite flowers, and McArthur – their gardener – had kept the house supplied with fragrant blooms winter and summer, courtesy of the heated greenhouses that were his pride and joy.

Angeline glanced at him as she passed the group of servants she regarded as family. McArthur's weather-beaten face was grim and his two lads, Seth and Bernie, who assisted their father in the upkeep of the two acres of land surrounding the house on the edge of Ryhope, had no cheeky smiles today. Myrtle, the housemaid, Lottie, the kitchen maid, and Mrs Davidson, the cook, were openly crying; and even Fairley, her father's butler-cum-valet, was struggling to keep back the tears. And poor Mrs Lee, who was standing with Angeline's governess, Miss Robson, looked about to faint.

Angeline paused at the woman's side and touched her arm. She'd wanted the interment of the housekeeper's husband to be incorporated in the service for her parents, but her uncle wouldn't hear of the idea, saying it wouldn't be seemly for a mere servant to be given such regard. She had tried to argue with him, but when Reverend Turner had agreed with her uncle, she had been forced to admit defeat. Simon Lee would be buried tomorrow, and his widow would have to endure a second funeral.

Her uncle's hand in the small of Angeline's back urged her forward. The subtle pressure had the effect of making her want to resist. Her father would have seen nothing wrong in publicly expressing empathy towards their housekeeper, who had been with her parents even before she was born. He'd always maintained that it was their duty to care for and protect their servants, and that each should be treated as a valued human being. She had grown up knowing that her father's father had been born in the slums of Sunderland's notorious, disease-ridden East End. Her grandfather had escaped by running away to sea at an early age, returning a rich man at the age of forty. After setting up as a wine and spirit merchant, he'd married the daughter of a local jeweller. Exactly how he had acquired his wealth was never discussed, and she had been forbidden to ask any questions on the subject by her mother, but she did know that when her grandmother had died giving birth to her Uncle Hector, ten years after her father had been born, her grandfather had wanted nothing to do with his younger son. She'd thought that very unfair.

'Come along, my child.'

Reverend Turner was holding out his hand to her and she stepped forward. She didn't like the Reverend. She had once heard her mother describe him to her father as a cold fish, when they hadn't thought she was listening, and she'd thought this a very apt description. The minister always had cold, clammy hands even on the hottest day, and his pale-blue bulbous eyes and fat lips reminded her of the rows of gaping faces in the fishmonger's window. She had said this once to her mama, and although her mother had reprimanded her, her eyes had been twinkling.

She bit harder on her lip as her heart and soul cried out, 'Mama, oh, Mama', but not a sound emerged. Her uncle had warned her that, out of respect for her parents, she had to conduct herself with dignity and propriety today, as befitted a young lady of fifteen years. Shows of emotion were vulgar and were only indulged in by the common people who knew no better. She had wanted to say that they were only a step removed from the common people, and that if her grandfather hadn't made his fortune, her father and uncle would most likely have been born in the East End instead of a grand house; but, of course, she hadn't. Mainly because she always felt sorry for her Uncle Hector. It must have been awful growing up knowing that your own father didn't like you and, furthermore, blamed you for your mother's death. Her grandfather had died long before she was born – her parents had been married for more than twenty years before she'd made an appearance, and her mama had often told her they'd given up hope of having a child – and in his will he had left everything to her father. Uncle Hector hadn't even been mentioned. It was as though he'd never existed.

Angeline's thoughts caused her to reach out and take her uncle's arm as they stood together, and she gave him one of the roses to throw on her father's coffin. Knowing what she did, it had always surprised her that her father and uncle got on so well, but then that was mainly due to her father. He had loved and protected his sibling all his life, and when their father had died, he'd set Uncle Hector up in his own business so that he could be independent and not beholden to anyone. Her father had been so kind, so good. Everyone said so.

When the first clods of earth were dropped on the coffins, Angeline felt as though the sound jarred her very bones. She had the mad impulse to jump into the hole, lie down and tell the grave-diggers to cover her, too. The shudder that she gave caused her uncle to murmur, 'Remember what I said, Angeline. People are looking at how you conduct yourself today.' Then he added, in a gentler tone, 'It's nearly over now. Hold on a little longer.'

The drive back to the house in Ryhope was conducted in silence. Angeline sat with her uncle and her governess in the first carriage, drawn by four black-plumed horses, followed by a procession of other carriages and conveyances. Drenched with misery, she stared unseeing out of the window of the coach. She'd always liked snow before this last week. It was so pretty, and she'd enjoyed taking walks in the winter with her mother, snug in her fur coat and matching bonnet. When they returned home they always thawed out in front of the blazing fire in the drawing room, with Mrs Davidson's hot buttered muffins and cocoa.

She hated the snow now, though. It had taken her parents, and she didn't know how she would bear the pain of their passing. It seemed impossible that she'd never see them again. Never feel her mother's arms around her or the touch of her soft lips. Never hear her father's cheerful call when he came home in the evening.

She choked back a sob, mindful of her uncle's words.

It was going to take every bit of her remaining strength to get through the next stage of the day, and she couldn't break down now. That luxury would have to wait until she was alone in her bed. Her uncle had invited friends and family back to the house for a reception following the church service, and she was dreading it. Not that there would be many family members; it would be mostly friends of her parents and business associates of her father. When her grandfather had returned to the town after being at sea, he had severed all connections with his siblings and other family members, going so far as to change his surname. Her mother had been an only child and, apart from two ancient spinster great-aunts on her side, there was no one else. No one but Uncle Hector.

She glanced at him, but he, too, was staring out of the window and seemed lost in thought. She wondered if he would go back to his own house tonight, now that the funeral was over. He had been staying with her since her parents' accident, and had seen to the arrangements for the service and other matters. This had included organizing for Miss Robson – who had previously come to the house every morning for a few hours, to take her through her lessons – to take up temporary residence and sleep in the room next to hers. This had been an added trial. She liked Miss Robson, but found her very stiff and proper, which was probably why her uncle had considered the governess an ideal companion and chaperone.

Angeline's bow-shaped mouth pulled uncharacteristically tight. She wasn't a baby. She was fifteen years old, and her father had always said she possessed an old head on young shoulders. She knew some girls of her age were flibbertigibbets and given to fancies, but she wasn't like that, possibly because her parents had had her so late in life that all their friends' children were grown-up, and so she had mixed almost entirely with adults. It would have been different if she had been allowed to go to the local school, but her father had been against it, and her mama had been equally against sending her away to boarding school. Hence Miss Robson. Not that she had minded.

She loved her home and being with her mother; her mama had been her best friend and confidante and companion. Some afternoons on their walks they had laughed and laughed until their sides ached.

This time a sob did escape, and Angeline turned it into a cough. If she could just get through this day she would be able to take stock. She felt as though she had been in a daze since the accident.

Nevertheless, in spite of her desolation, as the carriage swept through the heavy wrought-iron gates and drove up the long drive to where the house sat nestled between two giant oak trees, she felt a moment's comfort. Her parents had loved Oakfield House, and so did she. She had been born in one of the eight bedrooms and had never known another home. As the family business started by her grandfather had continued to go from strength to strength, her father could have moved to a much grander house, or so her mother had confided, but both their hearts had been firmly at Oakfield. The main building consisted of fourteen rooms over two floors, with a corridor from the kitchen leading to the purpose-built annexe housing the indoor servants. McArthur and his lads lived with his wife and the rest of the family somewhere in Bishopwearmouth. Angeline didn't know exactly where, but every morning the gardener and his lads were working before she came downstairs, and in the summer they often didn't leave until twilight.

It was a happy household. Or it had been, Angeline amended in her mind as the carriage stopped at the foot of the steps leading to the intricately carved front doors. Now nothing could be the same again.

Somehow she got through the endless reception. Her new black dress with its stiff little raised collar and long buttoned sleeves seemed stifling, and the corset that Myrtle had laced her into that morning was too tight. She had rebelled against going into corsets when she had turned fourteen, but her mother had told her that she was a young lady now and, along with privileges such as joining her parents when they had guests for dinner, there were sacrifices. Her childhood was behind her, and young ladies *always* had tiny waists. Her mama had brooked no argument on the matter, and that had been that.

Outside the house the overcast January day was bitterly cold with a keen north-east wind; inside, the huge fires burning in the basket grates of the dining room and drawing room where the hundred or so guests were assembled made the heat suffocating, at least in Angeline's opinion. All she wanted was some fresh air, or to get into a room that wasn't full of people. Nevertheless, she did her duty. She chatted here and there, accepted the words of condolence from this person and that, and behaved with the decorum her mother would have expected.

Finally, as the magnificent grandfather clock in the hall chimed four o'clock, the last of the company made their goodbyes and stepped into the snowy night. All, that is, but Mr Appleby, her father's solicitor. Before this day

Angeline had only known him as a friend and dinner guest of her parents, and on those occasions she had loved to sit and listen when her father and Mr Appleby had engaged in sometimes heated debates about social inequality and the like. These had usually finished with Mr Appleby calling her father a Socialist at heart – something her father hadn't minded in the least.

Angeline had always thought Mr Appleby's name suited him very well. Small and fat, with rosy red cheeks and twinkling brown eyes, she imagined that if an apple could take human form it would be exactly like the solicitor. Now, though, his eyes were full of sympathy when he said, 'Your uncle wishes me to acquaint you with the details of the will, Angeline', and he glanced at Hector, who was standing to the side of her.

'Now?' She asked the question of her uncle. He nodded.

'It is customary on the day of interment,' he said briefly.

Angeline didn't care if it was customary or not. She didn't want to think about the will – not today. All she wanted was to curl up by herself in front of the fire in her bedroom and cry. 'Can't it wait, Uncle Hector? I'd like to rest before dinner.'

If her uncle noticed the break in her voice, he ignored it. 'You have to understand the situation in which you find yourself, Angeline, and hear your father's instructions. It will pave the way for the arrangements that need to be made.'

She stared at him. Something told her that she wouldn't like these arrangements. 'Do you know what the will says?'

'Partly. Your father made me your guardian, in the event of something happening to him and your mother. This was a long time ago, just after you were born. Now, please, come along to the study, where Mr Appleby has the papers ready.'

It was a moment before she followed her uncle, Mr Appleby making up the rear. Angeline's head was whirling. It was stupid, but she hadn't thought about anyone being her guardian. She'd imagined that, once the funeral was over and her uncle and Miss Robson returned to their own homes, things would get back to normal.

Well, not normal, she corrected herself in the next moment. Things would never be normal again. How could they be? But if she had thought about the future at all – which she had to admit she hadn't really, not with her mother and father filling every waking second – she'd assumed that Miss Robson would resume coming to the house in the mornings, and Mrs Lee and the other servants would run Oakfield as they always had done.

The familiar smell of wood smoke from the fire and the lingering aroma of the cigars her father had favoured made her bite her lip as she entered the book-lined study. It was perhaps her favourite room of the house. From a little girl, she had stretched out on the thick rug in front of the fire and played quietly with her dollies, or had drawn or read books while her father worked at his desk, and as she'd grown she'd brought her needlework or crocheting and had sat in one of the armchairs at an angle to the fireplace. Her father was away so much in the town dealing with the business, and when he was home she liked to be with him, if she could. She had known that he liked having her there, albeit as a silent presence. Why had she never realized just how wonderful life was, before the accident? She'd taken it for granted, and now she couldn't tell them they'd been the best parents in the world and she loved them so much.

George Appleby walked over to her father's desk and sat down, as she and her uncle seated themselves in the two chairs that had been drawn close to it. He said nothing for a moment, his gaze on Angeline's face. He felt he knew what she was thinking, for her tear-filled eyes spoke for her, and his shock and sorrow at his dear friend's untimely death were compounded by his anxiety and concern for this young girl. Philip and Margery had been devoted to her of course, but in that devotion had come a desire to keep Angeline wrapped in cotton wool.

It was understandable – oh, indeed. He mentally nodded at the thought. They had been over the moon when they'd discovered Margery was expecting a baby, and when Angeline had been born, and her such a bonny and happy child, you'd have thought she was the most gifted and perfect being in all creation. And any parent wants to protect their child, if they're worth their salt. But George and Margery's decision to keep the girl in what amounted to a state of seclusion didn't bode well now – or for the future. She was the most innocent of lambs.

Hector Stewart cleared his throat, and George's gaze turned to him. As much as he had liked and respected Philip, he disliked his brother. The man was weak and ineffectual and uppish into the bargain, but he had always held his tongue about Hector, because Philip wouldn't hear a word against him. Which was commendable, he supposed, but sometimes not seeing the flaws in someone you loved could have far-reaching consequences. There were constant rumours at the Gentlemen's Club about Hector's drinking and gambling, and if even half of them were true, the man was on the road to perdition. Eustace Preston had told him only last week that it was common knowledge Hector took himself off to Newcastle these days to certain gambling dens where fortunes were regularly won and lost. Mostly lost, he'd be bound. And this was the individual to whom Philip and Margery had entrusted their beloved daughter.

Hector cleared his throat again even more pointedly, and George put his thoughts behind him and picked up the document in front of him on the desk. Addressing himself to Angeline, he said gently, 'This is the last will and testament of your parents, child. Do you understand what that means?' When she nodded, he continued, 'I will read it word for word in a moment, but essentially your parents left everything to you, which makes it simple. They appointed your uncle as your guardian, should they die before you reached the age of twenty-one and were unmarried. You will reside with him and have a personal monthly allowance, and your uncle will also have a sum of money each month for as long as you are in his care.'

Angeline stared at the solicitor. 'Leave Oakfield? No, they would never have said that.'

'I'm sorry.' George had been dreading this meeting, and it was being every bit as bad as he'd feared. The girl looked even more bereft than before, if that were possible.

'But why? Why would they want me to leave our home?'

'Angeline, you are fifteen years old.' Hector spoke firmly, but not unkindly. 'You cannot run a home on your own – the very idea is ridiculous. There are bills to pay, daily decisions to make, servants to keep in order, and umpteen other things.'

'The house runs itself under Mrs Lee, my mama always said so, and the servants don't need keeping in order. They . . . they're like family.'

Hector looked askance.

Realizing she'd said the wrong thing, Angeline swallowed hard. 'Miss Robson could take up permanent residence,' she said desperately. 'That way I'm not alone here, am I? She would keep everything and everyone as it should be, and she could report directly to you. And I could still live here.' Turning to the solicitor, she added, 'There's enough money for that, isn't there, Mr Appleby?'

Without giving the solicitor a chance to respond, and with a thread of impatience in his voice, Hector said, 'It's not a question of money, Angeline. Your father stated his wishes very clearly, and what you are suggesting is quite ludicrous. You will come to live with me within the week. That is the end of the matter. My final word. You may bring anything you wish, of course, and Miss Robson has agreed to continue to give you your lessons each morning. This house will be sold forthwith, and the proceeds added to the trust.'

'But Mrs Lee and Cook, and everyone?'

'The servants will be given excellent references and three months' wages in lieu of notice. The senior staff – the housekeeper, cook and butler – will receive six months' wages. This is very generous, believe me.' Her uncle's tone made it clear that if this stipulation hadn't been in the will, his treatment of the servants would have been very different. 'Now, Mr Appleby has pointed out that you will need a personal maid, m'dear. Which is not necessary at present, in my bachelor abode.'

Hector smiled his thin smile, but Angeline was too distraught by the turn of events to respond. Oakfield sold? And the staff dismissed? Just like that? This was their home, too – couldn't he see that?

'Mr Appleby suggested you might wish to bring your current housemaid with you in that capacity.' Hector's sniff of disapproval indicated that he couldn't for the life of him see why. A servant was a servant, after all. Now, if it had been a pet dog or cat . . . 'But I thought a maid already trained in that respect would be more suitable.'

Feeling as though she was drowning, Angeline caught at the lifeline that the kindly solicitor had provided. 'Myrtle attended to Mama when she had need of it,' she said quickly, 'and I would prefer her to a stranger.'

'So be it. Now, Mr Appleby, perhaps you would be so good as to read the will?'

When the solicitor eventually finished speaking, only two things had really registered through Angeline's turmoil. First, that she wouldn't come into her inheritance until she was twenty-one or married – whichever came first. Second, that she was a very rich young woman. This Mr Appleby had impressed upon her, adding that it was why her father had wanted to see to it that she was under her uncle's protection until she was mature enough to cope with such a responsibility.

'Your father has tied the trust up in such a way that no monies – other than your allowance and the stipend paid to your uncle for as long as you reside with him – can be extracted. By you or anyone else.' George Appleby's gaze flicked to Hector for a moment. He wasn't fooled by his blank countenance. Philip's brother had expected a bequest of some kind, although George couldn't see why. Philip had been amazingly generous to Hector when their father had died, setting him up in his own business and buying him a fine house and all. A different man would have been set up for life, but he rather suspected Hector was in trouble, despite his outward facade. Still, he'd make sure Hector didn't get his hands on one penny more than the amount Philip had settled on him each month for Angeline's keep.

Hector stared back at the solicitor. He was aware of George's dislike of him – a feeling he fully reciprocated – and had always resented the high regard in which Philip had held the little man, and the influence the solicitor had had upon his brother. Take this will, for instance. Hector's teeth clenched. He had no doubt Philip had left the mechanics of it to George Appleby, and the solicitor had been instrumental in determining that, even as Angeline's guardian, he couldn't use the trust money. *Cocksure little runt.*

George's eyes returned to Angeline's white face. 'Your father's main concern was to protect you, should the unthinkable happen. You do understand that, don't you?'

Yes, she did, of course she did, but losing Oakfield was almost as bad as the loss of her parents. Her voice unsteady, she whispered, 'Is there no way I can keep the house?'

'I'm sorry, Angeline.'

They looked at each other, and although she felt very small and lost, Angeline held herself straight, her chin lifting. Strangely her mind wasn't in a whirl any longer. Her mama had always said one had to have the grace to accept what couldn't be changed, and the sense to recognize what could. This was the former. Whatever her private feelings on the matter, it was kind of Uncle Hector to take her into his home and offer her protection. Her gaze now going to her uncle, she said quietly, 'I'll try and not be a bother, Uncle.'

'Of course you won't be. We'll get along just fine, m'dear.' It was too hearty, and Hector moderated his tone as he added, 'Your rooms are being prepared and will be ready shortly, so spend the next day or two deciding what you want to bring with you.'

*Everything*. She wanted to bring everything, because every single stick of furniture, every ornament, every picture, was part of her mother and father. But of course that was impossible. Inclining her head, she said flatly, 'Yes, Uncle.'

It was settled.

# *Chapter Two*

It took every ounce of Hector's self-control to remain civil in the time before George Appleby took his leave. Angeline had long since retired to her room when the two men walked out of the study into the hall, after discussing the finite details of the will. George had insisted in dotting the i's and crossing the t's with Angeline's guardian, determined that Hector would have no excuse in the future to try and wheedle money out of the estate by saying he hadn't understood how things stood. Hector was fully aware of the solicitor's motives. He would have liked to punch him on the nose and boot him out of the house. As this was impossible, he had played the devoted uncle and urbane host, albeit with gritted teeth.

Fairley appeared to help George on with his greatcoat and hand him his hat. He told him that one of McArthur's lads was bringing the solicitor's pony and trap from the stables. George thanked him, before pausing and saying, 'Bad business this, Fairley.'

'Indeed, sir.'

'Terrible shock for Miss Angeline, for us all.'

'Yes, sir. Knocked everyone below stairs for six.'

'I can imagine. Well, goodnight, Fairley.'

'Goodnight, sir.'

As George stepped out into the snowy night and walked over to where Seth McArthur was holding the pony's reins, he was thinking, 'Poor devils! They might think they've been knocked for six now, but once Hector breaks the news they're all out of a job, it'll be even worse.' Comforting himself with the fact that he'd at least been able to secure Myrtle for Angeline, he climbed up into the trap and, pulling the vehicle's thick horsehair blanket over his legs, clicked his tongue at the pony.

Hector didn't wait to see George depart. Turning on his heel on the doorstep, he swung round and barked at the butler, 'I want a word with you in the drawing room.'

Five minutes later Fairley emerged, white-faced and shaken – as much, he said later to the rest of the staff, after dinner had been served to Angeline and her uncle and Miss Robson in the dining room, by the master's brother's high-handed manner as anything else. 'He wants us out by the end of the month.' And, to the chorus of shocked gasps that followed this bombshell, he added, 'All, that is, except Myrtle, who's going to accompany Miss Angeline to Mr Stewart's residence. Myself, Cook and Mrs Lee receive six months' wages in lieu of notice. The rest of you, three months'.'

'And references, Mr Fairley?' Molly Davidson, the

cook, was clutching the collar of her frock as though she was attempting to strangle herself, her round, fat face stricken.

'Oh, we'll all get a good reference, Mrs Davidson. The master left instructions on that score, apparently.'

Hilda Lee wiped her eyes with a trembling hand. She'd been weeping on and off since the accident that had taken her husband, as well as her employers. 'I shan't need mine. My sister's offered me a home with her – the one that was widowed last year. Her Ike left her comfortably off and, with the nest egg I'll take with me, the pair of us will want for nothing. I said no to her when she asked me last week, after Simon' – she gulped audibly – 'after she heard the news. I thought I was set up here. But I'll have a word with her tomorrow, when she comes for Simon's funeral, and tell her I've changed my mind.'

The other staff looked envious. None of them were in such a fortunate position that they could choose not to work, and this blow was alarming. Each of them knew they'd be hard pressed to find another establishment like this one, where the mistress had been kind and the master fair and generous.

Myrtle was sitting very quietly, counting her blessings, as she glanced round the unhappy faces at the long, scrubbed kitchen table. The servants had just sat down to their own dinner when Elias Fairley made his announcement, and now plates of hot, steaming panackelty – made with meat left over from the funeral luncheon earlier in the day – sat untouched. Panackelty was one of Mrs

Davidson's specialities, cooked long and slow so that the sliced potatoes absorbed every bit of flavour from the beef or bacon or corned beef and stock, and the onions almost caramelized, and the whole lot went deliciously crusty at the edges. Tonight, though, the plates could have been piled with cardboard, for all the interest the others were displaying in their meal. Feeling somewhat ashamed that her mouth was watering, Myrtle listened to the ongoing conversation as patiently as her growling stomach would allow.

After all, she told herself guiltily, as question after anxious question was put to Elias, few of which he had an answer for, if she'd been told that she'd lost her job, she'd be feeling sick with worry, too. The eldest of ten children (the youngest of which was just three months old, and the brother next to her having just turned fifteen), Myrtle gave every penny she earned to her mother each month on her half-day off, when she went home to the two-up, two-down miner's cottage in Monkwearmouth. Even though her brother had got taken on at the mine with her father, Myrtle knew the family barely had enough to eat, and her mother was always weeks behind with the rent. She had been thirteen years old when she'd come to work for the Stewarts, nearly five years ago, and from the first day she had known that she'd landed on her feet, when she'd sat down to eat with the other servants. The food was good and plentiful, and she had gone to bed feeling that she had landed in heaven.

At last Mr Fairley picked up his knife and fork and

began to eat. This was the signal that the other servants might do the same. It was a sombre meal. Even Mrs Davidson's baked jam roll, golden and oozing with strawberry jam made from fruit from McArthur's walled fruit and vegetable garden near the small orchard, didn't bring forth the usual appreciative comments.

They'd almost finished their pudding when one of the row of bells fixed to the kitchen wall near the door rang. Elias glanced at it, before saying flatly, 'That'll be His Nibs wanting something or other.' Angeline and Miss Robson had retired to their rooms directly dinner was finished, but Hector had gone through to the drawing room, taking his coffee and brandy with him. Now Elias didn't get to his feet and answer the summons, as he would normally have done, knowing it was only the temporary master of the house calling them. Instead he looked at Myrtle. 'Go and see what he wants. Likely it's another bottle of the master's good brandy. He's been drinking his way steadily through the cellar for the last week.'

It was unheard of for the butler to criticize the family, and this more than anything brought home to the rest of the staff how drastically things had changed. They exchanged glances, but said nothing, as Myrtle did as she was told after a quick, 'Yes, Mr Fairley.' In the space of a week their calm, orderly world had been turned upside down. Suddenly life was precarious.

Myrtle was thinking the same thing as she hurried along to the drawing room, once again thanking her lucky stars that she wasn't in the same boat. If she was truthful, she wasn't looking forward to working for the master's brother, though. None of the staff liked him, mainly because he treated you as though you were less than the muck under his boots.

She paused outside the drawing-room door. Hopefully, if she was to be Miss Angeline's personal maid, she wouldn't see much of Mr Stewart.

After knocking once, she opened the door. 'You rang, sir?'

Hector didn't bother to look up from where he reclined in an armchair in front of the fire. 'I'm going into town shortly. See to it that the trap is brought round to the front door in five minutes.'

Myrtle hesitated. Since the master's fine big carriage had been smashed, and the two beautiful chestnuts that had pulled it had been put down, there was only the mistress's light, two-wheeled dog cart left, and the mistress's pretty little mare, Gertie. It was a bitter night, and Myrtle knew her late mistress would never have countenanced the pony standing waiting for hours in town, which no doubt was what Mr Stewart intended. Likely he was off to the Gentlemen's Club, or some other such establishment. Unbeknown to Mr Fairley and Mrs Lee, she'd overheard them talking about the master's brother's jaunts, and how Mr Stewart had been out nearly every night since he had been here. Furthermore, McArthur and his lads had gone home an hour ago and, the mood Mr Fairley was in, he wouldn't appreciate being informed that he had to get the trap ready himself. It was menial work.

'Well?' Hector's voice expressed his irritation. 'Don't stand there looking gormless, girl.'

Myrtle bobbed her head and hastily left the room. Mr Fairley would have to lump it, she told herself as she scurried across the hall. She knew which side her bread was buttered, and she wasn't about to rub Mr Stewart up the wrong way. She did feel sorry for poor little Gertie, though, and she'd tell Mr Fairley that the master's brother had said to put the pony's thick stable blanket in the trap, even though he hadn't.

It was half an hour later when Hector walked through the doors of the Gentlemen's Club. After the attentive doorman had fussed around him, taking his hat and coat, enquiring how the funeral had gone and generally ingratiating himself, Hector made his way to the lounge. He was greeted warmly by a number of the patrons, one or two of whom were important and influential names in the town, and by the time he had ordered his first brandy from the liveried steward, who was equally ingratiating, the feathers that George Appleby had ruffled so badly were smoothing out. The upper-class ambience of the exclusive establishment was soothing, and Hector drank it in, leaning back in the leather armchair and picking up the evening paper that the steward had placed at his elbow.

He would read for a while, have a couple more brandies

and then go through to the club's smaller lounge. This was universally recognized as the card room. Hector rarely differed from this routine. And he knew exactly with whom he would be playing, and where he would be seated. Regulars in the card room, like Hector, had their particular chair at a particular table. It was an unspoken rule, and one that no member would have dreamed of breaking. It engendered a feeling of belonging in Hector, a comforting sense of affiliation and kinship, something he had craved all his life, but never acknowledged.

On the dot of ten o'clock he joined the other three men who were settling themselves in the comfortable chairs around a table close to the blazing fire. Paul Duckworth, a wealthy landowner, was seated to his right, and on his left sat Robert Taylor. The small, heavy-jowled man's family was distantly connected to royalty, and Robert had never done a day's work in his life. The youngest son, and something of an embarrassment to his long-suffering parents, he drank and gambled away his allowance each month and regularly got into all kinds of trouble. But it was Oswald Golding, sitting opposite Hector, who was the undisputed leader of the quartet.

Since Oswald had inherited his large country estate and town house a decade before, at the age of twenty-six, gambling and riotous living had taken their toll on his fortune. Aristocratic to the hilt, Oswald's cold and callous nature was hidden behind charming good looks and a charisma that was very attractive to the fair sex. Unfortunately for him, these attributes were of little use in influencing his success at gambling, and he was rarely lucky. He had recently been forced to sell a farm at the edge of his estate and 300 acres, to pay his most pressing debts. This had sent him into a black rage for days. He believed absolutely that he was a superior being, and that God had seen fit to place him in a position of wealth and power, courtesy of the Golding lineage. To be taken to task by his creditors like any common man had been the height of humiliation.

Oswald glanced across at Hector as he lit a cigar. 'Didn't expect to see you tonight,' he drawled, before drawing the smoke deep into his lungs. 'It was your brother's funeral today, wasn't it?'

Hector nodded. He didn't want to discuss it.

Oswald's eyes narrowed slightly. He was aware that Hector was barely keeping his head above water. Oswald made it his business to know a lot of things. Hector must have been hoping that he would be remembered in the will, but it didn't look as though Philip Stewart had been overly generous to his brother. Of course Hector's reticence might be down to the fact that he was upset after the funeral. Oswald took another puff of his cigar. But he rather thought it was more than that.

His opportunity to find out more came later that night. Robert Taylor had consumed a bottle of brandy before he had even sat down to play cards, and by midnight he was too drunk to see what was in his hand, let alone talk coherently. Paul Duckworth, who had been on a winning streak all night and was worried his luck might change if he continued to play, offered to make sure Robert got home safely, and the two men left the lounge, Paul practically carrying the inebriated Robert.

Hector had stood up to leave at the same time, but when Oswald had taken his arm, saying, 'Fancy a nightcap, old chap?', Hector had been flattered into staying. Now he watched Oswald ordering coffee and a special liqueur that he favoured for the two of them, from the ever-attentive steward. Inwardly glowing that the influential and popular Oswald Golding had detained him, Hector smiled into the handsome face opposite. 'Paul was on form tonight,' he said, his tone light, but a thread of resentment that he couldn't quite hide colouring his words.

Oswald nodded. Paul, along with Robert, had been one of his friends for a long time, but it was a private source of annoyance that Paul – the only member of the quartet who could afford to lose and barely notice it – seemed to court Lady Luck far better than the rest of them. 'The blighter's cleaned me out,' he drawled, stretching his long legs in front of him and lighting his umpteenth cigar of the night. 'How about you?'

'The same.' And he had needed to win tonight; there were a couple of individuals in Newcastle to whom he owed money, and who had big mouths. There was no disgrace in owing money to a bank or some other establishment, but there was deep disgrace in being unable to settle your gambling debts. Hector was in over his head, and had been for some time, but for the life of him he could see no way out of his predicament. If only Philip had seen fit to leave him something – *anything*. He had thought for donkey's years that he'd be Philip's heir. Then Margery had surprised everyone by announcing that she was expecting a baby, when she was practically in her dotage. He'd comforted himself with the fact that a miscarriage was always possible; or that the child, if born, might be sickly or even an idiot – at Margery's age it wasn't unlikely. But no, she had gone full-term and had produced a bouncing baby girl. And Angeline was sweet enough, he had nothing against her as such; it was just that her arrival had meant he was cheated for the second time – first by his father, and then by Philip.

'So, how did the funeral go?'

'What?' It was a moment before Oswald's voice penetrated Hector's black thoughts. 'Oh, the funeral. It went all right on the whole, I suppose.'

'You don't seem overly sure, old chap.' The steward arrived with their coffee and liqueurs, and Oswald waited until the man had moved away before pressing the point by saying, 'Come on, Hector. You can tell me. We're friends, aren't we? What's wrong?'

The sympathetic tone, coming on top of George Appleby's treatment of him, and not least the amount of brandy he had swallowed during the course of the evening, loosened Hector's tongue. Shrugging, he muttered, 'As Philip's only brother, I was expecting to be remembered in the will, I suppose. Not in a big way, you understand,' he added quickly. 'A keepsake would have done.'

A keepsake, be damned! He'd been expecting a darned sight more than that, from the look on his face. Oswald took a sip of coffee. 'And there was nothing?'

'A trifling sum each month, for as long as my niece is under my roof.'

Oswald's thick golden lashes swept down, hiding the contempt in his grey eyes. There had been a definite whine to Hector's voice. The man really was a bore. But then, he reasoned, what could you expect? The Stewarts were 'new' money and only a generation or so removed from the gutter. 'You're the child's guardian?' he asked, without any real interest.

'Angeline is hardly a child – more a young woman, at fifteen years old, which carries its own problems of course. I have little insight into the female mind, nor wish to have.'

Oswald hid a smile. Hector's disinterest in the ladies had led one or two members of the club to speculate whether he was disposed in another direction, but there was nothing effeminate about the man. Rather, Oswald reflected, Hector was that rare freak of nature: a truly passionless individual, at least sexually. 'I take it that Philip left the lot to her?'

Hector nodded. 'The business, the house, stocks and shares – you name it. I had no idea Philip was worth so much, but then he always did have the Midas touch, like our father.' Now the bitterness was palpable. 'My niece is likely to be the wealthiest young woman this side of Durham, when everything's settled.'

Oswald sat up straighter. 'By wealthy, you mean . . . '

Hector shrugged. 'According to Appleby, the worth of the stocks and shares alone runs into six figures. He was quite a gambler in his own way, my dear brother. Then there's the business, of course; the house, bank accounts. He was canny, sure enough.'

Oswald stared at Hector. He had known Philip Stewart by sight. Hector's brother had been a member of the club longer than both of them, but Oswald hadn't spoken to Philip more than once or twice. The man hadn't gambled or had any known vices, and his circle had been men of the same ilk – pillars of the community, the lot of them. Consequently Oswald had considered Philip dull and uninteresting, with a provincial small-mindedness that reflected his origins. Now he could hardly believe what he was hearing.

Finishing his cup of coffee, Oswald searched his mind, trying to remember if he'd ever caught sight of the daughter, but to no avail. Not that it was likely. He spent a great deal of time at his London house, and when he was up at the estate his days were spent shooting or fishing, and his nights gambling and with other less-than-salubrious activities. He was well aware that his name had been linked with so many *demi-mondaines*, actresses and aristocratic women who'd been his companions and mistresses that it denoted scandal, but this had never concerned him. He and his circle of friends lived for pleasure: gambling, horse racing, shooting, womanizing, visits to the music halls and theatres, and trips to Europe. The balls, dinners, banquets and garden parties in London, along with the Henley Regatta, Ascot and Lords, made up his days and nights, and he wouldn't have had it any other way in the past.

But . . . Oswald's eyes narrowed as his mind ticked on. Having to sell the farm and land had come as something of a wake-up call, and he still had a mountain of debt. He accepted now that he had to marry into money – and fast. The problem was that although many a simpering young woman from good stock would have welcomed his attentions, their virtuous mothers would certainly be inclined to have a fit of the vapours at the thought of him as a son-in-law. And their fathers would want to know how he stood financially.

Carefully Oswald said, 'I would have imagined the inordinate responsibility of taking your niece under your protection was worth far more than a small allowance each month, old chap. Bit on the mean side that, if you don't mind me saying.'

Gratified that Oswald saw it as he did, Hector nodded. 'I'll do my duty, of course, but nevertheless . . . '

'Quite.' Oswald allowed a moment or two to pass. 'And young ladies of your niece's age are inclined to be somewhat . . . demanding, in my experience. I suppose it's only natural that, on the brink of entering society, as they are, their heads are full of the latest fashions, dinner parties and dances, and not least a dashing beau or two.'

Hector looked alarmed. 'Angeline isn't like that.'

Oswald smiled. 'My dear fellow, they're *all* like that –

take it from me. You'll see. Once the shock of her parents' accident has worn off, you'll have your work cut out to keep her entertained.' Casually he added, 'Is she a beauty?'

'A beauty? I don't know. I've never thought . . . Well, yes, I dare say Angeline is pleasing to the eye.'

'There you are, then. Recipe for trouble.'

'You really think so?' Thoroughly agitated now, Hector lifted his cup of coffee to his lips, missed his mouth and sloshed half of it down his shirt and waistcoat. He knew Oswald's reputation with the ladies, and didn't doubt for one moment that the man was fully conversant with the workings of the female mind.

'When they're that age, the trick is stopping them from getting bored and into mischief,' said Oswald with studied idleness. 'Give it a couple of years and she'll be easier to handle.'

'A couple of *years*?' Hector's voice rose on the last word.

'Look.' Oswald's voice was soothing. 'I'm planning a little get-together with a few select friends next month – nothing too formal, a dinner and perhaps a spot of dancing. Why don't you and your niece come along? It will give Angeline something to look forward to.'

Hector stared at Oswald in amazement. The only time they ever socialized was at the club, and then specifically in the card room. Oswald was gentry, and everything about him proclaimed that he was from a class that considered itself infinitely special. Until today, Hector wouldn't have been surprised if Oswald had looked the other way, should their paths have crossed outside the club's confines. But it wasn't only this that caused him to hesitate. He'd heard rumours about the high jinks Oswald and his set got up to, and if only half of them were true, then an evening hosted by this man was not the sort of occasion to take an innocent young girl to.

As though he knew what Hector was thinking, Oswald continued, 'When I say select, I mean mostly married couples like the Hendersons and Parkers, and I think Lord Gray is back from honeymoon with his new wife. Have you met Nicholas Gray? No? Oh, he's a fine fellow. Eton and Oxford followed by the Guards, and his estate in Scotland breeds the best grouse for hundreds of miles. Made a damn good speech in the House of Lords last year.'

Reassured by the mention of some of the most respectable names thereabouts, Hector breathed more easily. 'Wouldn't it seem a trifle soon for Angeline to be seen at something like that? Not that I'm not grateful, of course, but—'

'Good grief, Hector! We're not talking about a widow here, you know. The girl is young, she needs to be taken out of herself at such a time. Diverted, occupied by happier things. No one would expect anything less of a fond uncle.'

Still not wholly convinced, Hector nodded uncertainly. 'If you think so . . . '

'That's settled then.' Oswald smiled widely, revealing a

set of strong, white, even teeth. 'I'll see to it you're sent an invitation, old chap, for the pair of you. Now, where's that damned steward? More coffee and liqueurs, I think, before we venture out into this filthy weather. Did I tell you about the new hunter I bought last week? Magnificent brute, but headstrong. Took a bite out of the stable lad on the first day and . . . '

Hector let Oswald ramble on, as his mind attempted to assimilate what had just occurred. He didn't fool himself that Oswald's invitation was prompted by altruism, but for the life of him he couldn't see what other motive there could be.

The coffee and liqueurs came; Oswald continued to wax lyrical about the horses that were his pride and joy, and the heat from the glowing embers in the room's fireplace bathed Hector in a soothing sense of well-being. All of a sudden he decided to accept Oswald's benevolence at face value. It was just an invitation to a social gathering, he told himself – and what a social gathering! He could wait a lifetime before such an invitation came his way again. His money worries, the aggravation of having Angeline take up residence in his home with all the irksome irritations that would ensue, the fact that his brother had left him nothing but a paltry few pounds a week – all faded into insignificance. He stretched out his legs, settled himself more comfortably in his chair and shut his eyes, and within a moment or two was snoring.

# *Chapter Three*

Angeline stared at her reflection in the bedroom mirror. Myrtle had arranged her hair in glossy little curls and waves on the top of her head, with several white silk flowers set in the midst of them, and her new dress was the most exquisite thing she had ever seen, but still, she felt . . . odd. She nodded mentally at the word. She barely recognized the young woman in the looking glass, that was the trouble. But she couldn't voice her misgivings to Myrtle, not after the hours the maid had spent getting her ready for this dinner party – a dinner party, Angeline reflected, that she had no wish to attend.

'Oh, Miss Angeline.' Myrtle had tears in her eyes. 'You look beautiful.'

Angeline forced a smile. 'If I do, then it's all your work, Myrtle.' From the moment Myrtle had drawn her bath, liberally perfuming the water with rose oil, the maid had been on a mission to transform her young mistress into an elegant, sophisticated and fashionable lady. She'd mentioned several times during her ministrations the fact that Angeline had had her sixteenth birthday the week before, as though this had immediately turned her into Methuselah. After her bath, Angeline had been made to stand still while Myrtle dressed her from head to toe.

First, Myrtle had knelt before her, carefully drawing the fine silk stockings onto her feet and smoothing them carefully up her legs. With her silk chemise in place, Angeline had had to endure the maid fitting the long stays of white coutil, heavily boned, around her hips and slender figure. They exerted great pressure on her waist and diaphragm, forcing her small bust forward and her derriere out, in what Angeline considered a most unnatural way, and were twice as uncomfortable as her normal day-corsets. How she was going to sit down and eat when she could barely breathe, Angeline didn't know. Myrtle said that didn't matter.

Once the busk had been fastened down the front, after many adjustments, Myrtle had clipped the top of the stockings to the stay's suspenders, then the lacing had followed, beginning at the waist and travelling gradually up and down, until the necessary proportions had been achieved. The silk laces and their tags had flown in and out under Myrtle's deft fingers, accompanied by little gasps from Angeline and the odd protestation, which the maid had ignored.

Next came the petticoat, trimmed with Honiton lace, and then the pièce de résistance, the fine white and powder-blue chiffon and lace dress. Myrtle had selected an emerald necklace with matching earrings from the casket on Angeline's dressing table, but Angeline had baulked at wearing them. They had been a Christmas present from her father to her mother the year before, and it seemed wrong to put them on so soon. The whole idea of this dinner party seemed wrong. It was only when her uncle had become visibly upset at her refusal to attend that she had capitulated, and then with great reluctance. But she wouldn't wear the emeralds. Instead she had chosen a simple row of pearls from her own small jewellery box, and nothing Myrtle had said had been able to make her change her mind.

Angeline took a deep breath. Her uncle was waiting downstairs; she couldn't delay another moment.

'It'll be fine, Miss. You'll have a lovely time.'

Myrtle touched her arm and Angeline turned to face her. Myrtle's pretty little face was glowing, and Angeline knew that the maid was as excited as if she had been invited to the Golding estate. Inclining her head, she said, 'Don't wait up, Myrtle. I should imagine we'll be late back.'

'Oh no, Miss.' Myrtle looked shocked. 'Of course I'll wait up. Your uncle would expect it, and I need to help you to undress – you'd never manage otherwise.'

Stifling a sigh, Angeline smiled instead. Myrtle would expect chapter and verse on the evening, that was for sure, but how could she work up any enthusiasm? She didn't care that Oswald Golding was one of the most influential men in the north of England with connections in very high places, as her uncle had stated; or that an invitation to his home was a huge honour. And she certainly didn't see why she'd had to come out of mourning and abandon the black she'd worn since her parents' death for this night. When her uncle had said that to do otherwise would cast a pall over the evening, she'd retorted that in that case it was far better she stayed at home and he went alone. The argument that followed had been so upsetting that she'd cried till the early hours, once she was alone in her room. But she wished now she had stuck to her guns and refused to go. Oh, she did.

Leaving the room, she walked slowly down the wide staircase in the house that was now her home. She didn't like it. It had none of the warmth and feeling that Oakfield had had, and her uncle's housekeeper, Mrs Upton, and his 'man', Albert (who was also Mrs Upton's brother), were like their name: uppity. She had sensed their unfriendliness to Myrtle, but when she'd asked Myrtle about it, the maid had cheerfully assured her that she could give as good as she got, and with knobs on, too. Angeline thanked God every day for Myrtle. Life would have been unbearable without her bright face and chatter, and she knew, too, that the little maid was hers, which was infinitely comforting.

Hector was sitting on one of the two hard-backed chairs in the hall that had a small table between them, and his fingers were drumming impatiently on its polished surface. He rose to his feet at the sight of her, his face losing its look of irritation as he said with genuine sincerity, 'Why, Angeline, my dear, you look lovely. Quite the young lady.'

'Thank you, Uncle.'

He was holding a marabou-trimmed white cape, which he now placed over her shoulders, saying, 'A small present from me, to celebrate your first dinner party as a young woman. Shall we?' He bent his arm and she slipped her hand through it as they walked out of the front door, which Mrs Upton had opened for them. The cape was lined with fur and reached to her ankles, and Angeline was glad of this, as the icy air hit her, causing her to take a breath.

Albert was standing by her uncle's carriage holding a lantern, and at their approach he held it higher while keeping the door of the conveyance open. Her uncle helped her up the steps and followed her in. Albert closed the door and then climbed up into the driver's seat and, after he had clicked his tongue at the two horses, they were off.

Angeline caught a last sight of Myrtle, standing just inside the front door, beaming all over her face, but Mrs Upton was nowhere to be seen. Not that she had expected the housekeeper to see her off, she thought wryly. From the moment she and Myrtle had entered her uncle's house, Mrs Upton had made it plain she considered them usurpers. Once the woman's veiled resentment would have bothered her, but since her parents' death it was as though the worst had happened, and minor irritants like an unfriendly housekeeper didn't matter.

She bit hard on her bottom lip to quell the sudden surge of hot moisture at the back of her eyes. She couldn't cry. Not now.

Hector's five-bedroomed house was set in its own grounds on the outskirts of Bishopwearmouth, not far from Barnes Park, and as the Golding estate was to the west of Sunderland, not far from the village of Washington, they were soon on country roads and the wheels of the carriage were hitting large potholes. Angeline had heard of the village – some decades before, thirty-five men and boys had been killed in an explosion at the colliery, and her father had known one of the present owners, who had discussed the matter one afternoon when her parents had thrown a garden party – but had never ventured this way before. As it was, she could see nothing of the countryside they were travelling through, for it was pitch-black outside the coach windows.

Her uncle was not a great conversationalist, and often a whole meal could pass as they sat at opposite ends of the dining table and he said not a word, but now he kept up a commentary about the state of the roads, the cold weather and umpteen other tedious subjects. Angeline answered politely when it was expected, and wished he would stop talking so that she could concentrate on preparing herself for the evening ahead.

Then out of the blue, and apropos of nothing that had gone before, he said something that brought her full attention to him. 'It is extremely kind of Oswald to invite us to dine tonight, and I shall expect your manner towards him to reflect this. Do you understand, Angeline?'

His face was a dim blur in the darkness and she couldn't read his expression. She blinked. 'Of course.'

Hector shifted in his seat. 'It's just that you haven't seemed to grasp the honour that has been extended to us. True, he is a man of his time and, due to his wealth and influence, leads a very different life from most folk we know, but that doesn't mean . . . '

Angeline waited. When her uncle didn't speak, she said perplexedly, 'Doesn't mean what, Uncle?'

'Did your father ever speak of him?'

'Of Mr Golding? No, I don't think so.'

There was a shred of relief in Hector's voice as he said, 'I thought that might be the reason why . . . No matter, no matter. Well, he's a fine gentleman, Angeline, a very fine gentleman. There's a member of his distant family who's in the inner circle of the Prince of Wales, so I believe. What do you think about that?'

She didn't know what she thought about it, but it seemed important to her uncle that she thought well of his friend, so she said, 'That's wonderful.'

'Quite so. Quite so.'

This signified the end of the conversation, and the rest of the journey was conducted in silence, but Angeline sat mulling over what had been said. Clearly her uncle thought there was something wrong with Mr Golding, if he had to bolster him up to her like that. Was he ugly, was that it? Or grossly fat? Or disfigured? Perhaps he was foul-smelling. One of her father's friends had been like that, and her mother had had to open all the windows and sprinkle lavender posies about when he'd been for a visit, such was the smell. Her mother had said the gentleman in question couldn't help it, and that he had visited the top doctors in London to no avail. Maybe Mr Golding was afflicted with a similar complaint?

Her stomach quivered. She was possessed of a keen sense of smell.

Oh well. She sat up straighter, lifting her chin. It was one evening. She could get through one evening. She'd got through the last weeks, hadn't she?

It was another fifteen minutes before the coach bowled through two huge, ornately worked iron gates, which had a family crest picked out in gold and black. Large lanterns hung on either side of the gates and, as the carriage travelled along the gravelled drive, its way was lit by more of the same.

Angeline's breath caught in her throat at her first sight of the house. It seemed to stretch forever. The enormous forecourt, where several carriages were already standing, was brilliantly lit by lights streaming from all of the windows and, as they approached, the massive door at the top of the steps was opened by a liveried footman.

By the time the carriage stopped, the footman was there to open the door. Her uncle descended first, then gave Angeline his hand to help her down. She stood for a moment, overawed, and as she glanced at her uncle, she saw his face mirrored the same emotion. He recovered almost immediately, his voice brisk as he said, 'Come along, m'dear.' And then, unable to hide his gratification, he added, 'I do believe that's Oswald coming to greet us.'

Angeline stared at the tall, fair man bounding down the steps and, to her dazzled eyes, he appeared like a young god. He reached them, shaking her uncle's hand and then turning to her, both his hands outstretched as he grasped hers. 'This must be Angeline. I'm so glad you could come. I may call you Angeline? But I mustn't keep you out here, in the night air. How very remiss of me. Come in, do.'

Oswald was walking by her side now, after having tucked one of her small hands through his arm, with her uncle following a step or two behind them. When she stepped into the house, it was all Angeline could do not to stand and gape. The hall flowed away in front of her, with a grand, sweeping staircase curving upwards for two floors in the middle of the expanse, and glittering glass chandeliers overhead. And then she became painfully conscious of the man at her side again, and of the faint but delicious smell emanating from his person as he turned to her.

'Welcome to my home.'

He drew her eyes to his as he spoke. Aware that as yet she hadn't said a word, and fearing he would think she was a simpleton, Angeline pulled herself together. 'Thank you, Mr Golding. It was very kind of you to invite us,' she said sedately, aware that the fire in her cheeks belied her voice.

'Oswald, please.' He smiled, revealing a set of perfectly even, white teeth. 'And may I take this opportunity to offer my condolences on your recent loss. It was very brave of you to come tonight, and I'm sure it would be what your parents would have wanted. They would not wish you to hide away from life, but rather to take comfort from friends and family. Your father and I were members of the same club, along with your uncle here. He was a fine man.'

Eagerly Angeline said, 'You knew my father?' Her uncle hadn't mentioned that.

'But of course,' Oswald nodded, his voice smooth. 'And your uncle is a good friend of mine. I know he has been very concerned about you. Let us hope the evening brings a measure of enjoyment.' The footman had taken her cloak and now, as a maid in a black alpaca dress with a white lacy apron at the waist hovered to one side of them, he added, 'Peggy will show you to the ladies' room, where you can freshen up, and then bring you to the drawing room.'

'Oh yes, thank you.' Angeline's head was spinning as she followed the maid across the hall and down a corridor, and as they reached an alcove, the maid opened a door and stood aside for Angeline to go before her.

'I'll be waiting outside when you're ready, Miss,' the girl said brightly, before closing the door after her.

Angeline's heart was racing as she stood looking about her. Three small dressing tables with a dainty velvet-backed chair in front of each of them stood along one wall on the right, and on the left was a row of doors leading to separate enclosed cubicles. At the far end of the room was a large table holding several beautifully painted pitchers and basins, and at the back of these sat a pile of neatly folded towels. As far as she could ascertain, she was alone.

There were long mirrors on the walls on either side of the table, and now, her stomach fluttering with nerves, Angeline made her way towards them and stood surveying herself. She didn't want to wash her hands or use one of the closets, and there was nothing else to do. She put her hand to her hair and fiddled with a curl, wondering if she had been in the cloakroom long enough. She was a fish out of water here, and suddenly the desire to be safely back in her room at her uncle's house was strong. She felt very young and insignificant, and the longing for her mother was overwhelming.

*Don't cry. Don't cry.* She squeezed her eyes tightly shut for a moment. *It's just a dinner party, that's all – one evening that will soon be over.*

A knock at the door brought her swinging round, and the little maid stood there. 'If you're ready, Miss, I'll take you through.'

'Thank you.' She took a deep breath, keeping her head up and her shoulders back as she left the room, her sparkling vanity bag clutched tightly in one hand, so that her knuckles shone white through her flesh.

As she entered the drawing room it seemed full of people, and the buzz of conversation was loud. Her uncle was standing talking to a tall man and a beautifully dressed young woman some yards away and, as she hesitated, her arm was taken and Oswald Golding said, 'There you are, I was waiting for you. Come and meet Lord Gray and his wife. They're newly-weds,' he added, lowering his voice, 'just back from their honeymoon in Europe, and I do believe Gwendoline is only a year or so older than you. I'm sure you'll get on famously.'

He drew her with him, to where her uncle and the couple were standing, and said, 'Nick, Gwendoline, this is Miss Angeline Stewart; Angeline, Lord and Lady Gray.'

'How do you do?' Angeline inclined her head as she dipped her knee, hoping she was doing the right thing.

'Angeline, what a charming name!' Gwendoline Gray's voice was polite, but without warmth, and there was an edge of condescension as she added, 'Your uncle has been telling us of your misfortune, Miss Stewart. Please accept our condolences on your sad loss.'

'Thank you.'

'I thought you might be a branch of the Kirkmichael Stewarts. I came out with Lady Victoria's daughter two seasons ago. *Such* a dear girl. But your uncle assures us you are not acquainted with them.'

Angeline stared at the pretty, doll-like face. She had often heard her father talk with Mr Appleby about the mechanism through which elite society was controlled, and her father had been scathing on occasions. The ruling class was landed, hereditary, wealthy and leisured, and also interrelated and exclusive, he'd maintained, but the aristocracy and gentry were by no means adverse to new wealth acquired through certain channels. Banking, business or industry – provided it was transmuted in an approved fashion – could be the means by which dwindling coffers were restored, but this didn't mean that ordinary individuals who made their fortune in trade would be accepted. Slights, both real and imagined, had been discussed by the two men, with her father insisting that he'd rather walk barefoot on hot coals than associate with some of the upper-class personages he rubbed shoulders with, at his club or in business. 'And the women are the worst,' he'd said one evening, when particularly irate. 'They control access to membership of their supposed elite circle like a bunch of sharp-clawed, superior cats, whilst having the morals of their alley counterparts. Do you know what I heard today?'

Her mother and Mrs Appleby had shushed the men at this point, with a pointed glance towards herself, Angeline recalled, but the conversation had made an impact on her, not least because she had been incensed that anyone would upset or snub her father. But Lord Gray's wife was one of those ladies who her father had spoken about to his old friend. She didn't know about Lady Gray's morals of course, but the woman definitely thought both her uncle and Angeline herself were beneath her socially.

Unsmilingly she said, 'My grandfather changed the family name, for reasons of his own, before my father and uncle were even born, so I think it is highly unlikely we are related to any Stewarts you might know, Lady Gray.'

'Oh.' It was a surprised sound, and a trace of colour came into Gwendoline's pale cheeks.

Lord Gray cast his wife a glance that could have meant anything as he leaned forward, offering his hand as he said, 'It is very nice to meet you, Miss Stewart.' As Angeline placed her fingers in his, he raised her hand briefly to his lips, a twinkle in his eye as he murmured, 'Whichever Stewarts you are related to.'

They smiled at each other as his wife rustled indignantly in her taffeta and lace dress, and then, as a gong sounded in the hall, Oswald smoothly intervened, 'Ah, dinner, I think. Shall we?', his hand again at Angeline's elbow.

There were thirty seated at the vast dining table, which was beautifully laid with a fine white damask cloth, a battery of crystal glasses and regimented silver cutlery, placed just so, in order that plates and bowls could be put directly in front of each diner without having to rearrange the cutlery between courses. A snowy napkin, folded into an elaborate mitre shape, stood by each place, and silver condiment sets for salt, pepper and mustard were placed at regular intervals along the table. Heavy silver candelabra burned softly at either end of the table, wound around with ivy and small flowers; and a magnificent flower display took centre stage. Two footmen wearing an elaborate livery and patent buckled shoes stepped silently forward to pull out the chairs and seat the guests at table. The splendour took Angeline's breath away and, when she glanced at her uncle, she saw that he was equally wide-eyed.

Oswald, as host, sat at the head of the table with his back to the huge fireplace, in which a hearty fire was burning, and Angeline was surprised to find herself seated to his left, with Lord Gray on her other side. Her uncle sat on the opposite side of the table next to a stiff-faced Lady Gray.

Dinner was styled *à la russe*, which meant that each course was prepared on bowls or plates on the vast sideboard that stretched down one wall and was then handed to the guests by the footmen. A menu sat by each napkin, and Angeline was horrified to see that the dinner consisted of twelve courses. Her eyes took in the soup, fish, cutlets, fricassees, boudins, sweetbreads and pâtés that she was apparently expected to eat before the main roast, and she gave a little sigh.

A slight cough from Lord Gray brought her gaze to him and he said very quietly, 'Most of the ladies take a bite or two at most from each course; and some they wave away altogether.'

She smiled her thanks. He was nice, she thought. Not like his wife. She wondered how such a nice man had come to marry someone like Lady Gray.

Oswald made a point of drawing her into every conversation that he conducted during the meal, and by the time they came to the puddings she felt more herself, although a little hot and flustered. Whether this was from her first taste of wine – there were four glasses before her place at the table, and she had noticed that even the ladies drank all the different wines that were served with the various courses, although she only sipped the odd mouthful – or from the attention Oswald Golding was bestowing on her, she didn't know.

He was one of the most handsome men she had ever seen, that was for sure. His grey eyes rested constantly on her flushed face, sending a little thrill down her spine, and his silky blond hair gleamed in the candlelight. Of course he was only being kind, knowing that her parents had recently died, she told herself, but still . . .

The meal went on and on, the jewels of the ladies glittering as they talked and moved, the snowy shirt-fronts of the men glistening, and the silent servants coming and going as they handed out dishes and poured wine in the light of the many candles. The food was delicious and spectacular to look at, and the conversation ranged widely, laughter punctuating the talk of social events, sport and politics, most of which was above Angeline's head. She found it best to smile when others smiled and to look interested without venturing an opinion; her mama had always said silence was the best option, if one wasn't fully conversant with the facts. She avoided catching Lady Gray's eye; she had the impression that Lord Gray's wife didn't appreciate the attention he was giving to a little nobody, if her stony expression was anything to go by.

At the conclusion of the meal Angeline rose with the

other ladies as they adjourned to the drawing room. She had been dreading this moment, knowing it would have to come to enable the men to enjoy their port, brandy and cigars, but not wanting to be alone in the midst of so many women who all seemed to know each other very well. Admittedly several of the ladies had smiled kindly at her during the meal, but the feeling of being a fish out of water was back – and much stronger this time.

She didn't follow the main body of ladies into the drawing room, but instead made her way to the powder room again. This time she entered one of the cubicles and shut the door behind her with a thudding heart, as though she had escaped some peril. She stood with her back to the door and took several deep steadying breaths, all the while telling herself not to be so silly.

A large oil lamp hung on the wall at the back of the closet, over a wide shelf containing a row of glass bowls holding dried flowers that scented the air. The toilet itself was a wooden box structure, with a round porcelain seat surrounding the hole. Angeline continued to stand perfectly still, one hand resting on the pearl necklace at her throat and the other clutching her vanity bag. Slowly her breathing returned to normal, and she was just about to exit the closet and make her way back to the drawing room when the door to the powder room opened and what sounded like several women entered.

'But who *is* she exactly? I don't know of any Stewarts in his circle, do you?'

Angeline's hand was on the doorknob, but she paused

for a moment at the mention of her surname, uncertain whether it would be more embarrassing to make herself known if these ladies were discussing her or remain out of sight.

There was a tinkling laugh. 'Who knows, where Oswald's concerned?'

'But to seat her where he did! He's certainly made his intentions plain enough.'

'Maybe, but as I said: who knows with Oswald?'

'I think it's more significant who *isn't* here tonight,' a new voice put in.

'You mean the Jeffersons?'

'Who else?'

'So you think . . . '

'What I think, Camilla, is that the next little while is going to be very interesting.'

This brought more laughter, and Angeline's brow wrinkled. Those ladies were clearly talking about her, but she didn't understand what had been said.

There followed some rustling of dresses, and murmuring voices and laughter, then the door opened and closed and all was quiet once more.

She waited a couple of minutes more and then opened the cubicle door. Suddenly she felt utterly bereft. She wanted to go home. Whatever those ladies had been saying, it was spiteful, she was sure of it. There wasn't one person here that she liked.

No, that wasn't true, she corrected herself in the next instant, blinking back hot tears. Lord Gray wasn't like the rest of them; he had been kind to her. And Oswald? Her heart beat faster. He was . . . well, he was . . . She gave up trying to find words for what Oswald was.

He was sitting on one of the chairs in the hall when she left the powder room and immediately came towards her, saying, 'There you are, I've been waiting for you. We're finishing the evening with a spot of dancing, and I insist you dance the first dance with me. Oh, that's very rude of me' – he grinned at her, a boyish grin – 'for I should have said: would you do me the honour of the first dance?'

It was as she looked up into his face that a thought came to her, an impossible thought that caused a warm blush to spread through her body. Repudiating it – for why would a rich, handsome man of the world like him be bothering with someone like her, except out of a wish to be kind – she said, 'Thank you, I'd like that.'

His smile widened and his voice was soft as he said, 'I don't know if I will allow you to dance with anyone else, or is that rude, too?'

Angeline didn't know how to answer this and so she didn't try, but as he led her down the hall and through an anteroom into the ballroom, her heart was singing and the conversation she had overheard felt suddenly unimportant.

He liked her. She didn't know how it had come about, and she felt giddy at the thought, but Oswald Golding liked her. For his part, Oswald was telling himself this could have been much worse than it was. True, she was painfully naive and unsophisticated – two qualities that he abhorred in his women, finding such attributes irritating and inevitably boring – but, in this case, it suited his purposes. And she was much prettier than he had expected; one could say beautiful even, although her slender build was not to his liking. He preferred his women well rounded and voluptuous, with fire in their bellies. But she was clearly docile and biddable, which in the circumstances was a relief, if he was to get this business over with quickly. And a dutiful, meek wife was no bad thing. It would leave him free to conduct his life as he wished – and with whom. No, this chit of a girl would pose no problem. Even now he had her eating out of his hand.

And Hector? As Angeline's uncle came hurrying across to them, Oswald's shrewd gaze took in the other man's flushed face and bright eyes, and the way he was almost drooling with gratification at the quality of the company he was enjoying. Hector Stewart would offer no resistance to his advances towards Angeline, particularly when he offered the carrot of making it worth Hector's while. He would be tactful, of course. Hector was the girl's uncle after all, and it wouldn't do to offend him. Not until she had signed her name on the wedding certificate. After that . . .

# *Chapter Four*

'Oh, Miss, it sounds lovely.'

Angeline had just finished relating the details of the evening to an eager Myrtle. The maid had been waiting for her young mistress when the carriage arrived home after one o'clock. Angeline had described the house, every course at dinner, the ladies' sumptuous dresses and jewels and the wonderful ballroom, but she hadn't mentioned Oswald Golding.

Her heart fluttered madly at the thought of him. She'd had one or two dances with other partners, one of whom had been Lord Gray, but then Oswald had been at her side again, making it clear that he had eyes only for her. And, in truth, she had only wanted to dance with him. Her feet had hardly seemed to touch the floor when she was in his arms; he danced divinely, and she had felt she was floating around the ballroom.

Myrtle's fingers were busy releasing Angeline from the tight constraints of the corset and, when it fell away,

Angeline stretched, rubbing her ribs. 'That's so much better – I hate those things.'

'But you looked beautiful tonight, Miss,' Myrtle said reprovingly, as though only the corset had had anything to do with her mistress's appearance. Fetching Angeline's nightgown, she helped her on with it. 'What was he like, Miss? Mr Golding?'

Angeline didn't look at Myrtle. 'He . . . he's a fine gentleman.' Sinking down on the dressing-table stool, she added, 'I can manage now, Myrtle. You get off to bed, you must be tired.'

'Not as tired as you, Miss, I'll be bound,' said Myrtle cheerfully as she finished putting away the discarded items of clothing. 'I'll bring your tea later in the morning, shall I? Let you sleep in for a bit.' Bustling over to the door, she turned with her hand on the doorknob, 'Sleep well, Miss. Goodnight.'

'Goodnight, Myrtle.'

Once she was alone, Angeline breathed a sigh of relief. Myrtle had said she must be tired, but she had never felt less like sleep in her life. The blood was singing through her veins, and every pulse was throbbing with wild, exuberant life. Her eyes were starry as she gazed at her reflection in the dressing-table mirror, and she jumped up, twirling around the room until she collapsed on the bed, giddy and out of breath.

A sudden thought brought her sitting bolt upright, even as her head still whirled. Was it wrong to feel this way, with her darling mama and father so recently gone?

She had left this house earlier feeling full of hidden resentment at her uncle's insistence that she come out of her black mourning clothes for the evening and accompany him to a dinner she had no wish to attend. Her new evening dress, exquisite though it was, had brought her no pleasure – not until she had seen Oswald's gaze on her, that was. Then she had been glad she was looking her best. Was that the height of superficiality?

Falling on her knees beside the bed, she put her hands together. Her voice choked with tears, she prayed, 'I'm sorry, I'm sorry. I love you, Mama. I love you both, so much. Forgive me.'

She continued to berate herself for some little while, until the tiredness she had denied brought a kind of calm. Climbing into bed – a bed that was much too soft, due to a thick feather-filled mattress that made her feel she was being smothered each night – she told herself she wouldn't sleep. Within moments she had proved herself wrong.

It seemed as if she had only just shut her eyes when Myrtle's voice woke her, saying, 'Good morning, Miss. You're in the best place – it's snowing a blizzard out there.'

Blinking, she sat up, taking the cup of tea that Myrtle handed her, with a murmur of thanks. 'What time is it?'

'Gone ten, Miss.' Myrtle set about persuading the glowing embers of the fire in the bedroom's small fireplace into life. With Angeline's permission, she had told Mrs Upton that she needn't concern herself about any aspect of the young mistress's care and that she would see both to Angeline's room and to her person. She herself slept in one of the two rooms in the attics, the other one being the housekeeper's. Albert had his own quarters above the stables, but ate all his meals in the kitchen.

'Ten o'clock?' Angeline couldn't remember a time when she hadn't been up and about before eight in the morning, although her mother had occasionally risen late, normally after a dinner party or some other social gathering. This thought brought Oswald to the forefront of her mind, and her heart began to thump.

'Your uncle has already gone out, Miss. I thought you might like a breakfast tray up here, rather than sit by yourself in the dining room?'

'That would be nice, Myrtle. Thank you.'

'I'll bring it shortly.' Myrtle pulled back the heavy drapes at the window as she spoke, revealing a cold white world, the wind howling as it drove the thick whirling snowflakes in a demented dance of its own making. 'You snuggle down again, Miss. The fire'll soon take hold and warm things up.'

As Myrtle bustled out, Angeline smiled to herself. Since they had come to live with her uncle, Myrtle's manner had verged on motherly at times, and yet she was only a couple of years older than herself. Still, it was nice.

She ate everything on the tray Myrtle brought, finding that she was ravenously hungry, and then had a long hot bath and washed and dried her hair. Feeling refreshed and rested, she was dressed and sitting close to the roaring fire in the drawing room, reading, when Myrtle came in, her face beaming. 'These have just arrived for you, Miss.' She was almost hidden behind the most enormous bouquet of flowers Angeline had ever seen. 'And a *footman* delivered them.'

Angeline looked at the pink-and-white rosebuds, baby's breath, carnations and a whole host of other perfect blooms, and her heart began to race.

'Here, Miss.' Myrtle reached out a hand and gave her a small, embossed envelope with the Golding crest in one corner.

Opening it, Angeline read:

Dear Angeline,

Thank you for an enchanting evening. I have selected these from my own hothouses to bring a touch of summer's beauty to a cold winter's day, but may I say – and please do not think me too forward – that their beauty can in no way compare to your loveliness.

Your obedient servant,

Oswald

Myrtle's bright eyes were wide, and in answer to the unspoken question, Angeline murmured, 'They're from Mr Golding. Would you take them and put them in water, Myrtle, and we'll have them in here, I think. Perhaps on the small table by the window, away from the heat of the fire.'

For the rest of the morning her gaze strayed constantly to the flowers, which had required dividing into three vases, so many were there. When her uncle arrived home for lunch, she realized she hadn't read a page of her book.

Hector's eyes went straight to the table set between the two wide bay windows. 'Well, well, well.' He smiled at her. 'What do we have here?'

Knowing she was blushing, Angeline smiled back. 'They're from Oswald, from his own hothouses on the estate.'

'Indeed. I could see he was somewhat smitten last night.'

'Oh, Uncle, he was being kind, that's all.'

'And the flowers? Is that just being kind, too?'

'He . . . he knows about Mama and Father; he's being sympathetic.'

'Perhaps.' Hector's voice was hearty, expressing his delight. 'Well, let us go through for lunch, m'dear. With the weather so inclement I shall stay at home this afternoon, for the roads are getting treacherous. An afternoon keeping you company by the fire will be most agreeable.'

Angeline tried to look pleased. She would much have preferred to be alone with her thoughts.

The next few weeks were ones of savage snowstorms, bitterly cold winds, ice and unrelenting short days and long nights, but this bothered Angeline not a jot. Some days after the flowers had arrived, a carriage carrying a

Golding footman called again, this time with a box of crystallized fruit. The accompanying note was along the same lines as the first. Then Oswald himself took to calling two or three times a week, ostensibly to see Hector, but always with a small gift for Angeline. A first edition of Longfellow's *Song of Hiawatha*, after Angeline said she thought it the most beautiful of books; a box of delicious sweetmeats; a carton of big, black, sweet grapes from the Golding outhouses; and so it went on.

During this time Hector and Angeline were invited twice to the estate, first to a small soirée in the evening, when the guests listened to music after an excellent dinner, and then to an informal lunch, when it was just the two of them and Oswald showed them around the house.

This evening the carriage was calling for them at seven o'clock, when her uncle and Angeline were to accompany Oswald and an elderly aunt – who was paying him a visit from Scotland – to a play at the Avenue Theatre and Opera House. For once, Angeline was not anticipating the evening with excitement. It had been on leaving this very theatre three months earlier that her parents had met their deaths.

Myrtle, sensitive to her mistress's mood, said very little as she helped Angeline dress. She knew how her mistress felt about Oswald Golding – it was as plain as the nose on your face – but she didn't like him. Not that her feelings were of any account, she knew that, but there was something about him . . . He was wildly handsome, she'd give him that, and wealthy and influential to boot, if the talk that went on in the kitchen between the housekeeper and her brother was anything to go by, but why was he pressing his suit so ardently? It wasn't right, not so soon after the master and mistress had died. He wouldn't have behaved in such a fashion if the master was alive, and she didn't care what anyone said to the contrary.

She followed Angeline downstairs, holding her fur-lined cloak as Oswald stood talking to Hector in the hall, his aunt waiting in the carriage outside. Immediately he saw Angeline, Oswald smiled, holding out his hands as he said, 'You look beautiful, my dear.' He took the cloak from Myrtle, without looking at her, and she stepped back a pace, watching him as he slid it around Angeline's shoulders and then pulled the wide hood up over her hair, saying, 'It's cold outside.'

Angeline smiled up at him, her face alight, and Myrtle experienced the unease that she felt when seeing them together. Something wasn't right, but she was blowed if she could put her finger on it. Then, as Oswald ushered Angeline out of the front door, he turned for just an instant, the grey eyes raking down Myrtle's person from the top of her head to the soles of her feet. Mrs Upton shut the door behind him in the next moment, but still Myrtle stood where she was, shocked and shaken.

'What's the matter with you?' said Mrs Upton sharply.

'Nothing.' She forced herself to walk past the eagle eyes of the housekeeper and over to the staircase, making her way to Angeline's room, where a pile of clothes needed to be put away. Once the door was closed behind her, Myrtle sank down on the bed. Mr Golding had virtually undressed her, there on the doorstep. Her cheeks burning, she put her hands to her face. The filthy so-an'-so. And it hadn't been like when the butcher's boy gave her the eye, or when the odd lad whistled at her on her day off. She gave as good as she got then. No, this had been different. He'd made her feel dirty and ashamed – sullied.

She brought her hands down from her face, staring at the window. And this was the man Miss Angeline was fair barmy about. He was playing her like a violin, but why would he do that, with all his money and influence? He could have any woman he wanted. She didn't understand any of this, but one thing she did know: Miss Angeline wouldn't hear a word against him. Anyway, what could she say? That Mr Golding had looked at her – because in truth he'd done nothing more.

Slowly Myrtle slid off the bed and made herself start tidying the room, but her thoughts were with her young mistress, and they were fearful.

Angeline found the whole evening something of a strain, not because of the company, although the elderly aunt was deaf and consequently everyone had to bellow their conversation, but because the picture of her parents enjoying themselves in this very place – not knowing what was to befall them – was at the forefront of her mind. She endeavoured to hide her feelings, joining in the talk about the play at the interval and smiling and laughing, but by the time the little party of four left the theatre, a headache was throbbing at the back of her skull.

The Golding carriage had been waiting outside. Although the month of May was just around the corner, the odd desultory snowflake was wafting in the air and it was bitterly cold. Angeline pulled her cloak tightly round her and, once in the carriage, snuggled into the fur with the hood low over her face. Hector had invited Oswald and his aunt in for coffee and brandy and, much as Angeline lived for the moments spent in Oswald's company, tonight she would have preferred to go straight to bed.

As they entered the house Oswald took Angeline's elbow, letting the other two go on before them into the drawing room. 'Is anything wrong? Have *I* done anything wrong?' he murmured softly. It had been his constant fear over the last weeks that she'd hear something about him – about his past, some remark or insinuation or other comment – that would cause her to withdraw from him, but he had still felt that he dare not hurry things along any faster than he was doing.

'No, of course you have done nothing wrong.' Shocked that such a thought would enter his mind, Angeline was further emboldened to whisper, 'You . . . you could never do anything wrong. I have a headache, that is all, and . . . ' She paused, wondering if it would further spoil the evening if she mentioned her parents.

'And?' he prompted gently.

'I have been thinking of Mama and my father. It was on leaving the Avenue Theatre that the accident occurred on the way home.'

'Oh, my dear.' His tone and manner altered, and he caught her hand, pressing her cold fingers to his warm lips, before muttering, 'I didn't realize. Your uncle should have said, and we could have gone elsewhere tonight. I would never willingly do anything to cause you a moment's unhappiness. Can you forgive me?'

Angeline looked into the handsome face that fascinated her and filled her dreams, her heart in her eyes. 'There's nothing to forgive, Oswald. Truly, please don't distress yourself.'

This evening had rattled him. He had almost been sure she was turning cold on him. Her fortune would provide the injection of cash that was necessary to turn his finances around; he couldn't afford to let Angeline slip through his fingers. Telling himself that he might not get another chance like this for a while, he drew both her hands against his chest and, as she began to tremble, felt a moment's thrill of satisfaction. She was his for the taking – and to hell with convention. He had to get her up the aisle without delay. Tonight had been a warning.

'I think you have guessed how I feel about you, Angeline. From the first moment we met I haven't been able to hide my adoration, have I?' He smiled the boyish smile that he knew charmed the female of the species, from the cradle to the grave.

Angeline's blush deepened, but she made no reply.

'My dear, I want to ask you something. No, I *long* to ask you something. I think of little else, but Hector is your guardian, and propriety dictates that I must put my request to him first.' Oswald hesitated, as though unsure of himself. 'I think what I am trying to say, dearest Angeline, is: would you wish me to speak to your uncle?'

How could Oswald wonder for a moment if she wished for anything else? There was nothing in the world she wanted more. Her head bowed, Angeline nodded, trying to keep the flood of joy and elation from showing in her voice when she answered as demurely as her mother would have instructed, 'Yes, Oswald, I would wish it.'

'I shall return tomorrow morning.'

She kept her eyes on their joined hands. Hers seemed very small in comparison to his, which were long and strong, with thin fingers and meticulously clean nails. She loved his hands, she thought wonderingly; she loved everything about him. And he cared for her. Even now, after all these weeks, she could scarcely believe it.

'Come, they will wonder what is keeping us.' There was a lilt to his voice. 'I shall make my excuses and leave now' – and, at her exclamation of protest, his smile widened – 'and you must go to bed and rest, and nurse your headache, dearest, but I shall see you tomorrow. Each minute will seem like a day, and each day a lifetime, till then.'

He said such beautiful things. She accompanied him

into the drawing room and stood quietly as he helped his aunt to rise from her chair and they made their leave to Hector. What had she done to deserve him? Whatever had she done to deserve a man like Oswald Golding?

# *Chapter Five*

Hector stared at the man in front of him. He had suspected what Oswald had in mind when he had taken him aside on the doorstep the night before and asked if he could talk privately with him in the morning, but conjecture was different from hearing plain words.

'I think you may be aware of the reason for my visit this morning. I wish to ask for Angeline's hand in marriage.' This was what Oswald had just said, and now that it was out in the open, Hector had to admit he wasn't as pleased as he had thought he would be. The significance of the events of the past weeks hadn't been lost on him, of course, and he had actively encouraged Angeline's association with Oswald, basking in the reflected glory, but this was so soon, so . . . sudden.

They were sitting in Hector's study, with a cup of coffee and a plate of Mrs Upton's delicious shortbread biscuits in front of each of them, and now Hector took a sip from his cup to give himself a moment of time. He knew of Oswald's way of life – at least the way of life he had pursued up until a short while ago. Some would term it scandalous, others would say he was merely a man of his time and class. And Hector knew which way his brother would have thought. Philip wouldn't have let this man within ten miles of his daughter.

Awkwardly – for this was Oswald Golding, after all, and the last thing he wanted to do was offend him – Hector said, 'Can I speak frankly, as one friend to another?' And at Oswald's nod, he continued, 'I have to say I don't quite understand why a man of your standing and influence would want to marry a young girl like Angeline. I am very fond of her of course, and she is a young lady in every sense of the word, but brought up as she was by my brother and his wife in what amounted to virtual seclusion, she is unworldly and naive. I would have expected you to choose a wife' – he hesitated, having been about to say 'of your own class', but that would reflect on him, so he changed it to – 'who is well acquainted with society and perhaps a little older?'

Unsmilingly Oswald said, 'I *am* old enough to be her father, if that is what you are suggesting, but still in my prime at thirty-six, Hector. As for what you term Angeline's unworldliness . . . time will rectify that.'

'Of course, of course.'

Oswald's eyes narrowed. He hadn't expected this. He had imagined that Hector would be congratulating himself on being lifted into the upper strata of society, courtesy of his niece; not that he would develop a conscience towards the girl at this late stage. Or was he playing some game of his own? Perhaps attempting to find out what was in it for him? Oswald could understand this way of thinking, and it tempered his irritation. 'I have a great affection for Angeline, and my regard would certainly extend to her nearest and dearest, upon our marriage. Now, if I can be the one who speaks frankly, I thought it a great injustice that your brother did not see fit to behave honourably towards you in his will. As Angeline's husband, I would see that this is rectified.'

Red colour stained Hector's pale cheeks, a mixture of chagrin and outrage, but his mortification at the veiled suggestion that he could be bought was tempered by the weight of his debts. He licked his lips, seeing a way out of his money problems, which had spiralled out of control. Stiffly he said, 'My prime concern is Angeline's happiness.'

'Of course.' Oswald's voice was honeyed. 'As is mine. But, in our happiness, I would not wish to see someone she cares for deeply suffering an injustice of any kind.'

In a moment of piercing clarity, Hector knew that all the misgivings he had tried to bury over the last months about the character of Oswald Golding had just been confirmed. Who was it who had said that a leopard cannot change its spots? Whoever it had been, they were right.

He reached for his coffee, gulping at it.

But however suspect the man was, he clearly cared for

Angeline, for why else would he be so set on marrying her? And Angeline was in love with Oswald, of that he was sure. It would be cruel to stand in her way. She had lost Philip and Margery; could he be the obstacle to her finding happiness again? The fact that he would benefit from the marriage was a side-issue, that was all, and hadn't he taken Angeline into his home and looked after her as though she was his own daughter?

And so he quietened his conscience as Oswald stared at him with cold grey eyes, fully aware of what Hector was thinking, and hiding his distaste for the man who was Angeline's uncle behind a blank countenance.

Eventually Hector looked up, saying in a falsely jolly tone of voice, 'Of course the decision is Angeline's, and hers alone. I know nothing about young girls and their feelings, so I will leave the answer to her. If you would like to wait in the drawing room, I'll send her in to you shortly.'

Oswald smiled, finishing his coffee before he stood up and then, without saying a word, walked out of the study.

Angeline was pacing her bedroom in a fever of impatience. She had watched Oswald arrive from her window, and it seemed like hours ago that he'd disappeared with her uncle into Hector's study, even though her dainty little bedside clock told her it was only twenty minutes or so since his knock at the front door.

'Are you all right, Miss?' Myrtle had entered the room,

her arms full of fresh linen to change the bed, and had stopped dead at the sight of her young mistress's agitation.

'Oh, Myrtle, I shall burst if I don't tell someone.' To Myrtle's surprise, Angeline grasped her hands. 'Mr Golding is here, and he's going to tell my uncle he wants to marry me. He . . . he asked me last night if he could.'

Myrtle didn't know what to say, but her face must have spoken for itself because, her whole manner changing, Angeline let go of her hands and drew back, her voice expressing her hurt as she said, 'What's the matter? Aren't you pleased for me?'

Recovering herself, Myrtle stammered, 'I . . . I'm so-sorry, Miss. I never expected . . . What I mean is, you . . . you haven't known Mr Golding long.'

'Just over three months.' Angeline's voice was cool, signifying her pique. 'But sometimes these things happen in an instant.'

Aye, and give rise to a lifetime of regret. 'It's just so soon, Miss, after . . . '

'Yes, I know.' Her voice changing yet again, Angeline reached out and patted Myrtle's arm. 'Don't look like that, Myrtle. I think of Mama and Father often, and miss them, too. We were a happy household, weren't we?'

'Oh, don't cry, Miss.' Horrified that she had caused tears, Myrtle was beside herself. 'It's just that you are young and, if you'll pardon the imposition, Miss, you don't know anything about lads – men, I mean.'

Angeline wiped her eyes on her lace handkerchief and

gave a wan smile. 'I know what my heart is telling me, Myrtle. Doesn't that count for anything? And—'

Whatever she had been about to say next was interrupted by a knock at the bedroom door and the housekeeper's clipped voice calling, 'Miss Angeline? You are wanted in the drawing room.'

'Oh.' As Myrtle watched, her mistress's face was transformed. 'He's got permission to ask me.'

Myrtle hoped not. Oh, she did so hope Mr Stewart had sent Mr Golding packing and it was Miss Angeline's uncle who was waiting in the drawing room. The poor lass might cry and wail for a bit, but it would be for the best, Myrtle knew it in her waters.

Angeline whirled out of the room, leaving Myrtle staring after her, biting her lip. She tiptoed onto the landing and peered down into the hall, staring at the closed drawing-room door. When it didn't open again and no raised voices or protest were heard, Myrtle's heart sank into her boots. This was all wrong, she told herself for the umpteenth time. She might not know all there was to know about etiquette and codes of behaviour, but she knew enough to know this proposal was flouting every rule – happening so quickly after the lass's parents had been killed, and her being so young an' all. And him, Mr Golding, for all his wealth and looks, he was as shallow as a worm's grave and not the right one for Miss Angeline.

In the drawing room Oswald had taken Angeline's hand and drawn her to a couch set at an angle to the fireplace. Once she had sat down, and without letting go of her fingers, he went down on one knee in front of her. 'Angeline, dearest Angeline, will you marry me,' he said softly, 'and make me the happiest man in the world?'

She was too honest to play the coquette and her shining eyes were answer enough, even before she whispered, 'Yes, Oswald.'

'May I?' He had drawn a small velvet box out of his pocket, opening it to reveal an exquisite engagement ring. Angeline looked down at the gold band set with a half-hoop of diamonds and rubies, her heart racing.

Oswald took the ring from the box and slipped it on the third finger of her left hand. 'It was my mother's, and her grandmother's before her,' he murmured. 'Story has it that my great-great – I forget how many greats – grandfather acquired it, and other treasure, when he fought the Spanish whilst protecting England's shores. This ring was the prize of his booty and, on arriving safely home, he presented it to the lady of his choice and they became betrothed. I think he would be pleased to see it on your finger now.'

Entranced, Angeline lifted her hand and the ring sparkled brilliantly. It fitted perfectly.

Oswald stood up, drawing her with him and into his arms. She shut her eyes as he kissed her on the lips. It was a gentle kiss and only lasted a moment, but the feel of his mouth on hers brought the blood surging through her veins and hot colour to her cheeks. Unbidden, the thought of Queen Victoria's Golden Jubilee, three years ago, came to her mind and something her mother had said about the elderly Queen. They'd had a wonderful day joining in the celebrations in the town and a carnival-like atmosphere had prevailed everywhere: street parties, processions of school children in fancy dress, banners and Union Jacks flying from every house and shop, and a huge fair in Mowbray Park. Walking home in the evening between her parents, she had smiled up at her mother. 'It must be wonderful to be Queen Victoria and know you're so loved, not just here in England but all over her empire.'

'Perhaps.' Her mother had nodded. 'But the Queen has lived a large portion of her reign without the man she loved at her side. I would not change places with her.'

And then her mother had smiled at her father in the special way they kept for each other, Angeline remembered, and even then, at thirteen years of age, she had thought, 'I want that. When I marry, I want to love someone like that.'

And now she did.

She opened her eyes as Oswald said gently, as though he knew her thoughts had been with her mother, 'With your parents gone, I want to take care of you as they would have done, my sweet. Are you agreeable to a short engagement?'

She knew most engagements were of two or three years' duration, especially when the bride-to-be was as young as she was, but she didn't want to wait so long. Shyly she nodded.

'I'll speak with Hector.' Drawing her arm through his, he gave the wide, ingenuous smile that she loved. 'Let's tell him you've have made me the happiest man in the world, and then the three of us will lunch at the house and I will introduce you properly to the staff.'

She stared at him, something approaching alarm replacing the light in her eyes. 'Your staff? Is that necessary? I mean . . . ' For the first time it dawned on her what being a wife to someone as wealthy as Oswald would mean. 'What will I say?'

For a second she thought she saw disdain in the handsome face, but it was gone in an instant and his voice was soft. 'I'll be with you, and you don't need to say a word – merely act as the future mistress of my house. They will not expect any acknowledgement from you, for they are merely servants.'

Oh dear, that sounded so different from what she'd been used to at Oakfield, and from the way her father had behaved towards Mrs Lee and the other staff. She hoped she could live up to what Oswald expected of her, but she didn't like the thought of looking down on his servants, even if – as he'd insinuated – it was what they were used to. And then he pressed her to him, stroking back a wisp of hair from her forehead, and his touch banished the tiny cloud that had momentarily overshadowed her happiness.

Angeline found that she had to force herself to eat the delicious lunch; even the caramel pudding that followed the three other courses seemed to stick in her throat. It hadn't helped that, on entering the great hall of Oswald's house, her uncle had taken her aside and muttered, 'The going-on here is a different kettle of fish from anything you've been used to. Remember that, and take your lead from Oswald. If in doubt, say nothing and, whatever you do, don't be familiar with any of the servants – and by that I mean don't treat them like you did that lot at Oakfield. Do you understand me, Angeline? Today will set the tone, for you as well as them, because give 'em an inch and they'll take a mile, and laugh behind their hands while doing so.'

And now lunch was finished and she had to face the ordeal. Hector remained in the dining room, as he would not be accompanying them. Oswald walked with her into the hall where a long line of servants stood waiting. Numbly she heard him say, as they reached the first man, 'This is Palmer, my man, and Wood, the butler. Mrs Gibson, my housekeeper, will continue.'

The housekeeper was the very antithesis of Mrs Upton, being a large plump woman with rosy-red cheeks and a double chin, but her voice was circumspect as she stepped forward after bobbing her head and began to name names, which Angeline immediately forgot. Two footmen, housemaids, the cook, two kitchen maids and a scullery maid, a seamstress, a laundress and a boot-boy all bowed their heads or dipped their knees, and then the butler took over and pointed at various individuals, beginning with the coachman and grooms and finishing with the gardeners and a married couple who were the lodge-keepers. Angeline didn't have to worry about remaining aloof, for her brain was so addled she couldn't have spoken or smiled if she had wished to.

When they reached the end of the line Oswald took her elbow, saying in an aside to the housekeeper, 'We'll take coffee in the drawing room, Mrs Gibson' and to Angeline, 'Come along, my dear, a tedious ritual but necessary', as though they weren't within sight or hearing of the servants.

Once in the drawing room, where Hector was waiting for them, Oswald closed the door and said, his tone faintly surprised, 'One would have thought you'd been doing that all your life.'

She stared at him. There was something – the merest inflexion in his voice – that she didn't like, although she couldn't have said why. Nevertheless it jarred. And this came through in her tone, which was cool as she replied, 'I am glad you approve.'

Oswald's eyes narrowed, but in the next moment he had taken both her hands in his and turned to Hector. 'We must have an engagement party so that I can show Angeline off to the world,' he said jovially. 'A ball – yes, that's it. We'll have a ball. Have you been to a ball before, my dear?' he added, smiling down at her as he kissed her fingertips. 'No? Then I will make this one perfect, as you are perfect.'

Telling herself it was nerves making her imagine absurd things, and that Oswald would never belittle her in word or thought – for didn't he love her as much as she loved him? – Angeline smiled back. A ball, for her. Oh, her mama would have been so thrilled.

'And we will announce the date of the wedding, too. After the London Season, I think? Late August perhaps, or maybe September. September can be a beautiful month for a wedding, don't you think? Mellow and warm.'

Angeline could tell that her uncle was as amazed as she was; when Oswald had said a short engagement, she had expected it to last eighteen months, at the very least twelve.

'It's what we both want.' Oswald turned to Hector again. 'You have no objection, I presume? There will be time enough for certain legalities and . . . financial arrangements to be put in place.'

Hector blinked. His debts were pressing and the situation could only get worse month by month, but September? He looked at Angeline and said weakly, 'I have no objection, if that's what you want?'

She couldn't disappoint Oswald, and there was no reason to delay anyway. What did custom and convention matter? She wanted to be his wife, and if Oswald wished them to marry in September, so be it. Nodding, she said, 'Yes, it's what I want.'

'Then the wedding preparations will be put in motion this very week.' Oswald bent and kissed her nose. 'And you must busy yourself deciding how you want our private quarters refurbished. I confess they are very much a bachelor's taste at present, but I give you free rein, my sweet.'

The mention of this brought a blush to her cheeks. Their bedroom and private quarters were where *that* side of marriage went on, and although she had no idea what it entailed, she knew it was the means by which babies were made. When she had begun her monthly cycle two years ago, her mother had told her it was the natural preparation of a woman's body for marriage and bearing children, and that when she met her future husband she would explain further. In the meantime, her mother had said, she must not worry about such matters. Angeline hadn't been too anxious, as it happened, reasoning that if her beloved mother and father did whatever it was that they did, then it was nothing to fret about. Now she wished that she had asked more questions.

Oswald had noticed Angeline's reaction and had to curb his impatience. Nothing about her innocence attracted him; it was merely an inconvenience. His father had arranged his introduction into manhood when he was a boy of fourteen, and it had been some weeks later before he had realized that the lady in question – who had been well versed in the intricate variations of a man's needs and base desires – had been his father's former mistress. Oswald had enjoyed her services for some good time, before moving on to new pastures, and with the passing years had come a taste for depravity and lewdness. He had never been in love and had no wish to be, viewing the concept with distaste and suspicion. Sexual attraction was something else, and his present mistress – the wife of a friend he'd known for years – fitted his requirements in the bedroom perfectly. Mirabelle Jefferson was passionate and wanton and beautiful, and his body was aching for her. Since he had begun his assault on Angeline's affections he had kept Mirabelle out of the picture, but the London Season was beginning and he intended to visit his town house in the West End as soon as he could. He would make some excuse to Angeline for his absence for a while. The girl would believe anything he said.

He glanced at Angeline and Hector as Mrs Gibson came in with the housemaid, who was wheeling the coffee trolley. Provincial to the core, he thought irritably. Oh, for some decent conversation. Mirabelle was a clever hostess, and in any gathering of people she selected there were always one or two Cabinet ministers or a viceroy or some high official from a far-off corner of the Empire, along with a painter or architect and a group of musicians who played to the company after dinner. She only invited women famous for their beauty or wit, or both, who gave the conversation a sparkling turn or were wise enough not to interrupt the good talk; and scandal and gossip were always rippling like a current through the guests.

How long before he could escape? It had to be soon, or he'd be unable to keep this charade up for much longer.

But then in the next instant he told himself: steady,

steady. All was going so well, he couldn't rock the boat now. He had to remember that this particular boat was a treasure trove.

# *Chapter Six*

Angeline stood staring at herself in the bedroom mirror, much as she had done on that evening months ago just before she had met Oswald for the first time. Now, as then, she barely recognized the reflection looking back at her.

Myrtle finished adjusting the gossamer-thin veil and stepped back a pace to check her handiwork, and she, too, was remembering that other night and wishing passionately it had never happened. Not a trace of this came over in her voice as she said softly, 'You're beyond beautiful, Miss Angeline. I don't think there's ever been such a lovely bride.' When, in answer, she received a radiant smile from the fragile figure clad in pure white, who seemed too ethereal and celestial to be of this world, Myrtle had the wild impulse to throw herself at Angeline's feet and beg her not to walk out of the door.

She didn't, of course. What could she say, after all? Her only comfort was that she was accompanying her young mistress to the big house as her personal maid.

This had only come about because of Angeline's insistence that it be so. Myrtle was fully aware that Oswald Golding had wanted to employ a lady's maid of his own choosing for his new wife; he seemed intent on controlling every aspect – large and small – of her life, but in this one thing Angeline had stood up to him.

'Here, Miss.' Myrtle passed Angeline the small bouquet of pink rosebuds and baby's breath tied with white ribbons that she was to carry. 'Are you feeling all right? I could get you a tot of sherry to calm your nerves, if you like.'

Angeline's giggle dispelled the illusion of an angelic creature. 'I ought to be feeling nervous, I know. It's the done thing, isn't it? But the truth is that I've been awake half the night because I'm so excited. Is that terribly unladylike? Anyway, I don't care if it is. I want to be Mrs Golding, Myrtle, and to begin my new life.'

Myrtle forced a smile. Mrs Golding – and her not yet turned seventeen, and him twice her age. The old master and mistress would turn in their graves if they knew what Mr Stewart had allowed, and it wasn't only her who thought so. She'd heard what was being said when Mr Appleby had called some weeks back; you couldn't not hear it. Mr Appleby had been shouting like one of the stallholders at the market – he hadn't sounded like himself at all. Miss Angeline had been up at the house with Mr Golding (she suspected Mr Stewart had arranged it that way), and hadn't Mr Appleby given him what for. Course, it hadn't made the slightest bit of difference, and she had known it wouldn't. Mr Appleby had left in the end, red-faced and spitting bricks, and Mr Stewart had called her and Mrs Upton and Albert into his study. He had warned them that he didn't want his niece knowing about the solicitor's attitude. It would distress her, he had said, and cast a pall over the wedding preparations.

The three of them had walked through to the kitchen when they were dismissed, and for once Mrs Upton had let her guard down and been almost friendly. 'You can't blame Mr Appleby for saying she's too young – not with a name like Mr Golding's got, and Mr Appleby being a friend of the lass's father. You going to say anything to Miss Angeline?' she'd asked.

Of course she hadn't replied to that, she wasn't daft. She wouldn't trust the housekeeper as far as she could throw her. Instead she'd said, 'What do you mean? A name like Mr Golding's got?'

'Well . . . ' Mrs Upton had lowered her voice. 'Albert here hears things, don't you, Albert? From other coachmen, you know? If they're waiting outside with the horses for hours, they all get talking to pass the time, and' – her voice went a shade lower still – 'Mr Golding likes a pretty face and a turn of ankle, right enough.'

Myrtle had shrugged. 'So do lots of men.'

'Aye, true, but Mr Golding don't just look, if you get my drift? There's been some right goings-on, I can tell you, but the devil looks after his own, and he's got away with his shenanigans by and large. Now I'm the first to say that what the gentry get up to is their own business, and me an' Albert have always considered ourselves in clover here with Mr Stewart. But all this with the young lass sticks in my craw. I can't say I was over-pleased to hear she was coming, and I was wary at first – thought she'd be expecting to be waited on hand and foot, and would be full of airs and graces – but, well, she's a nice little thing.'

Myrtle had nodded. 'Aye, she is.'

'But young, very young for her years, and impressionable, you know? All this with Mr Golding, it don't seem right.'

Still not sure if the housekeeper could be relied upon, Myrtle had hedged, 'Well, she's fair barmy about him, and he seems smitten. Perhaps she'll change him.'

'A leopard changing its spots?' Mrs Upton had snorted. 'It don't happen. Still, like I said, we're in clover here, and I've had my say. My conscience is clear. It's up to you what you do or don't say.'

Now Myrtle gathered up the small train of Angeline's dress as her mistress prepared to leave the bedroom. Should she have said something? Voiced her misgivings? She probably would have done, had it not been for the way Miss Angeline had reacted on the day Mr Golding had come to the house to ask for her hand. Her attitude then had made it plain she wouldn't hear a word against him. No, if she'd repeated any of what Mrs Upton had confided, it would only have driven a wedge between her and her mistress; or, worse, she would have been dismissed. And with her da having been off work the last few weeks with his stomach trouble, she couldn't afford to risk losing her job, or it'd be the workhouse for them at home, for sure.

Nevertheless the sense of guilt weighed heavily as Myrtle followed Angeline down the stairs, to where Hector was waiting in the hall.

Hector's own conscience had been playing him up for weeks. On the one hand, he kept telling himself that Oswald was obviously genuine about his love for Angeline, for why else would he – a member of the landed gentry – want to marry a girl who, for all her wealth, couldn't be said to be his social equal? And yet his gut instinct told him there was more to Oswald's apparent affection for his niece than met the eye. And yes, he admitted in his truthful moments, he didn't want to probe too hard, for fear of what he might uncover.

When the still, small voice became too insistent to ignore – often in the middle of the night when sleep eluded him – he silenced it by telling himself that, whatever the rights and wrongs of the matter, Angeline loved Oswald and would be heartbroken if their nuptials didn't take place. It would be cruel, he reasoned, to stand in their way. This argument worked – mostly. Today, as he took in the sight of his brother's only child in the first blush of womanhood and with a smile on her face that tore at his heart, it didn't work. And when her expression changed and she fairly flew across the hall, careless of her finery, saying, 'What is it, Uncle? Are you unwell?', Hector felt as though burning coals were being heaped upon his head.

Recovering himself, he took her small hands in his. 'No, no, child, don't fret. You look so lovely, that's all, and your mother and father would have been so proud of you. Come, we must be away.'

Out of respect for Angeline's parents, the wedding ceremony and reception were to be a quiet affair. After a simple service at the parish church, a small handful of guests had been invited back to a wedding breakfast at the house before the happy couple left for Oswald's London establishment. Oswald had suggested – and Angeline had been happy to comply – that their honeymoon proper could take place early in the New Year, but a week in London when he could show her the sights, and they could visit the theatre and art galleries and perhaps meet friends for dinner once or twice, would be a brief precursor to two or three months' travelling around Europe in the spring. He had implied that it was out of regard for her parents' memory that they should delay their holiday a while, and Angeline had loved him all the more for his thoughtfulness. Also, he had added gently – clearly as an afterthought – it would enable certain financial legalities to be taken care of. Such matters were tiresome, but best dealt with swiftly and then forgotten.

Mrs Upton opened the front door for them, and her voice and manner were kind when she said, 'May I wish you every happiness, Miss Angeline. Every happiness, I'm sure.'

'Thank you, Mrs Upton.' Angeline smiled at the housekeeper, and then at Albert, as she walked down the steps with her uncle to where Albert was standing by the carriage, resplendent in the new livery her uncle had bought him for the occasion. Myrtle followed, still carrying the train, to avoid it brushing the dusty ground. August had been an unusually hot month and the earth was baked, and even now, in the second week of September, the hot spell showed no sign of abating. The sky was high and a clear vivid blue, without even the smallest cloud marring its expanse. It was a beautiful day. Angeline breathed in the warm air scented with shrubs and flowers. Life was beautiful. If her mama and father could have been here, everything would have been perfect.

Once Angeline and her uncle were settled in the carriage, Myrtle climbed up beside Albert and they were off. Mrs Upton forgot herself so far as to wave her handkerchief as the carriage trundled down the short drive and out onto the road. Angeline smiled to herself. If her uncle's housekeeper had been as nice when she had first come to live with him as she had been for the last little while, her early weeks in the house would have been different altogether. She had said the same to Myrtle a little while ago, and Myrtle had made her laugh when she'd said wryly, 'Perhaps it's because she knows she's getting rid of the pair of us shortly, Miss.' Dear Myrtle. She was so glad she would have someone of her own in Oswald's house; his staff were much more formal than she had been used to, but then that was the way Oswald liked it. And she supposed, with the house and grounds being so vast, it was necessary. As she'd said that morning, she was beginning a new life – one with different rules – but at least she could be the same with Myrtle as she'd always been. They'd both need that, because things would change for Myrtle, too.

Albert was saying much the same thing to Myrtle as the horses clip-clopped along the road towards the church. 'Going to be lady's maid to Mrs Golding, from this day forth then. Going up in the world, aren't you, living in the big house an' all?'

Myrtle glanced at him. His tone hadn't been nasty, but there had been some sort of edge to it that she couldn't place. 'Miss Angeline will still be the same, and so shall I, big house or no.'

'You say that now, but you won't want to know the likes of me when you're in with that lot up there.'

Myrtle twisted in her seat and studied his profile properly. 'What's the matter?' She had thought she was getting on all right with Albert and his sister for the last little while, since their chat in the kitchen. Particularly with Albert. Once he had unbent towards her, she'd discovered he had a wicked sense of humour that he kept under wraps most of the time, because his sister didn't approve of too much jollity.

'I'm just saying, that's all.'

'*What* are you saying, Albert?'

'That it's different looking after Miss Angeline, like you've been doing so far, from how it's going to be from now on. You'll be up there in the hierarchy with the butler and the valet, and you won't be wearing a uniform any more. You'll get your room cleaned for you by the housemaids, and all sorts of perks.'

Myrtle knew where all this had come from. His sister. Although Mrs Upton had been nicer in recent weeks, she hadn't been able to resist remarking that a lady's maid should be properly qualified for the post, and with an education superior to that of the ordinary class of female servants. Could Myrtle do fine needlework? Was she familiar with the useful and ornamental branches of female acquirements that Miss Angeline would need when she became Mrs Golding? Could she dress the new Mrs Golding's hair for grand occasions? And so it had gone on. Myrtle had let most of it go over her head and had tried not to get rattled, but now she was upset to think that Albert thought she would turn into an upstart. She wasn't like that.

'Albert, even if it's like you say, you'll still be my friend. How could you think otherwise?' she said, the hurt sounding in her voice.

Albert seemed to concentrate very hard on the road ahead for a minute or two. Then he said quietly, 'What if I want us to be more than friends?'

For a moment she thought she must have misheard him, but a glance at his tense profile told her otherwise.

'You . . . you mean . . . ' She didn't dare voice it, in case she had made a mistake.

'I like you, Myrtle. More than like.'

She didn't know what to say, and so she said the truth. 'I didn't know. I've never thought of you in that way, I suppose, not with how things were when Miss Angeline and I first came to the house. Your sister and you – well, you weren't very friendly.'

'I can understand that, and I regret it deeply. But now, would you consider thinking of me in that way?'

She looked at him out of the corner of her eye. Albert was nice-looking, in an earthy sort of way, tall and broad, and he had lovely curly hair. She knew Mrs Upton was fifteen years older than him – Mrs Upton had been the eldest in the family, and he'd been the last baby – because Albert had told her that one night, when they'd sat in the kitchen drinking tea after his sister had gone to bed to nurse a headache. He had confided that when Mrs Upton had taken the post of housekeeper to Mr Stewart, after her husband had died, she had got him this job. But Myrtle still didn't know exactly how old he was. Bluntly she said, 'How old are you, Albert?' He was one of those people about whom it was difficult to guess their age.

'Twenty-eight; and you were eighteen at Christmas, weren't you? Do you think I'm too old for you, Myrtle?'

There was ten years between her mam and da. Suddenly she knew she didn't want Albert to go out of her life. Softly she said, 'No, I don't think that. Miss Angeline has told me I'll get every Sunday afternoon off, unless we're at Mr Golding's London house or away somewhere. I . . . I could meet you then, if you want, and we'll see how it goes.'

'I do want.' He glanced at her – a swift warm glance – and Myrtle felt a tingle snake down her spine.

'All right then.'

'The first Sunday you're back from London?'

She nodded.

'You won't regret giving me a chance, lass, I promise you that.' And then he smiled. 'And if you can agree to walking out with me when I'm dressed up like a dog's dinner in these ridiculous clothes, it bodes well.'

Myrtle giggled. The livery was similar to that worn by the footmen at the big house, when they delivered bits and pieces for Miss Angeline from Mr Golding, but although it looked befitting on them, she had to admit it was out of keeping on Albert. He was too manly, that was the thing. To tease him she said, 'You wouldn't want to wear this sort of thing all the time then?'

'Heaven forbid!' He grinned at her, and then, his voice becoming serious, he said, 'I've been saving up for years to get a little smallholding, lass. That's me dream. Somewhere where I'm me own boss, and I don't have to bow the knee to anyone. A cow and a couple of pigs, a few hens and a nice allotment, and me own fireside of an evening.'

She liked the sound of that. Oh, she did. They were nearing the church and they didn't have time to say anything else, but as Myrtle climbed down from beside him she had a warm glow inside. Albert! Who'd have thought it? But he was a nice man. She just hoped Mr Golding was as nice, but she wouldn't put money on it.

Oswald sat waiting in the church, dusty golden shafts of sunlight slanting through the stained-glass windows and bathing the altar in a warm glow. Nicholas Gray was sitting beside him as his best man. He had cultivated his friendship with Nicholas since pursuing Angeline, not because he particularly liked the man – Nicholas was too strait-laced for his taste – but because Lord Gray and his wife added the stamp of respectability to any social occasion, unlike most of his former friends. It had been fortunate that he could use the ploy of Angeline's parents having so recently died to limit the guest list, too. Along with the Grays and two other reputable couples, and a couple of elderly great-aunts on his side, Angeline's uncle made up the sum total of invitees. He had promised his set a rip-roaring party in due course. Mirabelle had once referred to such beanos as being little more than orgies, and she was right of course.

Mirabelle . . . He lingered on the memory of their last meeting just a week ago. He had told Angeline he had urgent business in London, and had escaped from the North into Mirabelle's arms. Hell, he'd put her through her paces all right. They'd spent the whole day in bed and got through three bottles of champagne.

The sound of the organ signalled the bride's arrival, and as Oswald glanced round he was annoyed to see that

George Appleby and his wife had slipped into the back of the church. He had been to visit the solicitor in his offices a few weeks ago, ostensibly to thank the man for handling Angeline's finances so well to date, but Appleby had given him short shrift and Oswald was still smarting from his treatment. It had taken some tactful questioning of Hector to make sure nothing could stand in the way of Angeline's fortune coming into the Golding coffers once they were man and wife.

'She looks exquisite, old fellow. You're a lucky man.'

Nicholas's whisper reminded Oswald to play the doting groom as his eyes focused on the ethereal figure walking up the aisle on Hector's arm, and he schooled his features accordingly. Not much longer, and then this farce would be over, he comforted himself. Angeline would be content to play house in the country, and he could get back to his old life. For the sake of appearances he'd take her to town once or twice, and she would have to be part of the exodus to the grouse moors in the autumn for the shooting next year – it was expected of the wives – but he didn't see her impinging on his liberty as such. She would do what she was told.

She reached his side. Oswald lifted the veil back from her face to reveal the trusting brown eyes looking at him adoringly.

Yes, he'd have no trouble with Angeline.

# *Chapter Seven*

It was dark when they arrived at Oswald's large, elegant town house. They'd been met at the station by Harper, Oswald's man when he was residing in the city. Harper's wife, Ellen, was housekeeper and cook, and their daughters, Sally and Tessa, were maids. At the last moment, literally as they were leaving for the station, Oswald had told Myrtle that her mistress would not be requiring her to travel to London with them after all.

Angeline hadn't demurred until they were in the privacy of the carriage, and he had swept her objections to one side with his boyish smile. 'The maids will wait on you, my dear, and I want you all to myself,' he'd murmured, taking her hand in his. 'The girl is forever popping up and getting in the way. I fear she hasn't yet learned the art of a good lady's maid, which is to be invisible when necessary, which is most of the time. If she doesn't improve, we really will have to think about getting you someone more suited to the position, my dear.'

'No, I wouldn't do that.'

His tone and manner altered and, letting go of her hand, he said, 'You would do just that, if I decided on it.'

She stared at him. He had never used that tone of voice with her before. Taken aback, she stiffened, her body drawing away from his. There was absolutely no way she would dismiss Myrtle.

Immediately, his voice now low and appealing, he said, 'Oh, my sweet, I can't help it if I want us to enjoy our first days as man and wife alone together, can I? I thought you wanted that, too.'

Confused and feeling she had failed him in some way, she murmured, 'I do want that, of course I do.'

'Then it is settled. Your maid will apply herself to preparing for your return. Oh, you are going to adore London, my dear. I find it hard to believe you've never been to town before. There's so much to see and do, and – situated as we are, overlooking Grosvenor Square – we're at the hub of it all. Of course we've missed the Season, but no matter. If it was the height of summer we'd be riding in the Park. Hyde Park,' he added, seeing her look of enquiry, 'every afternoon. Everyone who is anyone meets for what is practically a daily Society garden party in the late afternoon, between tea and dinner, at a spot between Albert and Grosvenor Gates under the trees. As for the shops, every woman of my acquaintance loses herself for hours in sheer bliss.'

She had never seen him so animated. Feeling perturbed, but not knowing why, she listened to him talking about the theatres, opera houses, balls, garden parties, croquet and lawn-tennis afternoons, dinners and banquets he'd attended in the past in his life of gentlemanly leisure, all the way to the train station.

Once on the journey to London, he waxed lyrical on the subject of the Prince of Wales's pursuit of pleasure. Luxury and conspicuous consumption of all things fleshly were apparently to the taste of the heir to the throne, and Oswald seemed to approve, as far as Angeline could ascertain. He spoke contemptuously of the Prince's mother, Queen Victoria, whose court was a model of respectable bourgeois morality. As Angeline's father had held the Queen in some esteem, and Oswald had never hinted at such views before, she felt overwhelmed by bewilderment. Where was the suitor who had so ardently declared they were made for each other? And who had spoken of marriage as something mysterious and fine?

She had eaten little at the wedding breakfast; she had been too excited for one thing, and her corset had been so tight it had left no room for food. Now the rocking and bumping of the train were making her nauseous and her head muzzy.

After a while Oswald noticed her pallor and suggested she shut her eyes, which Angeline was thankful to do. She must have fallen asleep, because it seemed only the next minute that Oswald was rousing her to say they had arrived.

She glanced at him now as the carriage stopped outside a large three-storey terraced property, with black iron railings separating the yard or two of front garden from the wide pavement. Her sleep had refreshed her, but the churning in her stomach and the feeling of apprehension that had grown since the wedding breakfast were even stronger. One disturbing thought hovered constantly at the back of her mind: this Oswald seemed so different from the man who had declared his endless devotion to her only yesterday. But she countered it by saying to herself that she had to remember this was a big day for him, too. Nevertheless his attitude gave her no confidence for the moment when they would be alone together in the bedroom. Suddenly she felt afraid.

They were warmly welcomed by Ellen Harper and her daughters, one of whom took Angeline upstairs to the master suite, in order that she could freshen up after the journey. The room was beautifully furnished, and leading off it was a dressing room and a large bathroom with an indoor closet. Oswald had told her there were three more bedrooms on this floor, all with en suites. The top floor of the house was given over to the servants and was therefore more utilitarian.

When she came downstairs to the drawing room, it was to find Oswald on his second glass of wine, sitting sprawled on a chair in front of the fire. He stood up, saying, 'A glass of wine or sherry before dinner, my dear?'

Angeline was about to decline, for she rarely drank alcohol, preferring the taste of soft drinks or tea or coffee. Then, feeling that she needed something stronger for the evening ahead, she nodded. 'A sherry, please.'

She sat down on a sofa some distance from the fire, for the evening was warm and the fire had made the room quite stifling. Oswald joined her, handing her the glass of sherry as he said, 'We have been invited to dinner tomorrow night at the Jeffersons.' He gestured towards an open envelope lying on the coffee table close to where he had been sitting. 'I think one or two of my friends who are still in town for a short while would like to meet you before they retire to the country for the shooting.'

Jefferson. Where had she heard that name before? Realizing he was waiting for a response, she said, 'Do you want to go?'

'Of course.' His tone said: why ever not?

She had hoped their week in London would be spent getting to know each other properly, when she had thought about it before today, but now she realized that the idyll of being alone together every day was perhaps not what Oswald had in mind. Warily she said, 'I thought everyone had already left for the country?'

'Obviously a few have not.'

She took a sip of her sherry, feeling it warm a path down into her stomach. What had happened? she asked herself helplessly. This was not what she had expected – none of it. It all felt strange, disturbing. Did all new brides feel this way?

They sat at either end of the long, polished dining table during dinner and Angeline was relieved to find this room was not as warm as the one they had just left. The meal consisted of four courses, beginning with a clear soup, which was full of flavour, and ending with a lemon sponge pudding. Ellen Harper was an accomplished cook and, despite her nerves, Angeline ate well and drank a glass of wine with her food. Oswald seemed to have switched back to the man she had known over the last months, making light and amusing conversation and being as attentive as she could have wished for, and she found herself relaxing.

She loved him, she told herself, so very much, and because of that and the fact that she was somewhat overwrought after such a momentous day, she had been letting her imagination run away with her earlier. Nothing was wrong.

After dinner they went through to the drawing room and sat on the sofa together to have their coffee and the handmade chocolates that were Mrs Harper's speciality. Now the nervous fluttering in her stomach had returned at the thought of the night ahead, and Angeline found herself wishing she had defied him and insisted that Myrtle came with them. Oswald had picked up the newspaper from the coffee table once they had sat down, and Mrs Harper had left the room, so Angeline chose a magazine from the pile on the table – not because she had any interest in reading it, but because she was at a loss to know what to do. The thought crossed her mind that Oswald had been putting on an act throughout dinner for the servants who had been waiting on them, and then she told herself she was being unfair again. She had to stop analysing everything, or she would drive herself mad. Why was she suddenly doubting him like this?

She had finished her coffee and eaten three of the chocolates when Oswald's paper lowered and he peered over it at her. 'You must be tired. Why don't I ring for one of the maids to bring you a jug of hot water upstairs and help you undress?'

'Thank you.' She stood up as he rose and walked across to the bell pull, and he had barely tugged the long cord before there was a knock at the drawing-room door and Sally opened it.

'Mrs Golding is ready to retire. See to it that she has some hot water, and ask Tessa to bring me a bottle of malt brandy.'

'Yes, sir.' Sally stood aside for Angeline to pass and, once in the hall, said, 'I'll be up directly, ma'am.'

*Ma'am*. Angeline swallowed hard, as the girl disappeared in the direction of the kitchen. She was the wife of a wealthy gentleman, the mistress of a large country estate and a town house, and for a bewildering moment she wondered how it had all come about so quickly. Would she be able to be all that Oswald expected in a wife? She had so much to learn, she knew that, and tonight she didn't feel adequate for the task. She felt . . . She bit on her lip as she glanced about the beautiful hall. She felt out of her depth, and it was unnerving.

Realizing it would look odd if she was still standing here when Sally brought the water, she turned and quickly made her way upstairs. When the maid arrived, she asked her to place the water on the washstand in the bathroom and told her that she could manage her own undressing, once Sally had loosened the ties of her corset.

She didn't linger over her toilette, wanting to be sitting up in bed when Oswald came in. Her new nightdress was a lovely thing of chiffon and lace, and she brushed her hair so that it hung in long, burnished ringlets down her back, the red in it gleaming in the lamplight as she looked at herself in the mirror. Once in the big bed, she pulled the covers up to her chin, before forcing herself to lower them to her waist and settling back against the mound of pillows. She found she was trembling. Not with cold, for the room was over-warm, if anything, from the coal fire burning in the fireplace, but from the panic of the unknown that was coursing through her. Taking some long deep breaths, as her mother had taught her to do when she was nervous, she waited.

And waited . . .

Outside the window the occasional carriage or two trundled past, but the select residential street was quiet on the whole, as befitted this upper-class address. In the distance she could hear more noise, but it was muted and sufficiently far enough away not to intrude. After an hour had passed she slid down further into the bed, and after another hour had ticked by the exhaustion of the day fought her nerves and won. She slept.

*

At what time of the night she became aware of Oswald sliding into bed beside her, she didn't know. He had pulled most of the bedclothes off her as he lifted them to get into bed, and as she moved drowsily she realized it was pitch dark, there was an overwhelming smell of alcohol on his breath and he was pulling her nightdress up over her thighs. As her mouth was claimed by his, his knee nudged her legs apart and, without further ado, and without the slightest endearment or caress, he drove into her.

Angeline screamed, she couldn't help it, for the pain and shock of what was happening to her were terrifying, but he took her face between his hands as his body continued to rent her in two, and muffled her cries with his mouth. And then, mercifully soon, it was over and he was mumbling drunkenly as he rolled to one side, his words incoherent in the main.

Shaking from head to foot and with a smarting pain between her legs that felt like fire, Angeline lay quite still for a minute or two, unable to move, drained of life. Oswald began to snore, turning towards her in his sleep, and it was this that enabled her to scramble out of the bed away from him, her crying soundless as she sat trembling on the very edge of the mattress.

Shock was making her teeth chatter as she felt her way in the dark to the bathroom, bumping into a chair as she stumbled about and nearly falling headlong. But then the handle of the door was under her fingers. Once inside the bathroom, she sat for a long time on the edge of the roll-top bath, her eyes gradually becoming adjusted to the darkness so that she was able to pick out the shadows of various items.

The pain between her legs had settled into a throbbing ache, but she felt damp and sticky down there. Pouring some water into the bowl from the jug on the washstand, she dabbed at herself with a wet flannel for a while. It helped a little.

The floor of the bathroom was tiled, but a big fluffy mat stood next to the bath, and after she had dried herself she curled up on it, pulling one of the huge bath towels over herself. She couldn't go back into the bedroom and to the proximity of Oswald's body; he might wake up and reach for her again. Just the thought of it made her shake and feel sick. And he was her husband. *Oh God . . . God, he's my husband!*

With her two hands cupping her face, and her knees under her chin, she made herself as small as she could, all the time whispering to herself, 'Oh, Mama, Mama, what have I done? What have I done?'

# PART TWO

## *The Gilded Cage*

## 1892

# *Chapter Eight*

'I do believe the weather is brightening, ma'am, and not before time.' Myrtle stood back from arranging Angeline's hair, surveying her handiwork critically for a moment or two before putting the last touch – a jewelled comb – in place.

Angeline smiled. 'Does the bad weather make Albert's absence seem worse? Believe me, Myrtle, I've no wish to be here, either.'

It was late September and they were staying at Lord Gray's country estate. A fine Scottish rain had fallen for days, but now the clouds had cleared and a watery sun had broken through.

Myrtle grinned. She knew her mistress disliked as much as she did the annual withdrawal to Scotland when hundreds of game birds – grouse, pheasant, partridge, snipe – would be slaughtered every day for weeks in an orgy of shooting. Gargantuan meals with many courses and types of wine, elaborate wardrobes and frequent changes of costume, and hours of boredom for the ladies when the men were out sating their bloodlust was the order of the day. With the Tories having just fallen from power and the succeeding Liberal government led by Mr Gladstone in place, politics had dominated the dinner table for some nights, until several of the ladies had objected in no uncertain terms.

Angeline hadn't been one of them. In truth, she preferred listening to talk about *something*, rather than the inevitable spiteful gossip and inane chatter that prevailed most of the time. Unbeknown to Oswald, she often read the periodicals and journals he had lying about at home for show, and had been slowly forming her own opinions on a number of subjects. Over the last two years, since being married to Oswald, she'd come to understand the real meaning of what her father had grumbled about: that for hundreds of years Britain had been ruled by a tiny elite who owned most of the wealth, made all the important decisions and exercised exclusive class power. And it was unfair. She supposed it was only to be expected that this privileged position would not be surrendered easily, and despite the Industrial Revolution and the widening of the franchise, the gentry – of which she was now part, courtesy of her marriage – continued to dominate political and social life. Everything, in fact.

Angeline sighed heavily. She doubted if a single one of Lord Gray's other guests had the same thoughts as she did, but then outsiders like her were different. Different, but still expected to maintain values and codes of behaviour relating to taste, manners and refined living. The basis of the aristocracy's power was land; her husband's estate and those of most of his circle were large, not only giving employment to working-class individuals of both sexes, but wielding power and influence. And didn't they know it! She sighed again. The masters of all they surveyed.

She realized now that she had understood little of this when she married Oswald – in fact it hadn't even crossed her mind. She had been very young and naive, and trusting, and she had paid for her gullibility in a hundred different ways. She didn't fit into her new life, although outwardly she made a pretence of doing so, but she hated the endless round of what some would term pleasure – the London Season with its social whirlwind, the autumn of country-house parties providing opportunities for blood sports and all sorts of goings-on, the winter with more parties, balls and social functions. Most of all, she hated her husband.

'I think you're ready, ma'am.'

Myrtle's gentle intrusion into her thoughts reminded Angeline that she was daydreaming. Stifling a sigh, she nodded. This day would be no different from the ones before it. The assembled guests began the morning by breakfasting at ten o'clock. The meal would consist of many courses in silver dishes on the side-tables in Lord Gray's sumptuous dining room. Angeline knew there would be enough food to last a group of well-regulated digestions for a week, let alone a day. After they had all eaten, the men would go off shooting and then the emptiness of a long morning would follow. Groups of women would sit tittle-tattling about this and that, prattling on in order to hear the sound of their own voices, or would write letters at the host of small ornamental tables scattered about. Then would come yet another of the endless change of clothes, this time into sporty tweeds for the luncheon rendezvous with the men outside.

Angeline hid a shudder. Trophies of bloodied birds would be carelessly piled up, and she loathed this time of the day.

After the impossibly large luncheon, finishing with coffee and liqueurs, the ladies would return to the house for an afternoon nap, before changing into beautiful tea-gowns, most of which were far more lovely than their dinner gowns. Once downstairs and around the tea table, where Angeline felt they all looked like enormous dolls, the conversation would be spasmodic and even slumberous, but every gown would be noted by each woman present and its cost mentally calculated. Competition was fierce, but covert.

Dinner would be the occasion of the day and would last for hours, the men discussing their prowess against the defenceless birds, and the women expected to be decorative and admiring in their fragile concoctions of delicate chiffon, silk, lace and net, some of which might only be wearable on a couple of occasions before they began to wilt like hothouse flowers. Angeline had listened to several conversations over the last nights between women comparing the most fashionable London *modistes* with the Parisian couture houses. If she heard another such discussion she would scream, she told herself, as she left the bedroom. She had said as much to Oswald and it had caused another of their bitter quarrels, although now that she was expecting a baby he hadn't subjected her to what he called his 'reformation'. These bouts of verbal abuse, when he criticized everything about her – beginning with her parentage and finishing with her lack of refinement – always ended with him asserting his marital rights, no matter how she fought him. And she did fight.

Angeline paused before entering the dining room, taking a deep breath. Oswald had left their suite of rooms some twenty minutes ago, but she didn't doubt he would have saved her a seat and would play the doting husband, for Lord Gray's benefit. Nicholas Gray had made it clear from their first meeting that he liked her, in spite of his wife's condescending attitude – or maybe because of it, she thought ruefully. He was a kind man, generous and amiable with a natural gallantry. How he had come to be married to Gwendoline, she didn't know, but it was clear to everyone that he absolutely adored his wife. Nicholas would make a wonderful father. She touched the slight mound of her stomach, which was as yet unnoticeable. But Oswald . . .

She had been about to put plans to leave him into play when she had discovered a little while ago that she was expecting a baby. She'd had it all worked out. She would sell her jewellery, which would be enough to buy a little house somewhere; down south preferably, where she could disappear. Then she could perhaps give private lessons, as Miss Robson had. She'd thought about throwing herself on the mercy of her uncle – he and Oswald had had some kind of falling-out directly after the wedding, although she didn't know why, and since then the two men hadn't spoken. When she had defied Oswald's orders not to associate with Hector, and had gone to see her uncle, hoping to find out what had caused the quarrel so that she could pour oil on troubled waters, her uncle had refused her admittance to the house. It had distressed her greatly, for he was the last link with her parents.

Nevertheless, it hadn't been this that had made her decide not to involve her uncle when she fled the marital home; more the fact that she knew Hector's house would be the first place Oswald would look for her. Anonymity somewhere in a big city would be the safest thing, although the thought was frightening. It had been a desperate plan, but she *had* been desperate. She still was, perhaps more so, but in a different way, because now she was concerned about the innocent little person growing inside her, who had a monster for a father. A monster who had the Establishment behind him, in any fight for custody.

A footman came through the open doors of the dining room carrying some empty dishes and glanced at her. Pulling herself together, she lifted her chin and walked briskly into the low hum of well-mannered conversation. She was now approaching her fifth month of pregnancy and was thankful that the morning nausea, which had been severe at first, was now almost gone.

'There you are.' Oswald appeared at her side immediately. 'I was beginning to think you were indisposed.'

She stared into the handsome face, which had once thrilled and fascinated her. How foolish she had been. How stupid and witless. And because of her gullibility, her baby would be born into a loveless marriage, with a father who could be physically violent – and not just with her. Before they'd left for Scotland, Myrtle had told her that Oswald had laid about a groom the day before, for not saddling his hunter correctly, lashing the lad with his whip about the head and shoulders. Myrtle had confided that it was almost certain the groom would lose an eye. Horrified, Angeline had called the doctor to the house to treat the boy, paying him out of her own funds. Oswald had been furious, but she had stood her ground, and because they were leaving for Scotland his temper had soon cooled.

Turning away from the perfect features that now repelled her, she said coldly, 'As you can see, I am not.'

Oswald's mouth tightened before he forced a smile, for anyone who might be watching them. It hadn't been long into his marriage before he'd realized that he had underestimated Angeline. He'd expected her to be pliant and subservient, as she'd been so docile when he had been courting her and he had thought she would be easy to manipulate. Admittedly the wedding night hadn't helped. He couldn't remember much of it, for he'd been too drunk, but he'd obviously been a little rough and she had taken umbrage. But she was his wife – his property to do with as he wished. That's what she didn't seem to understand. Even after he had apologized she had still been stiff with him.

His eyes narrowed. She should be down on bended knees, thanking God that someone in his position in society had seen fit to marry her. He had wanted to tell her that at the time, but there had still been a few legal niceties to finalize, so he had promised himself he'd take her to task later. And he had. He'd taken it out of her hide all right. But still she defied him now and again, as in the matter of the groom. The lad was nothing – scum.

He watched Angeline now as she stood talking to Lord Gray and his wife, Gwendoline wearing the superior expression she always adopted with Angeline. This irritated him beyond measure, reminding Oswald that he had married beneath him.

'Careful, darling.' Mirabelle lightly tapped his arm as she joined him, a faint waft of the delicate perfume she had specially made for her teasing his nostrils. 'One could almost suppose you were the jealous husband, staring at your wife like that.'

He brought his eyes to the beautiful feline face, in which her startlingly green eyes surrounded by long lashes laughed at him. 'We both know that's not true.'

Mirabelle tapped his arm again. 'How ungallant, especially when you have such a lovely young wife. You men are never satisfied, are you?'

She was being deliberately provocative, he knew that, but he also detected a thread of disapproval in her soft voice. It amazed him – genuinely astounded him – but he knew Mirabelle liked Angeline. She had told him so on more than one occasion when they were in bed together. 'It takes a real woman to satisfy me,' he murmured, his gaze dropping to her red mouth. 'You know that.'

Yes, she knew that. Mirabelle looked away from him to where Angeline was now helping herself from one of the silver dishes. And she also knew why Oswald had married the girl; he had been quite frank with her, possibly, she suspected, because he had harboured the idea she might be jealous if he took himself a wife. She wasn't. Their affair was purely a thing of the flesh, on both sides. She loved her husband, but her needs were much greater than his and most of the time he couldn't satisfy her in bed. Oswald could. If she was being truthful, she didn't think she actually liked him as a man, but as a lover he was everything that she had ever desired – and more.

It had surprised her that Angeline was not as besotted with Oswald as he had led her to believe, before the marriage. When she had met the girl for the first time, when the newly-weds had been in London the week after the marriage, Angeline hadn't behaved like a young bride who was head over heels in love with her husband. It was some weeks before she was alone with Oswald and could ask him about it, and he had replied shortly that Angeline didn't like the intimate side of marriage.

Was he cruel to the girl? Mirabelle's green eyes turned to the hard, handsome face again. It was possible. She had never seen that side of him, but she had it on good authority that he could be a devil when something upset him. 'Go to her side,' she said very quietly, 'Nicholas will expect it. Does he know about her condition?'

'No. No one but you knows, for the moment.'

'Nevertheless, go and do your duty.' She softened the words with a smile, knowing Oswald didn't take kindly to orders. 'And you can do your duty to me later, in the summerhouse at the back of the rose garden. Slip away from the shoot for an hour or so after luncheon and I'll meet you there when the others are resting in their rooms.'

'I'll be waiting.'

Across the room, Angeline was aware of the two of them standing together, although she hadn't looked directly at them. For some time after she had married Oswald she had wondered about Mirabelle Jefferson and whether, in the past, she had been more to Oswald than a friend. There was nothing she could put her finger on, just a feeling, and if things had been different between her and Oswald, she might have asked him; but things weren't different, and such was the chasm between them that she wouldn't give him the satisfaction of thinking it concerned her. Then had come the night when, in one of his attacks on her when she had tried to fight him off, he'd accused her of being passionless and as cold as ice, not a real woman at all. 'Not like Mirabelle,' he'd growled in her face as he had forced himself upon her. 'She knows how to please a man all right.'

'Then go to her,' she'd cried back, through the pain of one of the many unnatural indignities he delighted in heaping upon her.

'I do, frequently.'

After that, so many things had fallen into place: the odd glance, a whisper here and there, a knowing smile.

She should hate Mirabelle, Angeline thought for the umpteenth time, as Oswald joined her at the table; but, funnily enough, she didn't. Maybe her heart was so full of hatred for Oswald there was no room to hate anyone else?

Across the table Gwendoline was holding court, as she was apt to do, given half a chance. The subject was the radical Joseph Chamberlain, who had recently thundered forth another attack against the Conservative Party, declaring that they spoke only for a class who were idle from the day they were born until the day they died.

'I mean,' Gwendoline trilled, 'everyone knows the world is quite simply divided into those who lead and those who are fit only to be led.'

'Or those who are born booted and spurred to ride, and a large dim mass born saddled and bridled to be ridden,' someone else put in. 'Intelligence is a direct result of breeding every time.'

'Exactly,' Gwendoline beamed. 'It would be a case of throwing pearls before swine to expect anything else. The country would flounder within months, if given over to the masses.'

'How do you know? How can you possibly know?' The words were ringing in Angeline's head, but she didn't realize she had said them aloud until the moment of utter silence that followed.

'I beg your pardon?' Gwendoline's face was almost comical in its amazement.

'My father used to say that it is characteristic of elites that they seek to preserve and justify their position through certain styles of living and codes of behaviour, at the same time inflicting an expected subservience on those who belong to the lower orders, especially on dependents in the village or servants in the house or estate, without any idea of who those people are or what they really think.' Angeline didn't know where the words were coming from; they must have been buried in her subconscious for years, courtesy of the debates between her father and Mr Appleby during dinner. 'We label them "the poor" and assume that, because they live in cramped, damp dwellings and work all hours of the day and night just to survive, they are unintelligent and have no calling on their lives. It might be that in the main these people could rise as high as any of us, given a decent education and a chance to think, rather than work, every waking moment.'

The silence continued to be absolute. It was a full ten

seconds before back-up came from the last source Angeline would have expected, as Mirabelle drawled, 'Was it Sir Lawrence Jones who said the aristocracy don't think of class, because class is something that is here, like the rest of the phenomenal world, and we expect it to be so? The poor just happen to be poor, and consequently couldn't be expected to dine off the best in the land, unlike the nobility; and the deference of servants provides a daily reinforcement of our self-assurance, superiority and self-perception as God-ordained leaders. He has a point, don't you think? And, speaking of God ordained, wasn't His Son born in a humble stable to poor peasant folk, and didn't He work as a carpenter for years, getting His hands dirty?'

Nicholas Gray recovered first, and his voice wasn't patronizing, but rather full of hidden amusement as he said, 'Well said, ladies, well said. I don't pretend to agree with all the sentiments you've expressed, but by golly, you'd give some of those in government a run for their money. I'm not even going to broach the subject of the woman question and the suffrage movement. I fear we've been shaken up enough for one morning, but the pair of you might like to read John Stuart Mill's *The Subjection of Women* some time. If I remember his words correctly, he said human beings are no longer born to their place in life and chained down by an inexorable bond to the place they are born to, but are free to employ their faculties and such favourable chances on offer, to achieve the lot that may appear to them most desirable. I fear this is not altogether true, but it is interesting, don't you think? And now, gentlemen, to the shoot; and let us leave the ladies to their own devices . . . '

Angeline sat where she was as the company began to disperse, pretending to finish the food on her plate. Oswald was furious with her; his face had been as tight as a drum as he left the room, and she knew what he was thinking. She had behaved in accordance with her heritage and upbringing and had shown her roots. The steely set of his mouth had told her that he would make her pay for her rebellion.

'That set the cat amongst the pigeons.' Mirabelle plumped down beside her and she was smiling. 'For once Gwendoline didn't know what to say.'

'Oswald's angry.' Angeline looked at the woman who by rights she should consider her rival, but for what? Her husband's affection? Mirabelle was welcome to it. 'Is Marmaduke annoyed with you?'

'Marmaduke?' Mirabelle laughed lightly. 'Good grief, no. He doesn't enjoy these shooting parties any more than I do, and he simply abhors Gwendoline and her endless prattle. From the wink he gave me when he left, I rather think he enjoyed the break from the endless monotony as much as I did.'

Angeline was taken aback. 'Do you mean that? About the endless monotony?'

'Absolutely, but one has to pretend. It's expected.' Mirabelle rose gracefully to her feet. 'And don't worry about Oswald. He'll have forgotten all about it after a day's shooting.'

No, he wouldn't. Angeline's face must have spoken for itself, because Mirabelle surprised her for the second time that morning. Bending down, she said softly, 'Don't look like that, child.' For a moment she seemed to consider something, and then she murmured, 'Humour him, Angeline. That's all you have to do, and you could learn how to manage him.'

'I don't want to manage him.' It was a flat statement.

'It would be better in the long run. He's that sort of man.'

'I know what sort of man he is.' This time no one could doubt her bitterness, and the two women stared at each other for some moments.

'Does he ill-treat you?' Mirabelle asked, even more softly.

Angeline didn't answer this. This woman was Oswald's mistress after all, and she had no idea whether she could trust Mirabelle or not, in spite of her coming to her aid that morning. Standing up, she said quietly, 'Thank you for what you said. No one else would have spoken for me. I know that.'

Mirabelle smiled. 'Maybe we're two of a kind.'

Angeline inclined her head, but said nothing before walking away. Two of a kind? They were poles apart, and Mirabelle knew that as well as she did. Mirabelle's family had royal connections and everyone wanted to be associated with her, whereas she – she had been unimportant before today, and now she would be considered something of a pariah to boot, although Mirabelle's championing of her against Gwendoline would not go unnoticed. Why had Mirabelle done it? Was it a little game of her own that Oswald's mistress was playing?

But it didn't really matter. Angeline's hand went protectively to her belly. Nothing mattered now but her child. Once the baby was safely born, they'd escape Oswald's clutches. Perhaps she should start thinking more laterally – why not France or Italy rather than simply the south of England? She could speak a smattering of both languages, thanks to Miss Robson. She could pretend to be a widow. She could do it, she knew she could.

*Oswald wouldn't have her baby.* Her mouth tightened. *Not while she had breath in her body.*

# *Chapter Nine*

The rose garden was devoid of the heavy perfume of summer, having been manicured to within an inch of its life by the estate's gardeners in preparation for the Scottish winter, but the earlier rain followed by the September sunshine had brought a fresh fragrance to the air as Mirabelle strolled towards the summerhouse that afternoon. She and Oswald had discovered the pretty little wooden building modelled in the fashion of a Swiss chalet at the start of their affair some years ago. They had made good use of it since then, for their clandestine assignations during the annual shoot – the danger of someone stumbling across them bringing extra spice to their lovemaking. Today, though, Mirabelle was finding that a hitherto unknown phenomenon was taking the edge off the prospect of the enjoyment to come; she was developing a conscience. Not about her husband, oh no. Marmaduke was fully aware he couldn't satisfy her needs and, by unspoken mutual consent, they had decided long ago that she could look elsewhere as long as she was discreet.

She paused, glancing up at the sky, which was now as blue as cornflowers after the grey of the last few days.

It was Angeline who was bothering her. She bit down on her bottom lip, worrying it for a moment with her small white teeth as she brought her eyes to the summerhouse once more. *Was* Oswald ill-treating his wife? Once she would have dismissed the idea as ridiculous, but not any more. Which in itself was a concern. And now the girl – because Angeline *was* still little more than a girl, in spite of having been married for two years – was expecting a child, when she seemed such a child herself.

When she reached the summerhouse she found it empty, and after kicking off her soft kid shoes and discarding her cloak, Mirabelle settled herself on one of the two upholstered couches, idly flexing her toes in the thick wool rug at her feet. The summerhouse was beautifully furnished in the style of a pretty miniature drawing room, and she had been enchanted when she first came across it. Today she found herself wishing she was somewhere else.

Should she end her affair with Oswald? It wasn't the first time she had considered it since his marriage to Angeline, but it *was* the first time she had admitted to herself the element of fear which the thought held. She had caught glimpses of another Oswald over the last months, glimpses that had persuaded her that the stories about his fiendish temper and dark side might be true. Perhaps she had always known it was so, but hadn't wanted to acknowledge the truth? Not while he met her physical needs so completely. This thought was even more disconcerting.

A sixth sense told her she was not alone, and she came out of her thoughts to see Oswald standing in the entrance to the summerhouse, his eyes narrowed and his handsome face unsmiling. In spite of her deliberations, his manly beauty sent a thrill of desire shooting down her backbone and she smiled at him, patting the space beside her as she murmured, 'Come and sit, I've been waiting for you.'

He didn't move for a moment, then he stepped inside and shut the summerhouse door, but still he remained standing.

Her smile faded. 'What's the matter?'

'What do you think is the matter?'

His tone brought Mirabelle stiffening. 'I have no idea, Oswald, and I do not appreciate being spoken to in this manner.'

'And I don't appreciate your collaboration with my wife in making me look a fool.'

Mirabelle's face stretched in amazement. 'What are you talking about?'

'I'm *talking* about that scene at breakfast, when you turned me into a laughing stock. The morning I've had' – he ground his teeth before going on, his voice little more than a growl – 'I've been the butt of every Tom, Dick and Harry's snide jokes. Do you know what that swine Braithwaite said to me? No? I'll enlighten you. "Too bad you can't control your wife, old chap, but it comes to something when you can't control your mistress, either."'

'Braithwaite?' Mirabelle flicked her hand. 'The man's a moron.'

'Moron or not, he said what the others were thinking.'

Mirabelle stood up, every inch the aristocratic lady as she said clearly and coldly, 'Angeline expressed a point of view and I did likewise, that is all. The conversation had absolutely nothing to do with you, as far as I can see. Marmaduke hasn't objected to my expressing my opinion, so I hardly see that you have the right to do so.'

'Marmaduke!' It was a snarl. 'You castrated him years ago, and everyone knows it. And what you and my dear wife said was all to do with me. She did it to make me look a fool, don't you see, woman? And you applauded her.'

'Don't "woman" me, Oswald. I'm not your wife and I don't have to put up with your tantrums. Can't you see Angeline was merely saying what she thinks, and why shouldn't she? Why shouldn't I? Women have got brains, too. Believe it or not, neither of us thought of you when we were speaking our minds. You were unimportant.'

Her words acted on him like fuel to a fire. 'Unimportant, you say? Unimportant! I'll show you how unimportant I am.'

For a moment Mirabelle didn't understand what he was about to do, not until he reached out and, grasping the bodice of her gown, ripped it in two. In her pampered childhood and youth, and even more in adulthood, she had never experienced another human being raising their hand to her in anger, and for a moment the shock rendered her helpless. Then his knee whipped her legs from beneath her and they fell to the floor, and she began to fight back with as much effect as a kitten defending itself against a savage dog.

She twisted and turned beneath him on the rug where in happier times they had sported, aware of the curses spewing out of his mouth as he attempted to hoist her dress and undergarments over her thighs. He slapped her hard across the face at one point, her head thudding back, and for a moment everything went black, but then she felt her silk drawers being torn away and she brought her knees up in an instinctive movement of self-protection.

She heard him gasp as her legs caught him in a sensitive place and tried to scramble away as his grip loosened momentarily, but then he was on her again, growling through gritted teeth, 'You need to be taught a lesson, my fine lady – one you won't forget in a hurry.' The next second he had flipped her over so that she was face-down, and his hands parted the rounded globes of her bottom.

Indescribable pain brought high-pitched screams, muffled by the thick rug, as he hammered into her, panic and horror and agony at what was happening to her reducing Mirabelle to an animal caught in a trap.

When it was over and she felt his weight roll off her, she couldn't move. She heard him say, 'You brought this on yourself, remember that. I won't be crossed and those who try live to regret it.' She knew he was standing looking down at her, and there was no resistance in her now; if he attacked her again she would be unable to put up a fight. Tears of shock were still seeping from her eyes as she heard him rearranging his clothes, but it wasn't until she knew she was alone that she found the strength to roll onto her back.

She lay for long minutes shaking with the pain and when she attempted to sit up at first it brought overwhelming nausea. She was sick several times, but when her stomach was empty she dragged herself to her knees. There was blood on the rug, and when she stood up she was aware of the darkness rushing in on her and had to hold onto the back of the couch for a full minute.

It was some time before Mirabelle felt able to leave the summerhouse after making herself as presentable as she could, tidying her hair in the gilt mirror and wiping all trace of tears from her face with scented water and a handkerchief from her vanity bag. The bodice of her dress was ruined, but her cloak would cover her until she could get to the safety of her room and dispose of her dress and undergarments. By now the other ladies would be taking tea in the drawing room, and the coast would be relatively clear for her to slip upstairs unnoticed.

It hurt to walk, but she encountered no one except a footman as she entered the house. The men were still out shooting, but Alice, her personal maid, was busy taking the last of the creases out of the evening dress Mirabelle had chosen to wear that evening, using a small iron heated by methylated spirits that Alice always brought with her when they travelled.

'Oh, I'm sorry, ma'am, I thought you would be taking tea for some time,' said Alice, flustered. 'I'll take this downstairs and—' She stopped, taking in her mistress's pallor. 'Are you all right, ma'am?'

'I . . . I've taken a fall.' Knowing she was about to faint, Mirabelle reached out as Alice came running to her, and as the maid took her weight, blackness descended.

She could only have been unconscious for a few moments, and even then not fully, because she could hear Alice murmuring, 'Oh, ma'am, ma'am', although she couldn't bring herself to respond as she lay on the floor of the room with Alice kneeling beside her. It was only when Alice made to rise to her feet that Mirabelle found the wherewithal to clutch at her and say, 'No, stay. He-help me.'

'Of course I'll help you, ma'am, but let me fetch some-one.'

'*No!*' Her voice stronger now, Mirabelle sat up with the maid's help and, as she did so, her cloak fell apart, revealing the state of her bodice.

'Ma'am . . . ' Alice's eyes travelled from the torn frock to the blood splattered on the skirt. 'Ma'am, who's done this?'

'I . . . I fell.' No one must know. Ever. The humiliation was so great it was crushing her. 'If you could ring for hot water I'll take a bath, but you must say nothing of this to anyone. I mean it, Alice. Not even Mr Jefferson. Promise me.'

'I promise, ma'am.' Alice had tears in her eyes. Something terrible had happened, but if her mistress wanted nothing said, she would rather have her tongue cut out than betray her. She had been with Mirabelle for nine years, and a degree of trust and closeness had developed between them; it was hard to attend to the intimate toiletries of someone without getting to know them fairly well. Over this time she had become the confidante of her mistress, sharing not only snippets about clothes and beauty, but gossip, excitements, anxieties and heartaches, too. Only Alice knew how distressed Mirabelle had been in the first years of marriage when one miscarriage after another had eventually determined that she would never have a child. A lady's maid was expected to be discreet and wise beyond her years, and loyal, regardless of how kind her mistress was; but Mirabelle had always treated Alice very well and, in so doing, had gained her maid's affection as well as her allegiance.

After settling her mistress in an easy chair by the window with her back to the room, Alice arranged for the housemaids to bring the hot water. Once the tub in the small bathroom off the bedroom was sufficiently full, she sprinkled into the warm water some of the floral bath-soak consisting of coarse salt, lavender oil, lavender flowers and small dried rosebuds that she made exactly to her mistress's taste and transported in a glass jar sealed with a glass stopper. After that she helped

Mirabelle undress, saying nothing about the soiled, bloodied clothes, but when she lowered her mistress into the water and a cloud of fresh blood spread out beneath her, she murmured, 'Oh, ma'am, ma'am' through her tears. For a while the barrier between mistress and maid disappeared as the two women embraced each other, Alice kneeling by the bath with Mirabelle's head buried in her shoulder.

Eventually Mirabelle drew away, her voice thick as she whispered, 'Cut them up and burn them in the fire in the bedroom, Alice' as she gestured towards the pile of clothes.

'Ma'am, you need a doctor—'

'No. No doctor, no one. You promised.'

'But you're hurt.'

'It will pass. Now do as I say.' As Alice went about her grisly task, Mirabelle lay back in the bath and shut her eyes, images of what had happened stark behind her closed eyelids. Alice had said she was hurt and she was right, but the physical pain was only part of it. The miscarriages had hurt, the agony of grief and pain and loss seemingly unendurable, but she *had* endured each one until she had come to accept the unacceptable. But this – this was . . . She could find no words for what it was, as hot tears coursed down her cheeks and she bit into the flesh at the base of her thumb to stop herself moaning aloud.

Only her hatred of him had stopped her walking into the lake and drowning herself when she had first left the summerhouse. She had thought about it, she had stood there and seriously considered it, but then he would have won.

Sitting up in the water, she brushed her hand across her eyes. She would have her revenge. When, how, she didn't know, but it would come. She would bring Oswald low, have him grovelling in the dust as he had made her grovel. She wouldn't rest until he was broken, defiled. She knew people – or rather Marmaduke did – men who could turn a game of cards into whatever they determined it would be. Skilful players who could strip the very bones of a man dry. She would intimate to Marmaduke that Oswald had offended her and, in doing so, had belittled him. No details, but she would insinuate that he had been playing to an audience when he'd derided her good name and had held Marmaduke up as an object of ridicule. It would be a slow process, but she could wait. Oswald would know what humiliation was.

Every movement made her wince, and when she stood up in the water it was tinted scarlet, but nothing would prevent her going down to dinner tonight as normal. She would be gay and sparkling and would put on the performance of her life, because the aim to destroy him began now. One day she would make Oswald Golding wish he had never been born.

# *Chapter Ten*

An agonizingly slow forty-eight hours had crept by and the final shoot had taken place. Angeline had been on tenterhooks the whole time. She had prepared herself for a verbal assault from Oswald for her temerity in challenging Gwendoline Gray, but his displeasure had taken the form of an icy silence when they were alone. In public he maintained the facade of a happily married man. Angeline didn't mind his ignoring her in the privacy of their room, in fact she welcomed it, but she was surprised and wary. Normally Oswald didn't rest until he had vented his anger.

On the last evening after dinner Lord Gray had arranged a musical soirée to entertain his guests. A fine Scottish choir from Edinburgh had arrived at the estate earlier that afternoon, and for once, as Angeline sat with the rest of the company enjoying the excellent singing, she found herself relaxing.

The firelight flickered in the magnificent drawing-room fireplace, casting dancing shadows on the walls;

the reflection of the lamps glancing off the jewels at the neck and wrists of the ladies made brilliant points of light; the men looked well fed and content after their days of wholesale slaughter, somewhat somnolent in their white tie and tails, and overall a peaceful and lazy atmosphere pervaded the air.

At the invitation of Lord Gray, the servants stood in the hall listening to the choir through the half-open door. They had served coffee and liqueurs before the entertainment had begun and were free to go to bed when they wished – all but the housekeeper and butler, who never retired before their master, and the ladies' maids and valets, who would help their respective mistresses and masters prepare for bed later on.

The ladies were sitting at the front of the semicircle of several rows of small upholstered chairs that had been placed in the middle of the room. Most of the men were sitting or standing towards the rear. Angeline was sitting in the second row and found her eyes constantly straying towards Mirabelle in the front row and to the left of her. She couldn't rid herself of the feeling that something was amiss with the other woman. Certainly Mirabelle was her usual vivacious herself and, popular as she was, she'd had her familiar group of friends clustered around her all evening, but since the incident with Gwendoline at the breakfast table two days ago Angeline felt there was a brittleness to the lovely redhead's gaiety. And at the dancing the night before, Mirabelle had openly rebuffed Oswald when he'd asked her to partner him. Angeline didn't know how many people had noticed, but she certainly had. Had the two of them had a tiff?

Angeline glanced behind her to where her husband was standing with a group of other men. He was half a head taller than anyone else and easily the most handsome man in the room. Her stomach curdled with distaste.

Turning round, she remembered his expression when Mirabelle had refused him. His features had tightened and his eyes had narrowed, before he had quickly stitched a smile on his face and sauntered off as though nothing had happened. But then he hadn't come to their room until the early hours, and she had assumed he might have made things up with his mistress and they had found a quiet corner somewhere. But now she wondered. Perhaps he had just continued to play cards and knock back the whisky, as he had been doing when she'd gone upstairs? He had been as drunk as a lord when he'd come to bed, and she'd been thankful that pregnant women repulsed him. He hadn't touched her in months.

As though her thoughts had conjured it up, she felt the faintest of flutterings deep in her abdomen. Instinctively her hands covered her belly. It had happened once or twice since they had been in Scotland, a slight but unmistakable movement of the baby in her womb. It had thrilled her beyond words. Each time it occurred the rush of protective love and tenderness it caused had taken her breath away.

Myrtle, who had been with her mother when several

of her siblings were born, even helping them into the world because the family couldn't afford a midwife, was familiar with all aspects of pregnancy and birth. It had been she who had gently suggested to her mistress in the early days that the nausea Angeline was experiencing, coupled with the non-appearance of her monthly cycle, probably meant that a baby was on the way. In spite of being married for more than a year, Angeline had had no idea, and when Myrtle had understood the extent of her mistress's ignorance, she'd sat with her one day and explained what Angeline might expect month by month, and how her body would adapt and change for the time when she would give birth, and how that would be accomplished.

Angeline had been embarrassed but grateful, and that day had strengthened the growing bond between the two women.

Myrtle would help her when she left Oswald after the child was born, Angeline thought now, her hands still splayed over her stomach. Her mother's jewellery and the pieces she now owned would fetch a goodly sum, and she had been saving for some time the monthly allowance for clothes and fripperies that Oswald allowed her. He was anxious that she didn't let him down, by not keeping up with the likes of Gwendoline and Mirabelle, but such was his disinterest that he didn't notice if she wore the same dress once or a hundred times.

She would ask Myrtle if she wanted to accompany her when she left England, and she would give Myrtle a sum of money to settle on her family before they left. It could work.

The tiny stirring of life inside her came again, and with it the resolve to carry through the plans she had been mulling over for months. Each time she considered them she grew more certain of what she was going to do, and with that came strength. It was up to her to protect and safeguard her child, and her father had always maintained there was no shame in good, honest toil. Whether he had expected his own daughter would have to support herself was, of course, doubtful. But she could do it. She just had to believe in herself.

As soon as Angeline was able, she made her way out of the drawing room, pleading a headache to Lord Gray, when he asked her why she was leaving the entertainment so early. As solicitous as ever, he told her he would send one of the housemaids to her room with a mild sleeping draught, despite her protest that she would be quite recovered after a night's sleep.

'It will ensure you do sleep well, m'dear, that's the thing,' he murmured as the choir sang on. 'I always find that rather difficult myself when I'm away from home, don't you? But then I am a creature of habit. Gwendoline is always telling me I need to be more spontaneous. I fear I can be a little dull at times.'

'I think you do very well just as you are.' Angeline smiled at him. 'And thank you. You are very kind.'

It came to her as she left the room that she had never thought of Oswald's house as home. It was a luxurious prison, a beautiful gilded cage that she had walked into willingly.

Nicholas Gray stood staring after Angeline after she had left him, the music and singers fading into the background of his thoughts. There was something terribly wrong with Oswald's young wife, but he was damned if he knew what it was. The first time he had met her she had been little more than a child, it was true, and immature for her years, but she'd had a light in her eyes and an inner serenity, and that in spite of having lost her parents only months before. Now that light was extinguished – that was the only way he could put it. He frowned, the sense of unease he'd felt about Oswald's marriage on several occasions strong. But what could he do? He could hardly ask a fellow pertinent questions about his wife and how they were getting on.

'Sir?' Nicholas's butler spoke softly in his ear. As his master turned to him, he murmured, 'With your guests leaving in the morning, I wondered what time you would like the vintage port served tonight?'

Nicholas Gray was generous with his guests and this generosity was reflected in the excellent food and drink he had served to them in huge quantities. However, there was a subtle difference between the excellent vintage port that had lain in his cellars for some twenty years and the good-quality port of a later vintage. The opening of the vintage port on the last day of the annual shoot in Scotland involved some ceremony, not least for the servants below stairs. It formed a crusty sediment over the years it was laid down in the massive cellars and, to avoid disturbing this, and to make sure that none of the cork crumbled into the port, the necks of the bottles were gripped tightly using iron tongs, heated red-hot in the coal fire of the range, and a feather dipped in icy-cold water was then passed over the neck of the bottles. Only the butler had the authority to open the vintage port and, being a difficult operation, the procedure was a nail-biting affair from beginning to end. Once the neck had snapped off in the required fashion, the port was then poured through a silver funnel into a linen-covered sieve, to further avoid contamination of the fine, rich liquid as it dropped into a crystal decanter.

Nicholas Gray, like his father before him, was well aware of the finesse entailed and of the agonies his butler suffered until the job was done. He himself had attempted the process once and it had been an unmitigated disaster. He smiled his gentle smile. 'Now would be a good time, I think, McKenzie. You have the ladies' glasses ready?'

The ladies were served an inferior, although still excellent, claret, as it was accepted that their less discerning tastebuds would not appreciate the delicate difference.

McKenzie nodded. 'Yes, m'Lord.'

As the butler bustled off, Nicholas glanced across the room to where Oswald was standing. He looked somewhat bored. Clearly the choir was not to his taste, Nicholas thought wryly, and certainly the man was not concerned about his wife's departure from the company.

Nicholas frowned. He could have sworn in the early

days that the Golding marriage was one made for love and not for convenience, but now it had all the hallmarks of the latter. Had he been mistaken all along, or had something happened to drive a wedge between the couple? He had spoken of his misgivings to Gwendoline and she had pointed out that, with Angeline not being of their class, she was perhaps finding it difficult to fit into the life that was expected of her as Oswald's wife. And of course that was possible. Angeline did seem on edge.

Nicholas sighed, flexing his shoulders and wishing the evening would soon be over. He was looking forward to getting out on the river with his ghillie, once his guests had departed, for a few days' uninterrupted fishing. Besides his private stretch of river, the estate boasted a large lake in the grounds, which was well stocked with prime brown trout. There he could forget any problems and concerns, especially ones he could do nothing about, like the Golding question. And probably he was imagining something that wasn't there anyway. He nodded mentally at the thought. When he had tentatively broached the possibility of Gwendoline having a little word with Angeline, his wife had flatly refused, saying that if the couple were experiencing any problems, it was their business and theirs alone. And of course Gwendoline was right. It was just that Oswald's young wife seemed so very alone . . .

# *Chapter Eleven*

It was nearing the end of an icy-cold, wet November, and the change in the weather of the last day or two heralded that December was around the corner. Rain and sleet had changed to hard frost in the mornings and snow was forecast.

Since returning from Scotland, Angeline had used the fact of her ever-increasing girth to remain in seclusion on the estate, and Oswald had not objected to this. He had continued with life as normal; accepting invitations to one or two weekend shoots in the Durham area, travelling down to London in the middle of October for a few days and, when he was at home, staying out till all hours drinking and gambling with his cronies. There were periods when Angeline did not see him for days at a time and she was thankful for this. She busied herself organizing the redecoration of the nursery wing, which comprised a day-nursery, a night-nursery, the nursery maid's bedroom and a washroom and closet. Within the next week or so she was due to interview a number of nursery maids, as she was now just seven months pregnant, with a view to the successful applicant taking up employment after Christmas ready for the birth at the end of January.

The last weeks had been ones of mixed emotions. Every time she entered the newly decorated nursery wing a part of her was saddened that her child would not grow up in such comfortable and luxurious surroundings, because she was still determined to leave Oswald when she could. She would wait until she was sure the baby was thriving and healthy and the first few months were over, and then she would take her child and Myrtle and would escape.

This morning Angeline awoke early in the room in which she now slept alone, Oswald having moved to his own quarters since they returned from Scotland. He claimed he didn't want to disturb her when he returned late to the house after she had gone to bed, and she had hardly been able to believe her good fortune when he had first declared his intentions. She suspected it was more that he found every aspect of pregnancy repellent, because as her shape had begun to change he couldn't hide his distaste, but that mattered not a jot. The fact of the matter was that she didn't have to endure the trial of his close proximity to her any more, and it was wonderful. He was due back from an overnight stay with some friend or other – she didn't know who and she didn't care – that afternoon, so as she sat at her window watching the winter dawn break in a pearly-grey sky streaked with dusky pink, she was surprised to see him galloping up the drive on his hunter.

Feeling apprehensive, but without knowing why, she continued to sit at the window until she heard his footsteps on the landing outside. He opened the door without knocking and stared at her as she stood with her hand resting on the easy chair, still in her nightdress and rose-pink dressing gown. Closing the door behind him, he walked to within a few inches of her, so close that she could smell the stale alcohol and cigar smoke emanating from his person. His words, when they came, were all the more sinister for being spoken softly. 'I could kill you for the trouble you've caused me.'

Angeline swallowed deeply and gripped the top of the chair tighter. 'I don't know what you are talking about.'

'No, I dare say you don't, Little Miss Holier Than Thou. So pure, so righteous, so touch-me-not. Spouting about matters you know nothing about and disgracing me into the bargain, but that's not all. Because of you and your babbling, Marmaduke Jefferson has been turned against me – and he's got influence. Two thousand I lost last night. *Two thousand*.'

Unable to follow the reasoning, Angeline stared at him. 'You were gambling?'

'Of course I was gambling, but I was played for a fool. They cheated me, and not for the first time. I've lost too much over the last weeks, and I see it all now.' He swayed slightly. 'Damn cheats, the lot of 'em.'

Unable to keep the distaste out of her voice, Angeline said, 'You are still drunk. How much did you drink?'

'What's that to you?'

'You probably lost the money because you were too inebriated to think straight.'

'Don't tell me why I lost. I know full well, dammit. Jefferson and his hangers-on are out to fleece me, and all because you couldn't keep your mouth shut.'

'You're mad.' She genuinely couldn't follow him. 'I've never even held a conversation with Marmaduke Jefferson.'

'You didn't have to. All you had to do was spout that drivel your father harped on about.'

Suddenly she understood. The morning in September when she'd disagreed with Gwendoline Gray and made her own views plain. That was what all this was about. But it was weeks ago. Why was he bringing it up now, and what did Mirabelle's husband have to do with it? Suddenly she felt furiously angry. 'You're seriously saying I'm to blame for you losing at cards? If Marmaduke really is annoyed with you, as you claim, it's surely over your affair with his wife? Everyone knows he worships the ground she walks on.'

'He does that all right.' His voice had risen and he seemed beside himself. 'But he's never objected to Mirabelle's dalliances as long as she's happy. But you put an end to that, didn't you! You made me lose my temper and—' He stopped, breathing hard, his face suffused with rage. 'She'll never forgive me, I see that now. Do you know what you've done? Do you? Marmaduke is a good friend, but a bad enemy, and who knows what she's told him.'

He was making no sense. Her face tight, she said, 'Well, either don't sit down at cards with Marmaduke again, or grovel to Mirabelle and put right what you've done.'

When Oswald's fist caught her straight between the eyes Angeline actually heard her nose crack. She went spinning backwards, to fall heavily across the chair she had been sitting on by the window. The wooden arm thudded into her back with such force that the pain rendered her unconscious, the echo of her piercing scream fading. She wasn't aware of the bedroom door being flung open and Myrtle running in, or of Oswald stumbling out of the way of the girl as he muttered, 'She fell. Dizzy spell. She fell.'

When Angeline came to again she was in bed, but the pain in her face was nothing compared to the agony in her belly, which was trying to tear her apart. Myrtle was kneeling beside the bed. The housekeeper and one of the housemaids were in the room, and it was Mrs Gibson who said, 'The doctor's on his way, ma'am.'

Angeline groaned, and as the pain in her stomach intensified and worked up to a crescendo before abating somewhat, she became aware that she was holding onto Myrtle's hand and that Myrtle had tears streaming down her face. 'Myrtle.' Through the pain, she forced the words out. 'He said . . . he said Marmaduke Jefferson has turned against him because he lost his temper with Mirabelle. Ch-cheated him. Gambling. Mirabelle Jefferson, his wife . . . '

'I know, ma'am, I know.' Myrtle knew full well who Mirabelle Jefferson was, and you'd need to be blind or barmy not to know what she was to Mr Oswald, an' all. Or had been, by the sound of it.

'He said it's my fault, Myrtle. Where . . . where is he?'

'Sleeping it off, ma'am. Don't worry, he'll not come in here again.' And as Myrtle caught the housekeeper and housemaid exchange a glance, she said fiercely, 'You hear me? He's not to come in here. He's done enough, the evil swine.'

'Myrtle, the baby. I think the baby's coming.'

'Don't worry, ma'am, it'll be all right. The doctor will be here soon.' Myrtle rubbed at her wet face with her free hand. 'You just try and lie still, ma'am.'

'Too . . . too early.'

'Oh, ma'am, don't cry. Try and sleep, and the pains'll stop.'

But another contraction was coming, and sleep was the last thing she could do. By the time the spasm had ended, each one of them knew the baby was coming and nothing this side of heaven could stop it.

The doctor arrived and he was grim-faced as he examined his patient. Angeline heard him say, 'And her face?'

'The master.' Myrtle's voice was equally grim.

'You're sure? Mr Golding has told me he was with his

wife when she had a dizzy spell and fell, cracking her face against the chair and floor.'

'Mr Golding can say what he wants, sir, but I know what I know. Look at her, for crying out loud. Look at her poor face!'

'You were in the room when it happened?'

'No.'

'Ah, in that case . . . '

And then the pain took over again and Angeline didn't know much about the hours that followed, except that the doctor didn't leave her side and neither did Myrtle. At one point she thought she heard Oswald's voice, and Myrtle – sounding quite unlike herself – screaming, 'Get him out of here! Get him out!' but she told herself that couldn't be, because for Myrtle to speak like that would mean instant dismissal, and Myrtle had her family to think of. Her wage meant the difference between surviving, and the workhouse for her parents and siblings.

The pain was raging out of control and the only thing in the world besides the agony was Myrtle's hand holding hers. She knew she was going to die. No one could survive such torment and live. And she didn't care about herself. But her baby . . .

By midnight she was so tired she couldn't tell what was real and what was not. The brutal pain, the ache in her head and eyes from her broken nose, and the bruises from the fall that were already making dark stains on her body combined to produce a state of collapse. The excruciating pains were practically continuous, and still the baby showed no signs of emerging from its place of safety into a world where its underdeveloped lungs meant that each breath would be a fight for survival.

As dawn broke, the doctor decided he would have to operate if he didn't want to lose the mother as well as the child. But no sooner had the decision been made than Angeline began to push. Twenty minutes later a tiny but perfect baby girl came into the world. Myrtle saw the doctor cut the cord, she saw the baby's head move as though searching for her mother, but there was no cry, no taking of breath. The doctor simply held her in his arms as he glanced at Myrtle and, long in the tooth as he was, he had tears in his eyes when a few moments later he shook his head.

And then Angeline began to haemorrhage. She hadn't really been conscious at the birth, not fully, but as Myrtle watched, the figure on the bed became as white as the bleached linen sheets, the crimson flow coming from beneath her the only colour in an ever-widening sea of red.

The doctor thrust the tiny body into Myrtle's arms, saying, 'Wrap her up', before he sprang to attend to the mother. Unable to comprehend the extent of the tragedy, Myrtle gazed down at the child in her arms. The minute face was so sweet, so pure, so delicate, devoid of eyelashes or eyebrows, for all the world like a porcelain doll.

Numbly she walked into the bathroom and reached for a towel, wrapping the baby in it, before holding her close to her chest. 'It's all right,' she whispered. 'Really, it's all right. I've got you.'

# *Chapter Twelve*

After the birth of her daughter, Angeline lay for almost a month hovering between life and death. Unaware of her surroundings or the daily visits of the doctor, she lay as still as a corpse being cared for by the nurse Oswald had hired on the advice of the doctor. Myrtle had been sent packing by a furious Oswald immediately after the miscarriage. He had threatened the maid with dire consequences if she repeated her assertion that he had struck his wife and caused the death of the child.

Heartsore and desperately worried about her mistress, Myrtle had left the estate on a bitterly cold, frosty morning, and made her way to Hector's house to see Albert. It was his sister who opened the back door at her knock, and when Myrtle dissolved into tears on the doorstep, she saw a different side to Olive Upton. Within five minutes she was sitting at the table with a cup of strong sweet tea and a plate of hot buttered girdle scones, with Albert on one side of her and his sister on the other.

Olive made her drink the tea and eat two of the scones

before Myrtle told the full story, and as Myrtle was near to a state of collapse herself, she didn't argue. She was crying again as she finished relating the sorry tale, and Albert had his arm around her as he said to his sister, 'We must tell the master. He's her uncle, after all.'

Olive, shocked to the core, nodded. 'That poor lass, and the bairn, too. A little girl, you say she was?' she added to Myrtle. 'And you think he hit Miss Angeline?'

'I'm sure of it, but I could tell the doctor isn't about to say so. He knows which side his bread is buttered.'

'What about the housekeeper?'

'She'll say nothing. She's frightened of Mr Oswald – they all are – and with the mistress at death's door, she can't say what happened. And the baby . . . ' Myrtle turned and buried her face in Albert's chest, her shoulders shaking. 'I can't bear it.'

It was decided that Mrs Upton would go and have a word with Angeline's uncle and put him in the picture, and then call Myrtle if he wished to speak to her.

Hector was sitting in his study staring at the mountain of bills on his desk, most of them pressing. Several of the tradesmen had made it clear they would supply nothing more until their accounts were settled in full; the bank was threatening to foreclose; and he had no money to pay Mrs Upton's and Albert's wages, which were already overdue by some weeks. He was ruined. He sat, his head thudding. His gambling had got more and more reckless as his debts had mounted; he knew it, but he hadn't been able to stop. It would all have been so different if Golding had come through on his promise to help him after the marriage.

Hector stood up abruptly, walking over to stand at the window, but without seeing the garden, clothed in sparkling white. The humiliation of that meeting, shortly after the newly-weds had returned from their week in London, would be with him till his dying day. He had waylaid Oswald at the club rather than go to the house where Angeline would be present, and right away he had sensed that Oswald was going to make things hard for him. What he hadn't expected was that Oswald would deny any knowledge of their arrangement. What he should have done was cut his losses at that point and walk away with a shred of dignity intact, but he had argued his case until he had been reduced to begging Angeline's husband, practically on bended knees.

Hector ground his teeth together, his hands clenched at his side. And Oswald had laughed at him. Taken great delight in it, too. Oh yes, great delight.

He had known then he would never be able to face Angeline again. Hector turned, looking at the mound of papers on his desk. His humiliation was too deep, too raw. He had betrayed his brother's trust in him and had sold his soul to the devil, because if ever the devil took human form he was there looking out of Oswald Golding's eyes that night.

The knock on the study door brought him back to the present, and when his housekeeper opened it after he had called 'Come in', she found him sitting at his desk once more.

'Sir, Myrtle – Miss Angeline's maid – is in the kitchen, and she's in a sorry state.'

Hector raised his eyebrows, but said nothing.

'I'm sorry, sir, but it appears Miss Angeline has lost the baby she was expecting and, well, I don't know how to say this, sir, but Myrtle thinks Mr Golding struck her and that's what caused the miscarriage.'

'*What?*' Hector half-rose from his chair and then sank back down again, staring at his housekeeper. 'Send her in to me.'

Myrtle was puffy-faced and red-eyed when she was ushered into Hector's study by Albert's sister moments later. After signalling for Mrs Upton to leave them, Hector surveyed the girl, whom he knew to be loyal to his niece. 'Pull up a chair' – he gestured towards two straight-backed chairs standing against the far wall – 'and tell me what you know. What you *know*, Myrtle. And think carefully before you speak. Mr Golding is a powerful and influential man, and the allegation you made to Mrs Upton is an extremely serious one.'

'I know that, sir.' Myrtle sat down after she had placed the chair opposite the desk, but she did not relax, keeping her body stiff and her chin raised. 'And if you're asking me if I saw him hit the mistress, no, I didn't. But he punched her in the face, as sure as eggs are eggs. I was born near the docks in Monkwearmouth, and I know what a woman looks like when she's been bashed like that. No fall against a chair could do what he did to her.'

Hector made no comment on this, but said quietly, 'Are you saying Mr and Mrs Golding were not on good terms before this incident?'

'The mistress came back from the week in London after the wedding a changed woman, sir. And no, they were not on good terms, but it wasn't Miss Angeline's – Mrs Golding's – fault. No one could have been happier on their wedding day than the mistress. But Mr Golding,' Myrtle's lips came back from her teeth for an instant as though she was smelling something foul, 'he's not what he seems, sir.'

Myrtle paused for a moment, taking a deep breath and trying to control her voice as she said, 'The result of him bashing her was that she lost the baby, and when I left this morning the doctor didn't know if she was going to be all right. Mr Golding wouldn't let me stay, not after I'd said to the doctor that he'd hit her and . . . and shouted at him.'

'You shouted at your employer?'

Myrtle's chin rose higher at the disapproval in Hector's voice. 'Aye, I did, and I'm not sorry. Miss Angeline didn't want him near her, after what he'd done.'

'What you *think* he did.'

She was going to get no help for Miss Angeline here. Throwing caution to the wind, Myrtle stood up. 'Everyone at the house is frightened of Mr Golding, so you won't get the truth from any of them, but he's a fiend when he wants to be and he's no gentleman, I tell you that. If Miss Angeline dies, he's killed her. She didn't deserve to be treated like he's treated her from the day they got married, not Miss Angeline.'

'All right, all right, calm yourself. Tears will help no one.'

'And he killed the babbie. A little lass, she was, and perfect, but she came too early, thanks to him. The old master and mistress must be turning in their graves at the thought of Miss Angeline being married to him.'

'*That's enough!*' Hector was at a loss to know how to deal with a hysterical female.

'It's wicked . . . wicked.'

Glancing with distaste at Myrtle, who was now beside herself, her nose running and mingling with the tears streaming down her cheeks, Hector rang the bell for Mrs Upton. In truth he was both astounded and horrified at what he had heard, but he still found it difficult to comprehend that a man of Oswald Golding's breeding would hit a woman, let alone his pregnant young wife. The man was a bounder and a liar – something he knew to his cost after all – but this was something entirely worse, and the maid must be mistaken. But something had happened, and it was clear Angeline was in a bad way.

When Mrs Upton put her head round the door, he said briskly, 'Take Myrtle to the kitchen and give her a hot drink. And tell Albert to bring the carriage round.'

'Yes, sir.' Olive looked at Myrtle, who now had her hands covering her face and was crying so loudly it was enough to waken the dead. Raising her voice above the din, she felt impelled to ask – although she would never normally dream of doing so – 'Where shall I say you want to go, sir?'

'To the house.' Hector didn't have to say which house; they both knew there was only one in question.

As Mrs Upton led Myrtle – who was crying even more loudly, if anything, at this unexpected turn of events – away, Hector shut the study door and stood with his eyes closed for a moment. If only half of what the maid alleged was true, he was likely to get short shrift from Golding, and in spite of himself his stomach churned at the thought of facing him again. He hadn't been back to the club since the ignominy of that last meeting, when Oswald had held him in such contempt, and their paths had not crossed in the last two years. His shame had prevented him seeing Angeline when she had called at the house shortly after his altercation with her new husband, and as the weeks and months had gone by, it had seemed impossible to bridge the chasm.

No, he must be honest here, he thought, opening his eyes and straightening his shoulders. He hadn't *wanted* to see his niece. He would not have known what to say to her because he couldn't have voiced the real reason he had quarrelled with Oswald. He had taken the easy way out, even knowing that Angeline would have been distressed and deeply hurt by his rejection of her. He had delivered her into Golding's clutches and walked away, that was what it boiled down to, although in his own defence he hadn't imagined for a moment that the man would ill-treat her.

When he walked out onto the drive, Albert was waiting, standing by the open door of the carriage.

'Bad business this, sir,' said Albert soberly.

'Yes, indeed, but let us not jump to conclusions until we have established the facts.'

Albert said nothing as he shut the carriage door after his employer and climbed up into his seat, lifting the horses' reins, but inside he was shouting, '*Jump to conclusions! Jump to conclusions?*' Myrtle had told the master the facts in plain English. What more did he want? And why did he think Myrtle would put herself in the position of losing her job – a job her family relied on to keep them out of the workhouse – if every word wasn't the truth? But then again, there was none so blind as them that didn't want to see. If blame was to be apportioned regarding this whole sorry affair, the master should be standing right there at the front of the line.

The sky had clouded over in the last hour and a few desultory snowflakes floated lazily in the morning air. Albert looked up at the thick grey clouds and clicked his tongue for the horses to go faster. They were in for a packet; he could smell the coming snow and he didn't fancy making the journey back from the big house in the middle of a blizzard. He wanted to get back to Myrtle, too. She was in a right old state about Miss Angeline and the baby, and worrying about how she was going to tell her mam that she'd got the push. He could understand that. The first time he'd gone home with her to the four-roomed cottage in Monkwearmouth, he'd had to hide his shock at the way the family lived. Not that the place wasn't clean – he'd been amazed at how spotless it was, considering her mam had her hands full with the bairns and the washing she took in – but it was tiny. The front room, into which you stepped from a square of hall that allowed only for the opening of the door, held a double brass bed and a rickety wooden cot. Here Myrtle's parents slept with the latest baby. From what Albert could gather, Myrtle's mother seemed to give birth every eighteen months like clockwork. Upstairs, the two small bedrooms had straw mattresses lying on the floorboards for the rest of the children – girls in one room, and boys in the other – with a line of nails driven into the wall for their clothes.

The family lived in the kitchen, which had a fireplace with an open black range, a kitchen table with an assortment of old chairs round it, a rickety dresser and a number of shelves down one wall. On either side of the fireplace in the two alcoves were more shelves with a cupboard beneath. The tap for water was at the bottom of a communal yard, which served a number of houses, along with a privy and wash house. Their existence was hand-to-mouth and the rent man was a constant spectre.

Since Myrtle's father had fallen ill, another son had left school and started work at the Wearmouth Colliery, but that was still only two wages coming into the house to support a family of twelve, counting the new baby who was only a few months old; and the few bob Myrtle's mother earned from taking in washing went nowhere. They needed Myrtle's money. Albert bit his lip. And Golding had dismissed her without a reference, which would mean she'd have to take any menial work she could find. For two years now, since she'd become Miss Angeline's personal maid, Myrtle had been earning double what she could expect anywhere else – Miss Angeline had seen to that. And every Sunday afternoon when he met her at the bottom of the drive of the Golding estate to walk her home to see her parents, Miss Angeline always made sure that Myrtle had a bag of food to give to her mam. And not bread or tatties, either. A cooked ham and other bits one week; a side of best beef and a bag of sugar another – in all the time Myrtle had been at the big house, Miss Angeline had never forgotten. And now the poor lass was at death's door.

Albert sighed heavily and then geed up the horses, which were apt to dawdle, given half a chance.

He felt sick to his stomach about what had happened to Miss Angeline, but he had to admit another part of his mind – perhaps the greater part – had been chewing over what this new state of affairs would mean for him and Myrtle. He couldn't see her family reduced to going to the workhouse, and without the generous wage she'd been earning that's what this could mean. The money he put aside each month towards the smallholding that was his own and Myrtle's future was now a tidy sum, but he couldn't in all conscience hold onto it and see Myrtle's heart broken. He was going to have to subsidize whatever Myrtle could earn, and put the dream on hold. By, he could swing for Golding – he could straight.

By the time the carriage clip-clopped along the drive leading to the house the snow was coming down thicker. Albert pulled up on the forecourt at the bottom of the steps leading to the front door and alighted, opening the carriage door. Then he stood watching his employer as he mounted the steps and rang the bell. He found himself praying that for once Mr Hector would show some backbone and be a man. Damn it, he and Olive had never understood why Mr Hector had married his niece off to Golding, but surely now a blind man could see it had been a huge mistake.

The door was opened and Hector stepped inside, and then there were just the horses snorting softly and the snow falling in big starry flakes, and Albert was left to his sombre, anxious thoughts in a quiet white world.

It had been Wood, the butler, who had answered the door, and only years of practice kept his face from showing any emotion when he had recognized the man standing on the doorstep. Every servant in the house knew why Myrtle had been dismissed – Myrtle had made sure she hadn't gone quietly – and each one knew better than to express an opinion about what had befallen Mrs Golding, or to speak of the situation to anyone but each other. Now the butler led the way across the hall, the floor of which was polished until it resembled a mirror each morning, saying, 'If you will come this way, sir, I will tell the master you are here', before opening the drawing-room door.

Once alone, Hector made his way to the massive fireplace and stood staring down into the great wooden logs ablaze there. From somewhere deep inside him strength had come in the last few moments. He had left Oswald like a whipped puppy that night at the club two years ago, but he was damned if he would let the man intimidate him again.

When the door opened he swung round. Oswald stood there, as perfectly groomed and suave as always. 'Hector, my dear fellow. You've heard? So good of you to come.'

It took him aback. Whatever he had expected, it wasn't to be greeted with open arms. Stammering slightly, he said, 'Th-the maid. She came to my h-house this morning.'

'Ah, the maid.' Oswald shook his head. 'I confess I didn't know what to do with the girl; she's been here on borrowed time for a while. I found her pilfering the odd trinket or two months ago, but when I tried to dismiss her Angeline was so upset I allowed her to stay. I can only surmise that once she saw her mistress so ill, she thought I might take advantage of the situation and get rid of her, so she made up the preposterous story that I had attacked my own wife, in the hope of blackmailing me. Of course, even for Angeline, I could not allow her to stay after that, and frankly the girl is fortunate not to be in the hands of the law today. If it wasn't for my beloved wife and the anguish such an action would cause her, after the grief of losing our child, I would not have restrained myself. The baggage wasn't even in the room when Angeline fell. Did she tell you that? But come, sit down. I've arranged for coffee and brandy to warm you; it's a filthy day and, with the shock, I'm sure you need it.'

'I want to see my niece.'

'The doctor's with her at present. It's touch and go, I'm afraid.' Oswald drew a hand across his eyes as though overcome. 'I don't understand, Hector. One moment we were so happy, expecting our first child, and now . . . ' His voice cracked. 'I can't go on without her, I shall go mad.'

Hector felt totally nonplussed. Slowly he sat down. Oswald turned away, as though struggling to compose himself, and after a few moments said thickly, 'Excuse me a moment, I won't be long' and left the room.

Once in the hall Oswald stood for a moment with his back to the door, his head lifting and his eyes narrowing. This needn't be the disaster he'd feared it would be, during the long night hours before the child was still-born. It looked as though the mother would soon follow the child, and with the maid out of the way and the doctor backing him, nothing would be said. He could manage Hector Stewart. The man was nothing short of a simpleton.

Oswald straightened his shoulders. Come the funeral for both mother and child, he would play the grieving husband and father to the hilt. After that he would be free to resume his old life once more. And after all, he'd barely touched Angeline; it had been her stumbling backwards and falling across the chair that had caused the damage. She was a scrawny, weakly little thing at the best of times; it was highly likely she would never have gone full-term anyway. She clearly wasn't meant to bear children.

As he stood there, the doctor came walking down the stairs, a housemaid trailing after him. From the look on the physician's face Oswald thought Angeline had gone already, and he aimed to keep the deep relief out of his voice as he said, 'How is she?'

The doctor shook his head. 'Prepare yourself, Mr Golding. It could be any time. The loss of blood was severe – the worst I've seen where a patient is still breathing. I fear,' he shook his head again, 'there is little hope. Your housekeeper is sitting with her at present, but with your permission I will arrange for a nurse to attend Mrs Golding while it remains necessary.'

Oswald inclined his head. Any time. Any time and he would be free of this marriage that had become like a lead weight around his neck. All he had to do was keep his head, placate that old fool Hector, and make sure the man passed on his threat to send the maid down the line if she didn't keep her mouth shut. What was the word of a common servant compared to his? And the way the chit had spoken to him, he could have wrung her neck. But he must be careful to do everything by the book till Angeline died. With that in mind he said quietly, 'My wife's uncle is in the drawing room and naturally he is very upset. Would you care to have a word with the poor fellow, and explain that you believe my wife fell and this brought on the miscarriage of the child?'

The doctor looked full into the handsome face. He was aware of what he was being asked to do, in collaborating Golding's version of events, but in truth there was no reason not to. The maid admitted herself that she had not been present when the fall had taken place, the wife was not long for this world and, as physician to the Golding estate, he earned a considerable amount of money each year, which would almost certainly cease if he fell foul of Oswald Golding. Whatever the truth of the matter, nothing could now be proved one way or the other. Nodding briskly he said, 'Of course' and walked across the hall and through the door that Oswald opened.

Hector listened to the doctor, and after the man had left he continued to listen to Oswald for some minutes more. Then he followed Angeline's husband out of the drawing room and up the stairs to his niece's quarters.

When he walked into the room with Oswald, the housekeeper who had been sitting by the bed rose to her feet, but Oswald motioned for her to sit again, saying, 'We are only going to be a moment, Mrs Gibson. Dr Owen is sending a nurse to take over shortly, when you will resume your duties as normal. Can you see to it that a single bed is brought in here when she arrives, and anything else she asks for?'

Hector walked over to the bed. Angeline appeared

deeply unconscious, her swollen, discoloured face made all the more shocking by the bloodless white of her hands, which were folded across her chest on top of the counterpane. She wasn't recognizable as the eager young girl who had left his house that morning two years ago to marry the man of her dreams. Could this amount of damage to her face be the result of a simple fall over a chair? Reason said no. And yet the doctor had appeared quite satisfied that it was so. But then again, Dr Owen was Oswald's physician and was unlikely to cause waves in the absence of concrete proof. But her face, her poor little face.

Hector gently lowered his head and kissed Angeline's forehead. It was icy cold. Straightening, he said to the housekeeper, 'Tuck her arms under the covers and bring a thick eiderdown, she is freezing.'

'There are hot-water bottles at her feet and sides, sir.'

'I don't care, it's not enough.'

Soothingly Oswald murmured, 'It's the loss of blood, Hector. There's little we can do,' before adding to Mrs Gibson, 'Ring for an eiderdown, Mrs Gibson, and the housemaid can make up the fire while she's here. Keep it blazing day and night for the time being.'

Hector glanced towards the fireplace where a good fire was glowing in the grate, small flames leaping up the chimney. The room wasn't cold; in fact it was stuffy, if anything. Suddenly he felt a deep heaviness in his spirit. All the eiderdowns and fires in the world wouldn't save her. She was dying.

# *Chapter Thirteen*

But Angeline did not die.

For a full month she remained oblivious of where she was or what had happened, cared for by the nurse Dr Owen had sent to the house. Fortunately for Angeline, Nurse Ramshaw was a strong and forthright northern woman who took no nonsense from anyone and was dedicated to her chosen profession. The patient was the only person who mattered to Nurse Ramshaw, and she rubbed Oswald up the wrong way from the first day. Consequently he stayed out of the sick room, confining his visits to a few minutes in the evening for the sake of appearances.

After three weeks all that remained of the injuries to Angeline's face was a small bump on the bridge of her nose, where the bone had become distorted, and the faintest of bruises. By the end of four weeks, when she began to show signs of returning to full consciousness, even those shadows had disappeared.

It was on the morning of Christmas Eve, when the

snow was thick on the ground and a bitter north-east wind had created great drifts that could swallow a man whole, that Nurse Ramshaw awoke to find her patient struggling to sit up. Before the nurse could speak, Angeline whispered, 'My baby?'

Nurse Ramshaw was not one for prevaricating. Gently she said, 'I'm sorry, Mrs Golding.'

She had known. Even in the strange deep sleep that had overtaken her, Angeline had known. This morning, when she had come to, her hands had moved to her flat stomach, and now she wanted to join her baby. There was nothing left for her in this world. With tears streaming down her face, she shut her eyes and slipped back into the darkness, but within the hour she was awoken by gentle but firm hands, the same hands she had been dimly conscious of in her dreamlike state. Nurse Ramshaw smoothed the eiderdown as she said, 'I've a nice warm drink for you here, Mrs Golding. Do you think you could manage it yourself?'

Through the fog in her head she could remember this voice and the taste of liquid on her tongue. Weakly she murmured, 'I don't want a drink.'

'Oh aye, you do.' The nurse bent over her, stroking a strand of hair from Angeline's forehead. 'We're going to get you well again.'

She couldn't argue. She was too tired to argue. She allowed the ministrations of the nurse without protesting unduly, including the washing of her body and the changing of her nightdress, and then she slept again. At one point she heard the nurse saying, 'I've *told* you, Mr Golding, she will probably sleep twenty-three hours out of twenty-four for the next weeks, and it's the best thing for her. She has turned the corner, and that's the main thing,' and realized it must have been Oswald's voice that penetrated the layers of sleep moments before. She made no effort to open her eyes or to move, but when he said something to the nurse and then the door opened and closed, a hatred so intense it caught her breath balled in her throat.

He had struck out at her and she had fallen – she remembered it all now – and then the baby had started coming. Slowly she moved her head and looked to where Nurse Ramshaw was sitting at the end of the bed. 'Where's Myrtle?'

'What's that, Mrs Golding?' the nurse asked as she came to stand by her.

'Myrtle, my maid. Where is she?' Dimly she remembered Myrtle shouting that Oswald must keep away, and it had been Myrtle's hand she had held through those terrible hours. She wanted Myrtle; Myrtle understood what had happened.

Nurse Ramshaw's brow wrinkled. She seemed to remember Dr Owen saying something about a maid who had been dismissed, but he had warned her not to get involved in the affairs of the house, not that she would have dreamed of doing so. Her patient was her only concern, besides which the staff here treated her with suspicion and wariness. She was an outsider and not one of them. Quietly she said, 'I'm sorry, Mrs Golding. I don't know a Myrtle. There has been no one here of that name since I have been taking care of you.'

'How long *have* you been here? How long have I been ill?'

'It's Christmas Eve, Mrs Golding.'

'Christmas Eve?'

'Yes, my dear. Now, now, don't get agitated. You have been very poorly, very poorly indeed, but you'll soon be strong and well. Take this medicine. No, don't shake your head. Open wide now, that's it. Go to sleep and you'll feel better each time you wake.'

It was late evening before Oswald came again, and after her evening meal of soup and a roll Angeline had made herself stay awake. She was sitting propped up against the pillows with her eyes closed when he came into the room, and he was looking at Nurse Ramshaw as she opened them, asking about the day. He seemed to glow with health and vitality, his blond hair shining in the light of the oil lamp and the flickering flames of the fire, and his clothes as impeccable as always. She remembered Reverend Turner preaching one Sunday about Lucifer, the fallen angel, saying how everyone always depicted the devil as a type of gargoyle with horns and a hideous face, but the Reverend had put the case that the Bible spoke of Lucifer being beautiful – the most beautiful and enchanting of all the angels, even in his fallen state. She believed that now. She was looking at him.

She had imagined she would be frightened when she saw Oswald again, and all day her dozing had been punctured by moments of real terror. Now, as she looked at him, she knew she was not. Her baby was gone. The worst had happened. Nothing else could hurt as much.

He turned his head and was at her side in an instant, his voice breaking as he murmured, 'Oh Angeline, my sweet, my darling. How I have prayed for this. Oh, my darling.'

In spite of herself she shrank back from him, pressing into the pillows, but her voice was clear as she said, 'The baby. Was it a boy or a girl?'

He had been about to bend over and kiss her, but something in her voice warned him to be careful. Instead he drew the bedside chair closer and sat down, taking one of her small cold hands in his. 'A girl. It was a little girl.'

'Where is she?'

'When it became clear you were so unwell we held a small service here, and she is buried next to my mother in the family graveyard.'

'So she had a proper burial?' She had been worried that the baby would be disposed of without any ceremony, as was very often the case with stillborn infants.

'Of course, darling,' Oswald murmured softly. He was aware of the nurse's eyes on him and would have liked to ask her to leave the room, but, fearing the woman would refuse, he held his tongue. Now that Angeline was conscious again he intended to get rid of Nurse Ramshaw at the earliest opportunity, knowing full well she disliked him as much as he disliked her. He wanted no cosy chats between nurse and patient.

'Have you asked for God's forgiveness?'

'I beg your pardon?' Oswald kept his voice low, but his fingers tightened, crushing hers. Angeline ignored the warning.

'I said: have you asked God's forgiveness for the death of our child, because I want you to know that even if He forgives you, I never will.'

'What? What are you saying? You're ill, my love, and—'

'Where's Myrtle? Have you had her sent away?'

'Now, sweetheart.'

'I think that is enough, Mr Golding.' Nurse Ramshaw was at Oswald's shoulder as Angeline began to weep, and to his absolute amazement and fury she manhandled him out of the chair, positioning herself between him and her patient as she said, 'It is best you leave now. You are distressing her.'

'I'm distressing *her*? Did you hear what she accused me of? Dammit' – he caught hold of himself, gaining control with some effort – 'I want to comfort her, to talk to her. She's clearly been in the grip of hallucinations, you heard her.'

'That is quite possible, Mr Golding, but no good will be served by upsetting her more tonight.'

'I don't want to upset her. I want to *talk* to her.'

'Not tonight.'

Determined brown eyes held his angry grey ones. Brown won. With a muscle working in his clenched jaw, Oswald ground out, 'Very well, but I question your judgement and I shall make that perfectly clear to Dr Owen.'

'That is your right, of course, Mr Golding. Goodnight.'

'I want to kiss my wife before I leave.'

Angeline made a strangled sound in her throat and again Nurse Ramshaw said, 'Good*night*, Mr Golding.' He had reached the door when she added affably, 'Oh, and merry Christmas, sir.'

Once the door had banged shut, Angeline said weakly, 'Thank you. I hope I haven't got you into trouble with Dr Owen.'

Nurse Ramshaw smiled. 'Don't you worry about that, m'dear. I'm going to ring for a warm drink for you and then we'll settle you down to sleep, and I shall be here all the time. All right?'

Angeline knew what the nurse was really saying. Oswald would have to get through Nurse Ramshaw to reach her, and she had already seen that the big-boned, hefty northerner was a match for him. 'Thank you,' she said again, and within moments she was asleep.

It was another few days before Angeline was considered well enough to spend an hour or so lying on a chaise-longue at the window of the bedroom in the afternoons. During that time Oswald stayed away. Then, on New

Year's Eve – the first day Nurse Ramshaw helped her to the chaise-longue and settled her with a book to read – he made an appearance. He stood staring at her from the doorway and Angeline stared back, refusing to be intimidated or to speak first. It was Nurse Ramshaw who broke the charged silence by saying, 'Good afternoon, Mr Golding. Mrs Golding is making good progress, as you can see.'

His gaze moving to the nurse, he said nothing for a moment. Then he smiled, 'Quite. Which leads me to explain why I am here. Dr Owen is waiting downstairs to drive you back to town. My wife is quite able to continue her convalescence without medical care. I have a houseful of servants who can attend to her needs. Gather your things together.'

'I'm sorry, but I don't think your wife *is* at a stage where she doesn't need medical care, Mr Golding.'

'Would it surprise you to learn that I am not interested in what you think?'

'Dr Owen—'

'Dr Owen agrees with me. When he examined Mrs Golding yesterday and was satisfied she could begin having an hour or two's change from the bed, I put it to him that it was time you left. Be downstairs in the hall in five minutes with your bag.'

He stepped back onto the landing and then paused in the act of closing the door. 'Oh, and as you will not be here tomorrow, happy New Year, Nurse Ramshaw.' He smiled again, his gaze moving to Angeline's white face for a moment before he withdrew.

Angeline and the nurse stared at each other. 'This is ridiculous,' Nurse Ramshaw said angrily. 'You're not well enough, in my opinion, and I can't believe Dr Owen would say otherwise. I shall go and have a word with him right now.'

Angeline watched the nurse march out, but she knew there was no point. Dr Owen would do and say as he was told.

Within minutes a distinctly ruffled Nurse Ramshaw was back. Angeline didn't ask what had been said, for it was obvious, and neither did she criticize the doctor, as Nurse Ramshaw worshipped the ground he walked on. Instead she reached out and took the nurse's hand. 'Nurse Ramshaw, now you are leaving, would you do me a great service? My maid – the one my husband dismissed, and no doubt without a reference – is walking out with a young man who is employed by my uncle. Myrtle was utterly loyal to me, and I am sure that's why my husband sent her away when I was too ill to know about it. Would you take something to her young man, if I give you my uncle's address, and make sure you put it into his hands, and his hands only? I . . . I owe her a great deal, for her support and kindness after my marriage, and she's been treated shamefully; in fact, I don't know what I would have done without Myrtle.'

'Oh, my dear, has it really been that bad?'

For a moment Angeline was tempted to tell the nurse

the truth about the day she lost the baby, but she knew Dr Owen would not support her. Oswald had the doctor in his pocket. He held all the cards. The day after Christmas, when Dr Owen had come to see her, she had heard Nurse Ramshaw talking to him on the landing as he had left, relating the scene with Oswald when Angeline had accused him of being responsible for the death of her baby. They hadn't known she could hear them, but her hearing had always been particularly acute.

Dr Owen had clucked for a moment and then said, 'Mrs Golding has been through a distressing time and it is natural she is over-emotional. It is not uncommon for women to shift the guilt that follows a miscarriage to another source, and in this case I fear it is her husband. She is very young, childlike even, and it is well known that the female reproduction role tends to dominate the thinking of some women. Mr Golding has told me his wife was looking forward to their first baby almost as though the child would be a live doll to play with; a little girl looking forward to Christmas morning and the special present she would receive. When that present was taken away – and, I understand from Mr Golding, through his wife tripping over a sewing bag she had left on the floor – like a child, she wanted to blame someone else.'

Nurse Ramshaw had murmured something she couldn't catch, to which the doctor had replied, 'I'm sorry my dear, and I know you have Mrs Golding's best interests at heart, but I think you have to accept that she is not herself at the moment. The loss she has suffered affects the mind every bit as much as the body. Mr Golding is prepared to be patient with her and has shown great restraint thus far; I have no doubt he is a caring, loving husband. Time is the best healer in cases like this. To come so close to death and not succumb has taken a great toll on body, soul and spirit, but come the summer I am sure this distressing episode will be behind them both.'

Remembering this now, Angeline chose her words carefully. 'My husband is not what he seems, Nurse Ramshaw. I think you have seen evidence of this while you have been nursing me? But with regard to my maid, could you fetch me pen and paper, so I may write to her? And I would greatly appreciate this staying between the two of us. Please help me, there is no one else.'

Nurse Ramshaw appeared to be having an inward tussle with her conscience. 'This is most irregular. I don't know what Dr Owen would say if he knew, Mrs Golding.'

Angeline thought the nurse knew only too well and there was no point in pretending. 'What do *you* say, Nurse Ramshaw?'

There was a moment's silence. 'I'll get the writing material.'

'Thank you, thank you so much.'

Angeline kept the letter short. In truth, she was so tired it was an effort to form the words and think straight. She wrote:

Dear Myrtle

It was with deep regret that I learned Mr Golding dispensed with your services when I was too ill to know. I shall always remember your kindness to me at a time when I needed a friend. I shall pray for you every day. Please pray for me. Accept the enclosed with my grateful thanks.

She hesitated for a moment as to how to sign it, then followed her heart: 'Love Angeline'.

Folding the letter into an envelope, she said to Nurse Ramshaw, who'd been gathering her things together, 'Would you pass me the musical box on the dressing table, please?'

As the nurse watched, Angeline lifted the beautifully engraved wooden and tortoiseshell lid, so that the tiny ballerina began to whirl and dance, and then pressed a hidden spring so that a secret compartment in the bottom of the box opened. Looking at Nurse Ramshaw, she said, 'My father bought me this for my tenth birthday and told me the secret was between him and me only, and I have never revealed it to anyone else.' She took out the wad of notes that the hidey-hole contained, putting them in the envelope and sealing it.

'Mrs Golding, that's a great deal of money. Shouldn't you think about this? You are still unwell.'

'I know my own mind, Nurse, truly.' She hesitated and then said, 'My monthly dress allowance is more than Myrtle's family can earn in a year. I say this not to boast, but to my shame. Something is very wrong in our society, don't you think? But I digress. Myrtle was dismissed unfairly and it will have hit her family hard. This is hers by right, because if ever anyone earned thanks, it is Myrtle. Will you help me, Nurse Ramshaw?'

The nurse nodded, taking the envelope on which Angeline had written Myrtle's name, care of Albert (she had no idea of his surname) and her uncle's address. 'I'll give it to' – she consulted the envelope – 'Albert myself, Mrs Golding. You have my word. I wish I could do more to help you.'

'That is far and away the best thing you could do for me.' Angeline smiled at the nurse, whose soft centre was hidden behind her strong, rather masculine features and forbidding countenance. 'And I'm very grateful.'

Once they had said their goodbyes and Nurse Ramshaw had left, Angeline sat looking out of the window. The snow was thick and a pearly-grey sky promised more, but it could have been a bright and beautiful summer's day for all the scene outside registered on her senses.

She had given Myrtle every penny she had saved over the last months, and she knew it would seem like a king's ransom to the maid and her family. On the last count there had been more than 500 pounds salted away in the musical box; there would have been more, but for the fact she made sure she bought a certain amount of new clothes now and again to avoid Oswald becoming suspicious. It might seem the height of foolishness to give all the money away, but it wasn't. Her dream of making a new life for herself and her child had died. It was over. She had nothing to live for now. Her only desire was to join her baby, her precious little baby girl. It was the beginning of a new year tomorrow. Well, she wanted none of it. Nurse Ramshaw had tried to explain the darkness of spirit that had overtaken her by saying it was natural in the circumstances. She had suffered a great loss, the nurse had said gently, on top of which she had nearly died. Body and soul needed time to heal. But she was young and healthy, and there was no reason why she shouldn't have more babies when the time was right. And the nurse had patted her hand comfortingly.

Angeline had listened quietly, eaten and drunk what she had been given, taken the sleeping draught the nurse had measured out each night and indulged in the relief of tears only when she was sure Nurse Ramshaw was asleep, but from the moment she had woken and felt her empty, flat stomach life had become pointless. She didn't want to stay in a world where good people like her mama and father died, and Oswald Golding prospered and thrived; where money and power and influence dictated might over right, and the capricious spitefulness of someone like her husband meant an honest, decent family could find themselves forced into the workhouse. Most of all, she didn't want to stay in a world that didn't hold her child.

Angeline glanced over at the ornate chest of drawers where she had hidden the new unopened bottle of sleeping draught that she'd taken from Nurse Ramshaw's bag when the nurse had gone downstairs to speak to Dr Owen. As she had expected, the nurse had not left the partly used bottle with her, saying that she would pass it to the housekeeper with instructions that Angeline be given a dose each evening for as long as she required it. Angeline hoped the stolen bottle would not be missed among the many pills and potions piled into the nurse's cavernous leather bag.

It was an hour later when Polly, one of the housemaids, brought Angeline her afternoon tea. Angeline had gone back to bed. She felt more exhausted than she would have thought possible, when all she'd done was to move from the bed to the chaise-longue. She felt like an old, old woman.

She glanced at the tray Polly was holding. It held a pot of tea, milk and sugar, a plate of daintily cut sandwiches and a small cake stand with assorted iced cakes and pastries. Lying back against the pillows, Angeline sighed wearily before she murmured, 'Just pour me a cup of tea, Polly, and then you can take the tray away.'

'Yes, ma'am, but Cook made the iced fancies specially to tempt you. Won't you try just one and perhaps an almond pastry? Cook's pastries melt in the mouth.'

'Very well, just one of the cakes then.' She took from Polly the cup of tea and the plate holding the cake and then said, 'Thank you' as she smiled at the girl. Polly seemed a good-natured, caring little soul and she reminded Angeline of Myrtle.

Polly stood hovering for a few moments and then all of a sudden burst out, 'We're all very sorry, ma'am, about . . . about the baby an' all. I'm not supposed to say, ma'am, but Myrtle came back just before Christmas to see you, but the master had left orders with Mr Wood that she was to be turned away. But Cook said she could have who she liked in her kitchen, and so Myrtle came in for a bit. She was ever so upset about you, ma'am, and' – Polly paused to take a breath – 'angry with the master. But like I said, I'm not supposed to say, cos Cook could lose her job an' all, if the master found out.'

'Rest assured I won't say anything, Polly, but thank you for telling me. I've been very worried about Myrtle.'

'Oh, she's all right, ma'am, and her young man's been ever so good. He asked your uncle to give Myrtle a reference so she can get another job – make out she's been working for him for the last couple of years like.'

'That's a good idea. And did my uncle agree?'

'Myrtle said her young man had to twist his arm a bit, but the housekeeper – her young man's sister – put in her two penn'orth and between them they managed it, ma'am.'

Angeline was feeling so tired it was an effort to smile and nod, and as the maid bustled out she placed the cup of tea on her bedside cabinet and shut her eyes. This lack of strength would have been alarming in other circumstances; as it was, with the knowledge of what she was going to do, it was merely an inconvenience. It was strange, but over the last hour or two all feeling seemed to have gone from her. There was an emptiness in her, a cold emptiness, and though she was pleased to have been able to send the money to Myrtle and to know that Albert was clearly looking after her, it didn't seem important. Perhaps because she had accomplished what she had wanted to do, courtesy of Nurse Ramshaw? It had been the desire to do something to help Myrtle that had focused what little energy she possessed. She felt now as though she were existing in a vacuum, a nothingness. And she welcomed it.

She had always been frightened of dying. That seemed laughable now. But in the past, life had held so many things she wouldn't have wanted to give up. And then she had met Oswald. When she looked back she could believe that all her feelings had been worn out since then. First she had loved unreservedly and unconditionally, and then eventually she had hated in equal measure, but in between had been a whole host of emotions. It was ironic that the man who had killed all love for him within her had inadvertently been the means of giving her something that made all other kinds of love weak by comparison. But then finally he'd destroyed that too, her little baby. Since Christmas Eve she'd felt her heart had been torn from her soul with the pain and bitterness consuming her; it was a relief to feel nothing now. She only wanted that: to feel nothing. To slip into the vast void and leave all emotions behind. It was cowardly and wrong, but that's what she wanted.

*

She must have slept because she awoke to the door opening and Oswald striding into the room. He walked over to the bed and stood looking down at her. 'From this day forth you are going to eat everything you are given,' he said with no lead-in. 'I will not have a wife who is an invalid, do you understand me? And in the afternoons you will come downstairs, starting from tomorrow. You may lie on the sofa in the morning room or on one in the drawing room – it makes no odds – but you *will* dress and leave this room. The weakness you complain of will only increase if you give in to it. It is mostly in the mind, as it is. You need to pull yourself together.'

Quietly she said, 'Is this what Dr Owen has said?'

'It is what I have said. I am your husband, and you will do what you are told. Other women go through what you have. You are not a unique case, so stop acting like one.'

Angeline was trying to hold on to her sense of vacuity, but something was happening inside. The void was being filled by a rage so intense that her voice shook as she said, 'I presume you are referring to the loss of my baby?'

'Of course. You can have more children; you are young and, after all, it was only a female child.'

The white flames of anger were truly alight and nothing could douse them. Her springing from the bed surprised them both, but then her hands were clawing at his face, her nails gouging the flesh as she screamed her hatred.

Her fingers had no real force behind them and she had

begun to fall even before he threw her back onto the bed, cursing and shouting as he did so. Vaguely Angeline was aware of other voices joining Oswald's, but she was feeling faint, the strength that had coursed through her when he had dismissed so contemptuously the death of their baby girl quite gone.

When the commotion died down, she knew it was Mrs Gibson sitting by the bed holding her hand, although the housekeeper's voice was uncharacteristically soft. Then everything was quiet for a long time. It was dark, and she didn't know if it was night or early morning when she became conscious of voices about her. It was Polly who whispered, 'What did he do to make her go for him like that, and her half-dead as it is.'

'I don't know, Polly, and if you don't want to be out on your ear, you won't speculate on the matter. Suffice to say she's played right into his hands, the poor dear.'

'What do you mean, Mrs Gibson?'

'Least said, soonest mended. If there's one thing I've learned since being here, it's to hold my tongue, and I suggest you do the same.'

'I can't believe Nurse Ramshaw was given the elbow. I'm no doctor, but even I can see the mistress needs looking after by someone who knows what's what. It wasn't so long ago she was at death's door, an' she's as weak as a kitten.'

'Not so weak she didn't mark him, more's the pity.'

'More's the pity? I didn't think you'd got any time for him, the same as the rest of us.'

A sigh followed. 'Think, Polly. If he needed evidence she's gone a bit doolally, then the marks on his face prove it.'

'The mistress?' Polly was indignant. 'She's no more doolally than I am, the poor thing. An' if Myrtle's to be believed, an' I think she is, that bairn ought to be on the master's conscience.'

'That's enough!' It was razor-sharp. 'You hear me?'

'Yes, Mrs Gibson.'

'That sort of talk leads to trouble, m'girl, so just you think on. The mistress is of the gentry, she don't need you to be in her corner, because she certainly wouldn't be in yours. They're a different breed, Polly.'

'The mistress isn't like that.'

'They're all like that, and don't you forget it. You think the mistress knows about a poor widow woman bringing up her bairns on four shillings a week from the parish; and lighting in her grate, from time to time, a piece of brown paper, in order that she and the bairns might warm their hands for three or four fleeting seconds, when the paper flames and roars in the draught of the crooked chimney? Well, that was me mam, an' out of the seven of us bairns, it was only me and me brother who come through the winter of '62. So don't talk to me about the gentry, Polly. Our Timmy used to walk nine miles every morning with his tool-bag on his back to the carpenter's shop where he was employed, and nine miles back of an evening, and him nought but a bairn at eleven years old. And you know what? Old Mr Ferry, the landowner who owned the carpenter's business and everything else an' all, used to pass our Timmy trudging home after knocking-off time and not once would it occur to him to let him sit alongside the driver of his carriage. Some of the landed gentry might think of their villagers or servants as "their" people, but only in the same way they think of their horses and hounds. In fact, not as highly as their horses and hounds, truth be known. So don't you go sticking your neck out for the mistress, nice as she is.'

'No, Mrs Gibson.'

'Now you get yourself off to bed, once you've helped me give the mistress her medicine.'

'What about you, Mrs Gibson?'

'I'll stay here for a bit. I don't sleep none too well as it is, so it's no odds to me.'

Angeline was half-lifted from the pillows and when Mrs Gibson murmured, 'It's your nightcap, ma'am, the one Nurse Ramshaw said to give you', she opened her lips obediently and swallowed the familiar bitter liquid.

Instead of the deep sleep that the draught normally induced, her rest was fitful, punctuated by nightmarish dreams and ghoulish, insubstantial images. At one point she thought she heard Oswald's voice saying, 'Mrs Gibson? What are you still doing here? It's two in the morning. I was just checking on Mrs Golding after her seizure earlier.'

'I thought I'd sit up with the mistress tonight, sir. She being so poorly an' all.'

Angeline detected a note of intense irritation in Oswald's voice, which he seemed to be trying to mask. 'That is not necessary. You need your sleep.'

'Nevertheless, I'd like to stay, sir. Just for tonight.'

'Very well.' And, as an afterthought, 'Thank you, Mrs Gibson. Goodnight.'

'Goodnight, sir.'

And then Angeline knew she must be dreaming when, after a minute or two, she heard the housekeeper mutter to herself, 'Aye, an' I've got your measure, Mr High-an'-Mighty. A pillow over her face would sort all the problems, wouldn't it?'

She must finally have gone deeply asleep because when she next awoke the white light of morning was pouring into the room and Mrs Gibson had gone. Polly was drawing back the drapes from the window and, when the maid saw she was awake, she said brightly, 'Good morning, ma'am. It's late so I thought I'd better wake you.'

'What time is it, Polly?' Angeline sat up, the events of the previous evening flooding back. Part of her was horrified that she could so far have forgotten herself as to attack Oswald. Another section of her mind, which was becoming stronger over the last days, told her he deserved far worse.

Polly handed her a cup of tea as she said, 'Gone eleven, ma'am, but Mrs Gibson said you were tossing and turning nearly all night, so we thought you could do with the rest.' The maid hesitated for a moment. 'The master left the house early this morning, ma'am.'

'Did he? Did he say where he was going?'

'I think' – again Polly paused – 'Raymond, the footman, heard the master tell Mr Wood he was going to bring Dr Owen back with him. They should be here soon.'

Angeline nodded, still sleepy and light-headed from the effects of the sleeping draught, which usually took most of the day to clear completely. Through the drug-induced fog in her mind she wondered vaguely why Oswald had gone to fetch the doctor himself, for he had never done that before, always sending a message with one of the footmen if he needed Dr Owen. After Polly had left the room she'd done no more than raise the cup to her lips before she heard footsteps outside the door. Oswald entered, with Dr Owen at his heels. Her eyes widened when she saw her husband's face. It was covered with scratches and, although they didn't look deep, some appeared quite red.

She hadn't done all that. She stared at Oswald. She knew she hadn't. The marks on his cheeks certainly, but his forehead, his nose, his throat? What was going on?

'Mrs Golding.' Dr Owen's voice was soothing. 'I hear you were a little disturbed after Nurse Ramshaw left yesterday evening. How are you feeling this morning?'

Angeline sat up straighter. 'I was *disturbed*, as you put it, by my husband saying the death of my baby was unimportant as she was a girl. Reason enough, wouldn't you say, Dr Owen?'

'That's not true,' Oswald said softly. 'As I said, I came in to spend a little time with her, and for no reason at all she suddenly attacked me, screaming and shouting. I had to fend her off as best I could, but as you can see' – he raised a hand to his face and then stretched both hands out, palms down, to reveal further welts on the backs of them – 'not without cost. She seemed to possess what I can only describe as superhuman strength.'

'Do you remember attacking Mr Golding?'

Angeline stared at the doctor. 'Yes, of course I remember, but that's not to say it happened as he says it did. It was his fault.'

'You see?' Oswald shrugged his shoulders. 'I have tried, believe me I've tried, but she needs help that I can't provide.'

'I didn't do that amount of damage to his face, Dr Owen. How could I?'

'So you don't really remember?' the doctor said gently.

Angeline tried to clear her mind. 'I've told you I remember what happened last night and I do, but all that' – she gestured towards Oswald – 'is not of my doing.'

'Mrs Golding, do you remember suffering from bouts of rage in the past when the focus of your anger was Mr Golding?'

'What? No. No, of course not.' Frightened now, she glanced at Oswald, who stared back impassively. 'I don't know what my husband has told you, but none of it is true. He's the one who can be violent, and because of him hitting me the baby died. He struck me and—'

'Always the same,' Oswald interrupted sadly. 'I confess I hoped having a child would calm her, so in that sense I am partly to blame. However, what one might once have described as childish tantrums have become more . . . serious. I hold the parents responsible to some extent. They must have detected some mental weakness in the past, but as far as I know spoke of it to no one. But then, a beloved only child – it is understandable.'

'What are you saying?' Angeline stared into the cold, calculating eyes. 'Stop it, you're lying.' Appealing to the doctor, she said, 'Please, Dr Owen, you must help me.'

'I am going to help you, my dear. We all want to help you. There are places where such maladies can be treated very successfully. Now, why don't we get you dressed and then we'll go for a little ride.'

He was talking as though she were a simpleton. Trying to keep her voice from trembling, Angeline said, 'Places? What places? What are you suggesting?'

'Now, now, do not agitate yourself, Mrs Golding. All will be well, you'll see.'

'I'm not going anywhere.' She was pressing back against the pillows, and then her terror mounted as Dr Owen called out, 'Blackett, Hopkins' and two bulky figures appeared behind the slight person of the doctor.

'Now come along, Mrs Golding. This is helping no one.'

As she scrambled out of the far side of the bed, the doctor motioned for one of the men to walk round to her. It was then that she began screaming.

# *Chapter Fourteen*

Betty Ramshaw had never felt such a conflict of loyalties. She admired Dr Owen greatly and was more than a little bit secretly in love with him, but when she had arrived at work earlier that morning and one of the staff had told her what had befallen Mrs Golding, she'd been horrified. Now it was lunchtime, and she stood outside Hector Stewart's residence in a fever of indecision, one hand fingering the envelope in her pocket.

If, as Dr Owen seemed to think, Mrs Golding wasn't in possession of her faculties, then she wasn't in a position to endow this maid with such a large sum of money. On the other hand – Nurse Ramshaw's brow wrinkled worriedly – Mrs Golding had seemed perfectly lucid to her. Frail and depressed and upset certainly, but in the circumstances was that surprising? As for the husband, he was a nasty piece of work. She wouldn't put much past that man, and if his wife had become an inconvenience, what better place to ship her off to than Earlswood Asylum north of Newcastle? Out of sight, out of mind.

The poor dear. Dr Owen had been hoodwinked by Mrs Golding's husband, she'd bet her last farthing on it.

Well, she couldn't stand here all day. It was now or never. Taking a deep breath, Betty marched up the drive and round to the back of the house, where she hoped to find the kitchen door. She intended to have a word with Mrs Golding's uncle before she left, but wanted to see the maid's young man first and any other staff employed here. She wouldn't mention the envelope in her pocket initially, but would get a feel for what was what. She prided herself on being a good judge of character, and if she felt in any way bothered by what she discovered here, she would leave without handing the envelope over. She could say she had come to tell them about Mrs Golding's admittance to the asylum, which was true in a way.

It was Olive Upton who answered the knock at the back door and she stared in surprise at the uniformed nurse standing on the doorstep. 'Can I help you?'

'I hope so. I've been nursing Mrs Golding, at the Golding estate, for the last weeks and she asked me to pass on her best wishes to Myrtle via her young man. She – Mrs Golding – was most insistent.'

'Oh, come in, come in.' Olive's austere face broke into a smile. 'How is Miss Angeline – I mean, Mrs Golding?'

Betty Ramshaw followed the housekeeper through a scullery and then into a large warm kitchen where a young couple were sitting at a table, cups of tea and half a large fruitcake in front of them. Olive turned, saying, 'You can speak to Myrtle yourself, she's popped in to see

Albert. Myrtle, this is the nurse who's been looking after Miss Angeline.'

Myrtle had jumped up and now she came round the table and clasped Betty's hand eagerly as she said, 'How is she? The mistress? Oh, I've been that worried. Is she feeling better?'

Betty looked into the bright young face and liked what she saw. Her voice gentle, she said, 'I think you'd better sit down, lass.'

'She's not . . . '

'No, no, nothing like that. But it's not good news.'

Albert had stood up and now took Myrtle's arm, making her sit down, before he said, 'You look like you could do with a cup of tea, Nurse. Take the weight off, and tell us why you've come.'

Betty plumped herself down, gratefully accepting the cup of tea from Olive before she said, 'Well, I've been nursing Mrs Golding, like I said, and she rallied at Christmas, came to herself so to speak, but of course she's very weak and poorly still. She was beginning to pull round when he – Mr Golding – suddenly announced yesterday that I'm to leave and she doesn't need a nurse any more. Which is nonsense, in my opinion. Anyway, when Mrs Golding knew I was going, she wrote a letter and enclosed some money and asked me to deliver it to your young man, as she didn't know where you were. But then this morning . . . '

'What?' Myrtle leaned forward. 'What's happened?'

'Well, I can only repeat what I've been told, lass. It

seems Mrs Golding attacked her husband last night, and this morning he saw Dr Owen and they've got the magistrate to issue a lunacy order. They've taken her to an asylum, I understand.'

Myrtle blanched. 'No, not the mistress. Not in one of them places. That can't be true. There's been some mistake.'

'Apparently her husband insisted on it.'

'But Miss Angeline isn't mad.' Myrtle appealed to Albert and Olive, 'She isn't, is she? Tell her.'

'I don't think Mrs Golding is mad, dear, or else I wouldn't be here. But folk are admitted for all sorts of reasons, and some of them . . . ' The nurse shrugged, indicating she didn't agree with the system, but was powerless to do anything about it.

'I have to do something.' Myrtle stared at Albert. 'It's him – that devil.' Turning back to Nurse Ramshaw, she said, 'She was swept off her feet from the moment she met him, but he never loved her, I know it. He caused her to lose the baby, Nurse. I can't prove it, but it's true. From the day she married him she's been a different person, and not in a good way. And now this. An asylum. And her the gentlest of creatures. Whatever he said she did, he's lying.'

'Well, my dear, that might well be true, but I'm afraid there is little you can do. Here' – Betty reached into her pocket and drew out the envelope – 'Mrs Golding wanted you to have this, for your kindness to her. She was very upset you had been dismissed. She thinks a great deal of you, you know, lass.'

Myrtle gasped in shock when she saw the money, but after reading Angeline's letter she burst into tears. When after some minutes she was still crying and would accept no comfort, Betty Ramshaw said briskly, 'Smelling salts, I think.' They had just held the vial under Myrtle's nose, causing her to cough and splutter, when a voice from the doorway into the hall caused every head but Myrtle's to turn.

'What on earth is going on here?' Hector stared in amazement at the scene in front of him. 'I could hear you in my study. Stop making that dreadful noise, Myrtle, and someone tell me what is wrong, for goodness' sake.'

'It's Miss Angeline.' Albert had not forgiven his master for allowing Oswald Golding to talk him round, the day after the miscarriage. When Hector had left the big house that morning and climbed back into the carriage without a word, Albert hadn't taken the hint and got up into his seat. Instead he had stood with the carriage door ajar and said, 'Sir? Miss Angeline?'

'She is most unwell, but they are doing all they can.'

'But him, Mr Golding? Myrtle said—'

'I know what Myrtle said, Albert, but she is mistaken. I understand from Mr Golding that he had occasion to reprimand Myrtle before, and could have dismissed her then, but did not do so out of regard for my niece's feelings for the girl. Do you know about this?'

'No, sir.'

'Then I suggest you ask the girl about it. It might put a different complexion on things. That aside, Myrtle herself admits she was not in the room at the time of the fall, and I see no reason to assume Mr Golding is to blame in any way.'

When he had asked Myrtle later what Angeline's uncle had meant, Myrtle had shaken her head in bewilderment. 'I don't know what he's on about, Albert, truly. I've never liked Mr Golding, I admit that, and he's picked up on it, I'm sure, and was always finding fault with me, but nothing specific was said.'

Remembering this now, Albert's voice was accusing as he went on, 'Mr Golding has had Miss Angeline committed to an asylum this morning. This is her nurse, and she came to tell us. He's had her put away, for no good reason. That's what he's done, and it could have been prevented if you'd listened to Myrtle. Golding's a devil, an' you handed her to him on a plate.'

Nurse Ramshaw stepped forward. 'Could I have a word with you, sir?' she said quietly, aiming to dispel some of the tension, which was palpable.

Hector was bristling with fury. To be spoken to like that by a mere servant was insupportable. Drawing himself up, he glared at Albert. 'You are dismissed. I want you out of this house by the end of the week, for which you will be paid in full.' Clicking his fingers at Nurse Ramshaw, he said, 'Follow me.'

He was halted in his turning when Olive Upton said, 'If he goes, I go an' all, sir.'

Hector looked at his housekeeper. In his temper he had forgotten that Albert was the woman's brother. Mrs Upton was excellent at her job and she suited him down to the ground; it had only been his regard for her that had persuaded him to write a reference for Myrtle when Oswald had dismissed her without one. But he couldn't be held over a barrel like this by a servant, even one as good as Mrs Upton. Stiffly he said, 'As you wish.'

Once in his study he closed the door after he had waved Nurse Ramshaw to a chair at the side of his desk. He didn't sit down himself, but stood with his back to the window. 'Tell me what you know, Nurse . . . '

'Ramshaw, sir. Betty Ramshaw.'

'Nurse Ramshaw. So where is my niece as we speak?'

'Earlswood Asylum, sir. It's on the outskirts of Newcastle.'

'She is sick in her mind?'

'I wouldn't say so. No, sir.'

'Perhaps you had better start at the beginning.'

Nurse Ramshaw started at the beginning. After a few minutes, when she stopped speaking, she stared at Hector. His eyelids were blinking rapidly and he jerked his chin up and down before he said, 'Correct me if I'm wrong, but you seem to suggest there is a possibility that my niece *has* been ill-treated, as the maid claims.'

'A possibility, yes, sir. Of course I was not witness to any physical assault, but Mr Golding's manner with his wife was uncharitable at best.'

He had known, hadn't he? Deep down he had known,

but he had tried to shut his mind to it, which was one of the reasons he hadn't gone back to the estate over the last few weeks. It had been easier to accept at face value what Oswald and the doctor had said. He had enough problems of his own; he didn't need further aggravation.

After questioning the nurse a little more he rang the bell for a grim-faced Mrs Upton to see the visitor out, and stood at the window watching her walk down the drive. Myrtle was waiting by the large open gates for the nurse, and as the two of them disappeared out of sight they were talking avidly.

Sitting down in his big leather chair, Hector put his elbows on the desk in front of him and dropped his head into his hands. He remained thus for some minutes. Then he rose and again rang the bell, and when Mrs Upton answered the call, he told her to tell Albert to bring the carriage round to the front of the house. 'I shall drive myself,' he added as the housekeeper turned with a flounce and a curt 'Yes, sir'.

It was beginning to snow in the bitter north-east wind when Hector approached the elegantly proportioned gatehouse entrance of the asylum more than two hours later. The journey on the icy, snow-packed roads had not been an easy one, for several reasons: Hector was not used to driving himself; the weather conditions were not good; and he had been unsure of the actual location of the asylum. He brought the horses to a halt and stared at the neoclassical half-circular arch, large and solid, over the tall barred iron gates, which incorporated a small pedestrian gate with its own key-lock. The harsh, architecturally sturdy lines were softened somewhat by the ivy that enveloped the upper parts, but Hector felt a shiver snake down his spine. A ten-foot-high stone wall stretched on into infinity on either side of the gatehouse, and it was impossible to see anything of the asylum itself from the road, but one of the men he'd asked directions of had told him it was surrounded by fields and farmland, where some of the patients worked.

'Them as are not too far gone,' the man added grimly, tapping the side of his head to emphasize his point. 'There's others who never see the light of day, if half the tales are true. Poor blighters. You wouldn't let a dog suffer like that, would you?'

The gatehouse-keeper came out after Hector had rung the bell attached to the side of one of the massive gates. And after Hector had given his name and explained that he was here to see his niece, the carriage was allowed through onto a wide drive that snaked through a small area of woodland, before opening up to reveal a snow-covered lawn beyond which stood the asylum. The huge, prison-style building had a high, square central tower with clock faces on each side and tall, narrow windows with semicircular brick arches at the top of each one. Hector felt the hairs on the back of his neck prickle as he gazed at it. He assumed, correctly, that the fields and farmland stretched away at the back of the asylum, but the forbidding facade that presented itself initially was enough to quell all hope in the most optimistic of minds.

After bringing the carriage to a stop in the courtyard in front of the building, Hector tied the horses' reins to one of the posts provided and walked up the wide stone steps. The massive front door had a well-polished brass knob and bell, and almost immediately swung open in response to his ring. After stating his business to the hall porter, he was asked to wait, and sat down on one of the chairs lining the vast expanse of green-and-brown-tiled floor. The doors opening onto the entrance hall were all closed, but in the background he could hear sounds, and once or twice a scream that curdled his blood.

The minutes ticked by and Hector was aware of the porter watching him, from behind his partly glazed cubby-hole. The chill of the place began to seep into Hector's bones, but it was a chill of the spirit rather than the body. And then, after more than ten minutes, a door at the far end of the hall opened and a tall, well-built woman dressed entirely in black walked purposefully towards him, her austere face unsmiling.

Hector stood up, holding out his hand as she reached him. 'Good afternoon. I am Hector Stewart, an uncle of Mrs Golding, and I understand she has been admitted here today and—'

'I am Matron Craggs, Mr Stewart,' the matron interrupted coldly. 'I have not been informed that you have permission to visit Mrs Golding.'

She did not shake his hand and after a moment Hector let it fall by his side. 'Permission? Of whom?'

'Mrs Golding's doctor, or her husband.'

'I wasn't aware that was necessary.'

'I'm afraid so. Particularly with new admissions, and ones that are as troubled and distressed as Mrs Golding.'

'Look, I just want to see my niece for a minute or two. Her parents died and she was my ward until she married Mr Golding. I won't stay long.'

'I'm afraid that is not possible.' Then, seeing his stricken face, the matron's manner softened slightly. 'Come along to my office, Mr Stewart. We can talk there.'

Feeling as though he had been offered a huge privilege, Hector found himself scurrying after the commanding figure of the matron as she led the way out of the hall and into the wide, high corridor with tiled walls and a stone floor. Pausing for a moment, the matron said, 'We have two identical wings that house the two sexes, with a dividing corridor right through the middle of the building, and within each social class the violent and the non-violent are segregated. We have mostly private patients here, but at the bottom of the scale there are a number of paupers who are, of course, kept quite separate from the other classes. Rest assured, Mr Stewart, your niece will not have to socialize with those beneath her. We pride ourselves that Earlswood is a hospital for the curable and a retreat for the incurable, but at all times the niceties of society are maintained.'

Hector didn't know what to say, so he said nothing as

the matron continued walking and talking over her shoulder.

'We follow the new guidelines here, and the patients are split into different categories depending on their condition. There are those persons of unsound mind, or whose balance of mind has been temporarily unhinged, and who require care and control. Then there are those who are mentally infirm and have become permanently incapable of managing their own affairs. Then there are the idiots who are defective in mind since birth, along with the imbeciles who are capable of guarding themselves against common physical dangers, but have no moral understanding. Then the feeble-minded, who may be capable of earning their own living under favourable circumstances and are on the whole non-violent – unlike the moral imbeciles, who are the most dangerous category and display some mental defect, with vicious or criminal propensities. And finally the epileptics, the inebriates and the deaf, dumb and blind.'

They had reached the end of the corridor and the matron opened a door that led into a large square, with more corridors leading from it. The smell that Hector had detected faintly in the entrance hall was stronger here and he found himself swallowing hard. Sounds filtered through, shouts and screams, and the matron turned briefly to say, 'Do not be alarmed. The restraint wards are kept locked at all times. You are quite safe. Here is my office, Mr Stewart. Would you care for a cup of tea?'

The matron's office was warm and well furnished, a coal fire burning in the grate and a comfortable chair for visitors opposite the large desk, but Hector didn't notice the creature comforts. Clearing his throat, he said, 'The restraint wards?'

'For those who may injure themselves or others.'

'When you say "restraint"?' He cleared his throat again, for the matron's face was not encouraging questions.

The matron was clearly finding his persistence annoying. In a clipped voice she said, 'When necessary we use straitjackets, muzzles to stop people biting, chains to fasten hands together, and so on. Each of these wards has a padded cell with restraining harnesses. It is necessary, Mr Stewart. We cannot have the staff harmed, or other inmates – or even the patients themselves. Safety for all is paramount.'

Hector found that a separate part of his mind was saying over and over again, 'Oh dear God, oh dear God. Angeline, Angeline!' But out loud he said, 'And my niece? I trust she is not in one of the restraint wards?'

'Mrs Golding is in the Admissions Block at present.'

Hector had noticed the slight hesitation before she had replied. 'And does this block have a restraint ward?'

'Of course.'

'And my niece?'

'I am sorry, Mr Stewart, but I cannot discuss Mrs Golding's treatment with anyone other than her husband or doctor. Suffice to say that we will have her best interests at heart in everything we do. Now, let me ring for a cup of tea before you leave.'

Hector wanted to shout that he didn't want a cup of tea. He wanted to get the woman by the throat and demand that she take him to Angeline. He wanted to get Philip's daughter out of this place, with its smells and sounds and nightmarish corridors. He wanted – he wanted to go back to the day of Philip's funeral and start again.

Instead he drank his tea when it came and made polite conversation with the matron in the five minutes she allotted him. When a big, buxom nurse knocked on the door and opened it, the matron rose to her feet. 'Nurse Skelton will see you to the entrance hall, Mr Stewart.'

'Will you tell my niece I came, and that I am thinking of her? I'm sure this is a mistake and—'

'I'm sorry, Mr Stewart, but I would have to check with Mr Golding before I agreed to that. We find reminders of the world outside can be upsetting for the patients, particularly those who have not been with us long.'

'I doubt Mr Golding would object. I am her uncle, after all.'

'That is not for me to say, but perhaps it would save you a fruitless journey in the future if you obtained Mr Golding's permission first?'

Hector stared into the cold, phlegmatic face and then looked at the nurse, who was equally detached. These were the kind of women who would be dealing with Angeline. Angeline, who had always been too sensitive and emotional and warm-hearted, if anything. She would feel utterly bereft. If her mind wasn't already unbalanced, it would be after a few days in this place.

He tried one last time. 'Mr Golding is not an ideal husband, Matron. My niece has recently lost a baby and needs to be in familiar surroundings with those she knows. I would be quite prepared to take her home with me and take full responsibility for her. I will sign anything you want me to sign and—'

'*Mr Stewart!*' This time the interruption was sharp and frosty. 'I see that I have failed to make the situation clear. Mr Golding is next of kin. He has full rights, and you have none. Nurse, see Mr Stewart out.'

The nurse said nothing as she led the way to the entrance hall. She opened the front door and stood aside for him to leave and, as Hector stepped out of the building, the door immediately closed behind him. He stood for a moment in the falling snow, breathing in the fresh, clean air to rid his nostrils of the faintly fetid smell of the asylum. It wasn't until he untied the reins and climbed up into the driving seat of the carriage that he realized tears were streaming down his cheeks. The words Albert had thrown at him were drumming in his mind as he left the asylum grounds. It was true, he *had* handed Angeline to Golding on a plate – and this was the result. What was she going to be like when she came out of that place? If she came out?

Only last week Hector had read a report in the paper which suggested that the somewhat 'mysterious disappearances' of certain people, who had become an inconvenience to their relatives or spouses, might well have become engulfments in the madhouse oubliette; forced into an existence which mirrors that of a prisoner in a dungeon. 'The number of sane men and women confined in lunatic asylums under the easy facilities of the Lunacy Act is a disgrace,' the article had gone on, giving an instance of one physician's statement, which apparently read: 'She had certain impressions with regard to certain other persons which are not accurate or true.'

He groaned out loud, staring ahead as the horses clip-clopped their way down the drive and out through the gates, which the gatekeeper had opened, obviously having been warned of Hector's departure.

He had thought Golding would be kind to Angeline, that she would have a life of ease in the higher ranks of society; he had acted for the best. He told himself the same thing over and over again, but tonight, in the heavy twilight that had fallen while he had been in the asylum, it was no good. He had been fully aware all along of the kind of man Oswald Golding was – the still small voice of his conscience accused him relentlessly – but the bait Golding had dangled, the promise of money to pay off his debts and wipe a number of slates clean, had been too great. Hector had been tempted and he had taken the apple.

He brought the carriage to a halt on a rise, and there, far away down in the valley, lay a small village. Smoke was rising into the snowy air from a number of chimneys and the spire of a small church rose into the white sky. His gaze became transfixed, as the remorse that he had held at bay for so long would no longer be denied. His gambling had become a curse, and God demanded retribution. He was ruined, financially and socially, but that day he had gone to see Angeline after the miscarriage had been his spiritual ruin. He had looked down into the bruised, swollen face and had known what he should do. If he had acted then, Angeline would not be in that living tomb and he would have retained some measure of self-respect. She was his one and only relative in this world – the same blood ran in their veins – and Philip had trusted his most precious thing into his care, and he had let his brother down.

*Philip. Oh, Philip! What am I going to do?* Hector looked around him wildly as though seeking an answer, but there was only the lengthening twilight and the silent snow falling in fat, feathery flakes.

The horses were breathing clouds and moving restlessly in the icy-cold air, shaking their heads now and again as the snow settled on their eyelashes. After a while Hector jerked the reins and they trundled off down the road that led to the hamlet, one of several he'd passed through on his way to the asylum after leaving the outskirts of Newcastle. He had seen an inn on the main road through the village and it was here that he stopped, securing the horses outside before walking into the warmth. He would need a drink – more than one – for what he was about to do.

An hour later he emerged into a night made light by its mantle of white, walking past the horses and carriage towards the end of the village, where the road led over a bridge with a fast-flowing river beneath. Walking to the middle of the bridge, he stared down into the black water.

He had never been able to master the art of swimming. Philip had tried to teach him; many summers they had gone out for the day together with their fishing rods and a packed lunch, and he had watched Philip swimming like an eel, but Hector had always sunk like a stone, despite his brother's help and encouragement. Those were the only happy times he had known – days spent alone with Philip, away from the oppressive atmosphere at home and the hatred in his father's eyes when they fastened on him.

He appealed to something outside himself now, unspoken words of remorse and self-loathing causing his lips to move. And then he climbed over the wooden side of the bridge and plunged into the icy depths below.

# PART THREE

# *Earlswood Asylum*

# 1893

# *Chapter Fifteen*

It was morning. She had twelve hours to get through before she could return to the relative safety of this room. Long, slow, soul-destroying hours. That was how she viewed each day now, Angeline thought, as the grey light of dawn encroached upon the shadows. Hour by hour. It was the only way.

She glanced at the tiny marks on the wall next to her bed, which she had made with her fingernail and were a record of how many days she had been incarcerated in the asylum. Today's mark would make thirty in all. She used her fingernail because they were not allowed any hairpins or sharp objects in case they tried to harm themselves, or others.

*Oh, God. God, help me!* She found she was praying almost constantly now, asking God to keep her sane amid the madness. *Help me get stronger, so I can find a way out of here.* It was the only thing that anchored her reason: the desire to escape from Earlswood.

She had spent only two hours confined in the strait-jacket in the padded cell in the Admissions Block. Then apparently she had had some kind of collapse – she remembered little of it – and had been rushed to the hospital wing because the bleeding that had followed the miscarriage had begun again. When the haemorrhaging had been brought under control she had lain for days too exhausted to do more than eat and sleep, but gradually, as some semblance of strength had returned, the horror of where she was had taken hold. She had been in a separate room off the main ward in the hospital wing and for this she had been grateful. Sometimes the sounds coming from outside her door had been terrifying.

The nurse assigned to her had been a brisk, no-nonsense type, but not unkind, and she had explained exactly where the asylum was located, the rules and regulations that were enforced at all times and the day-to-day routine, but in a manner that attempted to be sympathetic. Through these conversations Angeline discovered that the asylum was practically a small village in itself; besides housing staff and patients, the main building had kitchens, a laundry, a bakery and a large central meeting hall where, on special occasions, dances were held and the annual Christmas party. In the grounds of the asylum the nurse told her there was a chapel close to the main building, and some way from that a carpentry shed, a dairy, a brewery and the stables. Cows and sheep, along with pigs and chickens, were kept in the surrounding fields and looked after by the asylum's farm manager and his workers, many of whom were pauper patients. The ground-floor wards in both wings were reserved for the upper-class, non-violent patients and these led out to airing courts, which held lawns and flowerbeds and seating, surrounded by walls or ten-foot-high railings.

Angeline took in everything she was told, but said little and remained quiet and docile, the memory of the padded cell burnt into her mind. Dr Owen had visited the asylum once when she had still been in the hospital wing, and she had been unable to maintain the facade of calm resignation then. She had pleaded with him to help her, denouncing Oswald and his lies and insisting that her husband was the violent one. The result of this had been the staff administering medication for a few days, which had kept her drowsy and in a frightening half-world where her mind wasn't her own.

It had been a salutary lesson in going along with Dr Owen and the staff and keeping her own counsel.

After nearly two weeks she had been considered well enough to leave the hospital wing. As her manner had become circumspect, it was decided that she would be placed in one of the ground-floor wards, which were actually long rows of individual rooms leading off a corridor. Each room was simply furnished with a bed and chest of drawers, the small window had bars on it and a shutter in the door enabled the staff to check on their patients at all times. In the room next to hers Angeline had discovered that the lady there believed she was the Duchess of Windsor, and on the other side was an elderly woman who spent all her time slumped in stolid, unrousable immobility.

Now, as the shutter in the door opened, a voice said, 'Breakfast in half an hour, Mrs Golding.'

Breakfast was taken in the ground-floor dining room, but the floor above housed the violent patients and the shouts, shrieks and cries filtering through from above her head made mealtimes an ordeal, as did the underlying odour from the incontinent patients. And the habits of others. One young woman with beautiful golden hair and the bluest of eyes, who was apparently the daughter of a Member of Parliament, appeared perfectly normal most of the time, but as soon as she had eaten she would vomit into her dress and then eat it, if the staff didn't get to her to prevent it.

Angeline swung her feet over the side of the bed onto the tiled floor beneath and shivered. She was always shivering. Even in the dining room and the day-room where big fireplaces held substantial coal fires it was chilly, but in the corridors and especially in the cell-like bedrooms on the ground floor it was bitterly cold. She had asked for extra blankets for her bed and immediately got them, but the rawness crept into bones and muscles and could not be dispelled.

She dressed slowly. Most of her movements were slow these days and if she thought about this, it frightened her. There were so many inmates here who ambled at a snail's pace with a vacant smile on their face, as though all the life had been sucked out of them. At first she had assumed it was the drugs used by the staff to keep certain patients docile that made the women this way, but as the days had gone on and the rigid routine and monotony had taken their toll, she could see that it might be because they had simply given up hope.

After brushing her hair she wove it into one long plait at the back of her head, securing the end with the small band that the women were given for this purpose. Even the most trusted and quiet patients were not allowed pins or clips.

Exactly half an hour later the nurse opened the door and Angeline stepped into the line of women in the corridor, from where they followed the nurses in charge to the dining room. Patients took their meals around a number of large tables and ate using enamel plates and basins, with only a spoon. These were counted after each meal before they filed out of the dining room. They were served by the pauper inmates; some patients, like the elderly woman in the room next to Angeline's, had a nurse sitting with them to supervise their eating. Many of the women were nervous and fidgety, constantly twisting their fingers together and mumbling to themselves. One or two seemed in full possession of their faculties, and Angeline's eyes were often drawn to them. One woman, a tall redhead, reminded Angeline of Mirabelle and had caught Angeline's stare on a number of occasions and smiled at her. Now, as the first drink of the day was served – an enamel mug of sweet, sludgy cocoa – she again made eye contact.

Angeline smiled back, wondering what the redhead's story was. She didn't seem disturbed or ill in any way.

All had been relatively quiet from the floor above as the women had entered the dining room. Now, as often happened, an eerie wailing that turned into wild, passionate, despairing cries rent the air for some minutes, causing an uproar that included thumping and banging, before all became still again.

Angeline found that the slice of bread and jam that was served up with the cocoa was sticking in her throat. She couldn't stand another day of this, she told herself. The loss of self-respect, of liberty, and the constant fear would see her as mad as the poor ladies on the floor above before long. And somewhere in the world outside, which seemed a long way away, Oswald was going about his business after having her callously locked up. How could this be? How could the law allow it? After the incident when Dr Owen had come to see her in the hospital wing, one of the nurses had actually remonstrated with her and told her it cost hundreds of pounds a year for the first-class patients to be cared for, and that her husband must love her very much to do this. Angeline had looked into the self-righteous face and hadn't known whether to laugh or cry.

Once breakfast was finished the patients filed through to the day-room. Certain of the women were led away by nurses for what was termed 'treatment'. Angeline didn't know what this entailed and didn't want to know. Because of the inclement weather the doors that led to the airing courts were shut and bolted, and patients were encouraged to read, crochet or apply themselves to fancy needlework under strict supervision. Some merely sat staring into space or huddled by the fire, others rocked themselves to and fro whilst mumbling incoherently, and one middle-aged aristocratic lady positioned herself in front of the windows each day and refused to budge, saying that her son was coming to collect her shortly and she wanted him to see that she was waiting. One of the staff had told Angeline that the lady's son had been killed in a shooting accident in front of his horrified mother, and it was this tragedy that had caused her to become ill.

Angeline took a book from the small bookcase in a corner of the room. She pretended to read each morning so that the nurses were satisfied she was 'settling in', as they put it, but in reality she sat in a maelstrom of despair and turmoil. Retiring to the chair she favoured, which was one of two in a small alcove, she sat down. The alcove was well away from the fire, which was a pity, but as most of the ladies were drawn to the warmth it meant she was left in peace most of the time.

Today, though, a soft voice said, 'Do you mind if I sit with you?' and she raised her head to see the lady with red hair standing in front of her.

'Of course not.'

'Thank you. I'm Verity, Verity Fletcher.'

'Angeline Golding.'

'Please don't think me presumptuous, but I've been watching you and, unlike some of these poor dears, I've come to the conclusion you are no more mad than I am.' Verity smiled. 'Don't look so surprised.'

Recovering herself, Angeline smiled back, but she was still a little wary. Some of the ladies appeared quite normal until something disturbed them.

'You're married?' Verity was looking at Angeline's left hand, and at Angeline's nod, she said quietly, 'I'm not. In fact that is the reason I'm in here. Can you believe that? Well, it's true. My father could forgive me being a Socialist and a supporter of women's rights – just – but when I said I wanted to spend the rest of my life with my lover, who is a railway clerk, without marrying him, he imprisoned me in my bedroom at home. When I wouldn't give in, he and two of my brothers dragged me to a carriage in the middle of the night, tied me up with a rope and deposited me here. My father had a magistrate's order and two lunacy orders from his doctor and another physician, and that was all it took. My father said that because I was going to live with a man who is below me in station, and because I believe marriage is immoral, my brain had been turned by Socialist meetings and writings and I was unfit to take care of myself. He said it was social suicide and he was saving me from utter ruin by keeping me here until I see sense.'

Utterly shocked, not least because Verity had spoken so casually of wanting to live with her lover, Angeline said, 'How long have you been here?'

'Three months.'

'*Three months?*'

'I shan't give in. Edgar is doing all he can with our comrades in the Social Democratic Federation, but of course my father will allow no visitors. But somehow I will get out of here and, when I do, I shall publicize cases like mine.'

Verity's eyes shone with zeal, and Angeline had no doubt she would do what she said, if she got the chance.

'What about you?' Verity asked quietly, after she had glanced around to make sure none of the nurses were taking an interest in their conversation. 'Why are you here?'

Angeline told her, and was touched when Verity placed her hand over hers briefly when she mentioned the miscarriage.

'I shall never marry,' Verity said firmly. Looking keenly at Angeline, she added, 'That shocks you, doesn't it?'

'Well, yes. I'm sorry, but yes.'

'Don't worry. It shocked my father more.' Verity grinned. 'Father is an architect of some repute and simply rolling in money – the whole family is. On my mother's side there are connections to royalty, a fact we've had drummed into us from the breast. When I wouldn't do the London Season and continued with my education instead, Father threw a blue fit. I'm the only girl, you see, amid five brothers. As far as he's concerned, daughters are good for one thing only, and that's to marry well. We have never got on,' she said, stating the obvious. 'Father is one of those men who believes he was born to rule. You know?'

Angeline nodded. Oh yes, she knew to her cost.

'The terrible injustices to the poor, to women and children, have never held the slightest interest for him. Or to my mother and brothers. The nicest thing my father has ever said to me is that he considers me a cuckoo in the nest. I was so pleased about that. I couldn't have borne the thought he imagined that I was like them.'

Warming to her theme, Verity leaned closer. 'It's the same here: the divide between rich and poor. Did you know the pauper wards sleep fifty to a dormitory, with practically no space between the beds and no privacy whatsoever? And unless they are quite incapable, the paupers are expected to work constantly. The men mostly outside on the farm or in the fields and vegetable gardens; some of them in the carpenter's workshop or the blacksmith's next to it. The women do a little outside work, but mostly they're in the laundry and kitchens, or cleaning the wards and the rest of the asylum. May told me even the most infirm are made to sit picking lumps out of horsehair for mattresses, or making coconut-fibre mats. Apparently the matron and doctors maintain that the work is essential for their well-being and recovery – or simply to keep necessary control. A tired patient is less likely to cause trouble. Now possibly all that is true, but my argument is: why don't they give us proper work to do?'

Angeline didn't comment on this. Instead she asked, 'May?'

Verity lowered her voice still further. 'May is one of

the pauper patients. You might have noticed her – she's very striking, with jet-black hair and pure-green eyes. She helped serve our meals last week.'

'Yes, I think I know the girl you mean. She carries herself well and doesn't appear to be like the others.'

Verity grinned again. 'That's May. She has spirit. Well, we're not supposed to talk to the paupers, as I'm sure you've been told' – this was said with such disgust it left Angeline in no doubt how Verity viewed this rule – 'but one day I had a headache and was allowed to go back to my room to lie down. May was on cleaning duty that week, and she was in there. We started to talk a bit, and since then we've managed to exchange a few words now and again. She's a wonderful girl. The kind the Socialist Party would be proud of.'

'What is wrong with her?'

'Wrong with *her*? Absolutely nothing. It would be more in keeping to ask what is wrong with society.' Realizing her voice had risen, Verity glanced about her, before continuing more softly, 'She was in service and the son of the house noticed her. She spurned his attentions; he'd already got a previous housemaid in the family way, and so one night he got her on her own and forced her. When May found out she was expecting a baby as a result of the attack, she refused to go quietly like the other maid had done. May threatened to tell the son's fiancée what had happened and expose him for what he was. That night she was taken from her bed and brought here, where she was admitted for being "morally feeble-minded".'

Verity paused to let the full weight of the injustice done to May to sink in.

'For the first six weeks here she was kept in a restraint harness in a padded cell, because she wouldn't change her story and say she'd been carrying on with a number of the male servants, as the family she worked for claimed. Can you imagine what those six weeks were like?'

Angeline shuddered. She could imagine it only too well.

'Of course the inevitable happened, and at the end of the six weeks May lost the baby. Probably that had been their intention, I don't know. I might be doing them an injustice. But after she came out of the hospital wing she was put in the pauper ward and labelled a "morally unfit unmarried mother". That's why she has to wear the blue-striped dress. Have you noticed that?'

Angeline had been aware that among the pauper women who did the cleaning, serving and other tasks a couple of them, including May, didn't wear the asylum's grey-and-white striped frocks, but she hadn't really thought about it.

'She has been told she's in here for "reformative treatment". Matron told her that her wayward and irresponsible moral outlook would forever lead to harm to herself and others, and that until the authorities are convinced she has repented of her ways – and not least the slandering of the good name of the family she worked for, which they say was for financial gain – here she will stay.'

Angeline stared at the other girl. She had thought her eyes had been opened to the ways of the world since marrying Oswald, but over the last four weeks she had come to realize she hadn't known the half of it. She'd also come to realize that there was far more of her father in her than she had imagined. What had happened to her, and stories like May's and Verity's, was stirring an anger that was gradually overtaking the fear and hopelessness. She had wanted to die after losing her daughter. Left to her own devices, she would have used the bottle of sleeping draught that she'd secreted from Nurse Ramshaw's bag. But now . . . Now she wanted to fight.

'Perhaps you don't believe what May has alleged?'

Angeline's reply was quick and sharp. 'Of course I believe it.'

Verity made a small movement with her head. 'Good. Can I tell her about you and the circumstances under which you were admitted? You having lost your baby too would make her feel someone understands.'

Angeline nodded. She had found a friend, maybe two, and it made a difference. Verity had said it was society that was in the wrong for its treatment of women, the poor, the vulnerable, and she was right. And she could either lie down under the injustice of it all, as she had been thinking of doing, ending her life and taking the easy way out, or she could be her father's daughter and do battle. She had been thinking of him a lot lately, ever since she had repeated his beliefs and principles at Lord Gray's estate in the autumn. He had been a good man, a fine man, the very antithesis of Oswald. Her lip curled slightly at the thought of her husband.

Angeline drew herself up in the chair. Leaning forward, she said softly, 'Tell me more about the Socialist Party and what you believe, Verity.'

# *Chapter Sixteen*

Over the next days Angeline was conscious of a change taking root in her that had begun when she had talked to Verity. She and Verity conversed whenever they could, and as Angeline's eyes were opened to real social inequality and discrimination, to the oppression of women and children and the prejudices of the law, she felt as though she had been walking through life enclosed in a bubble up until now. Verity was passionate about the cause, and when Angeline spoke to May and heard her story at first hand, the divide between upper class and working class melted away.

Taking her circumstances into account, it was strange that the metamorphosis should happen in such dismal and frightening surroundings, Angeline thought one morning at the beginning of March. The patients had been allowed to walk in the airing courts for the last day or two, because although the air was bitterly cold and the nights were ones of heavy frosts, in the daylight hours the sun shone through and turned the frost and snow to glittering diamond dust. She stood now and breathed in the fresh clean air, taking it deep into her lungs to expel the cloying smell of the asylum, which seeped into clothes, skin, hair and even the books she read.

It was a beautiful morning. She stood watching a little robin as it hopped along the top of the airing-court wall, its red breast a vivid splash of colour. *The world was beautiful.* It was only humans who made it ugly.

Returning to her thoughts, she decided it perhaps wasn't so strange that it had taken incarceration in the asylum to wake her up. She had listened to her father and imbibed far more of his views and ideals than she had been aware of at the time, but although she had understood that the world was far from fair outside her own privileged circle, it hadn't stirred her as it should have done. There had always been too much going on and, once she had married Oswald, too much of a social whirl to contend with. Here, remarkably, she could think and meditate and decide for herself what she thought. If nothing else, she had time. Endless hours of it.

She had been waiting in a pre-arranged spot for Verity, and now, as she heard footsteps behind her, she turned.

May was holding a tray of warm, mid-morning drinks for the upper-class patients who were taking the air, and as she reached Angeline she said under her breath, 'Do you know about Verity?'

'Verity? No. What do you mean?'

'Her parents came yesterday and authorized her being

put in seclusion because she hasn't improved since being here. In other words, she won't do as they say.'

Angeline paled. 'What does seclusion entail?'

'Restraint, if the patient gets agitated. Injections of drugs. Purgatives. Hot and cold shower baths.'

'A padded cell?'

'You don't need a padded cell with seclusion patients, not when they've given them the drugs. They're mostly as quiet as mice.'

'Oh, May. How could they do that to their own daughter?'

'Quite easily.' Seeing a granite-faced nurse approaching, May said loudly, 'I can see if I can get you a cup of tea instead of the cocoa, ma'am' and quickly moved on before the nurse reached them.

'I trust you were not conversing with that particular pauper patient, Mrs Golding?' Nurse Clark stood staring after May, her thin mouth pulled tight with disapproval.

'No. I simply didn't want cocoa this morning.'

'I see.' The nurse stood with Angeline, watching May as she distributed the enamel mugs to the ladies, none of whom acknowledged May beyond the slight inclination of the head of a superior to an inferior. As May made her way back towards them, Nurse Clark reached out her hand and took one of the mugs that was left on the tray. 'It is not for you to decide what beverage Mrs Golding drinks or does not drink,' she said icily to May; and to Angeline, handing her the mug, she added, 'Tea is for the afternoon, Mrs Golding. Drink this up now and let us hear no more about it.'

May made a face behind the nurse's back as she continued on with the tray, but as the nurse walked away, Angeline stared after her. Nurse Clark had spoken to May as though she was less than nothing, and the nurses took that tone with all the pauper patients, but particularly with May and the other girl who wore the blue-striped frocks. May had told her that the paupers slept on straw mattresses with one blanket each, and the straw pillows smelt of cows, but they were fed well and extra rations of meat were provided for those working or those who were in the asylum infirmary. Many of the paupers had been starving in the outside world and therefore expressed something approaching contentment at their surroundings, but then after all, May said, most of them were as barmy as a monkey on a griddle.

It was later in the day before May managed to whisper anything more to Angeline. As they were lining up for the dining room, May and another pauper helper walked by, carrying bowls of freshly baked rolls to go with the soup they were having. May stopped by Angeline and fiddled with the back of one of her ugly hobnailed boots. 'Verity's definitely in one of the seclusion rooms,' she murmured softly. 'Nelly, me friend who's on cleaning there, said she's drugged up to the eyeballs and can't even talk. Wicked it is, what they're doing. I can understand it with someone like Lady Lindsay, who has voices in her head that talk to her, but not Verity. Here, I'd better go.

Sharkey's on the lookout for an excuse to have me locked up again.'

Sharkey was May's nickname for Nurse Clark, and only the week before the nurse had had May taken to the outhouse at the bottom of the paupers' exercise yard and chained there for twenty-four hours for some minor infringement of the rules. May hated the nurse with a passion, which Angeline could understand. What the nurse would do if she suspected Verity, and now Angeline, had so far forgotten their station in life as to befriend someone like May, let alone commit the heinous crime of being on first-name terms with her, Angeline dreaded to think, but she knew it would be May who suffered for it.

Angeline approached the dining room on leaden feet. She was desperately worried about Verity and missed her more than she could have imagined, considering that Verity had only been gone that day. The oppressive and often terrifying atmosphere of the asylum had been easier to take with Verity around, and she hated to think of the other girl's bright, intelligent mind being dulled and interfered with by the drugs the staff were administering.

She slept very badly that night and felt tired and anxious the next morning, but directly after breakfast one of the nurses told Angeline that she was wanted in the superintendent's office. Dr Rupert Craggs was at the top of the asylum hierarchy and was an esteemed doctor, and with his wife, the matron, he ran the asylum exactly as he wanted to. Although he reported to his Visiting Committee, which included prominent men such as magistrates, gentry and aristocrats who had supervised the funding and building of the asylum years before, his word was law. His annual report provided a wealth of statistics, ranging from the causes of illness to the number of patients working in various parts of the asylum, and the value of asylum farm and garden produce, but no one would have dreamed of challenging one word of it.

A dedicated but cold man, he and his wife had no friends among the senior staff of the asylum, by choice. The chaplain who took services in the asylum chapel, the assistant medical officer, the farm manager and the rest of the top team knew better than to allow even a suggestion of familiarity to colour their dealings with the superintendent and his wife, and everyone did exactly what was expected of them. Whilst many of the staff lived in the main building, Dr Craggs and his wife had a substantial house in the grounds of the asylum and it was to this that they retired while any staff get-togethers went on.

Angeline had met the superintendent only once some days after her admission, as by and large the matron looked after the female patients. He had marched into the infirmary and stood looking down at her for some time, without saying a word. Then he had cleared his throat. 'I am Superintendent Craggs, Mrs Golding, and I have been an acquaintance of your husband for some time, so rest assured that you are in good hands. Mr Golding's father and my father were on a number of committees together, and could even have been said to be friends.'

She had detected an element of pride in this last statement and wondered if there was anywhere or anyone that wasn't impressed by the Golding name or the flimsiest connection to it. She had made no comment, however, and after another moment or two he had cleared his throat again and turned on his heel with a brisk 'Good afternoon'.

Now Angeline wondered what the superintendent wanted with her, as she followed the nurse out of the dining room. The superintendent's office was off the main entrance hall and close to his wife's room and, as in the matron's office, a good fire was burning in the black-leaded grate. It was this – the warmth, after the chill of the asylum – that Angeline noticed first when the nurse knocked once on the brown-painted door and stood aside for her to enter.

Dr Craggs was sitting behind a large walnut desk in a big leather chair facing the door, a floor-to-ceiling bookcase filled with books behind him, and his wife was sitting at an angle to the desk in another big comfy chair. In the bay of the window stood a two-seater leather sofa and it was there that Oswald sat, his long legs stretched out in front of him and a cup of coffee in his hands. None of them stood up when Angeline entered, and as the nurse closed the door behind her Dr Craggs pointed to a straight-backed wooden chair in front of the desk. 'Please be seated, Mrs Golding.'

Angeline didn't accede to what was clearly an order, but she did hold onto the back of the chair, because seeing Oswald had made her feel faint. One of the nurses had told her in the early days that it had been decided she was to have no visitors until she had 'stabilized' – whatever that meant – but she hadn't queried this because no visitors meant she was spared Oswald's presence. Visitors to the asylum were only admitted on certain days and times, but as the asylum was in the countryside and difficult to reach on foot, it meant many patients, especially the paupers, could go weeks without seeing anyone from the outside world, and this was exacerbated during the winter months.

Nevertheless, for the last little while, visiting days had become something of a subtle torture for Angeline. She had feared Oswald would arrive at the asylum and they would deem her well enough to see him, but today her concern for Verity had occupied her mind to the exclusion of everything else. But now he was here. Hatred rose up as bile at the back of her throat, but she fought from showing any emotion, knowing that to do so would be misconstrued by the superintendent and his wife. Oswald held all the cards.

'Hello, Angeline.' Oswald's voice was soft and soothing, the sort of patronizing tone one would use with a fractious child. When she didn't answer him, but continued to stare coldly, he said gently, 'Do sit down, my dear.'

'Why am I here?' Angeline addressed Dr Craggs, ignoring Oswald.

'Why, to see your husband, of course. You do recognize your husband?' he added, as though he doubted her mental state in that regard.

'Yes, I recognize him, but I have no wish to see him.'

'Now, now, Mrs Golding,' Matron Craggs put in sharply. 'Mr Golding has come a long way to see you, because he has some distressing news he thought it better to break himself.'

'It's all right, Matron. I understand. It's the illness, not Angeline.' Oswald's voice was so forgiving that Angeline wanted to kick him, but she was more concerned about this distressing news of which the matron had spoken.

'What news?' She forced herself to look at Oswald as she spoke directly to him. His thick, fair hair gleamed in the light from the windows behind him, and he was dressed as immaculately as always. His leather boots shone, the collar of his dark frock coat was edged with satin and his trousers were perfectly creased. He looked every inch the handsome young gentleman Angeline had fallen in love with, what seemed like an age ago. Matron Craggs hadn't been able to take her eyes off him.

'It's your uncle,' Oswald said gently. 'You remember your uncle, my dear?'

Not dignifying this with a reply, she said crisply, 'What is wrong with my uncle?'

'I'm afraid he has passed from us.' Oswald was watching her closely, his eyes glittering. 'It happened some time ago, but the matron has only recently decided you were fit to be told. I am so sorry, my dear. He was a fine man, and I know you were fond of him.'

Gripping the back of the chair harder, she made herself say, 'How? I mean, what happened? He wasn't ill.'

Oswald's gaze went to the matron and then back to her, as though asking how much to say. 'It appears to have been an accident.'

'An accident? What kind of accident?'

'It appears, although one cannot be certain, that your uncle drowned, Angeline. He came to visit you here, just after you were admitted, but of course you were too ill at that point for visitors. On the way home he stopped at an inn and then took a walk down to the river and . . . ' Oswald shrugged his shoulders. 'He was found the next morning more or less where he must have fallen in. The edges of the river were frozen hard, but the middle was still running and very deep, I understand. He had become wedged against a large rock, or he would have been carried downstream. There were no signs of foul play, and his watch and money were still intact, so the police have ruled out an attack of any kind.'

There was something here she couldn't understand. 'My uncle doesn't like the water, be it a river or the sea. He couldn't swim. My father often used to tease him about it. Why would he take a walk to the river, on what was clearly a cold winter's night? It doesn't make sense.'

Again Oswald glanced at the matron. 'I said it *appears* to be an accident, my dear. There's always another possibility.'

'What? What is the other possibility, if not that he was attacked?'

'It was discovered after your uncle died that he was bankrupt. In fact he had massive debts and owed money to a considerable number of people. Gambling debts.'

Her head was swimming. Uncle Hector dead, and she hadn't known. A shaft of pain pierced her. He was her last link with her parents and she had always imagined that in time the rift between them, which had sprung up so suddenly and was beyond her comprehension, would be healed. And he had died on his way home from coming to see her here. Had he wanted to see her one last time before he took his own life? But no, she couldn't believe that. Not Uncle Hector. It had to be an accident. 'Perhaps he wanted a walk to clear his head after visiting the inn,' she said, speaking her thoughts out loud. 'You said there was ice, and ice can be treacherous. He could have slipped and slid in and been unable to save himself. The water would have been very cold and the shock of it . . . ' Her voice trailed away. She felt bereft, far more so than she would have imagined at losing her uncle. He was part of her father – it had been a tangible bond.

Looking Oswald straight in the eye, she said, 'Did you know he had money worries, before he died?'

Her directness threw Oswald. He hadn't been expecting the question. Completely taken aback, he muttered, 'I . . . yes. No. I mean, not exactly.'

'Did he come to you for help?' Like a mist clearing when the bright morning sun cast its light and warmth on it, the reason for the rift between her uncle and Oswald suddenly made sense. 'He did, didn't he, and you refused him?'

Oswald had recovered himself. Keeping his voice gentle, he murmured, 'Angeline, Angeline, how many crimes will you lay at my feet? I have no idea if Hector's death was an accident or if he took his own life, but I had nothing to do with it. You must try and get better, my dear, and then you will see things clearly. See *me* clearly.'

'I see you clearly now, Oswald.'

'Mrs Golding, please. Now calm yourself. This will help no one. Your husband loves you, and he is trying his best in what is a very difficult situation.'

'Difficult for whom?' she shot back at the matron. 'Not for him. He is not the one imprisoned against his will. He is free to do exactly as he pleases.'

'I am sorry you feel this way, my love.' Oswald shook his head sorrowfully. 'When you are better you will remember these times and wonder how you could have been so lost, but for the moment you must concentrate on getting better. That is all we want for you, the matron, the superintendent, everyone. We thought you were strong enough to hear about your uncle, but we were clearly wrong, and I take full responsibility for that.'

Angeline glared at him. The chaplain's sermon the previous Sunday came to mind, and her voice ringing with contempt she said, 'You are like one of the Pharisees Jesus spoke about. A whitewashed tomb on the outside, but inside full of filth and decay and corruption.'

'*Mrs Golding!*' Matron Craggs glanced at her husband as she said, 'I'm sorry, she has been so docile over the last weeks. I thought she was ready for this.' And to Oswald, 'Please don't take it to heart, Mr Golding.'

'Please don't distress yourself, Matron.' Oswald was at his most charming. He could afford to be. Everything was going even better than he had hoped. 'As I said, I am aware it is the illness – and not my wife – causing her to speak in this way.'

'I'm not ill.' Angeline swung to face him, spots of burning colour in her cheeks, but her voice now coming low and bitter and with terrible intent. 'And I tell you that you'll pay one day for what you did to our child and to me. Her blood is on your hands. Remember that. And keeping me locked away in here won't change it. One day God will demand an account from you for the wicked things you've done.'

The grey of Oswald's eyes were almost black, but his voice was quiet and controlled as he said to the superintendent, 'Is this part of the illness? Thinking she can speak for God Himself?'

The matron said agitatedly, 'She hasn't done this before, Mr Golding, and—'

'Please, Matron.' Oswald raised his hand. 'Might I perhaps have a word with my wife in private? I fear the presence of others could be aggravating her neurosis.'

'I don't think that is wise, Mr Golding.' The superintendent had stood to his feet, clearly disturbed. 'The puerperal mania that began your wife's illness seems to have developed into more than a passing animosity against your good self. I cannot agree to you putting yourself in harm's way, not after the last attack and the condition in which you were left.'

Oswald nodded regretfully, sighing. 'It is so sad, so very sad, but I will be guided by you, Dr Craggs.' He too had stood up, and before she realized his intent he took a couple of steps to bring himself in front of Angeline and bent towards her, as though to kiss her cheek, but whispering so that she alone could hear, 'You will be in here for the rest of your life, my sweet.'

She sprang back, as much from the nearness of him as from what he'd said. 'Keep away from me! Don't you touch me.'

'Please, Mr Golding.' The matron was as edgy as her husband. 'You can see that we can do no good here today. Perhaps in a month or two . . . ' She took Angeline's arm as though to lead her out of the room.

Oswald nodded, his voice seeming to break as he said, 'I had thought, when she became pregnant, that a baby would bring us closer together, but she doesn't seem to understand that I am grieving, too. I have lost a daughter after all.'

The hypocrisy was too much. Taking the matron by surprise, Angeline slapped Oswald hard around the face with her free hand, crying, 'Do not mention her! Don't you dare mention her. You're not fit to speak of her.'

In the next moment she found herself swung around by the matron's grip on her arm and practically thrown out of the door into the corridor outside, where the nurse was waiting. 'Help me take her back – and be careful, she's violent.'

'I'm not violent.' Angeline ceased to struggle in their grasp, but although she didn't protest as she was whisked back to the ground-floor ward so fast her feet hardly touched the ground, once they arrived there the matron issued orders that she be put into one of the restraint rooms.

Terrified at the thought of being fastened into a strait-jacket again, and knowing that she had played into Oswald's hands, Angeline tried to keep calm. 'I'm not violent, truly. Please, Matron, please.'

'Sedate her.'

Blind instinct took over. She started to fight to get away, to get out of the ward, as more nurses came to help the matron and nurse, but as before, she was soon rendered helpless. She felt the injection, but could do nothing to prevent it, and neither could she stop them strapping her into the harness and thrusting her into the windowless cell.

And then she was alone, and all became quiet except for the whimpers she could hear through her panic. It was only as the injection took effect, and she felt the whirling darkness begin to close in, that she realized the noises were coming from her own lips.

# *Chapter Seventeen*

'It's criminal, Albert, keeping the mistress locked away in that place. I can't bear it, I can't. An' them not letting me see her. What's that, if not downright cruelty?'

'Lass, lass, don't take on so.' Albert put his free arm round Myrtle, who was now sobbing as he drove the horse and cart down the drive of the asylum. 'We'll keep trying. You know that. And, to be fair, they're only obeying orders from Golding.'

'*Him!*' Myrtle rubbed at her wet face with the back of her hand. 'He's a wicked devil. All that's happened to Miss Angeline is because of him, and he drove Mr Hector to his grave.'

'I didn't think you liked her uncle?'

'I didn't, but what's that got to do with it? At least he came and tried to see her – that's something in his favour. And I don't care what anyone says about him being in debt and the rest of it. I think it was knowing Miss Angeline was locked away in that place that did for him. It was no accident, Albert. He topped himself, sure as eggs are eggs. His conscience saw to it.'

'Aye, well, if we're talking about consciences, mine and Olive's are none too happy about Mr Hector. If we hadn't said we were going, perhaps he might have come home that night. He was a funny old bird, but me an' Olive were the nearest thing he'd got to family, especially Olive. If we'd known the load he was under, with the debts an' all, I wouldn't have said what I did.'

Myrtle sniffed and scrubbed at her face again, before turning to Albert. 'We've been through this, Albert. You weren't to blame for him ending up in that river.'

'Maybe, maybe not, but what's done is done, an' it's no use dwelling on it, not with all I've got now.' His arm tightened as he hugged her close for a moment or two. 'It'd be like spitting in the face of the Almighty not to count me blessings – you being the most important one.'

'Oh, Albert.' Myrtle reached up and kissed his stubbly chin, then gave another little 'Oh' as the horse and cart passed through the gates of the asylum and into the lane beyond and one of the cart wheels bumped over a particularly large pothole.

Albert took his arm from around her, holding the reins of the big carthorse with both hands as they trundled down the lane. The cart was a heavy, open vehicle, wide and long and perfect for transporting goods and hay and farming equipment, but very different from the light, attractive conveyances with two wheels and springs that the gentry used for business or pleasure, or the smart carriages with two matching horses pulling them.

He glanced at Myrtle sitting on the wide, long, plank-like seat beside him. She was still clearly trying to compose herself and so he gave her a minute, but he hadn't been exaggerating when he said that she'd blessed his life. With her windfall from Miss Angeline and what he'd saved over the years, they had been able to buy the smallholding he'd dreamed of since he was a boy. Well, it was more than a smallholding, he qualified in his mind. It was a small farm, and over and above anything he'd thought he could aspire to. They'd got wed the day before he'd completed the transaction and moved in a couple of days later, at the end of March. They had invited Olive to come with them, but she'd maintained that she wanted her independence after working for someone or other all her life, and had rented a small cottage in the nearest village, about a mile or two from the farm. She'd been canny with money and had a sizeable nest egg to see her into her old age. But the landlord of the village pub had lost his wife the previous month and, when he'd come cap in hand to ask Olive if she'd take on the cooking for his customers in the evenings, she'd found that she liked the idea. Having her days free to potter round her cottage and small garden, and the evenings occupied and providing a nice steady income, suited her down to the ground, she'd told them.

'At least they promised they'd pass Miss Angeline my letter this time,' Myrtle said in a small voice after a few minutes had passed. They had been to the asylum once before, but hadn't got beyond the front door. This time the hall porter had taken pity on Myrtle and allowed them to come in and wait, while he found a nurse to talk to her. And after consulting the matron – who, with Myrtle's permission, had opened the letter and read it – it had been agreed there was no reason why Angeline could not receive it. 'She'll know we're thinking of her, and that she's helped us so much. That should do her good, shouldn't it?'

'Of course it will, lass. And like I said, we'll keep visiting, and one day soon they might let you see her. Golding can't stop her having visitors indefinitely.'

He probably could. Myrtle didn't say this out loud. It had been five months now since Miss Angeline had been locked away. Five months in that prison of a place. Myrtle shuddered in spite of the warm May sunshine. What would she be like when she came out? *If* she came out? She had no one to speak for her, that was the thing. No family, besides that wicked devil she'd married. Myrtle had asked about a bit, and it was apparent that the longer a patient stayed in one of those places, the less likelihood there was of her or his release. Someone had told her that less than one-third were released in under a year, and a growing proportion of most asylum populations comprised chronic, long-stay patients. When she had repeated this to Albert, he had said that as Miss Angeline wasn't a chronically ill patient, she'd be out in no timc. But she didn't believe that. Perhaps he didn't, either.

Myrtle glanced across the fields to where a large river was shimmering in the sunshine as they came to the top of an incline, then they were ambling down the slight hill and the river was lost to view. The afternoon was scented with the heady smell of May blossom and the wealth of wild flowers growing on the banks on either side of the road, and the sun was warm on her face. She took off her straw bonnet and let the breeze ruffle her hair, shutting her eyes as she searched her mind for a way to help the girl who had been so good to her.

She mustn't cry again, she warned herself as tears pricked behind her closed eyelids. It upset Albert, and really it did no good. Miss Angeline needed help, not tears, but she was at a loss as to what she could do. It wasn't as if Miss Angeline had any siblings or close relatives; even her friends and acquaintances had been Mr Oswald's, like the Grays. Except . . . Myrtle's eyes snapped open as a thought occurred. The mistress had said something about Marmaduke Jefferson turning against him, because Mr Oswald had insulted his wife or something, the awful night she'd lost the bairn. She'd said Mr Oswald had blamed her for it, that he'd had a falling-out with Mrs Jefferson. Even now, Myrtle's lip curled at the thought of the red-headed woman who had clearly been carrying on with Mr Oswald. Could she – dare she – go to Mr Jefferson and ask him for help? How would she even find out where he lived?

She continued to mull over the matter in her mind on the way home to the farm, which was situated west of

Sunderland near Castletown, and the beauty of the spring day – the wide, high blue sky, the trees swathed in blossom, the bluebells that were a thick carpet of pure cerulean in some places – added its weight to the conviction that she couldn't leave Angeline to languish in the grim confines of the asylum.

The sprawling, growing town of Gateshead was some six or seven miles behind them when eventually, two hours later, the road twisted and then divided. The main carriageway led on to a hamlet or two, before the bigger village of Castletown.

Old Ned, the horse, knew exactly where he was going and was as eager to get home as his owners. He gathered pace as he clip-clopped down the narrow wooded lane, shaking his big head with its flowing mane. After 200 yards the lane widened into a broader track and stretched gently downhill, and there, nestled in a small valley with fields containing a small herd of grazing cattle feeding on lush grass, was the farmhouse, a huddle of small buildings clustered around it.

Albert pulled Ned to a halt as he always did on returning home when they reached this point. They both gazed at the farm, the same emotion of deep thankfulness in their breasts. *It was theirs. All theirs. No one could take it away from them, and here they bowed the knee to no man.*

Furthermore – and Myrtle sometimes pinched herself on waking in the morning to make sure it wasn't just a dream – they had been able to bring her family with them, a double blessing in view of the fact that her father had died shortly after they had negotiated buying the farm. The oldest two of her four brothers – Daniel, who was eighteen, and Terry, who was fourteen and had recently joined Daniel down the pit – had been able to say goodbye to working in the bowels of the earth and were now Albert's farm labourers, and twelve-year-old Frederick would join them in the summer when he turned thirteen and was able to leave school, a day he was longing for, having an aversion to all things academic.

Sixteen-year-old Nell, who had been born with club feet and was a cripple, worked in the dairy on her crutches. She had been thrilled to be given an important job, after a lifetime of feeling useless. Consequently the dairy was spotless and was already proving a significant asset to the farm. Many an evening Tilly, Myrtle's mother, had to practically manhandle her daughter out of the place. Tilly assisted with the copious amount of cooking and cleaning, and even the little ones – apart from James, who was only a few months old and still at the breast, and Lily, who was nearly two – had their jobs to do when they were home from school.

It was still early days, and with every penny having been sunk into buying the farm and available stock, money was very tight, but all in all it was a supremely happy little family who lived at Crab Apple Farm. The lads had been content to work for bed and board until Albert could afford to pay them a wage sometime in the future, knowing full well that Myrtle and their brother-in-law had saved their mother and siblings from the horrors of the workhouse, and had taken the responsibility for the family off their shoulders. As Daniel said – frequently – who could put a price on working in the clean, fresh air after being entombed in Hades?

Albert and the older lads had whitewashed the two farm cottages inside and out. They stood behind the pigsties and stables and hen coops. The two-up, one-down brick dwellings were soundly built, and it had been decided the first would house Tilly and baby James in one bedroom, with the three older brothers in the other. Nell and her sisters lived in the second cottage, and again Nell had taken to the role of housekeeper and governor of her small brood like a duck to water.

The farmhouse itself was in need of some attention, particularly the roof. Albert had designated this a priority when funds were available. The building was composed of a large kitchen and a smaller sitting room, with another room off the entrance hall, which Albert was going to use as his study. Upstairs were four good-sized bedrooms, but three of them were in a very poor state. The windows were barely intact, the floorboards were rotten and more plaster had fallen off the walls than remained. The state of the ceilings provided the reason – if one had been needed – for the decay, but the fourth bedroom had escaped the ravages of the leaking roof and was habitable. Albert and Myrtle slept there, and for the moment Albert had decided to let sleeping dogs lie. One day the farmhouse would be restored to its former glory and his children would occupy the derelict rooms that the former owner – who was childless – had let slip into such disrepair. But for now every penny, every farthing, was needed to make the farm a success.

'It's beautiful.' Myrtle's whisper echoed his own heart. 'We're so, so lucky, Albert.'

'Aye, we are, lass.'

She turned to him, catching his sleeve. 'We couldn't have got this without Miss Angeline. You do see that, don't you? I have to do all I can to help her.'

'Aye, lass, I know. Don't take on.'

'What she said the night she lost the baby, about Marmaduke Jefferson turning against the master an' all – I feel that might be the answer. That he might help us.'

'Golding's not your master any more, lass.' Albert's voice was stolid. 'And gentry turning against gentry and helping the likes of us is a different thing altogether to them having some sort of falling-out.'

Myrtle said nothing when Albert tugged on the reins and the big carthorse obediently plodded towards the farm. Two of her sisters were sitting to one side of the track where it joined the farmyard, playing with one of the farm cat's kittens, and waved at their approach. Looking at their bright little faces, she said, 'No one should be locked away like a criminal when they haven't done anything wrong, Albert. I don't care what them doctors say. Miss Angeline is no more mad than you or I. It might do no good, I give you that, but I have to try to do something, and the only thing I can think of is seeing Mr Jefferson. If I don't, all this' – she waved her hand at the farmhouse – 'will turn to ashes. That's the only way I can explain it.'

'You don't have to explain it, lass. If you want to see this Mr Jefferson, that's what we'll do, all right? Now, now, no blubbering or they'll think we've had a row or something.'

Myrtle hugged him. 'Thank you.'

'Lass, I'd give you the sun, moon and stars, if I could. Getting you to see this Mr Jefferson is nothing.'

In the event, and to Myrtle's dismay, it necessitated a trip to London. To Myrtle, the visit to the asylum had seemed like travelling to the end of the world, and the thought of a long train journey to the capital and then finding the Jeffersons' town house was more than daunting. But her enquiries had yielded the fact that the Jeffersons were away in town and would remain there until the end of the season, whereupon the country-house parties would begin.

Much as she would have liked Albert to accompany her, she knew he was desperately needed at the farm and that an overnight stay in London would take him away for too long. Therefore she staunchly insisted that she would travel alone, and Albert just as vehemently said she would not. A compromise was reached when it was agreed that Frederick would take some days off school and accompany her. Two months away from his thirteenth birthday, Frederick was long and lanky and looked older than his actual age. Furthermore, the last years of having an ailing father and the family living from hand to mouth had toughened him up and, as Albert said with some approval, he had an old head on young shoulders.

So it was that, one morning towards the end of May, Myrtle and Frederick waved goodbye to the rest of the family and made the train journey south. Myrtle had not tried to make an appointment to see Marmaduke Jefferson, fearing she would be refused outright if she did so, so she left on the understanding that she had no real idea how soon she and Frederick would return, but hopefully they would stay in London only for one night.

Frederick was as excited as a bairn on Christmas Eve as the train journey unfolded, but was trying hard to maintain the adult pose expected of him as Myrtle's protector. Myrtle, on the other hand, was in a state of quiet trepidation at what she might face at the journey's end.

By the time the train puffed into King's Cross station in London it was three o'clock in the afternoon. As Myrtle and Frederick alighted – Frederick carrying the carpet bag with their overnight things, and the remainder of the sandwiches and cake they had brought with them and were saving for their tea – they looked about them in some confusion. The noise, the people, the general hustle and bustle were more than they had encountered before and it was all overwhelming. Myrtle settled her straw bonnet more firmly on her head, smoothed her summer coat free of the creases of the journey and slipped her arm through that of her brother. Albert had told her to find a taxi driver when she arrived at the station. 'Smile prettily,' he'd said with a grin, 'and tell him you can't afford his cab, but need to know how to get to a certain street. Then you can get a tram there.'

Her brain whirling, she said to Frederick, 'I think we both need a cup of tea before we do anything else, Fred. There's a station cafe over there. Let's go and have a sit down and get our bearings, and then we'll see about finding Lower Berkeley Street. We know it's off Portman Square in the West End, so that's a help.'

An hour and a half later they were standing outside the Jeffersons' grand terraced establishment, and Myrtle's heart was in her mouth. The stateliness of Lower Berkeley Street and all its neighbours proclaimed that the wealthy citizens and aristocrats of England monopolized the western half of the West End, as did the extraordinary ring of wide and pleasant parks that dotted the area. Myrtle had listened to Angeline talk about Oswald's London house and the shops and entertainment, the palaces, gentlemen's clubs, art establishments and museums in the capital, but she had never accompanied her mistress on her visits. Oswald had insisted that Ellen Harper and her daughters were on hand to see to Angeline's needs, and that had been that. Now, as the grandeur of the nobility's and gentry's summer rcsidences were in plain sight, she wondered how she'd had the temerity to think Marmaduke Jefferson would grant her an audience. *But she had to try.*

She glanced over her shoulder to where Frederick was waiting on the other side of the road. She had thought it better that she saw this last stage of the undertaking through on her own, but now she wondered whether to call him over. She felt very small and insignificant standing on the bottom of the four immaculate steps leading up to the gleaming front door, and glanced to her right, where a set of steps led down to what she assumed was the kitchen and the servants' entrance below ground level. Should she make enquiries there first? But probably they would just send her away with a flea in her ear.

She hesitated for a moment more and then took a deep breath and walked up the steps, yanking firmly on the bell pull. Her heart was now thudding so hard she didn't know if she would be able to speak when the door opened. It took a few moments and then the door swung open and an individual whom she took to be the butler was peering down his nose at her. He looked her up and down. 'Yes?'

No 'Miss' or 'Madam' or 'What can I do for you?' Strangely, his attitude put iron in Myrtle's backbone. She had decided to plead her cause to whoever opened the door. Now she straightened her shoulders and said coolly, 'I'm here to see Mr Jefferson.'

'Are you indeed. Do you have an appointment?'

Lying through her back teeth, she said, 'Of course.'

'And the name is?'

'I'm Mrs Golding's personal maid.'

'Well, Mrs Golding's personal maid,' he said with deep sarcasm, 'if you had had an appointment with Mr Jefferson, I would have known about it.'

Looking him straight in the eye she said coldly, 'Mr Jefferson must have forgotten to mention it, but I suggest you inform him that I am here.' She was banking on curiosity, if nothing else, prompting Mirabelle's husband to see her.

'Now look here—'

'No, you look! I have an appointment, and I don't appreciate being kept waiting.'

'I don't know what your game is, m'girl, but I do know you don't have an appointment with the master. Do you want to know how I can be so sure? Because he's—'

'Myrtle?' A voice behind the butler caused him to swing round, and Myrtle saw Alice, Mirabelle's personal maid, standing there. 'I was just crossing the hall and I thought I knew that voice. What on earth are you doing here?'

Myrtle gazed at Alice, her brain working furiously. They had met at various times over the last two years during the house parties in the autumn and winter, but it could hardly be said that they were bosom pals. Alice was a personal maid in every sense of the word and had made it clear she considered Myrtle far beneath her. A well-educated young woman in her own right, her qualifications and range of skills were excellent, as were her manners and deportment. It was well known that she was devoted to her mistress, and also that Mirabelle thought very highly of Alice and conferred privileges on her that made her like one of the family. All the other personal maids had been envious of her, and more than a little in awe of this paragon of virtue. Alice would know if Mr Golding had upset her mistress in some way and, if he had, Alice would be furious.

Throwing caution to the wind, Myrtle said urgently, 'Alice, I have to see Mr Jefferson about something Mr Golding's done. He's a devil, Mr Golding, and I think if Mr Jefferson knows—'

She stopped as Alice held up her hand, then said to the butler, 'I'll deal with this.'

He said not a word as Alice beckoned for Myrtle to follow her, and Myrtle reflected that all the stories about Alice's power within the household seemed to be true.

For her part, Alice was agog behind her calm, neat facade. She had put two and two together at the time of the attack on her mistress and knew full well Oswald was behind it, although nothing had been said between mistress and maid about that terrible incident from that day to this. The fact that her mistress's long-standing affair with Mr Golding had finished at that time, and the hate and loathing with which she had spoken of him since, were proof enough. And Alice knew that her mistress was aware that she knew; it was one of the many unspoken confidences they shared.

Alice led Myrtle into the morning room and shut the

door behind them. It was a beautiful room and spoke volumes about the Jeffersons' wealth and power, but all Myrtle was conscious of was the strong scent of hot-house lilies from the huge bowl of the flowers on an occasional table nearby. Thereafter she could never smell lilies without her stomach churning.

Without preamble Alice said, 'Well? What's happened?'

Myrtle didn't think about not telling Alice. There was only one way she would get to speak to Mr Jefferson and that was through this plain, reserved woman in front of her, who had always seemed more aristocratic than some of the high-born ladies. Again she repeated, 'Mr Golding, he's a devil, Alice. There's another side to him that's plain wicked. He hit Miss Angeline and caused her to fall and lose the baby before Christmas, and now he's got her locked up in one of them lunatic asylums and won't let anyone see her. Her uncle tried and he's dead – no one knows if it was an accident or what – and because I said what Mr Golding had done, he dismissed me.'

Alice was looking at her in amazement. Weakly, she said, 'You . . . you need a job?'

'No, no, it's not that. I'm married, see,' she held out her left hand, 'and we're nicely settled with our own farm, thanks in part to Miss Angeline – I mean, Mrs Golding. No, it's that he'll keep her in there, Alice. I know it. He won't let them release her, not ever. And she's as sane as you and me, so can you imagine what it must be like? Miss Angeline, of all people.' Her voice broke and her lip trembled, and she bit down hard on it with her top teeth, telling herself she mustn't cry. Not now. She mustn't appear hysterical or neurotic, or they wouldn't believe her.

Alice was still staring at her and it was clear she was completely taken aback. After a moment she said, 'We heard Mrs Golding had lost the baby, of course, and that she was dreadfully ill, but as far as I'm aware, everyone thinks she is being kept quietly at home until she regains her strength.'

'Aye, and I know why they think that,' Myrtle said bitterly. 'I suppose he put it about she don't want no visitors, either? The next thing'll be she's had a relapse or a breakdown, and then after that it'll be she's in a nursing home or abroad, or something; and by the time someone might find out where she really is, years will have gone by. She's got no one to speak up for her, Alice. No one to challenge Mr Golding. And he's got the doctors in his pocket.' Lowering her voice she said, 'She wasn't going to stay with him, you know, once the bairn was born. She hinted at it more than once.'

'A separation, you mean?'

Myrtle shrugged. 'Perhaps, or she might have just escaped somewhere, I don't know. Maybe he found out, or maybe he just wanted her locked away so he could carry on with his life regardless. He never loved her, but then you'd know that.'

Alice ignored the reference to her mistress's affair with

Oswald, but the expression on her face warned Myrtle not to say any more on that matter.

'I thought Mr Jefferson might speak up for Miss Angeline, Alice. I know there's no love lost between him and Mr Golding since they had a falling-out.'

'What do you know about that?'

Alice's voice had been sharp, but Myrtle warned herself not to reply in like vein. Quietly she said, 'Not much, except that it seems to have been the cause of Mr Golding's attack on Miss Angeline. He blamed her for it, by all accounts.'

They had been standing and now Alice waved to one of the chairs that the room held. 'Sit down and wait, and I'll see what I can do. I'm not promising anything, but I'll see.'

Myrtle wanted to throw herself on the other girl's neck and cry with relief. Instead she said softly, 'Thank you, Alice. Thank you very much.'

Myrtle sat in the morning room, which was tastefully and exquisitely furnished, for more than ten minutes, but when Alice returned, Myrtle couldn't for the life of her have described one item in it. Her whole being was willing Alice's mission to be successful. If Mr Jefferson refused to see her, she didn't know what else to do. And as Albert had put it, gentry turning against gentry and backing the likes of her was highly unlikely. But it wasn't *her*, she told herself, as though in the telling she could convince Mr Jefferson. It was Miss Angeline's well-being that was at stake here. If she could just see Mirabelle's husband and tell him that – explain how things were – he'd surely see that he had to do something? But then the upper classes were a different breed. Who knew how he would react?

She jumped to her feet when Alice came into the room.

'Come along.' Alice's voice was neutral.

'He'll see me?'

'Follow me and be quiet.'

Myrtle did as she was told. She had little option to do anything else.

Alice led the way across the hall and paused outside a door halfway down its vast expanse. After knocking once, she opened it and ushered Myrtle in, following her and then shutting it quietly.

Mirabelle Jefferson was sitting on a sofa going through the menu for a dinner party she was holding the next day, with her cook at her side. She glanced at Myrtle, then said to the cook, 'That's settled then, Cook. A selection of desserts including orange soufflé, compote of pears, sweet omelettes, and sweet and savoury jellies; and don't forget the ices with praline and sugared violets. Lady March is enamoured of your ices. Oh, and a selection of nougat and chocolate creams – strawberry, mint and coffee, I think. Is everything clear? Good. That's all for now. Just remember to cook Mr Riches's quail to a cinder, the way he likes it. Revolting, I know, but the man's a philistine when it comes to food.'

The cook bustled out, already looking harassed. Myrtle could imagine that by the time the meal was over the kitchen maids would be in tears and the cook would be tearing her hair out.

She had no time to reflect on the misfortune of those below stairs, however, not when faced with her own. It had been bad enough when she thought she was going to be confronted by Mr Jefferson, but Mr Golding's ex-mistress was ten times worse.

'So?' Mirabelle had been more than a little intrigued with the story Alice had discreetly whispered in her ear. 'Why did you lie to my butler, girl? Mr Jefferson has been in France for the last week and is not expected home until tomorrow afternoon. Even if that were not the case, I doubt my husband would have agreed to see you. Why should I believe the rest of what you related to Alice is true, if you lied about that?'

'*I had to lie about the appointment!*' The words came out too loud, and then Myrtle jerked her chin upwards as if in denial of the tone of her voice, before adding quickly, 'I'm sorry, ma'am. What I mean to say is that, if I hadn't said I had an appointment with Mr Jefferson, I wouldn't have got inside the door. I know that, ma'am. And I would have said or done anything to be able to speak to Mr Jefferson about what's happened to Miss Angeline – I mean, Mrs Golding. And it's true, it's all true, as God Himself is my witness.'

Aware that for all her bravado the girl in front of her was near to tears, Mirabelle's manner softened. 'Sit down.' She pointed to a chair set at an angle to the sofa on which she was sitting. 'And, Alice, would you tell

Routledge we are not to be interrupted and then return here, please.'

'Yes, ma'am.'

Mirabelle said not a word until Alice had reappeared and shut the door behind her. After motioning for her maid to come and join her on the sofa, Mirabelle fixed Myrtle with her vivid green eyes. 'Tell me from the beginning. Leave nothing out, but exaggerate nothing either, do you understand?'

Myrtle nodded. The beginning. Where did the beginning start? Long before Miss Angeline had married that fiend; probably that evening in Mr Hector's house when Mr Golding had assaulted her with his eyes. But she couldn't mention that here. Probably best to begin with how Miss Angeline had come back a changed girl after her week in London when she'd wed Mr Golding. She drew in a deep breath. 'On her wedding day Miss Angeline was the happiest bride in all creation. She fair worshipped Mr Golding, and he made sure he did and said all the right things.'

'You don't think Mr Golding's feelings were genuine?'

'He played her like a violin, ma'am.' Myrtle waited a moment, but when Mirabelle made no comment, she went on, 'When she came back from their week in London something had happened – something bad. She didn't talk of it, but I know her eyes had been opened to what he was really like. *Is* like.' Myrtle hesitated. This woman had been Mr Golding's mistress for years. What if she still carried a torch for him, despite their falling-out? She must have loved him, and love was a funny thing. What if she went to see him and told him all this? She'd be in deep trouble.

Myrtle caught herself. She had come too far – in distance as well as resolve – to mince words now.

Gathering her thoughts, she went on, 'Miss Angeline was terribly unhappy. I don't know what went on behind closed doors, but it's my belief he treated her harshly.'

Mirabelle leaned forward. 'Do you mean physically?'

'In every way, ma'am. He's . . . he's a bully. Like I told Alice, I think she was planning to leave him. She never said that in so many words, but she gave me the impression that was so. And then she found out she was expecting the bairn, the baby. He . . . he left her alone for a time after that. And then one day he comes home in a fury and he attacks her and she loses the baby. Bashed her in the face, he did, and she broke her nose—'

'You were there, in the room?'

That again. Myrtle tried to stay calm. 'No, ma'am, I came when she screamed, but it was too late then. He – Mr Golding – said she slipped and fell, but where I grew up there were plenty of women who looked like Miss Angeline did after their men had got paid on a Friday night and been to the pub. He hit her all right. Miss Angeline herself told me he was angry because, begging your pardon, ma'am, your husband had turned against him because you and Mr Golding had had a falling-out and he – Mr Golding, that is – blamed Miss Angeline for it. She didn't know what he was on about, ma'am.'

'You're saying Mr Golding assaulted his wife, which resulted in her losing the child, because of me?'

'No, ma'am; no, I'm not saying it's your fault, ma'am.' Myrtle was beside herself. Mrs Jefferson was her only hope in helping Miss Angeline, and she'd offended her. 'Please, ma'am, I didn't mean that. I'm sorry . . . '

Mirabelle waved her hand. 'I'm not angry, girl. I'm trying to get to the bottom of this.'

'It was something to do with Mr Jefferson and Mr Golding gambling – the reason Mr Golding was so angry, ma'am. He,' Myrtle gulped, 'he thought Mr Jefferson was seeing to it that he lost. He . . . he said he was being cheated.'

Mirabelle turned and looked at Alice and the two women exchanged a long glance for a moment.

'Please believe me, ma'am. I swear it's the truth and—'

Again Mirabelle held up her hand. 'I have no reason to doubt you . . . what is your name?'

'Myrtle, ma'am.'

'I have no reason to doubt you, Myrtle. And let me say it would not surprise me at all that Mr Golding ill-treated his wife. But to assault her when she was carrying his child is unforgivable.'

'It was a little girl, ma'am, the bairn. Perfect she was, but too small. Fitted in me two hands, she did. Oh, I'm sorry, ma'am.'

Mirabelle had made an anguished sound deep in her throat, and Alice glared at Myrtle, sounding quite unlike herself as she hissed, 'Shut up. Just shut up!'

'It's all right, Alice.' Mirabelle's first pregnancy had resulted in a miscarriage at six months, the longest she'd subsequently carried a baby, and the child had been a girl. She gave Myrtle no explanation, saying, 'Go on with your story.'

With a quick glance at the glowering Alice, Myrtle said hesitantly, 'Miss Angeline nearly died afterwards with the bleeding, but Mr Golding had me thrown out the next morning. I went back later, but I couldn't see her. And then the nurse who'd been looking after her came to Miss Angeline's uncle's house' – Myrtle had decided to leave out the matter of the letter to her, thinking it carried more weight if they believed the nurse had come to speak to Angeline's uncle – 'where my husband worked then, and told Mr Hector that Mr Golding had had her committed to the asylum. She, the nurse, said that although Miss Angeline was still poorly, there was nothing wrong with her mind. That . . . that was five months ago, ma'am, and Mr Golding won't let anyone visit or anything. I've tried, ma'am, but it's no good. It . . . it needs someone with authority, like Mr Jefferson, to speak for her. She's not mad, ma'am, I know she's not, but being in that place . . . '

'She could well end up so,' Mirabelle finished for her. 'Yes, I see that.' As Myrtle went to speak again, Mirabelle said, but not unkindly, 'Quiet, girl' and a silence fell on the room.

Mirabelle's head was whirling as she assimilated all she had been told. She didn't for a moment doubt that the girl in front of her was telling the truth, but nevertheless she was shocked and sickened that a man she had been intimate with for a number of years could behave so. And yet she'd had her eyes opened in the worse possible way as to how vile and vicious Oswald could be, hadn't she? Every day since, even after the injuries that he'd inflicted had healed, it had been as though the assault had happened just days, hours, before. The humiliation and shame had changed her forever, she knew that, and try as she might she couldn't rise above the burning hatred and desire for revenge that had turned her days joyless and her nights into a torment. Only Alice had any idea what was wrong with her, and the effort of pretending to everyone else – even Marmaduke – that she was the same gay, carefree woman she'd always been was beginning to make her ill. But it seemed as though Angeline had been as badly treated as herself, more so because the tender life of an innocent had been brutally snuffed out.

She bowed her head for a moment as the familiar pain of her barrenness, and all the heartache she'd suffered as baby after baby had come too soon, pierced her through.

When she looked at Myrtle again the mask she presented to the world was firmly in place once more, and the emerald-green eyes were as clear and hard as glass. 'I will speak to Mr Jefferson on his return and see that appropriate action is taken to secure the release of Mrs Golding.'

'Oh, ma'am, ma'am, thank you. God bless you, ma'am. Thank you, thank you.' Almost incoherent in her gratitude, Myrtle let the tears flow at last.

She was still thanking Mirabelle when, at a sign from her mistress, Alice led Myrtle out of the room, shutting the door behind them.

Left alone, Mirabelle sat gazing at the closed door. The girl had asked God to bless her, but only God Himself knew why she would make sure Marmaduke got Angeline out of that place, and with the maximum discredit to Oswald. She liked to think she would have done the same, if Oswald hadn't sodomized her and brought her so low that she knew she would never really rise again. But she would never know the answer to that for sure. And perhaps it didn't matter. What did matter was that every day she carried murder in her heart, and a holy God couldn't bless one such as she. But, even knowing that, she couldn't – no, she didn't *want* to – let the hatred and bitter fury die. It was the only thing that kept her going.

Alice knocked and re-entered the room, and Mirabelle raised her eyebrows as she said, 'Well, what do you think of that?'

'I think, ma'am,' said her very proper and refined maid, 'that Mr Golding might soon find himself like one of Cook's roast breasts of lamb – well and truly stuffed – and it couldn't happen to a nicer gentleman.'

Mirabelle stared at her maid in amazement and then burst out laughing. Perhaps the anger and loathing weren't the only things that kept her going . . . Thank God for Alice!

# PART FOUR

## *Breaking Free*

## 1893

# *Chapter Eighteen*

Angeline sat under the shade of one of the shelters in the airing court, ostensibly watching a game of croquet that two of the nurses were supervising between a few of the patients. In reality, her thoughts had soared way above the ten-foot-high walls surrounding the courts and the inmates they enclosed. The knowledge that Myrtle had come to the asylum a few days ago had been both heartening and weakening. Heartening because it had comforted her to know she wasn't completely forgotten by the outside world; weakening because the matron's refusal to allow her to see Myrtle for even a few minutes had brought home yet again how completely she was at the mercy of the asylum staff and, worse, Oswald.

Her fingers closed round Myrtle's letter, hidden deep in the pocket of her skirt. She didn't need to look at it to know what it said, for she had memorized every word. She had surmised – correctly – that Myrtle had written it with a view to getting it past the scrutiny of the matron, hence the fact that it was couched formally and didn't really sound like Myrtle:

> Dear Ma'am,
>
> Please excuse the impertinence of my writing to you like this, but if they won't let me see you, I hope they will pass this letter on. I am very well and I hope you are, too. Albert and I got married in the spring and, due to a windfall I received, we were able to buy a nice little farm near Castletown, so we will be forever thankful to my benefactor. My family are living with us too, and we have all settled in very nicely. I pray and think of you every day, and hope one day to see you again.

It ended, rather quaintly: 'I will forever be your obedient servant, your maid, Myrtle.'

A forlorn smile touched Angeline's lips. Dear Myrtle. And she was so glad the money had helped to secure the farm for Myrtle and Albert, and Myrtle's family. At least they were free of the shadow of the workhouse now. She wished she could share the news with Verity, for she would have loved to know that Myrtle and Albert had bought the farm and were prospering. One of her friend's absolute convictions was that there was no difference between the working class and the upper class except the capriciousness of fate, and that the working man was every bit as intelligent as the nobility in their mansions.

'I tell you, Angeline, the fatality of birth and the forced

repression of minds that could soar to great things, given a chance, is a terrible indictment of our society,' Verity had said more than once. 'And women are denied this basic right in every class, not just among the poor. I find it incomprehensible that, with a woman on the throne of England, we are not given our rightful place in society. But Queen Victoria positively promotes women's inferior status and the gross exploitation of the poor.'

Oh, Verity. The smile died. So many weeks had passed, and still Verity was locked away in seclusion. May had managed to have a word with her once or twice, when she had been on the rota to clean the seclusion rooms, and had been upset at Verity's deteriorating health. In protest at her treatment, Verity had refused to eat and was now being force-fed. May hadn't gone into details, but Angeline knew it was a brutal procedure.

But Verity's resolve to stand firm was still strong, May assured Angeline, with something like awe in her voice when she spoke of the other girl. Verity's heroines, who pioneered the right of women to higher education – Frances Buss, Dorothea Beale, Emily Davies, who all remained unmarried – were her inspiration.

Suddenly the quiet afternoon was shattered by Lady Lindsay, who had been playing croquet, having greatly improved over the last weeks, according to her particular nurses. At one time the voices in her head had ordered her to wrestle with an attendant or nurse, or to throw herself to the floor, and often the voices had given incomprehensible commands, injunctions, threats and insults, until she had stood and screamed and screamed at the contradictory orders. Lately, though, just one or two voices came and these were different and quite beautiful, according to Lady Lindsay. They gave her songs to sing and poetry to recite, and once they brought a hurdy-gurdy to encircle her bed and play a tune that made her weep with its loveliness.

Now, however, she had flung down her croquet mallet and was tearing at her hair, shouting that 'they' were all telling her to hit the wooden ball in a different direction, and that there were hideous faces grimacing at her from the grass. Before the two nurses supervising the four women could restrain her, she had taken off like a grey-hound across the airing court, her cries blood-curdling. Without pausing, and seemingly unaware that it was there at all, Lady Lindsay ran full tilt into the wall that enclosed the courts, knocking herself onto her back, whereupon she gave one terrible screech and then was still.

Pandemonium reigned. Several of the patients began screaming or weeping; the 'Duchess of Windsor' began giving orders to the nurses in a high-pitched holler; and more attendants and nurses came running from the building. In the midst of it all, one of the more excitable inmates who had been quietly playing croquet before the incident also ran amok, brandishing her mallet like a club. Unfortunately Angeline, who had been attempting to hurry to the relative safety of the asylum, was directly in the woman's path. Whether the woman intended to strike her or not was questionable – although Rowena Newton was highly strung and mercurial in her moods, she was not considered violent by the asylum staff – but, deliberate or not, the end result was the same. Angeline received a blow to the back of her head that felled her to the ground, and for a moment everything went black.

When she came to she was being carried on a stretcher, and one of the nurses was walking alongside it, saying, 'We're taking you to the hospital wing, Mrs Golding. You've received a nasty blow on the head', as though she didn't know her head was throbbing fit to burst.

Once in the hospital, she found herself in the small room off the main ward, where she had been ensconced for some time shortly after her arrival at the asylum. Within minutes Dr Craggs had examined the back of her head, tut-tutting as he did so and talking in an aside to his wife, 'No lasting damage, but this sort of thing really should not be allowed to happen. It's not good enough, Matron. Not good enough at all.'

In spite of the buzzing and aching in her head, Angeline was struck by the incongruity of the superintendent addressing his wife so formally. Were they like that in the privacy of their own quarters? she mused dizzily. Doctor and matron? It fitted into the insanity that was all around her, if nothing else.

Sounding extremely rattled, the matron said, 'It was nothing to do with me, Doctor.'

'Not good enough, as I said. You must keep a tight ship, Matron. Find out who was responsible for allowing

Lady Lindsay such liberty and send them to me. Now, sedation and bed rest for Mrs Golding, and I'll look in on her again tomorrow.'

'Very good, Doctor.'

The next hours were a blur. At some point quite soon after the superintendent's visit, Angeline was aware of one of the nurses helping her into a nightdress and then settling her in bed after making her swallow a bitter liquid. Not that she objected to that. Anything that made her excruciating headache bearable was welcome. Within minutes the sleep-inducing drug relaxed her taut muscles and produced a soporific calm.

Angeline didn't know when she became aware that the opiate no longer held her in its soothing, inactive stupor. Sounds penetrated the lethargy – awful sounds.

Fighting the desire to simply pull the blanket over her head and let sleep claim her again, she struggled to sit up in bed. Her head swam and her brain felt muzzy, and as the room had no window, the pitch-blackness added to the feeling of unreality. A bell was ringing somewhere and, now that she was more awake, she could hear shouts and screams, but they sounded different from the usual disturbances that occurred in the asylum.

Unable to orientate herself in the darkness, she sat on the side of the narrow iron bed for a few minutes and then stood up, feeling around the walls until she came to the door. Banging on it, she called out, louder and louder when she got no response, but to no avail.

Groping back to where she thought the bed was, she found it and sat on the edge again. Panic had given way to full-fledged fear. She could smell smoke.

It was only a minute or two later that Angeline heard the key turn in the lock, but it wasn't one of the nurses who spoke when the door opened, but May. 'Angeline, get up, there's a fire.'

'I am up.' She stumbled to May in the doorway, who held a bunch of keys in one hand. 'What are you doing, and what's happening out there? Where are the nurses?'

'They're trying to get patients out, but some of 'em have gone clean barmy because of the fire. Come on, this whole wing's burning and the smoke's terrible.'

'My clothes. I can't walk about in my nightdress.'

'You can – don't worry about that. The place is on fire, for goodness' sake.' May pulled her into the corridor, where thick black smoke was billowing from the direction of the seclusion rooms along with the crackle of burning wood.

'How did you get hold of the keys?'

'One of the nurses collapsed, so I pinched 'em.'

Hair-raising screams were coming from the end of the ward that led on to the seclusion rooms, and Angeline clutched hold of May. 'Is Verity still in there? We've got to help her.'

'I've tried, you can't get down that end for the fire.'

'But if Verity's trapped, we can't leave her.' Angeline's voicc caught in horror. A figure came shrieking out of the smoke, her nightdress and hair on fire. The woman fell to the ground before she reached them, still screaming, but as they ran forward the scream turned to a gurgling wail and then silence, although the body still twitched as the flames consumed it. Through the smoke they saw a wall of fire, an inferno.

May grabbed Angeline's hand. 'Come on, there's nothing we can do. It's impossible to get down that end.'

Her head swimming from the smoke and the sedative in her system, Angeline let May haul her along. 'How did you get out?'

'Our attendants led us out into the grounds, but then we could see the ground floor and above were on fire, and I thought of you and Verity. It's mayhem out there, it wasn't difficult to slip away.'

Once in the corridor beyond the hospital wing, they saw smoke seeping beneath the far door. 'We're trapped.' Angeline looked at May in horror. They couldn't go back and they couldn't go forward. She pointed to the window halfway along the corridor and set just below the ceiling. 'How can we reach it? If we could break the glass we could climb out.'

'Wait here.' May raced back the way they'd come and returned in a few moments, coughing and her eyes streaming, but carrying one of the straight-backed chairs from the nurses' station in the ward, along with a still-smouldering blanket. Positioning the chair beneath the window, Angeline steadied it as May climbed onto the seat and then onto the back of it and hoisted herself onto the narrow window ledge. Passing May the blanket,

Angeline watched as she wrapped it round her hand and arm, before punching the glass in the window as hard as she could. It shattered immediately, fragments of glass raining down on Angeline's uncovered head and into her loose hair, although the worst of it fell outwards into the courtyard, which housed the small outbuilding holding the shower-bath for the hospital wing and seclusion rooms.

Flames were now licking under the far door and the black smoke from the hospital wing was thicker. May had breathed in great gulps of the fresh night air, and as Angeline sank down onto the seat of the chair, coughing and choking, May positioned the folded blanket across the base of the window to protect them from any remaining shafts of glass and then leaned in, her arm outstretched. 'Come on, reach up to me.'

Still in the powerful grip of the sedative and with her chest aching from the inhalation of the foul smoke, Angeline shook her head. 'I can't.' She just wanted to lie down and rest.

'You must. Angeline, you must. For Verity, if not for you. Do you think she'd give up, in your place? Don't let her die for nothing. We can escape this place tonight – I know we can. Who will be able to say exactly who died and who didn't? This is our chance, and we have to take it.'

'We can't escape.'

'We can. When I came back in for you and Verity, the superintendent had already ordered the gates to be opened to allow in help from the village down in the valley, and messengers have been dispatched to Newcastle asking for aid from the fire brigades. The staff have got their work cut out with the patients who have managed to get outside – the hubbub is deafening. If we don't escape tonight, we never will. Your husband will make sure you rot in here, and they'll keep me as an unpaid skivvy for the rest of me days. I've seen it with other patients, lass. I know what I'm on about.'

Angeline looked up at May through blurry, streaming eyes. Something outside herself enabled her to climb onto the chair and reach for May's hand, but she still couldn't grab the bottom of the ledge or May's fingers.

'Wait a minute.' May swung her legs out of the window and turned onto her stomach, as her feet found a foothold in the old stone wall outside. Balancing on her belly and with both arms now reaching for Angeline, she said fiercely, '*Try*, damn it! Try, lass. You can do it, I know you can.'

Somehow Angeline managed to get one foot on the top of the back of the chair, but without anyone to steady it, as she had done for May, it slipped from beneath her. But May had grabbed her, almost overbalancing and falling back inside as she took Angeline's weight. Scrabbling with her bare feet up the wall, and with May dragging her upwards, it was only a second or two before Angeline was able to heave herself onto the ledge, but it felt as though she had run a mile. Hanging there, with May now steadying her, she gasped for clean air. And suddenly there was an almighty bang, as the door at the far end of the corridor seemed to explode and a huge ball of fire belched towards them.

May jumped down into the courtyard, pulling Angeline with her, and Angeline felt the fury of the fire singe her feet as she tipped headlong towards the stone slabs. But for the fact that she fell squarely onto May, whose body cushioned the impact, she would have done herself a serious injury. As it was, a sharp, shooting pain in her left wrist told her she hadn't escaped unscathed. May had had the wind knocked out of her and lay for a minute, fighting for breath, as Angeline rolled off her.

When May could speak again it was with her usual humour: 'Good job you weren't Big Bertha, lass, or I'd be as flat as a pancake on Shrove Tuesday. What have you done to your wrist? Ooh, that's broken, by the look of it. Everything else all right? Come on then, we have to find a way out of here without anyone noticing us.'

The pain in her wrist now excruciating, Angeline held it to her chest with her other hand as she stumbled after May. In one corner of the courtyard a small, narrow gate opened onto a row of greenhouses and beyond them stood the walled kitchen garden. May seemed to know her way about and led the way past the kitchen garden, taking care to stay in the shadows cast by the high brick wall.

As they walked, Angeline became aware that they were at the back of the asylum, but as they skirted more outbuildings, which May informed her were the men's workshops, and began to move down the side of the building, the shouts and screams and general hubbub became louder.

May stopped, drawing Angeline to her side. 'The water tower is at the back of the men's side of the building, and they've got everyone helping who is able, but the fire's got too much of a hold. That's why the superintendent's sent for help. We need to get down to the main gates while they're still open, if we can.'

Angeline gazed at May. 'But the gatehouse? The keeper isn't going to let us just walk out. They'll be watching for patients all the time.'

'I know, but we have to try – it's our only chance. Nothing like this is going to happen again.'

Angeline looked down at her feet, which were cut and bleeding from the glass in the courtyard. 'May, I've no shoes and I'm in my nightdress. How far do you think I'd get? You have to go by yourself. Everyone will know I'm a patient.'

May looked down at her own striped dress. 'They're not exactly going to think I'm Lady Whoever, lass,' she said wryly. 'But once we're outside, we'll manage somehow. Beg, borrow or steal.' Then she paused. 'I've an idea. Wait here.'

Before Angeline could stop her, she had disappeared back the way they had come, running like the wind. Angeline sank down to the ground, her head spinning and her wrist so painful it made her feel nauseous. Verity, oh Verity! She gave a little moan. Please, God, let the smoke have overcome her before the flames reached her. May had said she'd found it impossible to reach the seclusion rooms, but the echo of the terrible cries coming from that direction reverberated in Angeline's head.

She shut her eyes, willing the dizziness to subside, as the smoke and screams and shouts became a sickening cacophony that made her wonder if she *was* going mad.

How long it was before May returned, Angeline didn't know. It could have been minutes or hours, because she was sure she had slept in between. Then May was standing in front of her, her arms full of clothes and a pair of boots in one hand, dangling triumphantly from their laces.

'Courtesy of the clothes store behind the laundry.' May grinned at her. 'So you won't have to leave practically naked after all, and I will never *ever* wear anything with stripes again for the rest of me days.'

'How did you get into the clothes store?'

'I've got the hang of breaking windows now. These are clothes they have for the paupers who come in, so they're not what you're used to, lass.'

Angeline took the clothes May passed her. 'If we get out of here tonight, I *am* a pauper, May. Angeline Golding will have died in the fire. I can't go home and, even if I could, there's nothing there for me any more.'

They stared at each other. 'We can stick together, lass. How about that? I can't go home, either. Me da washed his hands of me when he found out I was expecting a bairn. It didn't matter to him that it weren't my fault.

Mind, I'm not sorry to see the back of him. Knocked us about something cruel when we were bairns, he did – me mam an' all. I've a brother in Newcastle. He left home as soon as he could, we all did. We could look Jack up. He's the only one who's come to see me since I've been here.'

Angeline had managed to pull on the petticoat and the coarse grey frock May had brought as her friend had been speaking, but May had to fasten the buttons. As she stuffed her feet into the ugly black boots she found they were a couple of sizes too big, not that it mattered. If by some miracle they really could escape tonight, nothing mattered. No one but May was going to help her get out of here, she knew that. And May was right: Oswald would see to it that she was incarcerated here for years, and how much insanity could you be party to before you lost your own mind? That was the thought that had become a constant torment of late.

May had changed her frock and now bundled the despised striped dress under one arm, saying, 'I'll get rid of this when we're far away from here. Don't want to leave any clues that we got out alive.' Then, taking in Angeline's chalk-white face, she proceeded to rip the skirt of the striped dress in two, making a rough sling, which she tied round Angeline's neck, before helping her to insert her injured wrist into the hanging fold of material. 'Better? Good. I know it's painful, lass, but if you can stand it, we need to go.'

They crept along the side of the building, and now the night was lit by the glow of the fire. Skirting under the cover of some trees, they stood for a moment looking at the scene in front of them. One or two ladders were propped against the building, and some of the male staff had entered windows on the first floor and were helping patients and nurses who had been trapped by the flames to climb down them. Patients of both sexes in their night clothes were standing, sitting or lying in the courtyard, with nurses and attendants – some of whom were also in their night clothes – attempting to take care of them and keep order. Quite a few of the figures lying on the ground appeared to be in an insensible condition, and a number of patients were clearly distressed, some being forcibly restrained by staff.

Even as they peered out from their hiding place, they saw one of the female patients climbing one of the fire escapes and then clambering along the guttering of a ward roof, followed by a uniformed nurse. As the nurse reached the woman, the patient clearly objected to being held, flailing her arms and struggling to get away. Flames were licking along the roof towards the two women, and some male staff left their fire buckets and stirrup pumps and ran to fetch a ladder from a few feet away. But as they hastily leaned it against the wall, both women fell, screaming, to the ground.

'Wait, May.' As May went to move off, Angeline grabbed her arm. 'Shouldn't we try to help?'

'Help?' May stared at her. 'Don't be daft. You can do nothing with that arm, and if you think I'm risking escaping this place to help them, you've got another think coming. God helps them that help themselves – that's what my da used to say, when he was thieving stuff down at the docks. And although I didn't agree with much he said, that rings true. You want to do another five, ten, fifteen years in here? Do you?'

Angeline shook her head and, as May moved away again, she didn't stop her, but followed after a moment or two.

Beyond the copse of trees they had sheltered in lay an open stretch of lawn, leading down to more trees and then the huge walls enclosing the grounds of the asylum. The drive that led down to the gatehouse was to their right. As they reached the edge of the trees, May stopped. The moonlight, added to the illumination provided by the raging fire, made it almost as light as day in the courtyard fronting the asylum; but even here, some distance away, it wasn't as dark as they needed it to be.

Angeline glanced at the girl who, together with Verity, had kept her going over the last months. Without the pair of them, she doubted she could have kept her mind focused and her will strong. May was staring ahead over the expanse of manicured lawn, her lovely face rent with doubt as her black hair wafted about her shoulders. 'May?' Now looking straight into the vivid green eyes, Angeline said, 'Anything is better than not trying. All their attention is on the fire. If we can get to the trees, we can try to climb one and get over the wall that way, rather than leaving by the gates. Let's do it. We've nothing to lose.'

'I haven't perhaps, but you?'

'I would rather die than become Oswald's wife again. One way or another, Angeline Golding is dead. If we succeed tonight, we start afresh. If not . . . ' She shrugged, wincing as her broken wrist sent a shaft of pain shooting up her arm. 'But we will succeed. I know we will.'

May's gaze searched her face. 'For Verity,' she said softly.

'For Verity.'

And together they left the shelter of the trees and began to run across the open space, expecting any moment to hear shouts and cries behind them and the sound of their pursuers.

## *Chapter Nineteen*

'No, oh no, Albert. How did it happen? Is Miss Angeline all right? How can we find out? How many people were hurt?'

'Whoa, lass, take a breath.' Albert put his arm round his wife's shoulders. Myrtle and Frederick had arrived at the farm minutes beforehand, after their overnight stay in London, and all day he had been dreading having to break the news to her about the fire at Earlswood Asylum. 'I only know what's in the paper. It being market day, Daniel went in to Castletown with the eggs and cheese and what-have-you, and everyone was talking about it apparently. He pricked up his ears when he heard it was an asylum that had gone up, so he went and bought a paper, to see if it was Earlswood.'

'And it was.' Myrtle's face was tragic. 'I shan't rest till I know Miss Angeline's safe. And this after Mrs Jefferson said she'd help to get her out of that place.'

'She did? Well, that's good, lass. Now, don't you go

thinking the worse. Likely Miss Angeline's as right as rain.'

'Let me see what the paper says.' Myrtle took it, sitting down at the kitchen table in her coat and bonnet and reading it avidly, while her mother made them all a cup of tea. It began:

**Fatal Fire at a Lunatic Asylum**

Early yesterday morning a fire was discovered at Earlswood Lunatic Asylum. The asylum receives insane persons for private treatment and also a number of pauper patients, and is run by Medical Superintendent Dr Rupert Craggs. The fire was discovered by one of the female attendants shortly after two o'clock, and an alarm was at once given, owing to the hold that the flames had already obtained on the building. The inhabitants of a neighbouring village assisted wherever they could and the Newcastle Fire Brigade was summoned when it became apparent the fire was out of control.

Commendable acts of bravery were reported, and foremost among these was Nurse Audrey Clark, who died attempting to save one of the female inmates who had climbed onto the roof of the building. Patients escaped the flames clad only in their night clothes, some of whom were badly burnt or suffered breathing problems due to inhaling the smoke, which was reported as being foul in nature. Other brigades followed the Newcastle brigade, and heroic efforts were made to extinguish the flames and save lives. However, it became

> apparent after some time that nothing could be done, except to save a number of the outlying portions of the building. Sadly many bodies are buried in the debris, and serious injuries to both inmates and staff have been reported.
>
> Details of those missing will follow in due course, after relatives have been informed, but among the injured in hospital are: Mr Adam Norris, the proprietor of the village inn, who sustained a serious cut on the head; Mr Ivor Longhurst, male attendant, concussion of the brain; Captain Howard, a patient, broken arms and fractured ribs; Mr Irvin Wright, a patient, broken spine and burns; Mrs Geraldine Middleton, nurse, injury to the foot and arm; Miss Cicely Hutton, patient, serious burns . . .

And so the list went on for more than half a page, before the article finished by saying:

> Those at the scene were indefatigable in their attention to the injured and dying. Many patients were in a state of great anxiety and confusion in consequence of the fire, but through the efforts of Superintendent Craggs and his staff excellent order was maintained. It is thought the removal of some dangerous walls and damaged parts of the building will commence once those persons buried in the debris are retrieved. Estimated damage: £45,000.

'She's not listed among the injured.' Myrtle took the cup of tea her mother passed her with a nod of thanks, as she added to Albert, 'That's good, isn't it?'

'Course it is.'

'I must write and tell Mrs Jefferson. She'll be able to find out what's what. They won't tell me anything, that's for sure. Oh, Albert' – Myrtle's voice caught in her throat – 'she has to be all right. Mrs Jefferson will get her out of that place, I know she will. It would be too cruel if Miss Angeline's died now.'

'Lass, you've done all you can, and more besides, and it's no good worrying. Now drink your tea and tell me how you got on. Young Fred look after you properly?' Albert grinned at his brother-in-law, who smiled back. 'And did you find the house all right?'

Myrtle filled him in on all that had happened, and later in the evening, when the rest of the family gathered in the kitchen, she told her story again. To a man they insisted that Miss Angeline would be fine and she mustn't worry, but Myrtle couldn't respond as she knew they wanted her to. She had the strangest feeling on her . . .

Oswald sat in the superintendent's parlour listening to the doctor rattle on about all that had been done to save each and every patient, and how the tragedy could not be laid at the door of the staff. 'When dealing with the insane, every safeguard is taken,' Dr Craggs said earnestly, 'but one cannot predict every eventuality. It seems one of the female patients, Lady Lindsay – who had run amok earlier in the day and had been taken to one of the seclusion rooms – overpowered the nurse who had been assigned to take care of her, sometime after midnight.' The superintendent didn't mention here that he had suspended Lady Lindsay's usual nurse, who was accustomed to the patient's ways, as punishment for the incident in the morning, in spite of the nurse begging him to reconsider due to the patient already being in a highly volatile state and needing the reassurance of familiar faces around her.

'Exactly what happened after that, we cannot be sure yet,' the superintendent went on, 'but in the past the lady's condition has led her to do strange and dangerous things, if not restrained.' At Oswald's raised eyebrows, the doctor added, 'She hears voices instructing her what to do.'

'I see.' Oswald didn't really care. The fact that he was now free of the burden of Angeline was enough. 'Besides my wife, how many people died in the fire?'

'Due to the sterling actions of my staff, a lot less than it could have been.'

'How many, Superintendent?'

'Along with Nurse Clark and several others, seven people died at the scene, but twenty-four are unaccounted for and believed to be buried in the debris. I'm deeply sorry for your loss, Mr Golding.'

'Thank you. And I am sure you and your staff did all you could, in the circumstances.'

'That is very gracious of you, Mr Golding.' The superintendent was clearly relieved. He had been receiving anxious relatives all day, and one or two had proved to be difficult, especially as it would be impossible to identify who was who for the burials. 'We are all quite devastated, of course.'

'Naturally.' Oswald stood up. After shaking the superintendent's hand, he allowed the man to see him out. He paused on the doorstep, turning to say, 'I will expect the payment I made this month for my wife's care to be refunded.'

'Of course, Mr Golding. And may I offer my condolences once again.'

Oswald walked across to the waiting carriage, his step lighter than it had been when he had arrived, to find out what was what. He'd hardly dared to hope that Angeline was one of the deceased. It had seemed too good to be true. But the fire having been started at that end of the asylum, it seemed she was in the wrong place at the wrong time. Or the right place at the right time, as far as he was concerned. He smiled to himself, pleased with his little joke, before pausing and breathing in deeply, expanding his chest and sighing with satisfaction. Then he climbed into the carriage and sat back in the leather seat, lighting one of his favourite cigars.

Randall, the coachman, shut the door and took his place in the driving seat, lifting the reins and clicking his tongue for the horses to move off. He was frowning. His guts had twisted at the look on his master's face. It was common knowledge among the staff at the house that Golding had had his young wife put away because it suited him, and to a man they were all heart-sorry for her. The young mistress was no more barmy than he was, Randall thought, and it was plain wicked to have her installed in one of these places. They were worse than the workhouses – and that was saying something.

He couldn't work out if the master had heard good news or bad, and he knew better than to enquire. The news would filter down from Wood or Palmer soon enough. But to come out of there looking as pleased as punch wasn't natural, however you looked at it. But then the master wasn't natural. Evil swine, he was.

He guided the horses through the open gates, nodding his thanks to the keeper, who began to shut them immediately they were on the road.

Yes, evil as the day was long, was Golding. Look at what he'd done to their Toby: taking his eye out because Toby hadn't fastened his horse's saddle properly, and the lad only sixteen. Toby would have been scarred worse than he actually was, if it wasn't for the young mistress sending for the doctor and paying for that expensive ointment, which had cost an arm and a leg. He'd put his brother forward for the position of groom, too, thinking another steady wage would help at home, but he'd regretted it ever since. And Toby wasn't the only one who bore marks of the master's temper. Now if it was Golding locked away in the asylum, there'd be plenty cheering their heads off; but no, it was the mistress, and her such a kind lass.

They say the devil looks after his own, Randall thought, squinting his eyes against the bright sunlight, and Golding was living proof of it. Likely he'd live to a ripe old age and die peacefully in his bed, damn his eyes.

He clicked his tongue for the horses to begin trotting, his face as grim as his thoughts. He, for one, lived in hope that the master got his just desserts this side of hell, *and* suffered plenty in the process. Every time he looked at their Toby's scarred face and the patch he wore over his empty eye socket, he prayed it would be so. And he wasn't the only one who wished it so, either, not by a long chalk. As much as the little mistress had been liked, the master was hated and feared. There wouldn't be one person who'd grieve Golding's passing and that was the truth. He'd lost count of the times he'd dreamed about doing him in, but he'd never get away with it, more's the pity. Still, a man could dream, nevertheless.

It was the afternoon of the second day after they had escaped from the asylum. The first day had been spent hiding in woodland not far from Earlswood, not because of Angeline's broken wrist, but due to May spraining her ankle badly when they had climbed up one of the trees whose branches overhung the wall and jumped down the other side onto the grass verge. May had been so intent on helping Angeline, who had found the procedure nigh on impossible with her damaged arm, that she hadn't taken enough care with her own safety. Within minutes her ankle had begun to swell and, after they had crossed the road from the boundary wall and found a gate into a farmer's field, May had had to sit for some time before she could limp on. They had reached the patch of woodland after an agonizing twenty minutes, and by the time it was light May's ankle had swollen to twice its normal size and she couldn't get her boot on.

A pure little stream gurgled through the heart of the woodland and, after slaking their thirst, both girls had sat on its mossy bank, May with her sprained ankle dangling in the icy-cold water and Angeline cradling her broken wrist in its sling. In spite of their precarious situation the knowledge that they were free was heady, and for a long time they simply breathed in the warm, earthy smell and listened to the water splashing over the stones and pebbles. They had dozed the afternoon away before moving under the shelter of a sturdy oak tree, and the night had been relatively warm and quite dry, so they had both slept as well as their injuries permitted.

They had awoken the next morning with the dawn chorus, stiff and sore and ravenously hungry, but the hours of inactivity the day before – along with the benefit of the icy water on May's ankle – meant the swelling had subsided enough for her to force her boot on.

As the sky had lightened they had washed their hands and faces in the stream and had a long drink, before leaving the protection of the woodland and setting off in the direction of Newcastle over the fields. They didn't dare take the easier route by road, where they might have been able to get a lift on the back of a cart, for fear that someone might put two and two together and surmise they were asylum inmates. Consequently the going was slow. May could only hobble a short distance at a time, and the pain in Angeline's arm was excruciating, especially when she stumbled or moved awkwardly on the uneven ground. Nevertheless, their spirits were amazingly high. They were together and they were free, and their liberty was everything.

They hadn't covered half of the distance they had hoped for when, at four o'clock in the afternoon, May finally admitted she couldn't walk any further that day. They were in open pastureland, and Angeline pointed to what looked like an old barn in the corner of a field. 'Can you make it to there? It's shelter of some sort and, once you're settled, I'll see if I can find something to eat.' They were both faint with hunger.

May snorted. 'It's spring, lass, not autumn.'

But as they made their way towards the barn she stopped abruptly. 'Look there.' She pointed down at their feet. Hidden from predatory eyes was a stone curlew's nest, ripe with eggs.

If anyone had told Angeline she would not only eat raw eggs but enjoy them, she wouldn't have believed them, but before they reached the barn they found two more nests containing eggs. She felt sorry for the parent birds, which swooped down close to their heads once or twice, calling their displeasure at the ransacking of their nests, but as May said: needs must. The eggs would barely have made a satisfactory meal for a hungry crow, but it was something in their stomachs after two days without sustenance.

On entering the barn, they found it wasn't as dilapidated as it looked and was clearly used for the storage of hay, a heap of which was stacked in one corner. May's ankle was like a balloon again, and when she finally managed to extricate her foot from her boot it was black and blue.

They made a rough bed with some of the hay and sank down on it, May falling asleep almost immediately despite her hunger. Angeline's wrist felt worse, if anything, and after a while she gave up trying to sleep and went to sit at the entrance to the barn in the evening sunshine.

The old barn adjoined a line of hedgerow dividing one field from the next, and sweet vernal grass and the scent of stitchwort, white dead-nettle, speedwell and other wild flowers hung in the warm, still air. The only sound was the hum of bees searching for nectar in the May blossom of the hedgerow trees, and the twittering of birds. Angeline rested her head against the warm wood of the barn and shut her eyes, drinking in the peace and serenity after the incessant noise and strain of the asylum.

*She would rather die than go back*. She held her wrist against her chest, her head bowed. She couldn't be shut up again and caged like an animal. Nor could she return to being Oswald's wife. From this day forth she had to forget her old life. Not her parents, she added quickly, as though they had heard her thoughts and were hurt by them. Never that. But she had to stand on her own two feet now, for better or worse. She had nothing; even the clothes on her back weren't hers. She was the poorest of the poor.

A little snore from the bed of hay behind her brought her head turning, and she smiled to herself. She *did* have something. She had May. And strangely that took away the fear she might have felt, and brought a sense of – if not excitement, then hopefulness. There was something curiously liberating about having reached rock bottom, which she couldn't have explained, even to herself. She was hungry and tired and in pain, but right at this moment there was nowhere else she would rather be than sitting here in the sunshine in an old barn in the middle of nowhere. She wasn't silly enough to expect this feeling of euphoria to last, but right at this moment it was welcome.

She looked out over the field again, her eyes drawn to the edge of it, where the hundreds of tiny, individual five-petalled flowering clusters of cow parsley whitened the hedgerow in a delicate lace-like mist.

She had told May that if they escaped the asylum, Angeline Golding was dead, but that hadn't happened the night of the fire. It had been happening for a long time – probably since the day of her marriage, but culminating the night her baby had died. The old Angeline had been an innocent, gullible girl, foolish and ridiculously romantic, with her head in the clouds. Her mouth tightened, a hard look coming over her face. She was glad *that* Angeline was dead. She had been weak, and because of her weakness she had only bitter memories to take with her into this new life.

She shut her eyes, letting the sunbeams dance over her face as she slowly relaxed and her breathing became deeper. Within a few minutes she, too, was asleep.

Angeline didn't know what it was that woke her, but when she opened her eyes it was to see a plump middle-aged woman with rosy-red cheeks and jet-black hair pulled tightly into a bun staring at her. May must have roused at the same time, because she heard a movement behind her and her friend saying, 'We're not doing any harm, Missus. We're just resting awhile.'

'You know you're on private farmland?'

'No . . . well, yes, I suppose so, but like I said, we're just resting for a bit before we move on.'

The woman's eyes swept over Angeline's sling and then to May's foot, which had turned all the colours of the rainbow. 'Looks like you two have been in the wars?'

'We had an accident – fell down a bank in the dark. We're . . . we're trying to get to a town or big village to find work. Our da died and it was a tied cottage, so we had to get out.'

'You sisters then?'

May nodded.

'Where's your mam?'

'She died years ago. There was only us and our da.'

Angeline rose to her feet, wincing as the movement hurt her arm. She sensed the woman didn't believe May. 'We're not doing any harm,' she said softly. 'We just wanted to shelter for the night, but we'll move on if you tell us to.'

The woman's eyes narrowed. 'If you're sisters, why don't you talk like her? Come on, I'm not daft and I don't like being lied to. You're an educated lass – a cut above.'

Too late Angeline realized she should have kept quiet. Miss Robson's elocution lessons had rid her of all but the slightest of accents and had given her the diction and pronunciation of a young lady (something her mama, in particular, had been adamant about), but right at this moment it wasn't helpful, to say the least.

'She was sent away to school,' May began, but Angeline gestured for her to be quiet.

'You're right,' she said even more softly. 'We're friends, not sisters.'

'You from that asylum place that caught fire?'

Angeline blinked. She heard May struggle to her feet, but before her friend could deny it, as she was sure May would, she nodded. As the woman took a step backwards, Angeline spoke quickly: 'Neither of us is remotely mad, I promise. I know that's probably what people who are mad *would* say, but it's true. My husband had me locked away so he was free to live his life without the encumbrance of a wife, and May—' She stopped abruptly, not sure if May would want to share her story.

'The son of the house where I worked forced me, and when I said he was the father of the baby I was carrying, the family had me put away,' May finished for her.

'When the fire started, we saw our chance to escape and we took it.' Angeline glanced behind her at May and saw that she looked as frightened as she herself felt. 'You have no idea what it is like to be somewhere like that when you are perfectly sane. It . . . it's beyond words. We'll leave now, this minute, but please don't tell anyone that you've seen us and give us away. People were trapped in the flames and died, and they'll think we're there, under the remains of the building. It's our only hope.'

There was a pause while the woman's gaze moved several times to both faces. Then she said, 'This husband of yours? He sounds a right so-an'-so.'

There was bitterness enough in her tone to convince the most sceptical mind that she was telling the truth when Angeline said, 'He is.'

The woman nodded. 'Gentry, is he? Aye, I thought so. I've no time for the gentry. Come riding over me husband's land on the hunt, all dressed up in their finery, and never mind the crops or anyone who gets in their way. No, I've no time for any of 'em.' Again the keen brown eyes searched their faces, and then the woman smiled. 'You two seem all there to me, and I'm no bad judge. I'll not give you away, don't fret; but perhaps better me husband – he's the farmer, Farmer Burns – don't know you're here. Had a spot of trouble last year with folk stealing the beet and what-have-you, and he's been a mite touchy since then, if you know what I mean. You can sleep here tonight, but just the one night, mind. I want you gone in the morning.'

Angeline inclined her head as she said, 'Thank you, thank you so much. You're very kind.'

'I've been called a lot of things in me time, lass, but rarely kind.' The woman chuckled to herself. 'What have you done to your wrist then? Painful, is it?'

'I've broken it, I think.'

'Broken, you say? Let's have a look, lass. When I was bringing my six lads up there was rarely a few months went by without one of 'em breaking something.' The farmer's wife helped Angeline take her arm out of the sling and then gently felt her wrist. 'Aye, it's broken all right, but it seems a clean break to me. You want me to see to it? I used to sort my lads out myself – them quacks charge a fortune. What about you, dear? Want me to look at your foot?' she added to May, examining her ankle before pronouncing, 'Nowt but a sprain, but they're painful enough. I'll strap that up an' all, when I come back after I've given my lot their dinner. Suppose to be out looking for one of our goats, I am. She's a wanderer, Eliza is. Won't stay with the others and is forever finding a way out of the pen.'

Angeline was feeling giddy, whether from lack of food, the pain in her wrist or simply relief at the way things had turned out she didn't know, but when she said faintly, 'I need to sit down' and slid to the floor with her back against the barn, the farmer's wife looked at her intently.

'When did you two last eat something?'

It was May who said, 'A couple of days ago.'

'I'll see what I can bring later. You're lucky it's a warm May this year. Last year there was snow on the ground even now. Still, every cloud has a silver lining. That's what Farmer Burns always says, and he's rarely wrong.'

With that the little woman bustled off, leaving the two girls staring at each other. May hobbled over to Angeline. 'Do you think we can trust her? Perhaps we should go now? She might bring her husband or one of her lads back with her, or send them to fetch the authorities.'

It was beyond her to go anywhere tonight. Weakly Angeline murmured, 'May, let's take it Mrs Burns is the silver lining in our cloud, all right?'

A soft, scented twilight was falling when the farmer's wife returned carrying an enormous wicker basket. Setting it down next to where Angeline was sitting, Mrs Burns said softly, 'Lass, I won't pretend this isn't going to hurt like the dickens, but it needs to be done, if that wrist is going to heal properly. Now I've got to make sure the two ends of the bone are lined up and then strap your wrist to this splint. All right? I'll be as quick as I can, and your friend will have to help me, cos it'll need two of us.

Then we'll see to your foot,' she added to May, 'and after you can both have a bite and sup tea.'

Afterwards Angeline was glad she hadn't known what was in store. Halfway through the procedure she must have fainted, because when she came round her wrist was bandaged to the wood and May was looking at her with a white face and anxious eyes. Mrs Burns was just tying the knot in her bandage, her voice cheery as she said, 'All done, lass, and it's going to feel better now it's held firm. Here, drink this.' She delved into the basket and brought out a bottle. 'A couple of good swigs will help.'

'What is it?' Angeline said as May helped her to sit up.

'Laudanum. It'll dull the pain and help you sleep, and you'll feel much better in the morning.'

Turning her attention to May, Mrs Burns swiftly and expertly bandaged her ankle before returning to her cavernous basket and bringing out a cloth on which she laid a whole egg-and-ham pie, a crusty loaf and a pat of butter, and a baked jam roll and pot of thick cream. Setting two plates and a handful of cutlery in front of them, she then added a jug with a lid on it, full of tea, saying, 'It's already got milk and sugar in it', and two tin mugs. 'Now, I'll leave you both to get on the other side of that lot, but I'll be back in the morning to see how you're doing. They think I'm collecting the last of the eggs from the hen house, so I'd better get going. Now, now, the pair of you – no blubbering. You get stuck into your grub, all right?'

'I . . . I don't know how to thank you,' Angeline managed through her tears, as May openly sobbed at the side of her. It was the first time she had seen the tough, resilient May cry and it shocked her, although of course it shouldn't, she told herself. May might be made of stern stuff, but she was only human, and the unexpected kindness was overwhelming.

They ate every morsel of food and drank every last drop of the sweet tea, before snuggling down on their hay bed as the moon and stars came out in a velvet-black sky. They were asleep even before they said goodnight to each other.

# *Chapter Twenty*

Mrs Burns was as good as her word. They were still fast asleep when she woke them in the morning. Angeline had stirred once in the middle of the night when something furry had run over her legs. Normally that would have been enough to have her jumping up and screaming, but she was so tired she had merely thought, 'Hope it's a mouse and not a rat' and had gone straight back to sleep.

'Rise and shine!' The farmer's wife stood smiling down at them, basket in hand.

'What time is it?' May murmured sleepily as she sat up, rubbing her eyes and yawning.

'Gone eight, lass. I had to wait till my lot were in from milking and what-have-you, an' had had their breakfasts and gone out again, before I came. Likely one or the other of 'em will be along this way later, so I wouldn't dilly-dally once you've eaten.' She had taken two dishes out of the basket as she'd been speaking, one with several slices of thick ham and a few sausages in it and the other full of scrambled eggs. This time the accompanying jug was full of thick, sweet, milky cocoa. 'How's the wrist?' she asked Angeline as she finished setting out the meal on the cloth. 'Feeling better?'

'Yes, yes, it is. Thank you.' Angeline was staring in wonderment at the food. In spite of the big meal last night she realized she was hungry enough to eat a horse.

'I'm a dab hand at fixing bones, if I do say so myself. Had plenty of practice with my lads. You were lucky it hadn't come through the skin. Always more of a problem when that happens. My Robin nearly lost his arm when it got infected when he was a bairn, but he's six foot three now and got arms on him like a wrestler at the Michaelmas Fair. Now tuck in, the pair of you. I'll wait and take the plates and everything back with me, so no one knows you've been here.'

Mrs Burns continued to chatter non-stop as they devoured the food, telling them all about her lads, the oldest of whom was thirty and the youngest sixteen. The six of them lived at home and worked on the farm with their father, although the eldest two were betrothed to twin sisters and planned to get wed as soon as the cottages they were helping their father build close to the farmhouse were finished. They sounded a happy and contented family, but then – as Angeline remarked to May later – how could they be anything else with someone like Mrs Burns as mother hen?

Once they had cleared every scrap of food Mrs Burns produced an old canvas bag from the basket. 'There's some cheese sandwiches, fruit cake and a bottle of my lemonade in there for the journey,' she said offhandedly, and as they thanked her again she added, 'Don't be daft, it's nowt. A farm can always spare a bit of food.'

'It's the world to us, Mrs Burns.' Angeline swallowed deeply. 'We were at the end of ourselves last night. And it's not just the food – wonderful though that is – but the fact you listened to us and believed us. We'll never forget you, and your boys are very lucky to have you as their mother.'

'Go on with you!' Mrs Burns flapped her hand to hide her pleasure. 'It's little enough, lass; but if we women can't stick together, it's a poor old world. Now, you get on your way and go careful, mind.' She grinned at May. 'No more falling down banks, eh, lass?'

May went red. 'I'm sorry, Mrs Burns. I shouldn't have lied to you. We hurt ourselves getting out of the asylum, as I suppose you've guessed.'

'Aye, I *had* worked that one out for meself, lass. Still, you didn't know me from Adam, and likely I'd have done the same thing in your shoes. It's hard to expect the best from folk when you've been through the mill, like you two.' Her voice losing its briskness, she said softly, 'I'll say a prayer for the pair of you from this day forth and ask the good Lord to bless you.'

Close to tears again, Angeline and May made their goodbyes. Mrs Burns directed them to a narrow bridle path that skirted the farm and wound across countryside towards Newcastle.

They passed the farm's orchard at one point. Pink and

white blossom, snow-like, loaded the boughs of apple and cherry trees and they stood for a moment gazing over the old dry-stone wall, just drinking in the scene. A dizzy fragrance wafted over them on the warm breeze and the glinting bright blossom was a firm promise of the rich harvest to follow. The farm seemed another world from the one they had been forced to inhabit.

More to herself than to May, Angeline murmured, '*This* is real, the flowers and the birds and the trees. You can trust this. This doesn't lie.'

It didn't really make sense, but May must have known exactly what she meant. She put her arm round Angeline for a moment, nodding as she said, 'The world would be a grand place without people in it. But we can trust each other, lass. That is a certainty for the rest of our lives, come thick or thin.'

They smiled at each other, a smile of perfect understanding.

'I wish Verity was standing here with us now. If there was any justice, she would be,' Angeline said. If Verity hadn't introduced her to May, May would never have come looking for her. Verity had been the connection that had brought them together. She doubted she would even have spoken to May, without Verity introducing them.

'I know. But it was impossible. I think the fire must have started close to the seclusion rooms, because everything was blazing when I reached there. It was like a furnace.'

Angeline remembered the woman who had come stumbling towards them, a ball of fire, and shuddered. It seemed impossible right at this moment, with the blossom typifying the beauty of England – a season her mama had always declared her favourite of the year – that such horror had happened. And even now, right up and down the length and breadth of the land, there were men and women interned in places like Earlswood who were like Verity and May and her – not mad at all, but rather an inconvenience to someone close to them, someone more cunning or powerful than they.

Angeline shivered in spite of the warmth of the spring morning. 'We've some way to go before nightfall. Let's move on.'

They ate their lunch in the greenest of dells, beech trees unfolding their soft, silky leaves on boughs that stooped so low they were almost lost beneath the sea of bluebells. Immediately they had sat down on the grass May took the boot off her injured foot, and once again the walking had made it swell, despite Mrs Burns's bandage. Angeline's arm was throbbing, but felt much better with the support of the splint. Looking at the lines of pain at the sides of May's mouth, she said, 'We can rest for a few hours – even until tomorrow morning.'

'No.' As soon as she had eaten, May forced her boot on again. 'I could be wrong, but I think the sky's beginning to cloud over. Best we keep moving.'

May wasn't wrong. By the time they reached the

well-to-do sprawling outskirts of Newcastle later that afternoon, a fine and misty but penetrating drizzle meant they were soaked through. It had turned colder, too, with a biting wind that chilled to the bone. Jesmond was a prosperous suburb situated in the area to the north of Sandyford Road and east of the North Road, and in spite of being born and raised in the town, May had never been in this part of Newcastle where the wealthy and influential could afford to live, far away from the festering slums. Before she had gone into service May had lived in the tenements on the north side of the Tyne, close to the quayside in Sandhill. The bridges high over the gorge meant that Sandhill and Pipewellgate and other slums had not been cleared by railway development, as in some other towns. Squalor and disease had been May's childhood companions, and the proximity of the slaughterhouses was another continuing health hazard. Six of May's siblings had been buried before they had reached the age of one.

They passed large, gracious terraces and grandiose detached houses set in their own grounds, and although May hobbled along without seeming to be affected by her surroundings, for Angeline it was a strange experience. She was wet and grubby and dressed – if not in rags – in clothes even one of their servants at home would not have worn. Her boots had caused large blisters on both her heels, and beneath her frock and rough petticoat she wore no underwear, no drawers or stockings. For the first time she really became aware that she was one of the destitute, a nothing, a nonentity, less than the muck under the fine shoes of the inhabitants of these roads they were walking along. Between Clayton Road and Jesmond Road a large carriage pulled by two magnificent chestnuts passed them, its wheels sending a spray of filthy water arcing into the air, which covered them from head to foot, but the driver didn't even turn his head to look at them. It was as though they were invisible, Angeline thought as she bowed her head, and for the life of her she didn't know whether to be glad or angry. Maybe she was feeling both.

They hadn't gone very much further when May stopped, brushing her wet hair out of her eyes. 'I'm sorry, lass, but I don't think I can make it to our Jack's place tonight.'

Angeline nodded. When she'd last glimpsed May's ankle the flesh was bulging over the top of her boot and it was clear her friend was in a lot of pain. 'Don't worry, we'll find somewhere to shelter. You'll feel better in the morning.' In truth, she didn't know how they would fare when they did reach May's brother's house. Apparently he rented a room in a house in the warren of streets close to the wharfs, not far from where May's family still lived, but May had made it quite clear they couldn't ask her parents for help. 'Me da didn't lift a finger when they had me put away,' she'd said the night before, when they were discussing what to do. 'In fact I reckon the family I worked for saw to it he was paid off not to make a fuss. He's a swine and Mam's not much better. Apart from me an' Jack, there's Andrew and Reg, and they both ran away to sea as soon as they were able, and three little ones still stuck at home, poor little blighters. He'll be leading them a hell of a life, for sure.'

May's face was white and pinched and she had lost her usual bravado, and just how wretched she was feeling was highlighted when she murmured, 'I'm sorry, lass. At least you were dry and well fed in the asylum. I don't know how we're going to manage—'

'Stop it!' Angeline put her arm round May's waist as she spoke. 'I'd rather starve than be back there, and so would you. We're going to be fine.' There was a park to the left of them opposite the row of terraced houses on the other side of the road, and now she led May into it, saying, 'Come and find a bench and sit for a minute.'

It was a very neat and manicured park, as befitted this superior part of the town, but due to the inclement weather they were the only ones around, and to Angeline's delight she saw a bandstand in the middle of the lawned area surrounded by flowerbeds. After helping May up the steps they found it to be relatively dry, the small wooden walls providing some protection to about four feet high, although from that point up to the fancy wooden roof it was open to the elements. On the far side of the park there looked to be a cemetery stretching away as far as the eye could see, but at least no one from there was going to bother them, as Angeline said with ghoulish humour.

May managed a weak smile. It took her a few seconds

to ease her boot off her swollen foot, but when she did both girls stared in dismay. Not only was her ankle black and blue, but it was so distended the skin was stretched tight and was very inflamed. Angeline wondered if Mrs Burns's diagnosis had been wrong. Maybe the ankle was broken after all.

Huddling together for warmth, they spent a damp, cold, uncomfortable night in the dubious shelter of the grandstand, dozing now and again but not really sleeping, and longing for the warm bed of straw in the barn and for Mrs Burns's hot milky cocoa. But not once did Angeline wish herself back in the asylum. She had meant what she'd said to May: she would rather starve to death than be transported back to Earlswood. Her wrist was paining her, she was hungry and chilled to the bone, and had no idea what the next day would hold, which made her stomach churn as much as the hunger. But she was alive and she was free. It was enough. No – not enough, she corrected herself in the next moment. It was everything.

At some point in the night it stopped raining and by the time a weak, watery dawn began to make inroads into the dark sky it was clear May was going nowhere. There was no chance of pushing her bloated foot into her boot, for one thing, and even if that had been possible she wouldn't have been able to walk more than a few steps. As the birds began to sing in the trees surrounding the park and the sky lightened to a rain-washed blue and the sun came out, Angeline made a decision.

'Give me Jack's address and I'll go and at least leave a message with someone, if he's at work, before I come back here and we decide what we're going to do. You can't walk on that foot today, May. Look at it.'

'But your arm . . . '

'I don't walk on my arm.' Angeline smiled, although in truth the thought of trying to find May's brother by herself was terrifying. At home she had never stepped out of the house without a chaperone in the person of her mother or Miss Robson, and since her marriage Myrtle had been at her side even when Oswald was absent. You told the coachman your destination and then settled back and waited to arrive – it was as simple as that – and young ladies *never* ventured out unescorted.

But she wasn't a young lady now, Angeline told herself. She was one of the faceless poor, a nothing, a nobody; and in that lay her protection against Oswald finding her, even if he suspected that she hadn't died in the fire.

'Lass . . . ' May's voice was hesitant. 'You're not used to what it's like – where I come from, I mean. It's rough and ready enough in the centre of town, but down by the riverside it's worse. There's good folk there an' all, don't get me wrong, but there's plenty of the other sort alongside them. You . . . well, you'll stand out like a sore thumb, if you don't mind me saying so.'

'Not unless I open my mouth, like I did with Mrs Burns, and I'll try not to do that unless I have to. I'll be all right, May. I mean, look at me. No one is going to think I'm anything but dirt-poor, not dressed like this.'

'Aye, but . . . '

'What?'

May didn't know how to put it. She didn't want to frighten Angeline, but how could she warn her that someone as bonny as Angeline would be eaten alive if she wasn't well versed in the ways of the world? And her friend was anything but that, in spite of what she'd been through with that swine of a husband. There were always men looking for new flesh for the whore-markets that littered the docks, and they had plenty of ways of luring a lass to her doom. Then there were the sailors and other ne'er-do-wells, who would think nothing of pulling a young lass on her own into a doorway or down an alley and having their way. You had to appear as tough as old boots to be safe, and before she'd gone into service May had thought nothing of carrying a knife to show she meant that No was No, if she was out after dark.

Weakly she said, 'There's always men who try it on, lass, and you're not used to that. Better we stick together.'

'I know that would be best, but it's not possible. You need to rest your ankle, but it might be days before you can walk. I have to try and see if your brother can help. If not . . . Well, we'll face that together. I'll be as quick as I can, but I have to go.'

May nodded, still clearly unhappy. 'His name's Jack Connor, and the last time he came to see me at the asylum he was living in a house in King Street, but that was months ago. He might have moved, for all I know. He's pulled himself up by his boot-laces, has our Jack,' she added with some pride. 'He's always been a one for learning and books, despite our da trying to knock it out of him and make him work in the docks, and he got himself taken on as a clerk in a solicitor's office last year.' Then, as a thought occurred, she said quickly, 'If you do see him, perhaps better not say who you really are, lass. Or that we've skedaddled from the asylum. Him being on the side of the law, so to speak, he might not see it like we do.'

Angeline stared at May. 'What *shall* I say, then?'

'We can say we met at the asylum, which is true enough, but that we got released on the same day. He might not know about the fire, but if he does we'll make out that it must have happened after we'd been let out. You was in the pauper ward, same as me, and you were in because . . . ' May wrinkled her brow for some moments. 'Because the family you worked for as a governess to the bairns said you were stealing, but you maintained it was the daughter of one of the mother's friends, because you'd seen her at it. We had a lass in the ward for that reason – Grace her name was. Grace Cunningham. That's who you are. Grace had educated herself and learned to talk proper, so she could rise in the world. Poor lass,' she added. 'She topped herself one night in the privy. Hanged herself with her own nightdress that she'd torn into strips.'

Angeline's eyes widened in horror. 'And that's who I am?'

May nodded. 'She was nice enough,' she said, as though that made it acceptable. 'And bonny. And it explains the way you talk. Jack's got no time for the gentry, that's the thing. The reason he wants to become a solicitor is to fight for the poor in the courts an' such. Goes on about it for hours, if you let him. Tell him we've been working in an inn for a while, but there was a fight between some of the customers and we got hurt. That's when we decided to get out and come back to Newcastle.'

Angeline shook her head. 'I'm not much good at lying.'

'In this case it's necessary, lass.'

'But what if the authorities write to your parents to tell them you're presumed dead?'

'They won't. It was the family I worked for who had me admitted. They might let them know, but they won't care. And even if they did write to my parents, neither of them can read. It'll be all right – just do as I say.'

Suddenly everything seemed a lot more complicated, but Angeline could see that May was right.

'Now,' May went on, 'keep walking south for a couple of miles and you'll come to Melbourne Street, with Manors station. The prison is a stone's throw from there, so you'll know you're on the right track. Make for the river; it's no good me telling you the names of the roads cos you won't remember them all, but just keep going south and you'll come to the river and the wharfs. Walk along by the side of them till you come to King Street. If you come to Aberdeen Wharf you've gone too far. Can you remember all that?'

Angeline nodded. She couldn't speak just at that moment for the fear that had gripped her.

'You'll be all right, lass.' Suddenly realizing she hadn't exactly been encouraging, May's voice was over-hearty. 'Just keep your eyes and ears open, and don't panic. All Saints' Church isn't far from King Street. If you get lost before you get to the wharfs, ask someone where that is – but a woman, mind; not a man. And don't answer any questions. Act simple, if you have to.'

May continued in this vein for some minutes, and by the time Angeline left the bandstand her brain was whirling. As she exited the park she looked back to see May standing up and holding on to the edge of the bandstand as she waved forlornly. Angeline waved back, but was glad when trees hid May from view. Her friend had sapped what little courage she had with all her instructions and dos and don'ts.

On leaving the area she found a sign that read 'Portland Park' and the road she was walking down was Portland Terrace, so at least she would know where to aim for, on the return journey. Before long the grander houses had vanished and she found herself in a grid of terraced streets that all looked the same. But the sun had come out and although the blisters on her heels had opened up again, she felt better for *doing* something. There were fewer people about than she had expected, and after a while the church bells told her why. It was a Sunday. And before long she passed a Church of England church where men dressed in their Sunday best and women in neat, dark dresses and bonnets were filing in. A little later it was a chapel, and here the bonnets of the ladies weren't nearly so fine, but their prim faces and subdued manner were the same. Few folk spared her a glance, but when they did it was invariably a man and, remembering what May had said, she found herself walking faster on those occasions.

After an hour or so of following her nose without really knowing where she was going, she saw two girls, arm-in-arm, coming towards her. They were giggling and deep in conversation, dressed in rough serge skirts with woollen shawls about their shoulders, but they looked friendly enough. When she was abreast she nerved herself to say, 'Can you direct me to Manors station?'

They stopped dead, their faces expressing their surprise as they looked her up and down, no doubt thinking her voice didn't match her appearance. It was a moment before one said, her accent denoting that she was Irish, 'Manors station you want, lass? Well, you're not too far off. Keep straight on at the crossroads into Argyle Street and you'll come to it, so you will. You not from round these parts?'

Angeline shook her head. 'I'm . . . I'm from the country.'

'Oh aye?' They nodded, but Angeline walked on,

willing herself not to hurry. She heard one say something to the other and then laughter, but she didn't turn round, and it wasn't until she was a good distance from them that she stopped. The blisters the boots had rubbed on her heels were raw and bleeding, but she had noticed neither of the girls was wearing anything on her feet. Stepping out of the boots, she picked them up by their laces with her 'good' hand and began walking again. The relief was magical – beyond words – and suddenly the day got a whole lot better.

She came to the crossroads and then Argyle Street, and eventually, joy of joys, Melbourne Street and Manors station.

The nearer she got to the waterfront, however, the more uneasy she felt. There seemed to be a public house every few yards, and after a while she put her boots back on, painful though it was, because of the muck and running filth in the roads. And the smell; she had no name for it, having never smelt the odour of extreme squalor and overcrowding and stinking privies before, coupled with the ever-present stench of the slaughterhouses.

Mindful of all May had said, she kept her head up but her eyes straight ahead as she walked, but she was aware of women standing on their doorsteps talking to neighbours while their children, some too young to walk, played or crawled in the gutters and on the filthy pavements. Appalled by the dirt and the stench, she tried to keep her face blank, but it was hard, especially when she saw a dead cat slowly decaying and alive with maggots just yards from where a bare-bottomed, curly-haired infant sat sucking her thumb, big sores on either side of her rosebud mouth.

Terrified, she found she was praying silently now as she walked along the wharfs, just one refrain: 'Help me, God; help me, God; help me, God.' Twice, a man bumped into her – one leaving a public house and, a few yards on, one entering – and on both occasions she felt it wasn't an accident by their leering faces, but she didn't acknowledge them or slow her pace, hearing one laugh as she marched on.

She was picking her way along the rough cobbles by the side of the tracks on which the engines shunted the wagons to unload the boats that moored at the wharfs, but as it was a Sunday the river was quiet. Just after she passed a landing stage, which was floating in the grimy black water, she came to the bottom of King Street and could have cried with relief, although the street looked as bad as any she had passed. The sunshine had brought out the bairns and there were plenty of them playing their games up and down the mucky, slimy cobbled road.

May hadn't known the number of the house where her brother lodged, so a few yards into the street Angeline stopped in front of two young girls sitting on the pavement with their backs to the grey tenement wall. They were nursing their dollies – two lumps of wood with faces carved on them – which they had wrapped in bits of rag. A little further on a group of children were skipping with a piece of old rope, their voices chanting:

'House to let, apply within
Lady put out for drinking gin
Gin, you know, is a very bad thing
So Jeannie goes out and Mary comes in.'

Bringing her attention back to the two in front of her, Angeline bent down, saying quietly, 'Do you know where Jack Connor lives?'

They shook their heads, their hair white with nits, but a young lad of eight or nine who was leaning against the wall a couple of feet away said, 'Yes, you do. She means the penny-a-liner.' And to Angeline: 'We call him that cos he can read an' write, an' if anyone needs a letter writin' or somethin' reading, they come to Jack. He's got a room in that house there.'

Angeline nodded and smiled. 'Thank you.'

'Come on, I'll show you.' And with that the boy turned and ran to a house a few doors away. The front door was open, and Angeline followed her little guide into a squalid hall and up the bare wooden stairs of the three-storey building to the second floor. The lad rapped on a door at the end of the landing. 'Jack? There's some-one wants to talk to you. A lass.'

He knocked again a few moments later, and when Angeline murmured, 'Perhaps he's not in?' he grinned at her, revealing brown-stained teeth.

'I ain't seen him go out, so he's likely abed. Works six days a week in town, an' then he's always at his books an' such till the early hours, is Jack. Barmy 'bout learning, he is.' Lowering his voice, he added, 'He's teachin' me to read an' write' as though there was something shameful about it.

'Don't you learn that at school?'

The boy stared at her as though she was from another planet. 'I ain't never been to school. I help me da at the docks. I'm a runner. Best runner there is.'

'I see.' She didn't have a clue what he meant.

'Me da's not for learnin',' the boy went on. 'Says it only gets you into trouble with the gaffers.'

'But you want to read and write?'

The boy shrugged. 'I want to be like Jack,' he said, as though that was the end of the matter.

Angeline heard a bolt being slid from inside the door and the next moment it had opened. A man stood there, naked to the waist and obviously just having got out of bed, his black hair ruffled and with stubble on his chin. His eyes were as green as May's and shaded by thick curling lashes, and his rough-hewn face wasn't smiling.

Angeline stared at him, shock curling in her stomach. She had never been in the presence of such raw masculinity before. Oswald had been handsome, even beautiful, but also graceful and elegant and charming. This man was clearly none of those things. The picture she had formed in her mind of May's brother had been of a scholarly, mild schoolmaster type, small in stature; an earnest intellectual whose books were his passion. Nothing had prepared her for the real Jack Connor.

He looked her up and down in a way that caused her

breathing to quicken and her cheeks to flush, and although she knew she ought to say something it was beyond her.

It was Jack who spoke first, his deep voice having an edge of huskiness, which again caused her stomach to flutter: 'Aye, and what can I do for you, my bonny lass?' And to the boy: 'All right, Joe, you scarper now', softening his words by fetching a penny out of his pocket and throwing it to the lad, who caught it deftly and pocketed it in an instant.

As Joe disappeared down the stairs, Angeline felt panic grip her, before she pulled herself together. 'I'm a friend of May's. We . . . she . . . We need your help.'

His face expressed the same surprise that the two girls on the road earlier had shown, but he recovered instantly, opening the door wider and standing back as he said, 'You'd better come in then and tell me all about it.'

# *Chapter Twenty-One*

Jack Connor prided himself on the fact that nothing in life surprised him. Having been reared in the tenement slums of Newcastle, he'd seen life in all its raw vulgarity from a babe at his mother's breast. A violent, drunken father and a mother who was only interested in avoiding her husband's fists had set the course of his childhood. Three brothers and a sister born after him had died through disease and neglect, and twin sisters had gone the same way before he was born. His two older brothers had been his rough childhood companions before they ran away to sea when he was eight years old.

May had been born when he was six, and from the first he had loved his baby sister, protecting her from the worst of their father's rages as she'd grown and making sure she got enough to eat, even if it meant going without himself.

May had left to go into service when she was twelve years old, and the same day he had walked out of the family home and into lodgings, knowing it was the time to follow his dream. His father had had him set on at the docks when he was eleven years old, but although his schooldays had been cut short, they'd planted in him a voracious desire for education. For the next five years he had worked at the docks during the day and studied at night, spending all his money on books and bettering himself. And finally, two years ago, a solicitor in the town had agreed to take him on as a clerk. It was the first rung of the ladder to becoming a solicitor.

He occasionally called in on his mother and the three boys who had come along after May, but in truth he had little time for his younger brothers, all of whom bore a marked resemblance to their father in looks and nature. May was different, and when he'd found out she had been raped and then cast into the asylum he'd been beside himself, especially when he had been able to do nothing to secure her release. Each time he had visited her he had told her he was working towards the day when he was qualified and could fight to get her out of the place, but they had both known that day was a long way off.

But now this young woman with the cultured voice, but who was dressed in little more than rags, was telling him May was free. He only had one chair and a small table in his room besides his bed, so he had directed her to the chair while he sat on the bed as she told her story. He stared at her, taking in her face, as her soft, pleasant voice flowed over him. She was a beautiful lass; even her nose, which had clearly been broken at some time or other, didn't detract from her beauty, but rather gave a uniqueness to her looks that was captivating. Her liquid brown eyes, under eyebrows that curved well beyond the bone formation of the eye sockets, constantly fell away from his, as though she was shy or frightened, or both. He had pulled on a shirt before he sat down, sensing that his bare torso had startled her, but she still was as jumpy as a cat on a hot tin roof.

His gaze moved to her hair, secured in a long plait at the nape of her neck, but even that couldn't hide that it was amazing. It wasn't brown or red or bronze, but a mixture of all three, and thick and silky, the tiny tendrils that drifted round skin like blushed milk curling in wispy ringlets.

The last two years had trained him to take in everything about people – their body language, appearance, inflections of voice – whilst ingesting every word they spoke. Mr Havelock had told him more than once it was one of Jack's strengths, added to the sixth sense that every good solicitor needed to cultivate, which told them if a man or woman was telling the truth – or, at the very least, the whole story. But somehow, with this young woman, and to his great surprise, Jack only felt confusion. Added to which he was very aware of his dishevelled appearance, which annoyed him. He should be feeling only relief that May was free and concern that she was injured, but instead a whole host of emotions were in play.

As Angeline finished speaking he leaned forward and

said, 'So May's waiting at Portland Park?' and was further annoyed at the slight recoil she made, before she collected herself. 'And you have nothing, you say? Not a penny between you, and merely the clothes you stand up in? Why didn't you take your things with you when you left the inn where you were working?'

Angeline had never felt more ill at ease in her life than now, lying to this man who was May's brother. 'We did, but they were stolen one night.'

Jack nodded. It happened. Softly he said, 'Is your arm very painful?'

'Not since it was strapped up.'

'Good.' Standing up, he pulled on his cap and jacket. She had explained about the elocution lessons, but he was finding that the way she spoke made him feel . . . he wouldn't allow himself to think 'inferior', instead substituting 'uncomfortable'. 'Make yourself a drink' – he waved to the small kettle on a steel shelf over the hot coals that the tiny fireplace held – 'there's tea and sugar on the shelf, but no milk I'm afraid. I'll get something to eat for the three of us after I've got May home.'

'But don't you want me to come with you?'

'Not necessary. I know where the park is.'

'Very well.' Angeline inclined her head. 'If you are sure.'

There it was again. It wasn't just her voice – it was her manner, too. Not exactly uppish, more . . . He found he couldn't put his finger on what it was, which again irritated him.

Once May's brother had gone, Angeline sat exactly where she was for some minutes. She felt as though she had come through a great trial, which was ridiculous really, when she had only found her way to this house. But that was how she felt. The reaction had her wanting to drift off to sleep where she sat, but after a while she kicked off her boots and made herself a cup of tea. It was the first drink she had made in her life, and she had no idea how much tea to put in the mug sitting next to the little tea caddy. Consequently it was very weak, but in view of the fact there was no milk, it was better than being too strong.

She sipped the tea, wondering how many books Jack had altogether. Books were piled high against every wall, the old bookcase along one wall long since having been overwhelmed. They were stacked under the one window the room boasted, and then on the windowsill itself, to halfway up the glass. So the room was darker than it might have been. Volume upon volume stood on the table itself, along with reams of handwritten notes and other papers. She reached over and picked up one of the handwritten pages, entitled 'The evil of unregulated capitalism and landlordism'.

Another wad of papers bound together had a front page that read:

> Henry Broadhurst, secretary of the TUC Parliamentary Committee, speaking at the Trades Union Congress, 1877: 'They [the men] had the future of their country

> and their children to consider, and it was their duty as men and husbands to use their utmost efforts to bring about a condition of things, where their wives would be in their proper sphere at home, instead of being dragged into competition for livelihood against the great and strong men of the world.' Discuss the merits of this statement, and the woman-question in general.

Intrigued now, the tiredness slipping from her, Angeline reached for another stack of papers tied with string. It was entitled: 'The condition of the people and the Education Act of 1870':

> This was not an Act for a common universal education, but an Act to educate the lower classes for employment on lower-class lines, and with specially trained, inferior teachers who had no universal quality. Elementary education is not a stage in the educational process, but a minimal education for those who cannot afford to pay for something better. Examine the system and the changes from then to now, and discuss.

Suddenly realizing that these papers might be private, and that May's brother might not like her going through them, Angeline put them down as though they had burned her. Walking over to the bookcase, she glanced at some of the titles: *How the Poor Live* by G.R. Sims; *All Sorts and Conditions of Men* by Walter Besant; *Struggles for Daily Bread* by Richard Rowe – the books went on and on, but she could see few novels or poetry books.

Thoroughly intimidated now, she sat down again at the table. When May had said that her brother had no time for the gentry, she hadn't said the half of it. What would Jack say, if he knew who she really was? He would despise her, that much was crystal-clear. And he would probably be right to do so. How could landowners and the aristocracy ignore what was right under their noses? But then, she had.

She bit on her lower lip, feeling wretched. She was weary and at this moment there was no fight in her. Shutting her eyes, she let the heavy mantle of sleep slip over her.

Jack walked to Portland Park, but after an emotional reunion with May, he flagged down a horse-drawn cab for the return journey. It being a Sunday, the tram service was limited. They were on their way when he said casually, 'And this Grace? What do you know about her?'

'All I need to know. She's been a good pal to me, Jack. The best. Somewhere like Earlswood has a way of bringing out the real worth of a person, believe me, and Grace is a diamond.'

'She's certainly done a good job convincing you.' A corner of his lips was pulled up in a one-sided smile.

May shot him a keen look. 'Don't you like her?'

'Don't be daft, I don't know the lass.'

'Well, I do. She's been through a lot and she's inclined

to keep herself to herself, and who can blame her? But we've both decided the past is the past, and we're not going to dwell on it. The future is what matters now.'

'Is that a sisterly way of telling me to keep me trap shut and mind my own business?'

May grinned. 'If the cap fits . . . '

'Aye, all right, I get the message. She's a saint, and I won't do anything to upset her. Now what about Mam an' Da? You want them to know you're back?'

Now May's voice was bitter as she said, 'I don't want to see them again for the rest of my life. If they'd stood by me, the Franklins wouldn't have dared put me in that place.'

'So it's you an' me an' St Grace?'

'Don't call her that. Jack, I know you're in one room, but if we could just stay till we get work and can rent a room ourselves? Please? It'll only be for a few days, till I can walk on this ankle and—'

'Lass, you don't have to beg. There's not enough room to swing a cat, but we'll manage. There's five of 'em living in the room next door, poor devils. What's your pal going to think about it, though?'

'She'll be grateful, same as me.'

'If you say so.'

'Thanks, Jack. I don't know what I'd have done without you.'

'Lass, it's eaten me up inside, knowing you were in that place and what he'd done to you. I'd have given ten years of my life for five minutes alone with that Franklin swine. I found their estate, you know – Hexham way, isn't it? Waited about all one Sunday and caught one of the housemaids going back after her day off. Got her talking, made out I was interested in seeing her again, and she told me the son of the family had just got married and was on his honeymoon in Europe. Doing the tour, she said, and wouldn't be back for months. First and last time in my life I'd carried a knife when I went there that day.'

'Oh, Jack.' May stared at him, horrified. 'You wouldn't have?'

'Do you know, lass, I would have. If I'd seen him that day I would have – and gone down the line for it. It would have been worth it.'

'No, no, it wouldn't.' May took his hand, pressing it to her face. 'How can you say that? You've always said the way to fight injustice and oppression is in the courts, to get laws changed and men in government who are for the ordinary people. You said—'

'I said a sight too much, May, standing on my lofty ideals and preaching from my soapbox. It's different when one of your own is treated with less consideration than their damned dogs and horses. Perhaps I needed to learn that. Not that I don't still hold with doing it legal, like, but action's needed sometimes, too. I can understand how a man can get so angry and frustrated that he can do murder now. I couldn't before.'

'But murder – violence can never be right, Jack.'

'I didn't say it was right, lass. I said I understand it. Now, now, don't look like that. I haven't done anything rash, like following the swine to Europe, now have I?'

'It's not funny, Jack.'

'Believe me, I'm not laughing. Nothing about Franklin and the rest of his kind makes me laugh.'

May said nothing, resting her head on his shoulder as the coach rumbled on. Jack was her big brother and the one person she loved in all the world, and she had never kept anything from him before. But it had been right to hide who Angeline really was. She had felt bad about it all morning; she still did in a way, but Jack was so very black-and-white about some things. Angeline belonged to the enemy camp, in his opinion, and nothing she could do or say would change that. And her first loyalty was to her friend. Jack wouldn't understand that. She wasn't sure if she understood it herself, but what she and Angeline had been through together – the asylum, Verity, their support of each other, and especially the last few days of escaping and tramping the roads – had forged a bond that was stronger even than her love for her brother. With each of her younger siblings she had longed for a sister. Now she had one.

Jack unknowingly heaped coals of fire on her head when in the next moment he murmured, 'Now don't worry, lass. You're home, that's the main thing. An' you're right, the past is the past, and it's the future that counts. If you can look at it like that, after all you've been through, I'm damn sure I can. I'll nip to the pie shop and get the three of us something to eat once we're back, an' ask if they know of any rooms coming up round about.'

'We've no money, Jack.'

'I've got enough to tide you over, till the pair of you are back on your feet and working.'

'We'll pay you back every penny, I swear it.'

Jack's big hand covered hers. 'Don't be daft – you're my sister. I don't want paying back.'

'Nevertheless, we will.'

'We'll see.'

If anyone had told May that she would look fondly on the docks and the filthy streets of her childhood, she would have laughed in their face. But as Jack lifted her out of the cab after paying the driver, she had a lump in her throat. She was home. She was safe. Even the rank smell permeating the air was comforting, and infinitely preferable to the odour of the lunatic asylum.

They had taken two years of her life in that terrible place, but she could begin again, she told herself as they entered the house and Jack carried her up the stairs in his arms. And as he fumbled with the door and it swung open and she caught sight of Angeline, fast asleep at the table with her head resting on her arms, she thought: *we* can begin again. Angeline was the sister she'd never had and they were in this together now, for good or ill.

Angeline opened her eyes, a look of relief on her face as she said, 'Oh, he's got you, thank God!' And as she jumped up and touched May's arm, May put her arm round Angeline's shoulders, drawing her close, and just for a moment the three of them were joined, their heads together and their bodies close.

# PART FIVE

## *Though the Mills of God Grind Slowly*

## 1900

Though the mills of God grind slowly,
Yet they grind exceeding small;
Though with patience He stands waiting,
With exactness grinds He all.

HENRY WADSWORTH LONGFELLOW,
'Retribution'

## *Chapter Twenty-Two*

In the seven years that had passed since the day Angeline had arrived on Jack's doorstep, she had changed beyond recognition. Not in her appearance; although she had matured into a poised, reserved young woman, her beauty was still as fresh and radiant as the day she had stepped into King Street. It was in her self-confidence and capability that the real change had taken place. She was now twenty-five years old, and her new life had given her self-respect as she had learned to stand on her own two feet. Whenever she thought about the old Angeline, it was with a feeling of pity for the childlike, ingenuous girl who had married Oswald so trustingly and been so ill-used. The new Angeline – or Grace, as she was known to everyone – was a different creature altogether. And if she sometimes felt a pang of regret that the sweet, naive girl had metamorphosed into a woman who was wary and guarded and who kept folk at arm's length, it was gone in an instant. Only May knew her secret, and that was the way it had to remain. And she was content in her new life – or she would have been, but for the ever-present ache in her heart concerning Jack Connor.

She glanced over at him now, sitting by the fire on the other side of the sitting room with May. The new century had been rung in the night before, amongst much celebrating; and today, the first one of the new year, most people had a thick head and were feeling the worse for wear. Her gaze lingered on Jack before moving round the room, and as always she felt a little thrill of pleasure that this was her home and she had the key to her own front door. It hadn't always been that way.

On their escape from the asylum she and May had spent a few days with Jack, but as it had meant Jack sleeping on the floor and she and May sharing his single bed, it had been a relief for all three when a room in a neighbouring house had become available. The previous residents, an Irish couple with a young baby, had been clean and respectable, and as they were going back to Ireland to be with family, Jack had bought the three-quarter-sized bed and two small armchairs the room had held, along with a kettle and a few pots and pans.

May's ankle had healed within a couple of weeks and she had got work in a rope- and wire-making factory on the other side of the river. Jack hadn't been too pleased – the women from this particular workplace were notorious for their foul language, which was worse than any sailor's – but, as May had commented, a job was a job, and beggars can't be choosers. It had been nearly two months before Angeline could use her arm, and as May's weekly wage of five shillings a week barely covered the one-and-sixpence rent and their food, she had been anxious to get work, although secretly terrified at the prospect.

May had flatly refused letting Angeline try for a job at the rope factory – 'They'll rip you apart, lass, the way you speak an' all. Anyone a bit different an' they're on them like a pack of dogs' – and so they had decided on shop work. They had borrowed four shillings off Jack and kitted Angeline out at the second-hand clothes market near Castle Square with a matching dress and coat and a pair of shoes. May had gazed at her in admiration. 'By, lass, you look the ticket, you do straight. An' the way you talk could work wonders in the right job. You ought to aim high.'

Aiming high had meant applying for a job in a draper's establishment, one of a row of shops in the centre of town near Ginnett's Amphitheatre off Northumberland Road. She had walked in on the morning of her interview, looked at the other girls waiting in the small room at the back of the shop and nearly walked straight out again. When she had left the premises an hour later, she'd got the job. As the slim, elegant manageress had confided some months later, 'As soon as you opened your mouth, it was yours, Grace. Adds a bit of class to the shop.'

Her starting wage of four shillings a week rose to seven once she was trained, and she and May didn't spend anything on themselves until they had reimbursed

Jack fully for every penny he had laid out since the day they had arrived in Newcastle.

The shop hours were long – from eight in the morning until eight at night, six days a week – but Angeline loved every minute. The shop prided itself on selling the latest fashions, but at a much cheaper price than the exclusive establishments that the gentry patronized. The women who frequented it tended to be the wives and daughters of white-collar workers, or other shop owners and the like.

Angeline had been at the draper's for just over a year when she and May had moved into the downstairs of a house a short distance away in Dean Street, further from the wharfs. Here they had a front room, which they used as their bedroom, and a kitchen with a range and room for a table and chairs and two armchairs. A pair of spinster sisters occupied the top floor of the two-up, two-down terrace; quiet, clean women who worked at a laundry in the town. It was bliss after being confined to one room and having to share a privy with the other tenants of the house, who hadn't been too particular in their habits. Now the privy in the small back yard was kept fresh and sweet with daily buckets of ash by the four women, and the days of clearing up other folk's excreta – including vomit on a Friday night when the men got paid – became a thing of the past. King Street had been a harsh baptism into her new life, but it had taught Angeline plenty.

Shortly after she and May had settled into their new

home, Angeline had heard that the shop next door to the draper's, a bakery, would soon require another assistant, when one of the two girls employed by the baker and his wife left to get married. After putting in a good word for May with the baker's wife, with whom she often passed the time of day when buying her daily loaf, Angeline persuaded her friend to go and make herself known to the couple. The result was that May was offered the position and started work at the bakery the day after the other girl left. The rope factory had been hard, rough and exhausting work, and the women workers who did the same job as the men got paid half the wage of their male counterparts, something that had always rankled with May, although most of the other women seemed to accept it as natural.

The bakery didn't pay as much as May could earn in the factory, but Angeline had recently had a rise at work, which covered the shortfall, besides which she desperately wanted to see May leave the factory behind. Even after a year May's hands had been raw and bleeding at the end of each six-day week, and her friend had slept each Sunday away in an exhausted stupor.

There had followed a period of calm routine, and after the events of the previous years their run-of-the-mill days and nights had been pleasant and welcome. Angeline and May had enjoyed their little home, and although May sometimes went to the picture house with the other assistant at the bakery or out for the day on a Sunday with Jack and his group of friends, Angeline never accompanied them. She had bought herself a Remington typewriter and a book by Isaac Pitman, who had developed a new shorthand system, using signs for sounds, but being unable to really afford the shorthand and typing courses that the local school board was running in the evening, had decided to teach herself in any spare time she had.

Although she genuinely wanted to learn shorthand and typing, secretly it was also something of an excuse for her hermit-like behaviour, once she was home. She confided to May she was always worried that she might be seen by someone who recognized her from the past, but again that wasn't the whole reason for her withdrawal. The main reason was Jack Connor. It had been some months after she had met him, and whilst she and May were still living in King Street, that they had gone to hear him speak at a meeting down by Castle Square at the back of the fish market. It had been a cold but dry October evening, and the smell of fish had been strong, but once Jack had begun speaking he had held his listeners enthralled, in spite of the odd heckler, who was more often than not one of his pals. Jack had talked about a better future for the unborn children of the working class; a country without employment of workers at starvation rates, without rack-renting of insanitary tenements and an absence of opportunities for education of the poor; a land where the death of a child before it was one year old wasn't determined by the area in which it was born.

She had stood with her arm linked in May's, her nose pink with the cold and her feet numb, and had seen Utopia. Jack had captured her imagination in a way no one else had ever done, and at one point in his discourse, when his green eyes had looked over the crowd and straight into hers, she knew he had captured her heart, too. She loved him. She had been frozen in shock. May's brother, Jack Connor, who despised and loathed the upper classes and all they stood for, and who was contemptuous of the sort of woman she had been. 'Empty-headed dolls,' he'd called the society ladies once, when he'd been talking with his pals, 'not fit to be called women at all.' And when one of his friends had asked him if that wasn't a little harsh, Jack had said how else could you describe a breed of female who could stand by and see the wretchedness of little ones begging in the gutters for a penny or two, when their own children were dressed in furs and lace and had umpteen servants to cater to their every need? 'You've seen what our women contend with,' he'd said. 'The unending struggle with poverty, the stillbirths, the miscarriages, and the old wives who butcher their own sex who've gone to them in desperation, to get rid of another unwanted mouth to feed. Mothers leading their bairns into the workhouse, cos it's that or seeing them starve. You've *seen* it. And what woman with bairns round here doesn't look twenty, thirty years older than she is? And you talk to me about being harsh? Wake up, man!'

Angeline had left May that night pleading a headache,

and had gone home to weep for hours. And then she had put the lid on that box in her mind and had stored it away deep in the heart of her. Jack thought her cold and unapproachable – she'd heard him describe her that way to May once, when he hadn't known she could hear; but better that than the truth. Warm and loving as he was to May, with her he was invariably cool and reserved, even taciturn on occasions. It hurt her, causing an ever-present gnawing ache that flared into exquisite pain when she was in his presence, but there was nothing she could do about it. She lived in fear of the day when one of the girls who, according to May, were shameless in their pursuit of Jack would catch his fancy, but again that was outside her control.

And then, a year ago, yet another phase of her life had begun. May had met and married the miller's son who supplied the bakery with flour, and a month or so before the wedding, Angeline had decided to try for an office post. May's impending nuptials had been the catalyst for change. Her friend's leaving would create a huge hole in Angeline's life. A new job would, of necessity, be a channel for her time and thoughts. She knew her shorthand and typing skills were good, but having no experience of office work and being happy at the draper's and at home with May for company, she'd resisted spreading her wings and leaving the safety of the niche she had carved out for herself.

After buying a newspaper she had replied to two

advertisements, one for a copy typist at the town hall and the other for a secretary to the manager of an engineering works just across the river, not far from the rope and wire works where May had once been employed. The town hall had written a polite letter saying they'd already been suited, but thanking her for her application, and the engineering works had granted her an interview the very next day. She had been thrown into a state of panic, and later that night when Jack had come round to share their evening meal – a regular occurrence twice a week, which was a source of mixed pain and pleasure for Angeline – he had found a very different person from the cool young woman he was accustomed to.

He had recently passed the last of his examinations to qualify as a solicitor, but had been turned down by two firms in the town – probably, as he himself admitted, because he didn't fit the middle-class image they were looking for. He was an oddity, working-class and proud of it, and not to be trusted. Consequently, and frustratingly, he was continuing in the same position as clerk to his present employer. That night, however, he had put his own disappointment and resentment aside and had risen to the occasion. He had been encouraging and reassuring, warm and even tender when Angeline had disgraced herself by weeping all over him and insisting she was out of her depth.

For the first time since they'd met he'd held her close, murmuring that she could do anything she put her mind to. May had fussed about making a pot of tea. Angeline had been conscious of the controlled gentleness of Jack's big male body, of the clean, soapy smell of him and of never wanting the moment to end. The strength of her feeling had terrified her, and as soon as she could she'd made the excuse of a headache and had retired to the front room to go to bed.

The next day she had attended the interview and had been offered the job and a starting salary of twenty-five shillings a week, fifteen shillings more than she had been earning at the draper's. It ought to have made her ecstatic, but all she could think about as she had walked home was how it had felt to be in Jack's arms and what a terrible mess she had made of her life. She was living a lie. Grace Cunningham didn't exist. Angeline Golding, on the other hand, was a married woman who was in love with another man – a man who could never know who she really was. Her career would have to be her life. She would grow old, childless and lonely, destined to be an aunt to any children May might have, but never holding her own little one in her arms. It was her bleakest hour.

She had gone and bought a cup of tea and a cake she didn't want in a dingy little cafe, returning home much later to find Jack and May waiting to hear how she had got on. She had accepted Jack's congratulations with a polite smile, and when he had given her a brief hug she had stepped back quickly, her body stiff and her face tense. From that day to this he had never touched her again.

Within weeks of May's marriage, Angeline moved across the river. She had found a small two-up, two-down terraced house in Garden Street close to the engineering works, which she rented for four shillings a week. She had gradually furnished it the way she wanted, and with the new job proving to be interesting and absorbing, she told herself she was lucky. Sometimes, especially the nights when she didn't work overtime and the evening stretched before her endlessly, she had to tell herself more fiercely than usual that she was lucky.

May's husband was a nice man and brought his wife to see Angeline once a week, taking himself off to meet up with pals at a public house in Newcastle so the two women could have dinner together and a good natter. After a while Jack had taken to joining them, ostensibly so that he could walk May back across the river and deliver her safely to her husband. It had seemed churlish not to invite him for dinner after he'd done this a few times, and thereafter a pattern had been set. Every Monday, without fail, the three of them would eat together and chat for a while, before Jack and May left to make their way across the bridge into Newcastle. Last week Angeline had told them she didn't expect them the following Monday, it being New Year's Day, but they'd both assured her they would come.

Now she carried the tray of coffee that the three of them always had after their meal across the sitting room and put it on the coffee table, around which was placed a three-piece suite. It was a cosy room, and unusual in as much as Angeline hadn't decorated it with the dark, serviceable colours most folks favoured; nor had she chosen a stiff horsehair suite and solid, heavy furniture, with the inevitable aspidistra in front of the window. Instead the walls were painted a pale yellow, the same colour as the flowery curtains at the window, and there were no starched nets. The sunny theme continued with the three-piece suite, which was made out of bamboo, with big, plump seats in gold brocade that were comfortable enough to doze in. A thick patterned carpet in the varying shades of autumn leaves covered the entire floor, and the bookcase and coffee table were also fashioned from bamboo. A large picture featuring a woodland scene sat on one wall and a gold-framed mirror hung over the small fireplace, but otherwise the walls were bare.

When May had first seen the newly decorated room she had secretly wondered where the tablecloths and runners, antimacassars and cushions, pot plants and vases and porcelain figurines were. And just one picture on the wall? A front room was a showpiece, for those fortunate enough to have one. She had been further surprised when it became clear that Angeline intended to use the room every day, and merely cook and eat in the kitchen with its big scrubbed oak table and four chairs. She had said as much to Jack, and when he had quietly replied that he thought the room was perfect, she had said no more.

She glanced at her brother now as he sat with his legs stretched out, puffing on his pipe, his eyes half-closed. He appeared perfectly relaxed and maybe he was, but it was difficult to tell with Jack. There had been the odd occasion once or twice – just a handful of times in all – over the last years when May had thought he might be sweet on Grace. Not that Jack had ever intimated it, quite the contrary in fact, but nevertheless . . . She had said as much to Howard and he'd laughed his head off, before telling her she was imagining things. And maybe she was. Certainly Grace wasn't interested in Jack, or any other man for that matter, and who could blame her after what she'd been through?

May accepted her cup of coffee from Angeline with a smile, thinking how pretty she looked with a slight flush to her cheeks, no doubt from the cooking. It was a shame Grace would never have her own husband and bairns, though, even if she seemed happy enough with her job and her home. But then, she *did* have a husband. May kept forgetting that. They had decided early on that even when they were alone she should call Angeline 'Grace', it was safer that way, and as time had gone by, it had become second nature – to the extent that she didn't think of her as Angeline any more, or that she was a married woman with a husband.

Mentally shaking her head at her rambling thoughts, May put down her coffee cup. 'I've an announcement to make, and seeing it's the first day of a new year, it couldn't be a better time.'

Angeline was sitting with May on the sofa, Jack being in a chair opposite, and now she turned to her friend and said softly, 'It's happened?'

'Aye, at last!'

'Oh, May, I'm so pleased for you.'

'I know you said it would, but with the past an' all I was beginning to wonder.'

As the two women hugged each other, Jack said plaintively, 'Have I missed something here?'

Laughing through happy tears, May said, 'You're going to be an uncle, lad. Uncle Jack. What about that?'

'You're in the family way?'

Jack was beaming, and it wrenched Angeline's heart. He would make a lovely father one day, but oh, she couldn't bear the thought of it. As if her friend had picked up on the thought, May now said to him, ''Bout time you settled down and thought about family life, isn't it? What happened to that last lass you were walking out with? Esther, wasn't it? She seemed nice enough.'

Jack shrugged. 'It wasn't serious.'

'Not on your side mebbe, but she was fair gone on you – anyone could see that. Why do they never last for more than a few months with you, anyway?'

He shrugged again. 'I'm not the marrying type. You've hit it lucky with your Howard, but there's not many who could say the same. I'd rather be miserable on me own than miserable tied to some lass or other.'

'Oh, you!' May flapped her hand at him before turning back to Angeline. 'It'll be born at the end of July, beginning of August, so a summer baby will be nice, won't it? We told Howard's mam an' da yesterday, an' they're tickled pink – first grandchild and all that.

Howard's mam has already started knitting, and his da's said they'll turn that ramshackle cottage at the back of the mill round for us. Get it nice before the baby comes. Not that I've minded living with them, but it'll be grand to have our own place whilst still being near to Howard's mam.'

Howard was the eldest of four boys and his mother had embraced May as the daughter she had always longed for. 'You're so lucky to have such nice in-laws, May.'

'Don't I know it! After me own mam an' da, I thank God every day for Howard's. Like I said to Howard . . . '

As the two women chatted on, Jack sat quietly watching Angeline, his feet resting on the gleaming steel fender of the fireplace, and curls of smoke from his pipe wafting over his head. He had been chary about lighting his pipe in her bright, clean house at first, but she had assured him that she loved the smell of pipe tobacco because it reminded her of her father. She hadn't elaborated on that and he hadn't asked her to; he'd learned in the past that any questions about her previous life would be met with monosyllabic answers or evasion, or just cold silence.

What would she say if he told her he lived for the few hours each Monday when he could be in her presence? But then why ask the road you know – she'd run a mile, and thereafter the door to this house would be closed to him. Once he could admit it to himself – and it had taken a long time, he thought wryly, his mouth curling in its lopsided smile – he had known he had fallen in love with

Grace the moment she had stood on his landing asking for his help. It had been as quick and as deadly as that. He hadn't been in love before that day, in fact he hadn't known if he believed in the forever-after kind of love between a man and a woman, not having seen much evidence of it in his life. Oh, there was the passionate, heady kind of love, where all that mattered was bedding a lass and having your way with her, but he'd seen too many of his pals fall for that and live to regret it, once the first thrill faded and they were stuck with a wife and a handful of bairns. And some marriages were plain hell – like his own mam an' da's. Of course there was the odd couple who seemed to get it right, like old Mr and Mrs Benson who'd lived a few doors up from them when he was a bairn. Done everything together, they had, and he'd fair worshipped the ground she walked on and there'd been no one like him for her. He remembered going into the two rooms that were their home when he was a bairn and wanting to stay there forever, such was the sense of peace and happiness there.

' . . . be nice to see them, don't you think, Jack?'

He came out of his reverie to find both women looking at him and realized he hadn't heard a word May was saying.

'Sorry.' He sat up straighter. 'I was daydreaming.'

'Still dozing off the effects of your shenanigans last night, more likely,' said May with sisterly disapproval. 'I was *saying* that they've got some more fireworks tonight over at Castle Leazes, the football-ground end near St

James's Park. Me an' Howard are going to see them when I meet him; why don't you and Grace come, too? Howard can give you a lift back to the bridge after, in the horse and cart, and you could walk Grace back here.'

Anything that meant more time with Grace was fine by him. Jack nodded. 'I'm game.'

'I don't think—'

'Oh, come on, Grace. You missed the fireworks and fun last night, and it's not every day a new century happens. By tomorrow everything will be the same again – it's just one night.' May played her trump card. 'It can be a celebration of the baby, how about that? They'll have the travelling fair there, and the hot potato man and everything. Please come, for me? Please?'

Against her better judgement, Angeline gave in. The evening would be bitter-sweet, as any time with Jack was, but the thought of being out with him, almost as a couple, was as thrilling as it was scary. Scary, because she would die a thousand deaths if he ever guessed how she felt about him. Thrilling, because in the seven years she had known him she had never been out with him in this way, even if it was as a foursome.

And then she checked the thought swiftly. It wasn't a foursome, not in that sense. May was his sister, and she was May's friend. *That was all.*

Later, though, when she excused herself and went upstairs to get ready and looked at herself in the bedroom mirror, her eyes were bright and her heart was racing. Shutting her eyes tightly for a moment, she murmured,

'Stop it, calm down. You know he barely likes you; if you weren't May's friend, he wouldn't give you the time of day; and even if he did like you, it's impossible. It was May who suggested this. It means nothing.'

Nevertheless, when her hand reached for her winter coat, it paused and then moved to the new coat she had recently treated herself to, but not worn yet. The colour was a little daring, being a deep cherry-red, but it had suited her so well in the shop she hadn't been able to resist it, and the fur-lined hood complemented the slim fit of the coat beautifully. She had bought a neat little hat in the same colour, along with black leather gloves and stylish black boots, even though at the time she'd told herself it was an indulgence, as she had nowhere to go to show the outfit off.

*But now she had.* She looked at herself in the mirror, once she was dressed in the coat and hat. She looked different – more like Angeline than Grace – and for a moment she almost took the coat off. Almost. But it suited her too well and something inside, a recklessness, wanted to make Jack notice her tonight as a woman, rather than as good old Grace, May's pal.

She felt ridiculously shy as she joined May and Jack who were waiting in the hall, brushing off May's oohs and aahs as her friend enthused about the coat, and being deliberately brisk as she marshalled them out of the front door into the bitterly cold street beyond. It had been snowing on and off for weeks, but with each fall had come a period of thawing before more snow had come along, the severe weather that had been forecast for after Christmas holding off. Now it was snowing hard again, and as she stepped down into the street after locking the front door, Jack raised her hood and dropped it over her head so that it framed her face. 'That's better,' he said, very softly. 'You look like the spirit of winter, like the rosehip berries. I love to see those specks of scarlet shine in the barrenness of a desolate countryside, don't you? They're like a promise of what's to come.'

May spoilt the moment by snorting derisively. 'Poetic, aren't we? You've definitely still got the effects of last night's carousing in your system, our Jack.'

He smiled, tucking one of May's hands and one of Angeline's into the crook of his elbows. 'Not at all. Do you know the month of January is named after Janus, the two-headed god of vigil? It's appropriate, because January looks back on the old year, yet at the same time advances towards spring.'

Another snort from May followed as they began to walk along the frozen pavement. 'All I know is I'm in danger of ending up on my backside. These pavements are like glass.'

Jack chuckled. 'You've no soul, lass. That's your trouble. Haven't you ever marvelled at the beauty in a frozen landscape? It intensifies every colour and shade, from the wisps of silver in a winter sky to the purple and bronze of the bramble bushes. I've often wished I was a painter. I'd love to capture what I see and hold on to it.'

'Huh, if you seriously think you could sell paintings of old bramble bushes, you're dafter than I thought.'

'May, May . . . Have you nothing of the artist in you?'

'Since when did paintings of bramble bushes provide bread for the table? There's more beauty in one of my Howard's sacks of flour than all your silver skies and what-have-you, my lad, so think on.'

Angeline listened to their good-natured bantering as they walked, but inside her Jack's words had stirred the ever-present ache into an actual physical pain. How often had she seen what he saw? Hundreds of times. And this other side of him, the side that saw beauty in such natural, everyday things – springtime primroses; wind-racked elms beyond a corn field shimmering in a summer's haze; a grey winter's landscape grizzled with sleet and many other things he had talked about in the past and which she had held close to her heart – this hurt her more than anything. It was the antithesis of the determined, even ruthless campaigner and reformer, the fierce individual who insisted that nothing less than radical social change was called for, whatever the cost to the individual.

Not that she didn't agree with him, for she did; but it was the militant, even aggressive side of things she baulked at. Unbeknown to anyone, she had investigated for herself the beliefs and values of the Socialist Party that Verity had believed in, along with other political organizations, and not least the female suffrage movement. Gradually she had sorted out where she stood on many issues, and with that had come a desire to do something. As her father would have said, she wanted to get her hands dirty, not attend this or that meeting or join one of the Socialist sects. She wasn't a political animal, that much was for sure, but exactly what she wanted to do wasn't clear. Or even what she would be allowed to do, as a young, supposedly unmarried woman.

'You're very quiet.'

Jack looked down at her, a smile on his face, and suddenly instead of the polite remark she had been about to make, she tilted her head at him and spoke in an accent as broad as May's as she said, 'Aye, well mebbe that's because I can't get a word in edgeways, with you two jawing on, m'lad.'

Jack stopped dead, a look of absolute amazement on his face, and then threw back his head, as peal upon peal of unbridled laughter sounded in the icy-cold air, causing a group of young lads and lassies in front of them to turn round and grin. Angeline felt the colour sweeping her face, but May and Jack were laughing so hard it was infectious. Soon the three of them were helpless, so much so that when an elderly couple passed them and the woman said in a tone meant to reach their ears, 'I don't care if it *is* New Year's Day, it's disgraceful being intoxicated at this time of the evening', it made them worse, not better.

It was a while before they gained control, and Jack was the last to stop spluttering. He wiped his eyes, before again pulling the girls' arms through his as he said, laughter still evident in his voice, 'Talk about a dark horse – where did that come from? Come on, let's go and meet this husband of yours, May.' And the three of them walked on, slipping and sliding on the icy pavement with its thin layer of fresh snow.

# *Chapter Twenty-Three*

Angeline was still glowing with the joy at having made Jack laugh, when they reached the inn not far from King Street where Howard was drinking with his pals. He downed his pint on their arrival and came straight out, which Angeline was relieved about. She had never set foot inside a public house, although she knew May had done once or twice in the company of her husband.

It had almost stopped snowing, with just the odd desultory flake or two floating in the cold air, and once Howard had brought the horse and cart round from the back of the inn, Angeline and May squeezed up beside him on the narrow plank-like seat and Jack sat in the back of the cart on a pile of old sacks.

The other three kept up a steady stream of banter as the horse clip-clopped its way through streets that would normally have been fairly empty at this time of night on a winter's evening, but which, due to the holiday atmosphere pervading the town, were relatively busy. Angeline was content just to listen and to hug every moment of the evening to her, knowing it wouldn't – *couldn't* – be repeated.

They heard the fair before they saw it, as the horse plodded along Newgate Street and then Gallowgate, and then they came into the bottom of the enormous area of land that was Castle Leazes. This was one of the common pastures of the town, where certain citizens had the right to graze their cattle and where, some decades before, the first public park was opened – Leazes Park – in the middle of the pastureland. It was a popular area with Newcastle folk, having bowling greens, tennis courts and a fine bandstand and fountain, with a football ground being situated at the foot of the hundred-plus acres of ground, in a tiny park called St James's Park. To the left of this the fair had set up, a spectacle of colour in the white world around it. The tantalizing, comforting smells of baked potatoes and roasting chestnuts were thick in the air as they approached the fair, after Howard had tied the horse to one of the big posts at the edge of the open space.

'Isn't it grand?' May was quivering with excitement. 'Come on, Grace, let's go on the carousel first, and then Howard can try and win me one of those teddies on that stall across there, for the baby. Oh, listen to the hurdy-gurdies, I love hearing them, don't you? This is better than the Michaelmas Fair, don't you think?'

Without waiting for a reply, May dragged Angeline over to the brightly painted carousel, the two men following in their wake. Howard lifted May onto one of the wooden horses, and Jack did the same with Angeline, and when the music started and the revolving circular platform began to turn, it wasn't the carousel that had brought the colour into Angeline's pink cheeks.

The feeling of mass gaiety was something Angeline had never encountered before. Her mama had not considered the travelling fairs a suitable environment for her daughter, and the dances and balls and other social events she had gone to as a young wife had been staid affairs compared to this. This was exhilarating and thrilling, it stirred the blood and quickened the senses, and for a little time at least she felt as one with the folk around her. And the sense of belonging was heady. Throwing caution to the wind, she began to enjoy herself with everyone else.

Howard won May her teddy, and at the same time Jack spent a fortune attempting to do the same for Angeline. After six attempts at throwing the darts at the dartboard, on a whim Angeline took the three darts from him and, never having held a dart in her life, scored a bullseye on her first throw. Howard promised he would never let Jack forget it.

May and Angeline screamed and clutched hold of Howard and Jack on the swing seats, which whirled above the heads of the crowd; screamed some more in the haunted house and on the helter-skelter; and had two big toffee-apples apiece in between the rides. Whether it was the magic of the evening Angeline didn't know, but it seemed perfectly natural for Jack's arm to be around her waist, or for her arm to be through his as they wandered about the fairground. For the first time in years she felt truly happy and it was more intoxicating than any wine or beer.

They had just bought some paper cones of hot chestnuts and were standing to one side of the brazier, laughing and talking as they ate them, when Angeline felt a touch on her arm and a voice say, 'Miss Angeline, is it you?'

Afterwards she thought of a hundred things she could have said or done, but as she turned and looked straight into Myrtle's shocked, wide-eyed face, she simply froze. Albert was standing behind his wife and his face expressed the same incredulous disbelief. For what seemed an eternity, but was in fact just a second or two, Angeline found she couldn't speak, and then somehow she murmured, 'Myrtle.'

'Oh, it is you! Oh, Miss Angeline! Everyone thought you were dead. I can't believe it.'

Angeline was aware of May leaving Howard's side and coming to stand with her, her arm going about Angeline's shoulders, and of Jack on her other side standing quite still, but the fairground and the crowd, the noise and the music had melted away and the world had narrowed into the young woman staring at her as though she were a ghost. Which to Myrtle she must have seemed. With a strength she hadn't believed herself capable of, Angeline reached out and hugged Myrtle briefly, saying at the same time, 'Hello, Albert. How are you?'

'I'm all right, Miss,' he said, his deep voice squeaky with shock.

'I . . . I don't understand, Miss.' Myrtle's eyes flashed to the others, before coming back to Angeline. 'We thought you'd died in the fire – there was a funeral and everything. Mr Golding' – she stopped abruptly before going on – 'he said you'd died. He . . . he had you buried next to the baby.'

'Mr Golding?' Jack's voice was as thin and sharp as a scalpel.

Without looking at him, Angeline said, 'My husband.'

'Your *what*?'

'Jack, it's not like you think.' May's arm had tightened round Angeline. 'He was a monster—'

'You knew about this?'

'Aye, I did, an' it was me who suggested she call herself Grace, and the rest of it, if you want to know.'

'I don't want to know.' Jack turned his furious gaze on Howard. 'Were you in on this an' all?'

'Don't start on him.' May's eyes were flashing as much as her brother's. 'And no, he didn't know about Grace – Angeline – no one did. It was better that way. He only knew what we said to you: that we met in the asylum and teamed up.' Turning round, she said to the bewildered Howard, 'I'm sorry, lad, but it had to be that way. Anyway, I thought you'd had enough to take on board, when I told you what had happened to me and the baby an' all.'

Ignoring the rest of them, Angeline again reached out

to Myrtle, who now had tears running down her face. 'Oh, Myrtle,' she said softly. 'I've missed you. I'm so sorry I couldn't tell you I was still alive, but barely a day's gone by when I haven't thought of you and Albert and the farm.'

'Oh, Miss . . . ' Sobbing openly, Myrtle hugged her back and they stood together in the midst of the gaiety and laughter and crowds, Myrtle with a hundred mixed emotions tearing through her breast, and Angeline with a curious feeling of calm. The worst had happened, and somehow she had always known it would. But she wouldn't be locked away again. She wasn't the broken young girl she had been when she'd been incarcerated in Earlswood; she was her own woman now, and she had proved it. She had a job and a home, which no one had given her but herself; she had worked for it and it was her blood, sweat and tears that had made it happen. But Jack, he would hate her.

Still holding Myrtle, she turned her head and looked at him, and the blazing green eyes in a face that had become as bleached as linen stared back at her, the look in them cutting her to the bone. 'I'm sorry,' she began and then stopped when he said, contempt and rage dripping from every word, 'Who are you anyway? I don't know you. Everything about you has been a lie.'

She couldn't deny it. 'I'm sorry.'

'So you said.'

She couldn't do this with him, not here, not now.

'Myrtle, will you and Albert come home with me? Are you able to?'

'Now, Miss? Well, aye. Me mam's got the bairns, and we came into Newcastle for the day, as a treat like. Just the two of us. Aye, we can come back; it don't matter to me mam what time we get home.'

Angeline turned to May without looking at Jack again. 'I'll see you another day, May. If Howard is still agreeable to us being friends, that is?'

Howard, bless him, immediately piped up, 'Whatever you've done or not done in the past, lass, is water under the bridge, as far as I'm concerned. Anyway, I couldn't stop May seeing you if I tried, which I wouldn't dare to.'

'I'll come tomorrow evening.' May's face was bereft. And to Myrtle and Albert she added, 'See she's all right, won't you?'

Angeline wondered if Jack would stop her as she walked away with Myrtle and Albert, but no one caught her arm or called out. Telling herself she couldn't think about him now – that would have to come later when she was alone – she kept her head up and her back straight as they left the park.

In spite of the circumstances, Myrtle couldn't keep a note of pride out of her voice as she led Angeline over to a small horse and trap waiting at the edge of the grass. 'Albert made this himself, Miss,' she said, pointing at the two-wheeled carriage, 'and we keep the cart for the farm produce an' that. He's made some bits for inside the house an' all, beds an' that, and a lovely crib for the babies.'

It was a squeeze on the seat of the trap, which was only meant for two, but once they were on their way Angeline said, 'How many children have you got, Myrtle?', preferring to keep the conversation on them until they were home.

'Three, Miss. Two lads an' a little lass.' Shyly now, she added, 'We called her Angeline, Miss. I hope you don't mind. In memory like.'

'Oh, Myrtle.' The emotion was weakening and she didn't want to cry, fearing that once she got started she would never stop. Swallowing hard, she said, 'I'm honoured, really. Is she a good little girl?'

'Well, to tell you the truth, Miss, she runs me ragged. The two lads are no trouble, never have been, but she's a little madam, an' as bright as a button.' This was said with some ruefulness. 'She's comin' up for three now and can already write her name, an' there's the two lads still have trouble with their ABCs.'

'How old are the boys?'

'They're twins, Miss. Like two peas in a pod, and they're six years old, but like I said, they're not ones for learning. They'd rather be out with their da and me brothers on the farm, but they're good little lads.'

Myrtle continued to chat about the children and life at the farm on the way back to the house, for which Angeline was grateful. She only had to put the occasional word in now and again and it gave her time to compose herself.

Twice, in the middle of her discourse, Myrtle stopped and said softly, 'Oh, Miss, I can't believe this, you being here. It's the answer to my prayer, it is straight', before carrying on with her tale, and each time Angeline was almost reduced to tears. To know she hadn't been forgotten, to know she was thought about with such affection, was balm to her sore soul.

When they neared Garden Street Angeline directed Albert to drive the horse and trap down the back lane so that the horse could wait at the end of the back yard, so they entered the house via the small scullery that led into the kitchen. Myrtle had become silent as they'd neared the house, and now, as she followed Angeline into the kitchen, she said, bewildered, 'You live here, Miss Angeline?'

'Grace Cunningham lives here, Myrtle,' Angeline said with a smile, to soften what she was about to say. 'Angeline Golding died in the fire at the asylum. Or that was the way it was before today. Look, go through to the sitting room and I'll make a pot of tea and explain.'

'*You'll* make the tea?'

'I do all sorts of things now, Myrtle. Cook my own food, clean my own house, work as a secretary and take care of myself.'

'Miss Angeline! And you a lady. What would Mr and Mrs Stewart say? It's not right.'

'Being a lady isn't dependent on your station in life,

Myrtle. Believe me, when I was married to Mr Golding – well, I suppose I am still married to him, come to that – but when I was living that life, I saw plenty of high-born women who were far from being ladies in their speech and conduct. As for my parents, I hope they'd be proud of what I've achieved. And Myrtle, it is right. For me.' She glanced at Albert. 'Go through, the pair of you, and I'll be with you in a minute.'

Once she was alone, she didn't immediately set the kettle on the hob to boil, but stood with both hands palm-down on the kitchen table as she bowed her head and shut her eyes. Jack couldn't have found out the truth in a worse way. 'Miss Angeline.' If anything was guaranteed to alienate him for the rest of her life, it was that. He would never forgive her. And if he was just May's brother it wouldn't matter so much, but he was much, much more than that.

She raised her head with a gasp as though she was emerging from a bottomless sea of misery, feeling as though she was weeping from every pore of her body, although her eyes were dry. They had been getting on so well tonight, too. And then she immediately overrode that thought with: so what? So what if they had laughed and talked and he'd seemed to like her for once? It could never have come to anything, she knew that. And now her secret was out in the open. Would he betray her to the powers that be? And even if he didn't, could she ask Myrtle and Albert to say nothing to anyone? There was

Howard, too. She rubbed her hand across her eyes. *What was she going to do?*

By the time she had made the tea and fetched out a fruit cake, she'd pulled herself together again. She had to be calm and controlled when she talked to Myrtle and Albert. How they must be feeling she didn't dare think. It had been a terrible shock for poor Myrtle, and she must be feeling hurt and bewildered, and probably resentful too, now it had all had a chance to sink in.

When she carried the tray into the sitting room they were sitting side by side on the sofa in front of the fire, although they both stood up as she walked in. Angeline told them to sit down and then said straight away, with no preamble, 'I'm so sorry I couldn't tell you I was alive, Myrtle. But for one thing I didn't know where you lived, and for another I didn't think it was fair to put that sort of burden on you. If I could have told anyone, it would have been you, truly.'

And then Myrtle showed the real depth of her affection when she said, 'Oh, Miss Angeline, how can you think for one moment I care about that, now I know you're alive and well? After all you did for me – for us. We can never repay you for your kindness, I know that, but anything we can do for you, no matter what, would be a pleasure. But how did you come to be here?'

'It's a long story.' Angeline had poured three cups of tea and cut the cake, which she now offered to them. 'You see, it was like this . . . '

Myrtle and Albert didn't interrupt once as she related

everything, from the moment she had found herself in the asylum to the present day. She left nothing out, although her voice faltered when she came to Verity's death. When she finished speaking they sat in silence for a moment or two, and then Myrtle said, 'Miss Angeline, I don't know how to tell you what I need to say.'

'Is it about Mr Golding?'

Myrtle nodded. 'Me and Mrs Gibson correspond now and again, and in her last letter she wrote that he's going to marry the daughter of some rich lord or other. Been after her for a while, because the father wasn't too keen at first, but he's won him round, apparently. There was a big engagement ball a few weeks ago.'

Ridiculous, but she had never thought of Oswald marrying again. Then again, she never thought of him at all, if she could help it. Faintly she murmured, 'How old is she?'

'I don't know, Miss, but young, I think. She's the only child – the apple of her father's eye – and rich in her own right.'

Another innocent to the slaughter? But even if this girl wasn't as young and naive as she had been, she didn't deserve Oswald. And he was married. She would be condemning this girl to a marriage that wasn't legal.

'I'm sorry, Miss Angeline.' Myrtle looked as though she was about to cry again. 'But I thought I should tell you.'

'Of course, Myrtle. You did the right thing. It's just' – Angeline glanced about her home, which had become even more precious – 'I thought I could remain Grace Cunningham forever, I suppose.'

'Miss, you don't have to say anything. What I mean is, me an' Albert would rather be hanged, drawn and quartered than give you away.'

Angeline smiled at the dramatic statement. Dear Myrtle! 'Thank you for that,' she said softly, 'but I think we all know I don't have a choice. My conscience would give me no rest if I let it happen, Myrtle. And perhaps it's time to face my demons. I've hidden away long enough.' She took a deep breath, feeling light-headed with the suddenness with which her life had taken yet another turn.

'What will you do, Miss?'

'Whatever I have to do, to stop the marriage happening. I have a little money put by, enough to see a solicitor and ask for advice.'

'But Mr Golding? I mean, once he finds out you're alive . . . '

Angeline stared at Myrtle. She knew exactly what she meant. Oswald would be beside himself. Nevertheless, she couldn't put another woman in the position of being involved in a bigamous marriage. 'I'll see a solicitor,' she repeated, 'and go from there. Mr Golding can't accuse me of being mentally impaired, not after the life I have made for myself.'

Myrtle's face expressed her doubt. 'Begging your pardon, Miss, but I wouldn't put anything past him. And what about your job and your reputation and all? What are folk going to say, when they find out you're not who you've said you are?'

'A wise man once said that reputation is what others think of you, and character is what God is interested in, and I concur with that. I shall make it clear what Mr Golding's character is, and if in doing so my reputation is tarnished, so be it. My character is what matters, Myrtle. That and being right with myself and God.'

Myrtle didn't look at all convinced, but after a moment she said, 'There's something else, Miss. It . . . it's a bit awkward. When they wouldn't let me see you in the asylum, I remembered what you'd said about Mr Golding saying Mr Jefferson was trying to ruin him because of . . . '

Angeline nodded. 'Go on.'

'I thought if he had it in for Mr Golding, so to speak, he might help you get out of that place, just to spite him, you know? So . . . so I went to London to see him.'

'You went to *London*?'

'Aye, I know, Miss. I surprised meself, to be honest, but our Fred came with me, so it wasn't too bad. Anyway Mr Jefferson was abroad, but I saw her, Mrs Jefferson, and – well, she was ever so nice, Miss. She promised to speak to her husband and said they'd get you out of the asylum and . . . '

'Yes? What is it?'

'I could tell that whatever had gone on between her and Mr Golding in the past, she hated him now. She didn't say so in as many words, but the air fairly crackled with it, and Alice, her maid, was the same. Mrs Jefferson would have got you out of Earlswood, I saw it in her face, and I think if you needed anyone to speak up for you against Mr Golding – someone with influence, I mean – she'd do it.'

Angeline stared at Myrtle. It was her turn to be surprised. After a moment she said softly, 'Thank you for what you did, Myrtle. It means more to me than you'll ever know. It was so terrible to be kept in that awful place, feeling everyone in the outside world had forgotten you.'

'Never, Miss. Not for a minute.'

'And I'll think about what you said regarding Mrs Jefferson.' Even as she said it, Angeline knew she would never ask Mirabelle to help her. She felt no grudge towards her, but she had been Oswald's mistress even during the time they'd been married. Mirabelle belonged to that different life anyway – a life that was so at odds with her own that there was no way to cross the chasm. No, Mirabelle Jefferson would be the last person she would expect to help her, and seven years was a long time. Whatever had transpired between Mirabelle and Oswald to make her turn against him might well have been put right by now, for all she knew.

The three of them talked a little more, but it was getting late and Myrtle and Albert needed to get back to their family. They made their goodbyes, Angeline promising she would visit the farm very soon, now that she knew where it was.

It had begun to snow again when Angeline opened the back door – big feathery flakes falling from a laden sky. The thick snow that had been forecast had arrived at last and it looked as though they were in for a bad spell.

Angeline and Myrtle hugged tightly on the doorstep, Myrtle saying with a break in her voice, 'Miss Angeline, there's a home for you with us any time, we want you to know that. For good, if you want, or just to escape the hoo-ha if things get difficult.'

'Thank you, Myrtle.' Angeline knew Myrtle meant well, but she was determined that Oswald wouldn't make her run and hide a second time, however unpleasant things got.

Nevertheless, after she had waved them goodbye and closed the back door, she plumped down at the kitchen table and rested her head in her hands. In spite of her brave words to Myrtle and Albert, she felt very small and insignificant. Oswald was wealthy and influential, but more than that, he was cunning and unscrupulous, which gave him the upper hand in a battle with him, however you looked at it.

She crossed her forearms tightly against her waist, drooping her head until her chin lay on her chest as she struggled not to give in to the flood of tears mounting in her breast. She didn't want to cry, she had cried so many tears in her life. Tears for her parents, for her baby, for Verity; countless tears during the time of her marriage and whilst she was imprisoned in the asylum, and for

Jack. For what might have been, if she had been a working-class girl and he had liked her.

Jack. Oh, Jack! She shook her head, the feeling of immense aloneness that had been with her since the death of her parents unbearable right at that moment. He hated her – she had seen it in his face.

## *Chapter Twenty-Four*

Jack watched the woman who had been Grace's maid – no, Angeline's, he corrected himself; he had to think of her as Angeline now – being helped up into the trap by her husband. He was standing in deep shadow some way along the back lane, hidden from sight, and couldn't see into Angeline's back yard from where he was, but he saw the woman and her husband wave and call goodbye, before the horse and trap trundled off along the snow-covered cobbles and disappeared out into the road beyond.

He had been waiting for more than an hour and was frozen inside and out, but he hadn't wanted to knock on the door while they were still there. Now that they had gone he still stood in the falling snow, nerving himself for what he was about to do. If she banged the door in his face it would be no more than he deserved. He groaned softly, bunching his hands into fists in the pockets of his coat. And nothing she might say to him could make him feel worse than he did right now. Fate had given him a chance tonight to make her notice him as a man – a chance to be strong and supportive and understanding. It was the first rule of a good solicitor that you didn't make hasty judgements; you listened and got all the facts and figures and the arguments clear. He groaned again, the anger and frustration at the way he had handled things feeling like a lead ball in his chest.

He had been so full of rage that he was shaking with it when Angeline had walked away at the fair. And May had looked at him, her face stony as she'd said, 'Are you proud of yourself? Are you?'

'Me?' For the first time in his life he had wanted to strike the sister he adored.

'Aye, you. Since when were you judge and jury anyway? You don't know a thing about it – and you behave like that.'

'Like what?'

'Like no better than her swine of a husband, that's what. He used to knock her about, Jack. Force her to sleep with him; rape her, if you want the full picture. And when she was pregnant with their first bairn, he hit her so hard he broke her nose and she lost the baby. She nearly died then, but he didn't care. Not content with that, he had her shipped off to the asylum within weeks, claiming she was doolally. That's why she's like she is, keeping every man at arm's length. And we weren't let out of the asylum, as you've probably gathered. There was a fire and we escaped, making out we'd died – or she'd be there still. Me too, probably. But you stand there spitting hellfire and damnation, when she needs something else from all of us. You make me sick, you really do.' May had swept round, turning to Howard. 'Come on, we're off.'

Howard had stared at Jack, totally at a loss as May had stalked off. 'Jack . . . '

'Go on, go after her, man. It's all right. I'll come to the mill in a day or two, when she's had a chance to cool down.'

'I didn't know.'

'Don't worry about it. Look after May. Go on, man.'

Howard had patted him awkwardly on his arm and then hurried after May, who was lost to sight in the crowd.

Jack had stood there for some minutes, his head swirling. Why had he gone for Grace like that? But that was it: she wasn't Grace Cunningham. She was another woman – a woman called Miss Angeline – and she had a husband. And the lass she'd called Myrtle had clearly been a servant of some sort, her maid most likely.

He found he had to sit down suddenly on the grass, his legs turning weak. That's why she spoke like a toff: she *was* one. Damn it, she'd made a fool of him for years with this story of being a working-class lass. How could he have been so blind? But a *husband*!

He sat there for some time, ignoring the odd glance from passers-by who clearly thought he'd had too much to drink. He wished he had. He wished he was blind-stinking-drunk and could just lie back and shut his eyes and be out of it.

As his anger had cooled, the full import of what May had flung at him hit home and he hunched his shoulders against it. Two lassies walked by, one turning and giving him the eye as she said, 'You should take more water with it, lad. Want a hand up? You'll catch your death sitting there.'

He shook his head, turning away and getting to his feet and walking off without a word. He heard her say something about 'uppity so-an'-so' to her pal, but he didn't look back. He knew where he was going.

Before he was halfway to Garden Street it had started to snow in earnest, the streets emptying as the snow got thicker. He walked on in the sparkling whiteness, which deadened all sound and made him feel like he was the only man alive. The smoke-blackened houses, filthy roads and pavements and the ever-present stench of the town was gone, lost under the gleaming virginal spotlessness. The house roofs were white, their windowsills and their doorsteps, and the air was icy-cold and clean. It brought the blood surging through his veins and sharpened his instincts, bringing an awareness of the moment, of the vital force that beat in his breast – of life.

He had to tell her how he felt about her: that he had loved her for years. It probably wasn't the right time – hell, he knew it wasn't the right time. Something like that should be done with flowers and when he was dressed in his Sunday best. But he had to tell her now, tonight, that it had been jealousy that had made him act the way he had. Jealousy that she'd had another life she wouldn't share with him; jealousy because she had shut him out and didn't need him, and he needed her so much; jealousy that another man had made her his. Most of all, that. A husband! Dear God – he raised his eyes to the white sky and called out silently, with every fibre of his being; he'd go mad thinking about it. Stark staring barmy.

By the time he was within a stone's throw of Garden Street he had changed his mind for the umpteenth time in as many minutes. He wouldn't tell her how he felt; there was no point. It would merely mean more embarrassment. She didn't give a fig for him and, by the sound of it, this husband of hers had put her off men for life. He would merely apologize for the way he had behaved, blame it on shock and say that he was always there for her as a friend.

He was suddenly aware of someone shuffling down the back lane, and saw it was an old man with a scruffy little dog at his heels. As he came level with Jack, the man eyed him over the top of his pipe. 'How do.'

Jack nodded, hoping the man would walk on.

'Cold night for standin' an' takin' the air, ain't it, lad?'

'I'm waiting for someone.'

'Oh aye? Well, I doubt if she'll come out the night, lad. Courting's best done in the warm, if you get my drift.'

'It isn't like that. I mean, I'm not courting a lass.'

'No? Surprising. Wouldn't have thought anything but

getting your oats would keep you waiting in this.' He gave a chesty chuckle. 'What say you, Buster?' he added to the little dog, which stared up at its master, clearly wishing it was home curled up in front of the fire rather than having its private parts dangling in this nasty, cold, white stuff.

On impulse Jack said, 'I've let someone down, and I need to put it right, that's all.'

'A lass.'

It was a statement rather than a question, but Jack answered it anyway. 'Aye, a lass, but we're not courting.'

'But you'd like to be.' The wheezy chuckle sounded again. 'I was young once, lad, believe it or not. Want my advice?'

Jack felt he was going to get it, whether he wanted it or not. He nodded.

'Faint heart never won fair lady. Is she fair, this lass? A looker?'

'She's perfect.'

'Oh aye, like that, is it? Look, lad, you don't get to be as long in the tooth as me without learnin' a bit as you go along, all right? An' one thing I've learned is that women like to know where they stand. If you mean business with this lass, say so. If you want a bit of slap an' tickle, an' then it'll be goodnight, Josephine, don't promise the other. Never does in the long run. But there's not many lassies who can resist a man wooing her when he's got marriage on his mind. Makes 'em weak at the knees, that does.'

'She's not like that.'

'No? Everyone wants to be loved, lad. And love breeds love. My Ava was fair gone on me brother when we were youngsters and living next door, and when he upped and married another lass, she took me as second best. She didn't say that, mind, but I knew. But I loved her enough for both of us, you know?'

Jack nodded. He knew all right.

'But I tell you, lad, and this is no lie, before we'd even had our first bairn she told me she loved me. And I knew she did – same as I'd known when she didn't. We had fifty happy years together before she passed on last Christmas. We raised seven bairns and they've got umpteen bairns of their own. I couldn't tell you how many; Ava knew all that. And now it's just Buster an' me, but that's all right. I had me time of loving.'

That's what he wanted. His time of loving. He stared at the old man who was fiddling with his pipe, which had gone out. As the dog whined plaintively, Jack bent down and patted it, getting a growl for his efforts.

'Don't mind him. He's an awkward little cuss, but we rub along well together, probably because I'm the same. See you, lad.'

'Aye, an' thanks. Thanks.'

As the old man shuffled on up the lane, Jack turned and walked straight into Angeline's back yard, not giving himself time to think. He thought he caught a glimpse of her through the window, sitting at the table, but he knocked on the back door – or hammered on it to be more accurate.

When she called out, 'Who's there?' he realized he'd probably frightened her, and his voice was soft as he answered, 'It's me, lass. Jack. I need to talk to you.'

'I . . . I'm just going to go to bed.'

'It won't take long. I want to apologize, face-to-face.' It cut him to the quick that her voice held a note of fear even though she knew it was him, but then what did he expect? She probably thought he wasn't through with ranting and raving. When the door opened she was holding herself straight and her chin was up, but again he saw fear in her eyes. 'Can I come in, lass?'

For answer she turned and walked into the kitchen, leaving the door open, and he followed her, his heart pounding. She didn't sit down, but faced him saying, 'You don't need to apologize – there's nothing to apologize for. It's me who should—'

'Grace.' He stopped. 'Angeline,' he went on, 'I need to make something clear to you and, when I do, I want you to know that I expect nothing, hope for nothing, because I know how you feel, but I have to say it. It's not the right time and everything is all wrong, but . . . ' He stopped again, drawing in a deep breath. She was standing as stiff as a board, and the guarded expression on her taut face wasn't encouraging. But for the old man and his Ava, Jack wouldn't have gone on. 'I love you, lass,' he said simply, 'be you Grace or Angeline, or whoever. I've loved you for a long time.'

She still didn't make a sound, and not a muscle of her face moved.

'May's told me a bit of what's gone on in the past, and I just want you to know' – he searched for the right words – 'that you're not alone. What I mean is, you can count on me as a friend. No strings attached. And whatever you decide to do about,' he swallowed hard, 'your husband, I'll support you. I . . . I was jealous, lass. When I sounded off, I mean, but I don't want you to think I meant it, when I said I didn't know you. I know all I need to know—'

'Please stop.'

'What?' Her whisper had been so faint that he stepped forward a pace, bending towards her.

'I . . . I'm everything you despise.'

'You're everything that I love.'

'Jack, don't—'

'I have to say it, lass. I should have said it years ago.' An idea had come to him. An idea so preposterous, so impossible, it couldn't be true, but it gave him the courage to reach out and pull her into his arms. For a moment she remained stiff and unyielding, and he thought he'd made a terrible mistake. And then she melted against him, her face turning up to his, and he was kissing her with all the passion and all the longing he'd kept hidden for seven years; kissing her until they were breathless and gasping as they swayed together in an agony of need.

It was a long time later – a time spent in murmurings

and wondering words of love and more kisses mixed with tears – that Jack whispered, 'You love me? This isn't a dream?'

Her arms tightened around him. 'For a long time.'

'Oh, my love.'

'But I thought you'd hate me, if you knew the truth.'

'How could I hate you?'

'But there's so much you don't know.'

'Then tell me.' He lifted her chin, kissing her full on the mouth, with such love in his eyes that she couldn't doubt it. 'Tell me all of it. I want to know everything about you; every tiny thing from when you were born till now. But let me say one thing: I promise you that whatever I hear, it won't affect what I feel for you. And I love your name . . . Angeline. My Angel. That's what I shall call you from now on: Angel. Has anyone else ever called you that?'

'My mama sometimes, when I was a little girl.' Mama. It reminded him that she was from a different world, but their two worlds were merging and he would make sure she never had cause to doubt him again.

# *Chapter Twenty-Five*

Mr Havelock of Havelock & Son, Solicitors, stared at his trusted clerk and the young woman Jack had brought in to see him. She had told an astonishing story, but he didn't doubt for one moment that it was true, or that the lady in question, who had gone by the name of Grace Cunningham for the last few years but was in fact Mrs Angeline Golding, had been severely ill-used.

However, he doubted he could say anything to her that would bring her any comfort; and if the situation escalated into a legal battle with the husband, she had absolutely no chance of winning. It wasn't this that really concerned him, though. He had grown fond of Jack over the years, and admired him for his principles and his determination to succeed, even when he found those same principles and views contrary to his own. The poor had always been poor and would remain so. It was the nature of things. Jack's desire to change the world and take on the Establishment through legal means was commendable, but misguided. And unpopular within the profession. He hadn't been at all surprised when, on qualifying as a solicitor, Jack had been unable to find a practice willing to take him on in that capacity. Not with the idealist views he held. Visionaries were all very well in their right place – in the Church as missionaries, for instance – but when it came to making money . . .

That said, he would hate to see his clerk making a fool of himself over a woman. Jack could lose everything he had worked for, and it could easily happen in this case, if he was linked with scandal. And what a scandal this could be: a wife returning from the grave just as her husband wanted to remarry. He cleared his throat. 'I trust you are aware, Mrs Golding, that the world in general could well see Mr Golding as innocent in this affair, if he genuinely thought you were dead?'

'Jack – Mr Connor – explained that, Mr Havelock.'

'You say he committed adultery all through your marriage, with a certain lady of your social circle. Can you prove this?'

Angeline shook her head. However sympathetic to her plight Mirabelle might have been when Myrtle went to see her seven years ago, she knew without a shadow of a doubt that Mirabelle would not admit to adultery with Oswald. It would ruin her husband, for one thing, and the stigma would be too great to bear. 'No, the only way would be for the lady in question to come forward and say so, but that would mean social suicide.'

'Quite so. The Matrimonial Clauses Act of 1878 facilitates legal separation and maintenance for badly used wives, which is an improvement on anything before that time, but only if the husband has been convicted of physical violence in a court of law. Is this the case?'

'No.'

'Likewise, whilst your husband could divorce you for adultery alone, if you had had an affair, for you to divorce him you need to prove adultery combined with desertion, cruelty, incest, bigamy or practising an unnatural vice.' Mr Havelock sighed. 'What I am trying to say, Mrs Golding, is that the law favours the man in every regard. Even if you obtained a separation order, which is highly unlikely, you would not be free to remarry and you could find yourself in an untenable position socially. I'm sorry, but I have to make this clear to you, unpleasant though it is.'

'I understand.' Angeline kept her gaze on the solicitor. 'But when I inform my husband that I am alive, I know he will want revenge, Mr Havelock. When I married him my fortune, which was considerable, was swallowed up within the estate, and my liberty and well-being came under the dictates of my husband. In a happy marriage, that would not have been a problem to me. But it was not a happy marriage, not from my wedding night onwards. Under the protection of the law, my husband ill-treated me physically and emotionally, ultimately causing the death of the child I was carrying, after which he had me shut away in a lunatic asylum. He is capable of anything. I have to inform him I am alive – I know that – but at the same time I need protection from him until somehow I can find proof of his adultery in the past and of his cruelty.'

'You think you can do that?'

'I don't know, but I want to apply for a judicial separation at the same time as I inform him I am alive. At the very least I feel it will show him I mean business.'

'Such petitions are not necessarily granted.'

'I know.'

'And, forgive me, Mrs Golding, but your husband might claim you are still mentally unfit and gain an order to have you recommitted to an asylum.'

'Over my dead body,' said Jack grimly.

'Mr Havelock, I have paid a thousand times over for my naivety in marrying a man I had a romantic, foolish infatuation for. I don't intend to go on paying for the rest of my life. I would like this to go to court so that I can have my say, and believe me, I won't come across as mentally unfit.'

The solicitor nodded. He could see what it was that had captured his clerk's heart. 'If your husband is as ruthless as you say he is, the weeks ahead could be highly unpleasant for you, Mrs Golding. In many ways. Are you prepared for this?'

'I am, and Mr Connor tells me you're the finest solicitor in the north of England, Mr Havelock, and more than a match for anyone. If you agree to take the case, I am more than happy to put myself in your hands. I don't want money or financial gain. I want a legal separation, and for the world to hear what Oswald is really like.'

'Revenge?'

'Justice. For myself and my child.'

'My dear, if you speak as well as this in court, we have won the case already.' He smiled, aiming to boost her morale after all the negativity.

Angeline smiled back – the first smile since entering Mr Havelock's office. 'Does that mean you will represent me?'

Oh yes, he could certainly see what Jack saw in her. 'Of course. It won't be easy, and I regret that I will need to ask you some pertinent questions in preparation, but that will be nothing compared to what you may have to face in court. By the very nature of your . . . ' he gave a little cough, 'disappearance for so long and your life under the name of Grace Cunningham, this case will arouse a lot of interest.'

Angeline nodded. She hadn't mentioned May's part in her escape from the asylum, nor did she intend to. There was no need for May to be dragged into this. Howard knew the full facts, but May's in-laws had no idea of that period in her life. Kind as they were, to the miller and his wife respectability was everything.

'And Jack?' Mr Havelock turned his gaze on his clerk. 'I don't need to tell you that it would complicate matters if Mr Golding got wind of your friendship with Mrs Golding. Until this is settled, discretion is the word.'

Jack nodded. 'My sister is Mrs Golding's close friend. I will only see her in May's company.'

'Better not at all.'

Angeline stared at the solicitor. 'But . . . '

'No buts, Mrs Golding. You are paying for my services, and I have to advise you as I see fit. Forgive my bluntness, but whilst most folk might privately admit that marriage can be a far-from-perfect institution, any hint of an illicit relationship on the part of the wife is fatal. Men are expected to stray; women are not. It is as simple as that.'

Angeline's cheeks were fiery, but as she opened her mouth to protest, Jack said quietly, 'Mr Havelock is right, Angel.'

'But it's so wrong.'

'I agree, but he is right.'

She looked into Jack's beautiful green eyes and saw that he meant it. 'It's so unfair.'

He smiled the smile that made her weak at the knees. 'It will only be for a short while, because Mr Havelock will do all he can to bring the case to court as quickly as possible. Isn't that right, Mr Havelock?'

Jim Havelock nodded. If this pair managed to follow his advice for more than a week he would be amazed, so time was definitely of the essence, but there were procedures to follow and regulations to adhere to, and a summer hearing would be the earliest they could hope for. Or maybe late spring. He leaned forward in his chair and opened his notebook. 'Now, Mrs Golding, let's start at the beginning . . . '

*

When Angeline left Havelock & Son later that morning she was able to keep herself together until she was out of sight and sound of the office; she felt she owed it to Jack to do that. She had cried on him enough over the last day or so. It was strange, but knowing he loved her made this all the more terrifying. She had so much more to lose now, if everything went against her. Mr Havelock had voiced the fear that plagued her every waking moment: that somehow Oswald would be able to have her locked away again. She kept telling herself it wouldn't happen – she had managed to make a new life for herself out of nothing, and had a responsible job and a home of her own. How could someone who was mentally infirm do that? Whatever Oswald said, surely the court would see the truth when it was under their nose? But thinking about how the law was weighted on the side of the husband kept doubt alive and well.

She wasn't expected back at work until after lunch; she had called in first thing that morning and explained the situation to her boss, who had nearly fallen off his chair in shock that his reliable, reserved secretary was someone else entirely, but he had told her to take as much time as she needed to sort out her affairs and that her job was safe, however things turned out. She had appreciated that.

As she walked along Northumberland Street, where Havelock & Son had their offices, she realized she was trembling, the threat of tears paramount again. Reliving the tawdry details of her marriage for Mr Havelock, the death of her baby, and not least the nightmare of the asylum had brought emotions to the surface that she normally kept buried. It had stopped snowing, but the sky was heavy with the promise of more, the wind cutting through her like a knife and the faces of passers-by as they hurried about their business preoccupied and scrunched up against the cold. Suddenly she felt very alone again and frightened; frightened of the enormity of what she was doing, of the scandal that would result, of seeing Oswald again and facing his venom. She wanted Jack, she thought desperately. She couldn't do this on her own. She needed his strength and reassurance.

She turned so swiftly on the packed snow beneath her feet that she almost went headlong, but for a pair of strong arms catching her. And then she looked up and Jack was there, pulling her against him, careless of the shoppers and the folk around them. 'Hey, I've got you,' he said softly. 'You looked upset when you left, and I thought you could do with a warm drink and a sticky bun, and most of all this.' He kissed her long and hard, as though they weren't in a busy street in full view of the world and his wife. It was the height of impropriety, but she didn't care.

When she could get her breath she said weakly, 'What are you doing here? You're supposed to be at work. And Mr Havelock said—'

'I know what Mr Havelock said, and it's good advice. I would say the same to a client in his place, but if you think I can stay away from you for a few days, let alone weeks and months, you've got another think coming. Golding hasn't even got Mr Havelock's letter yet, and after he has we'll be discreet – I'll make sure of that – but we're seeing this through together. All right?'

She nodded mistily.

'And don't worry about Golding. He's already beaten, he just doesn't know it yet. Come on, you need a cup of tea.'

He drew her arm through his and they started walking, but if Jack had thought to reassure her, it had the opposite effect. She wanted to tell him that he had no idea what Oswald was like – just the jaunty way Jack had spoken proved that. Oswald was vicious and immoral and devious, and he had no conscience, and this last made him more dangerous than anything. He believed that, as one of the ruling elite, he was untouchable, and because he believed it without a shadow of a doubt, he made it so. He was capable of anything, and how could a good, decent man like Jack – or Mr Havelock for that matter – get into the mind of someone like that and fight them on an equal footing? They couldn't, and she realized that was what had frightened her so much this morning. She was frightened for Jack, for the new life they were planning together; and yes, for herself, for who knew what revenge Oswald would take if he was thwarted? She was going to shatter his plans to marry again and was going to ruin his reputation, and even he wouldn't be able to survive such scandal unscathed.

So, a little voice in her head said quietly, what are you

going to do? Back down, disappear, hide away again? Let him win?

She glanced up at Jack as they walked and he caught her eye, smiling down at her as he moved her closer into the protection of his body.

No, she answered, even as her being quivered at the thought. She was going to fight.

# *Chapter Twenty-Six*

Oswald Golding had grown distinctly heavier in the last seven years, but it suited him. Now forty-six years of age, he had a presence that caused heads to turn wherever he went. The slight touch of silver in his fair hair was unnoticeable; his complexion was good, despite his many indulgences; and his handsomeness had a maturity that was very attractive. It was only his eyes which revealed the true nature of the man, and these were gimlet-hard, the grey having taken on the consistency of polished steel.

Fortune had not smiled on him in recent years, and he could trace the rapid decline back to the incident with Mirabelle at Lord Gray's Scottish estate. Before that his gambling had never been lucrative, but since that time his lack of success had become legendary. Of course, he should have stopped when he knew Jefferson was out to ruin him, but the gambling was a fever in his blood and he always told himself that things would level out. A few good wins, that was all he needed. But they had never come, and two years ago he'd had to face the fact that he was in danger of losing everything. And then a friend had tipped him off that, when he sat down with certain acquaintances, his drinks were more potent than they should be. He'd heard of that on the continent, of course – drinks being doped so that one would gamble wildly – but he had never dreamed it could happen to him. Not in England. Not among gentlemen.

He had been to see his accountant and then his bank manager, and with the latter he had used his charm, his name and an introduction to the higher echelons of society to hold back the wolves from the door. He had gained time. He knew exactly what he was going to do; he had done it once before and got himself out of trouble. This time with his marriage would come not only money, but influence and power. Angeline had been a nobody and of little account, which had suited his purposes at the time, but now he would marry a girl whose family could open avenues to unlimited wealth. And so he searched out his prey very carefully and decided on Lady Wilhelmina Argyle, whose father was a lord and whose mother numbered the Prince and Princess of Wales among her close friends.

It was unfortunate that the mother was a beauty and the daughter was not. Wilhelmina had buck-teeth the size of headstones, and a nose that was large and bony and that dominated her thin face; both of these traits she had inherited from her father. A father who, incidentally, adored his only offspring, and did not consider Oswald

Golding a suitable husband for his precious baby. And so had begun a steady, tenacious wooing of Lady Wilhelmina, who had fallen head over heels for Oswald from the start. He rather suspected the mother liked him, too, and when Lord Argyle was being particularly difficult, Oswald had comforted himself with the fact that in the future, once Wilhelmina was his wife, he would have the mother, too. It would be a most satisfactory revenge for the way he had been made to jump through hoops.

From the moment he had begun his advances to Lady Wilhelmina, Oswald had stopped his gambling and his escapades with the more notorious of his friends. In effect, he became a reformed character, so much so that Lord Argyle could no longer hold out against the combined pressure of his wife and his lovelorn daughter, and reluctantly – very reluctantly – agreed to the match.

So it was that, one morning in the middle of an icy and snowy January, Oswald came down to breakfast feeling very satisfied with himself. The engagement ball before Christmas had been a resounding success, and although Lord Argyle had tried to persuade his precious ewe-lamb to wait a full year before the nuptials, Wilhelmina and her mother had had their way and the wedding was to take place in May.

'Such a beautiful month,' Wilhelmina's mother had cooed when they had discussed it a few days before, 'with the promise of hot days and long, warm evenings to enjoy.'

He had smiled at the still-lovely woman who was only

two years older than himself. 'And sultry nights,' he had said softly, his eyes sending a message that was just for her. She had given her tinkling laugh, her cheeks flushing slightly, and Wilhelmina had chattered on, oblivious of his courting of her mother.

Now Oswald seated himself at the dining table, thinking of the day ahead. He had indulged himself and bought a new hunter after the engagement ball, a handsome beast that had yet to be fully tamed. He would do battle with the stallion today; he always enjoyed mastering a horse until it came at his whistle, although he never used force. That was the way to break a horse's spirit, and it was never such a noble beast afterwards. He used persuasion and intuition and patience, and it never failed. He stretched his long legs, encased in their leather riding boots, and glanced at the silver tray holding the morning's post, which the butler had placed to one side of his cutlery. When he was dining alone he didn't bother with a selection of covered dishes, but ordered his requirements the night before. Now, as Wood placed a plate of devilled kidneys and scrambled eggs in front of him, Oswald slit open the first letter with a silver paper knife.

For a moment the neat typewritten words didn't register. What they said was so bizarre, so preposterous, as to be unbelievable. Oswald made a sound deep in his throat, which caused the butler and housemaid who stood waiting at one side of the room to glance nervously at each other.

*She was alive? Angeline was alive? And asking for a separation order? It was here, in black-and-white, but it was impossible.*

He pushed his plate away, sending the contents scattering over the table, and jumped to his feet. Yelling at Wood to get the coach brought round, he strode out of the room.

Oswald read and reread the letter, and the enclosed papers that the envelope had held, as the coach made its way into Bishopwearmouth, where his solicitors had their offices. The letter heading showed Havelock & Son, Solicitors, followed by a Newcastle address. Swearing and cursing, he stared out of the window into the whirling snow. From his initial feeling of incredulity, now he didn't doubt it was true. Angeline was alive. The little scut was alive. Not only that, but she had the damn effrontery – the gall – to inform him of the fact through a solicitor's letter and ask for a separation, of all things. Where the hell had she been hiding for the last seven years?

As the carriage jolted him almost out of his seat, when it passed over a large pothole in the road concealed by the snow, he let loose a tirade of foul language at his coachman, before settling back in his seat again. Angeline! Hell and damnation: *Angeline*. And Wilhelmina . . . He groaned, grinding his teeth in fury. How could you be dead for seven years and then resurrect yourself, returning from the grave to wreak havoc? Well, he'd make sure she was dead again, and this time six feet under, with a body with her face on it to prove it; rather than a black, charred lump of meat that could be anyone.

What was he going to do? He stared blindly out of the window. If Argyle caught a whiff of this, it would be the death-knell for any hopes in that direction. Damn and blast her – Angeline had picked her moment well. How long had she been planning this?

By the time he reached Fawcett Street, the town's commercial centre, dignified by such buildings as the Liberal Club and the Town Hall, Oswald was barely able to contain his rage. There followed a shouting match with his solicitor, when Oswald wouldn't listen to reason and stamped about the office, his language so offensive it gave the solicitor's secretary a fit of the vapours. After this, Oswald told the man that he was dispensing with his services, in language colourful enough for a sailor, and returned to his carriage, telling the coachman to drive to Newcastle.

It was noon when he arrived at the offices of Havelock & Son, but far from cooling him down, the journey had given him time to stoke up his anger to boiling point.

Jack was sitting in the outer office, with the solicitor's secretary and the office girl, when Oswald flung open the door, startling them all. And even before Oswald opened his mouth, some sixth sense told Jack who it was.

'I've had a letter.' Oswald held the crumpled envelope in his fist, temper causing the veins to bulge in his forehead. 'Where's Havelock?'

'Have you an appointment, sir?' the secretary asked,

knowing full well he had not, at the same time as Jack rose to his feet.

'Appointment be damned! Where is he?' Oswald looked at the two offices leading from the outer office, one of which was Mr Havelock senior's and the other his son's. 'Tell him I want a word with him.'

Jack motioned with his hand to the secretary, coming to stand in front of Oswald as he said, 'And you are?' with not a shred of the politeness he would normally show to someone walking through the door.

Murderous grey eyes met clear, cold, green ones.

'The hell who I am,' Oswald ground out through gritted teeth. 'I want to see Havelock, and if you know what's good for you, you'll tell him so.'

'I asked you your na—'

'Get out of my way.'

The two men were equal in height, but Oswald was a good two or three stone heavier than Jack. However, as he made to thrust the younger man aside, he suddenly found himself whirled round, with his arm bent painfully behind his back.

'For the third time, sir, what is your name?' Jack hissed softly, twisting Oswald's arm until it was on the verge of breaking.

Oswald groaned, but Jack didn't release the pressure, and it was only the secretary saying, 'Mr Connor, *please*' as she pointed to Jinny, the little office girl, who looked as though she was about to swoon, that persuaded Jack to relax his grip slightly.

It was at this point that Jim Havelock opened the door to his office, having heard something of the commotion outside. He, too, had no doubt about who Oswald was, but this was due more to the fact that his clerk had murder on his face than it was to intuition. Walking over to the two men and putting his hand on Jack's arm in a silent warning, he said quietly to Oswald, 'Do I take it you wish to see me, sir?' And when Jack still didn't release him, he added, 'Thank you, Mr Connor. I think the gentleman will behave now.'

When Jack stepped back, Oswald was grey with pain, and for a moment he couldn't speak as he held his injured arm. Then he muttered, 'Damn it, he's broken my arm.'

'Strained it, I think you will find,' said Mr Havelock, sincerely hoping Golding wasn't right.

'I'll have the law on him.'

At this point the secretary said quietly, 'This gentleman was most obnoxious, Mr Havelock, and Mr Connor was forced to restrain him. Both Jinny and I were witness to this.'

'You the Havelock who wrote this letter?' Oswald continued to massage his arm after he'd thrust the letter at Jim Havelock. 'My wife has been dead seven years, and then I get this. How do you expect me to react?'

'Come into my office, Mr Golding, but there is little I can say, beyond what is written in the letter. I would advise you to give instructions to your own solicitor, so that matters can proceed. Mrs Golding is my client, you understand?'

'Matters can proceed?' Oswald glared at the solicitor. 'Oh, believe me, matters will proceed all right. My wife – if in fact this woman *is* my wife, which is yet to be proved – is deranged. If it is her, she needs locking away, and quickly. She escaped from a lunatic asylum, seven years ago. Did she tell you that? All this time I've thought she was dead, killed in the fire that night; a fire she probably started herself, thinking about it. I have doctors who will confirm that she's mentally unfit.'

'If you haven't seen her for seven years, how do you know she is mentally unfit?' Jack couldn't stop himself, earning a cautionary narrowing of the eyes from Jim Havelock.

'Come into my office, Mr Golding,' the solicitor said again. 'Can I get you a coffee before you go?'

'Damn your coffee!' Oswald swung round to Jack. 'And you – you haven't heard the last of this.' Looking at the solicitor again, he snarled, 'You ought to be careful who you employ. Someone like him could get you into a lot of trouble.'

'I am more than happy with my clerk's services, Mr Golding,' Jim Havelock returned calmly. 'And if there is nothing more we can do for you . . . '

'You take this on, you'll regret it.' Oswald's voice quivered with fury. 'I'll see to it that you're ruined, I promise you that. Representing a madwoman – you'll be a laughing stock. You hear me?'

The solicitor, his countenance still imperturbable,

stared back at the man whom his client had described as evil. And he could see why. Oh yes, indeed. 'Good day to you, sir.' He glanced at Jack. 'If you could show Mr Golding out, please.'

With a harsh oath, Oswald turned and wrenched the door open, banging it violently behind him as he left. For a moment the four of them remained still, and then Jim Havelock let out a long breath, just as his son, who had been in court with a client that morning, came in, saying, 'Who the dickens was that, who just left here? Nearly knocked me off my feet. In a devil of a temper, wasn't he?'

Devil was right. Jack was too wound up to speak, his neck muscles taut and his body rigid at the self-control he was exercising. For the second time in his life he had wanted to do murder, but unlike the time when he had attempted to face May's abuser, this time the man had been right in front of him and he had let him go.

As though he knew what Jack was thinking, Jim Havelock said quietly, 'We'll fight him in court, Jack, where it counts.' And to his son, 'He's Golding – the man I told you about – and he's everything Mrs Golding said, and worse.'

Yes, they'd fight Golding in court, but would they win? For the first time since Angeline had told him of the life she'd led with her husband, Jack acknowledged that doubt had crept in. Not about what she had declared – never that, he told himself, as though someone had suggested it; but now he could see for himself the sort of adversary Golding was, and he was formidable. He wished he had dealt with him here today. He wished he had put his hands round Golding's throat and squeezed and squeezed until the breath left his body. He would have been doing the world a favour, because it would be a better place without Golding in it. And he would have relished doing it. Before God, he would.

'Jack?' Jim put his hand on his clerk's arm, bringing him back from a dark place. 'Violence begets violence. You know that; that's why you've sacrificed much the last years, to challenge men like that in the courts.'

'Aye, and where's it got me? I'm still a clerk,' Jack said bitterly. 'They've got the money and influence to make black into white, if they want. The system's flawed, from top to bottom, and weighted in their favour every time.'

'You won't always be a clerk – your chance will come – but if you'd done something stupid today, Golding would have won. How many times have you said to me that the traditional attitudes of fatalism on the part of the working class, along with political scepticism, have to be changed from the inside out? Bright young men, like you, have to do that, Jack. No one else will. And every time someone like you resorts to violence to prove a point, it puts change back many years.'

'It wouldn't have been to prove a point,' Jack smiled mirthlessly. 'It would have been simply because he doesn't deserve to draw breath.'

'So men have argued through the centuries. But it's for the judicial system – be it a magistrate or twelve good men and true – to make such decisions, not the individual. Once we lose sight of that, whether we're an aristocrat or a common working man, we're no better than animals.'

'But the aristocrats rarely have to answer for taking the law into their own hands – you know that as well as I do.'

'All the more reason to bring about legal reformation, something that will be for the good of the whole and will affect the rich man in his castle *and* the pauper in his hovel. It's the only levelling process that has any chance of bringing about real change.'

Jack had preached the same many times, and he believed it, he really did; but, faced with Oswald Golding, a primal desire to avenge the grievous wrong done to one who had been without blame had risen up from somewhere dark and primitive inside him. He took a deep breath and nodded. 'I want him shamed and ruined. I want to see him eat his words and choke on them.'

'I think we can agree on that.'

'But can we do it?'

That was the thing. Jim Havelock gazed at the young man in front of him. He'd never lied to him and he wasn't about to start now. 'Come into my office,' he said quietly and, after telling Jinny to make everyone a cup of coffee, he followed Jack in and shut the door. 'The maid Mrs Golding spoke of – Myrtle – I think we need to go and have a chat with her and acquaint ourselves with the full facts regarding every aspect of Mrs Golding's former life. I'm interested in contacting the lady of whom the maid spoke, who was willing to speak to the authorities on Mrs Golding's behalf when she was in the asylum. At the very least we need to ascertain whether this lady would be prepared to act as a witness for Mrs Golding, because you do realize, Jack, that this is not going to be an easy case? However, Mrs Golding has made it plain she does not want this particular lady approached, so it would be better if this was done . . . discreetly.'

Jack nodded. Angeline was wrong not to arm herself with every means at her disposal, and if contacting this lady had to be done on the quiet, so be it. He was sure the maid would see it this way, after he had talked to her.

'I promise I'll do my best to expose Golding in court for what he is, Jack. Is that good enough?'

Not really, for Jack wanted a promise of sure-fire certainty, but he knew Mr Havelock could make no guarantees. He inclined his head. 'Yes, sir.' There was nothing else he could say, but he knew the months leading up to the court case were going to test his resolve to abide by the law. Every minute of every day.

Within two weeks Jack was deeply regretting he hadn't exerted a little more pressure and broken Oswald's arm – if not his neck – that day in the office. Mr Havelock received a letter from a leading London barrister whom Oswald had engaged to represent him, stating that his client, Mr Oswald Golding, was seeking a divorce from his wife on the grounds of her insanity. They were asking for a Decree of Nullity in which a marriage might be declared null and void if there was insanity at the time of the marriage. If this was granted, it would be as though the marriage had never taken place.

'Your husband,' Mr Havelock explained to a distraught Angeline, 'will be completely free to marry again. By implication of the court deciding in his favour, you would be detained in an asylum. The family doctor is willing to testify for Mr Golding, along with a London doctor who attended you at the time.'

'There was no London doctor.' Angeline could hardly believe her ears. 'I promise you, Mr Havelock. As for Dr Owen, he will say exactly what Oswald wants him to say.'

'This is serious, Mrs Golding. Your husband is alleging that you were mentally disturbed from the beginning, although he was initially able to control your "outbursts" within the home. After the miscarriage, he claims things escalated and you became physically violent – a danger to yourself and others – attacking him several times. They're also suggesting the fire at Earlswood, which caused the deaths of many people, could have been caused by you.'

'But it's not true.'

'I never for one moment thought it was.' They were sitting in Mr Havelock's office. Jack was holding Angeline's hand and his face, like hers, was as white as a sheet. 'But now we have the measure of what we're up against, Mrs Golding. You must do nothing, say nothing, and make no approach to Mr Golding. You understand? Mr Golding's barrister is pushing to get the case heard early because of the circumstances – his proposed marriage, and so on. Mr Golding's fiancée is apparently standing by him, so no doubt they hope this will impress the judge. But don't despair, my dear. Truth is on our side after all.'

# *Chapter Twenty-Seven*

*Don't despair*. Mr Havelock's words came back to Angeline many times over the ensuing weeks. Fortunately, for she had enough to cope with, one of the blessings of her new life was that she was sufficiently removed from upper-class society for the avid tittle-tattle that ensued in high places not to reach her.

Gossip and scandal, the twin sisters of disgrace, were adept at ingratiating themselves into the fine houses and great estates where the idle rich had too little to occupy themselves with. Long before the court case in the middle of May, it had become common knowledge that the late Mrs Angeline Golding wasn't deceased at all; nor had her supposed death been caused by a rapid decline after the tragic miscarriage of her child. No, it was whispered behind pale soft hands in splendid drawing rooms, her husband had had her committed to a lunatic asylum. Could you believe it? How deliciously shocking! Not only that, but he had believed her dead for all this time, only for her to appear just as he was set to marry Lady

Wilhelmina Argyle! What a rumpus that had caused. Lord Argyle was rumoured to have wanted Lady Wilhelmina to break off the engagement, but she had insisted that she would stand by Golding, whom, she maintained, was the injured party and guilty of no wrongdoing.

An attempt on the life of the Prince of Wales by a sixteen-year-old anarchist at the beginning of April was talked about briefly, but as the Prince had escaped uninjured, it really could not compare with the ongoing drama of the Golding affair. Even Lillie Langtry's portrayal of a dissolute courtesan in *The Degenerates* in London, which caused a sensation – several ladies of the aristocracy fainting clean away – was merely a play after all, a theatrical piece, whereas this was real life, with enough histrionics to keep the most bored socialites interested.

Angeline, oblivious to most of this and safe in the anonymity that Grace Cunningham afforded her, at least until the court case, carried on her normal life. She was fully aware this state of affairs would come to an end, however, and was mentally preparing herself for what would ensue.

On Mr Havelock's advice, she travelled down to London and consulted one of the top physicians in mental health in his rooms in Harley Street. After a lengthy consultation during which she explained the facts to him, keeping nothing back, he put her through a rigorous series of tests and examinations, at the end of which he declared her sound of mind and agreed to appear in her defence, if asked to do so.

Mr Havelock's investigations unearthed the fact that, after the fire at Earlswood, the asylum had been closed for more than a year. After this time it had been rebuilt and opened as a private nursing home. Superintendent Craggs and his wife had taken up an appointment in another part of the country, again in charge of an asylum, and when Mr Havelock had written to them, they had made it clear they wanted nothing to do with the present proceedings. He certainly could not comment on individual patients, the superintendent had written back. To do so would be highly improper. Nor would he venture an opinion on the family of such patients. Besides which, most of the records of the patients and their treatment had been lost in the fire, and one could not be expected to remember details relating to seven years ago. Which was all very well, Mr Havelock said privately to Jack, as long as the man didn't pop up like an unwelcome jack-in-the-box and speak up for Golding.

Spring came and it was a warm one. Almost overnight, flowers were blooming and the skylarks were singing their sweet, liquid melody in blue May skies. The day before the court case, a Sunday, Angeline and Jack spent together. They had been careful not to be seen in public together, at Mr Havelock's insistence, but this day was their own. Jack arrived at her little house at eight o'clock on a beautiful sunny morning, and when she opened the door he was standing next to a bicycle with two sets of pedals and two saddles, arranged one behind the other. 'It's a tandem,' he said, grinning at the expression on her face. 'A bicycle made for two.' He pointed to the basket at the front. 'A picnic, also for two.'

They set off amid much wobbling and little screams from Angeline. She had never ridden a bicycle before; her mother would have considered such a thing with horror, and totally unsuitable for the female sex of any age. But with Jack steering and keeping the bike upright, she soon found she was enjoying herself, the more so when they left the town behind and reached open countryside. There followed a day Angeline knew she would remember for the rest of her life.

In quiet pockets of wayside vegetation in the hedgerows and verges the drooping, bell-shaped heads of bluebells vied with buttercups, daisies and a whole host of spring flowers. The day was comfortably warm, with a gentle May breeze heavily scented with blossom, and butterflies and honey-bees were busily going about their business. They passed the odd hamlet and small village, thatched cottages with small front gardens bursting with colour, as pretty as any picture on a chocolate box, and wherever they went folk stopped to stare and smile and wave.

After this had happened several times, Angeline decided it was because a tandem was such a novelty, but Jack insisted it was her beauty that caused such a stir.

The stench and dirt of the town with all its industry, tenements and poverty seemed a million miles away, the deeper they travelled into the countryside along dirt lanes ridged by cart wheels and horses' hooves, and already the clover and rye grass had started to seed and farm lads were going about their scything in the fields. Overhead the sky got bluer and the temperature steadily rose, and by the time they ate their picnic lunch in a flower strewn meadow the distance was partly obscured by a trembling heat-haze.

They lingered there all afternoon, talking, laughing, loving, the time bitter-sweet. Neither of them mentioned the following day, but its shadow made each moment all the more precious. Angeline didn't want ever to go home, back to the black smoke of factory chimneys, the grids of streets, the dank and often foul-smelling river and the incessant noise and bustle of thousands of people packed into a small area of thriving humanity. She said as much to Jack as she lay with her head on his chest in the sweet, green grass, and he was quiet for a few moments. 'It's where I'm called to be, lass,' he said after a while. 'There in the midst of it all, with my ain folk. One day I want to set up as a solicitor myself, but among them – the people who matter – taking on cases that the fancy lawyers won't, for folk who haven't got two pennies to rub together.'

'I know. Oh, I know.' She knelt up, looking down into his green eyes. 'And I want that, too, I want to be with you. But' – she smiled ruefully – 'I want this, too. The peace and quiet, and the smell of newly cut grass and flowers.'

'It's not so romantic in the winter, lass. Not when you're knee-deep in mud and the fire sends the smoke back down the chimney to choke you, and you're hungry and tired. You think the pay's bad in the steel works and mines, but some farmers pay their men a pittance for a day that begins when it's dark and ends when it's dark. I know of farm labourers who—'

'Shush.' She touched his mouth with the tip of one finger. 'Let me have my dream, Jack, and see it as beautiful today.'

He sat up at that, pulling her fiercely into him. 'I don't want to spoil your dream, lass, and I promise you there'll be days like this in the years ahead. It'll be up to us to make them happen and escape the town now and again. We'll bring the bairns and let them run free, little lassies with ribbons in their hair who look just like you.'

'And little boys who are the image of their father.' She smiled at him, not wanting to spoil the moment. But if things went against her tomorrow, who knew what would happen? And even if Oswald's petition was thrown out of court, and he was shown up for who and what he was, it would mean that she was still married to him – a separation order being the most she could hope for in the future, unless at some point she was able to prove evidence of his adultery and cruelty and so obtain a divorce.

But she wouldn't think about the ifs today, she told herself resolutely. Not when she was with Jack and each minute was speeding by so quickly. All she could do was put herself in the hands of God. God, and Mr Havelock, she added wryly.

'It will happen, lass,' Jack said again, kissing her long and hard until every other thought went out of her head and there was only Jack – Jack and this wonderful, stolen day.

They cycled home in a mellow dusky twilight broken only by the songs of the blackbird and thrush and the cooing of wood pigeons in the trees bordering the lanes. All too soon they were approaching the outskirts of the town, and then on into the densely packed streets and industry.

Jack left her on the doorstep; he had to return the tandem to the friend he had borrowed it from that evening, but long after he had disappeared Angeline stood staring after him.

He had kissed her before he rode off, holding her close and whispering that she had to trust him that everything would be all right, and she had nodded and said all the correct things. But she was frightened. So frightened.

Once indoors, she made herself a hot drink and forced down some supper, only to go to bed and lie awake most of the night, cat-napping now and again and then waking with a start from nightmarish dreams. When a faint glow in the sky told her dawn was breaking she was glad to get up, and as she washed and dressed a calm descended. The day she had dreaded was here. No more waiting. Mr

Havelock had told her that Oswald would be in court, but there was nothing she could do about it.

May had wanted to be present for moral support, but as she was as big as a house with suspected twins, Howard wouldn't allow it. Angeline had expressed her thanks to May, but in actual fact she was relieved at how things had turned out. If there was the faintest chance of May being recognized by someone from the asylum days, it would be a disaster. Far better that she was out of the picture altogether. Myrtle and Albert were leaving the farm in the care of the family and meeting her at court, and of course Jack would be there, in the guise of Mr Havelock's clerk.

Angeline looked at herself in the bedroom mirror before she left the house. The day out in the open air had put a touch of colour in her cheeks, for which she was thankful; she suspected she would have been as white as a sheet otherwise, the way she was feeling inside. She had dressed carefully in a smart grey suit with a pink blouse, and her little hat was the same hue as the blouse. Neat and respectable. She nodded at the thought, oblivious of the startling beauty of her reflection.

She had arranged for a horse-drawn cab to pick her up and transport her over the river to the county court, situated at the foot of Westgate Hill at its junction with Fenkle Street. It wasn't too far and she could easily have walked the distance, but Mr Havelock had advised her to arrive by cab in case the weather was inclement on the day. As it happened, it was raining slightly when she left the house and she was glad she had taken the solicitor's advice.

She had been to look at the court building and make sure she knew exactly where it was some weeks before, and now, as the cab deposited her at her destination, her gaze was drawn to the five female heads carved on the window keystones. The one set under the date of the building was Justice wearing her blindfold. She gazed at Justice for a few moments, her heart thudding like a drum, and when she lowered her gaze there were Myrtle and Albert and Mr Havelock, and Jack was coming towards her to take her arm. And so she walked through the arched entrance surrounded by people who cared about her.

And then she saw Oswald. He was standing some distance away, talking to a man who was clearly his barrister, and a young, well-dressed woman was hanging on his arm, with an older man on the woman's other side.

She stared at him, taking in every detail of his appearance in the few moments before he noticed her. He was as well groomed and fashionable as she remembered, although stouter, but he carried himself with the same effortless panache. Perhaps it was her gaze that drew his, because suddenly the cold grey eyes were looking straight at her, and for a moment she was back in the asylum, listening to him pretend that he had cared about the death of the baby, in his charming, empty way. *He was everything she despised, everything she hated.* She stared back at him, her face expressing exactly what she was feeling, and it was his eyes that dropped from hers. He must have said something about her, because the next moment his three companions had turned to look at her, and Angeline noticed that the woman in particular was glaring. Wide-spaced eyes over a nose that was like a sharp beak raked her from head to foot, deliberately offensive. It was only the older man swinging the woman around and saying something that broke the contact.

'Angel?' Jack's voice penetrated the whirling emotion. 'Don't let them unnerve you, sweetheart. All right? All you have to do is speak the truth today and, however good this man from London is, he can't trip you up. Do you hear me?'

She heard him, but for a moment she couldn't respond. She had suffered at Oswald's hands, and since the first moment she had met him he had been in control. She had never seen it so clearly. Somehow she managed to turn to Jack and say, 'Don't worry. He can't—' She had been about to say, 'He can't hurt me any more', but legally he could, if the case went his way. Instead she changed it to, 'He can't frighten me any more' and, as she spoke the words, she knew them to be true. For years she had lived in fear of Oswald Golding, but however things went today, his hold on her was broken. He had done his worst and she had survived. She had Jack, and she had good friends. She glanced at Myrtle and Albert, and thought of May and Howard. The bond between herself and her friends had been forged in the fire of adversity and it wouldn't break. She doubted if Oswald had one person in the world he could say the same about.

Raising her chin, she smiled at Mr Havelock. 'Let battle commence.'

# *Chapter Twenty-Eight*

The courtroom was unusually crowded for a civil case. But this was no ordinary case, and anyone who had got a whiff of it was there. The local justice of the peace, Justice Cook, seemed somewhat annoyed about the interest. Staring across the court, he opened with, 'I trust everyone in this room agrees that marriage is the very basis of society, something to be held together at all cost. We are a civilized nation, a great nation, and the Empire stretches round the globe, bringing enlightenment to native lands and peoples. It is our sacred duty.'

Lowering his head, he consulted the papers in front of him.

'Golding versus Golding. I understand an initial request by Mrs Golding for a judicial separation was responded to with a petition for nullity by Mr Golding. For those present, let me clarify. Nullity enables a marriage to be declared null and void; a separation does not dissolve the marriage, and neither party can marry again. Every Decree of Nullity or separation is in the first instance a decree nisi, the grounds having been proved, and this is not made absolute until the expiration of six calendar months. So' – he raised his head again, his gimlet eyes raking the court – 'let us begin.'

The court soon discovered that Oswald Golding's London barrister was an eloquent speaker. He described how the late Mr Hector Stewart had introduced Mr Golding to his niece, the then Miss Angeline Stewart, shortly after her parents had died. It was immediately clear the girl had led a very sheltered life, but at the time Mr Golding – deeply in love and wishing to see only the best in his beloved – assumed it was simply a devoted mother and father being over-protective that had led them to keep their daughter hidden away from society. Of course, looking back now, the signs of madness were already there; but, as everyone knows, hindsight is a wonderful thing. The courtship was brief – again, in hindsight, it had become clear that Mr Hector Stewart knew of his niece's affliction and was anxious to rid himself of the responsibility of caring for her. The marriage subsequently took place and, from the very day of the wedding, Mr Golding's wife began to exhibit worrying quirks and mannerisms – her disposition becoming, on the one hand, withdrawn and non-communicative with Mr Golding and, on the other, prone to bouts of violent temper and unreasonable behaviour.

The barrister went on to explain how, because Mr Golding cared deeply for his poor wife, he had done everything he could to find a cure for her mental deterioration, but to no avail. Some of the time she appeared perfectly normal, and he found himself hoping she was getting better, but then – particularly when they were alone – her mood swings could be described as extreme. The doctors he approached proved to be unable to help, beyond suggesting the benefits of an asylum, but this he was loath to do. The barrister paused here, his voice dropping as he said, 'He cared for her, you see, despite the fact that by now he realized he had been tricked into marrying a mentally sick woman.'

Justice Cook cleared his throat. 'Keep to the facts, sir. You know better than that.'

The barrister bowed in acknowledgement, before going on to say how things had gone rapidly downhill when Mrs Golding became with child – one fit of rage causing such extreme behaviour that she fell, losing the child, and almost her life. After this she became completely unhinged, attacking Mr Golding so badly that the doctor had to be called to the house, after which she was taken to Earlswood Asylum. There she continued to display aggressive behaviour, so much so that several times she was put in a padded cell.

Angeline felt, rather than heard, the intake of breath from those listening.

'At other times,' the barrister said, 'Mrs Golding could appear as normal as you or I, which is perhaps the most disturbing aspect of this sad affair. After some months a fire broke out at the asylum in which over twenty people lost their lives. It couldn't be ascertained how this began, but Mrs Golding was detained in the area in which the fire took hold.'

Again Justice Cook warned the barrister, who graciously apologized to the court.

'Mrs Golding was assumed dead in the fire, and Mr Golding was left trying to rebuild his shattered life.' The barrister paused again, glancing around the court and then at Oswald, who sat with his head in his hands, the picture of dejection. 'Some years later he meets the lady sitting next to him today, a lady who made him believe in love again, who infused in him the will to trust another woman sufficiently to take the momentous step of marriage. And what happens? Mrs Golding, who we can only assume has been waiting and watching for reasons of her own – reasons that must seem acceptable to her poor, damaged mind – makes herself known to him. After seven years. *Seven years!* Your Honour,' the barrister now looked straight at the JP, his voice ringing out in condemnation as he said, 'Mrs Golding's illness has made her dangerous and cunning. My client feared for his life many times in the past and he fears for it now, if she is left to her own devices. This was never a real marriage; from the first Mr Golding was her carer, her nurse, her warder, if you like. Never has a Decree of Nullity been more deserved, and for her own sake – her own protection – Mrs Golding must be detained in a secure place indefinitely. Let us not lose sight of the fact that, but for the tragedy of the fire that killed so many innocent people, she would still be in Earlswood today.'

Turning back to the court, he went on, 'I would like to call the family doctor who attended Mrs Golding at the time of her marriage, along with others who can testify to the truth of the attacks on Mr Golding by Mrs Golding.'

Angeline had sat as still as stone during the barrister's discourse. Mr Havelock had warned her before the case began that she must be calm and circumspect at all times, and that any show of emotion or anger would be used by Oswald's counsel against her. Now, as she looked over to where Dr Owen was preparing to speak, she was assailed by so many terrible memories of the time when she had lost the baby that for a moment she thought she was going to faint.

Dr Owen spoke quietly – so quietly that he was asked to repeat certain statements – but his description of her mental state was damning. Another doctor, a London man whom Angeline knew for sure she had never set eyes on in her life, took the stand and said much the same. He was followed by one of Oswald's friends, Robert Taylor, a plump cocksure little man who described an incident when he had had to pull Mr Golding's wife off him as she had tried to scratch his eyes out. His crime? Taylor asked sadly; Mr Golding hadn't been sufficiently enthusiastic about a new frock she was wearing.

Oswald had persuaded people to lie for him. Angeline's eyes were drawn to where he sat, and just for a moment he looked at her, one eyebrow slightly raised. *You don't stand a chance*, that eyebrow said. *You cannot win. I will crush you as I would an ant, and with as little feeling.*

She turned to Mr Havelock. Jack was sitting on the solicitor's other side, for Mr Havelock had not wanted them next to each other and had warned them, more than once, not to look at each other or communicate during their time in court. Now, as she caught sight of Jack's face, she prayed he wouldn't do anything foolish. Mr Havelock must also have noticed his clerk's murderous expression, because he murmured something in Jack's ear, and Jack lowered his head, pretending to fumble with some papers in his lap.

'Mr Havelock?' Angeline touched the solicitor's arm. 'The second doctor, he's the one I haven't seen before. And the incident Oswald's friend described never happened.'

Mr Havelock nodded, but said nothing, and after a moment she sat back in her seat.

The next person to speak was Mrs Gibson, Oswald's housekeeper and, unlike Robert Taylor, she seemed reluctant. With the barrister prompting her, she related what had happened the night before the morning Mrs Golding was taken to the asylum. 'And you saw Mrs Golding attack her husband, leaving him with severe lacerations to the face and throat?' the barrister intoned solemnly.

There was a pause, and Mrs Gibson's eyes moved

from the barrister to Oswald and then back to the barrister.

'Mrs Gibson?' Justice Cook spoke gently and firmly. 'I'm sure this is an ordeal for you, but please answer the question.'

'I . . . ' Mrs Gibson was twisting her hands together and then, as though she had made up her mind about something, she straightened. 'I did not see it, no.'

'You did not?'

'No.' Seemingly undeterred by the barrister's tone, Mrs Gibson went on, 'When I came into the room, Mrs Golding was lying across the bed. The master was shouting and carrying on, but I didn't actually see her attack him.'

'Let me phrase my question differently. When you came into the room, was Mr Golding's face scratched and bleeding?'

'Aye. Aye, it was.'

'And was there anyone else in the room besides Mrs Golding?'

'No, it was her bedroom.' Mrs Gibson sounded faintly scandalized at the question. 'And she'd been very poorly. None of us expected her to pull through and—'

'Quite. And had Mrs Golding been unpredictable and emotional for some time before this violent assault on her husband?'

Mrs Gibson stared at the highfalutin London barrister with the pompous voice. She stared at him for some moments. Then she said, 'The mistress was seven months gone when her baby, a little lassie, was stillborn, and after that she was out of it for a good month and not expected to recover. When she came to herself, we had to tell her the baby was gone. Yes, sir, she was emotional.'

'That is not what I meant.'

Mrs Gibson made no reply to this, but her chin went up a notch.

'Thank you, that is all.'

Oswald had been staring at his housekeeper, and he continued to stare at her as she nodded at the barrister and resumed her seat, but she did not glance his way.

The barrister continued to speak for some minutes more, contriving to paint a picture of a loving, desperate husband trying to cope with his demented wife. Angeline didn't recognize any of the characters in the fairy story he was telling so persuasively, but she was sick with fear. One of Jack's most bitter criticisms of the upper classes was that they had the money and power to make black into white, and it was happening here in front of her. The barrister was good, very good, and if she had been sitting in the court listening to him and didn't know any better, she would be feeling sorry for the poor man who had been hoodwinked into marrying a deranged madwoman.

She felt Jack's eyes on her more than once, but she didn't dare reach out for the comfort he was trying to give soundlessly. If she met his eyes she would break down, she knew it, and she must not. Mr Havelock had stressed that she must not give way, but must maintain a dignified silence, and she could see why.

At last the London barrister came to the end of his summing up, and Mr Havelock stood up. He did not cut such a commanding figure as his adversary, who looked every inch a polished man of the world, but from his first sentence he had the attention of everyone in the room.

'"What a twisted web we weave, when we first practise to deceive." I don't know who said that, but never has it been more true than in the case of my client's husband, Mr Oswald Golding. He has told my learned colleague who is representing him a pack of lies – lies that are grievous and wicked in nature. Grievous, because it is sad to see how far one human being will go in pursuit of his own ends; and wicked because, should his lies succeed, they will commit an innocent woman once again to the horrors of a lunatic asylum. And I say "once again" advisedly because – and let me stress this – Mrs Angeline Golding is not, and never has been, mentally infirm. What she was, and she admits this herself, was foolish and young when she met Oswald Golding, naive and ingenuous, a true innocent in every sense of the word.'

Mr Havelock turned, looking straight at Oswald. 'It has been said Mrs Golding led a very sheltered life before her parents were tragically killed in a coach accident, and this is true, but not for the reason my learned friend implied. She was simply the only, treasured child of loving parents – parents who were aware of the beauty in the child that we now see in the woman, and who feared for her in this fallen world in which we live. They protected her, as any parent worth their salt protects their children, but there never was, or has been, the slightest suspicion of insanity. With Justice Cook's permission, I would like to challenge every point Mr Golding has made. And with that in mind I would ask Miss Selina Robson to take the stand.'

Miss Robson proved to be a calm, unruffled speaker who stated categorically that the young Angeline Stewart had been intelligent, biddable and enjoyable to teach, and was, she emphasized, as sane a girl as anyone could wish to meet. Furthermore her uncle, Mr Hector Stewart, was very happy to become her guardian and take her into his home, and it was only Mr Golding's insistence on marrying Angeline at the earliest opportunity that rushed the marriage into being.

Mr Havelock then called Dr Owen, but spent little time on him, beyond establishing that his position as family doctor to Oswald Golding was a lucrative one. The London doctor was a different kettle of fish, and from the first Mr Havelock went on the attack. Where did he examine Mrs Golding, and how many consultations were there? Six examinations took place at the Golding estate? Now that was strange, because none of the servants could remember even one such visit by the good doctor. Oh, they might have taken place in London? And there were records detailing this? Records are only kept for five years? Surely not! In fact, impossible to believe. And so on. Mr Havelock savaged the man – there was no other word for it. Angeline was in awe of Jack's employer.

By the time the doctor stood down, he was sweating and red in the face. Mr Havelock was as fresh as a daisy. As the Harley Street consultant whom Angeline had recently seen came to the stand, Angeline tugged on Mr Havelock's sleeve. 'How did you manage to talk to the staff at the house, without Oswald knowing?'

'I didn't.' Mr Havelock was pleased with himself. 'But you were sure you hadn't seen him, so I thought I'd try a bluff.'

He then proceeded to verify from the Harley Street consultant that Mrs Golding was mentally sound and in possession of all her faculties, which the good doctor was only too happy to elaborate on, with Mr Havelock encouraging him.

Nurse Ramshaw was called next. She described in harrowing detail how desperately ill her patient had been, and how very detached Mr Golding had seemed, both with regard to his wife's condition and to the loss of his daughter. She also repeated Mrs Golding's accusation that her husband was responsible for the tragic miscarriage.

'Did she say what had happened?' asked Mr Havelock.

Nurse Ramshaw shook her head. 'Not exactly, but Mrs Golding had sustained a broken nose, equivalent to being punched in the face by a man's fist.'

Objections from Oswald's barrister followed.

'Did your patient exhibit any symptoms of madness during this period?' Mr Havelock asked, when the furore in court had subsided. The reply was a definite No. Grief, pain, distress aplenty, along with extreme physical weakness, but that was all.

Mr Havelock thanked the nurse and pretended not to notice the argument Oswald was having with his barrister, who was trying to calm his client down. Clearing his throat, Mr Havelock looked across the court. 'At this point I would like to make it clear that Mrs Golding was wrongfully incarcerated in Earlswood Asylum on the orders of her husband, and state that the fire which proved so devastating was not – and could not have been – started by her. In fact an inquiry sometime after the event suggested that another patient, one Lady Lindsay, who had run amok that same day, was probably responsible. Also, my client was only twice locked in a padded cell: once on the day of admission, when she was naturally terrified and horrified to find herself in such a place, and again after a visit by her husband sometime later, when he proved most objectionable. Yes, she escaped on the night of the fire, but may I ask: wouldn't each one of us take such an opportunity, if we were wrongfully imprisoned with no hope of appeal?'

The court was perfectly quiet, with most eyes on Angeline's pale but composed face.

'And this supposed madwoman then not only survived, on finding herself thrust into a hostile environment, penniless and reduced to pauper level, but over the last seven years has risen to the point where she holds down a responsible job and has a comfortable home of her own. Why, you may ask, did she not make herself known to Mr Golding before now? Again, I ask you: would you have done so, knowing with absolute certainty that he would attempt to have you forcibly locked away again? It was only when my client discovered her husband was planning to marry again that she knew she couldn't remain silent any longer, because if she had allowed him to commit bigamy, she would not have been able to live with her conscience. She would not wish another woman to live through the hell she has been through at the hands of this man – a violent, cruel and totally unprincipled man who married her simply for the fortune that came with her. Yes,' Havelock said, as a stir swept through the room, 'I have it on good authority that, due to his profligate and dissolute lifestyle, Mr Golding needed an injection of money into his estate, and needed it fast.'

This time the objections from Oswald's barrister came thick and fast, with Justice Cook adding his weight as he asked if Mr Havelock could prove such accusations.

For answer, and with drama worthy of anything seen at the theatre, Mr Havelock said in ringing tones, 'Would Mrs Mirabelle Jefferson please take the stand?'

Angeline had known nothing of this, and now she half-rose in her seat, while Jack leaned round Mr Havelock to say, 'Sit down, and say not a word. He knows what he's doing.'

Mirabelle here? Angeline stared at the other woman, who had swept in with such dignity and aplomb. Mirabelle was looking every inch the noble lady, perfectly coiffured and dressed, as only unlimited wealth and good taste could produce. For an instant – just a moment – the emerald-green eyes met hers, but Mirabelle's lovely face showed no expression beyond a haughty expressionlessness, which continued as Mr Havelock began his questioning.

Angeline's gaze searched the room for Marmaduke, and there he sat, at the very back of the court, his eyes fixed on his wife. Even from that distance it was clear how much he adored her, and Angeline was amazed he had agreed that Mirabelle should come here today.

Oswald was now sitting up straight, his back rigid and his face as dark as thunder, and Angeline noticed that the father of his fiancée was leaning forward in his seat, his gaze locked on Mirabelle.

And what Mirabelle said was damning. With no prompting by Mr Havelock, after stating her name and address, she said in a voice that easily reached the back of the room, 'I was not asked to come here today to speak for Mrs Golding, but when I found out about this case, I contacted her solicitor and asked if I might do so. My husband and I have known Mr Oswald Golding for some years – longer, in fact, than we have known his wife. At the time of his marriage to her, he told my husband and me that he was in a fix financially and needed a great deal of money. He gambles,' Mirabelle paused before adding, 'among other pursuits. He was quite candid that he was marrying Angeline for the fortune she had inherited from her parents, and spoke about her with little feeling. Coldly, in fact.'

Angeline found her eyes going to Marmaduke again. Oswald might well have confided in his mistress at the time of her marriage, but in Marmaduke? Never. Nevertheless, he was nodding slightly as she spoke and was clearly supporting her story.

'From the time he married her he was obnoxious and cruel, and although he was our friend at that point, his behaviour to a young innocent whom he had coaxed to fall in love with him both disgusted and appalled us. Furthermore, to his shame he displayed no pangs of conscience about his treatment of her, which was abominable – so much so that my husband and I were forced to take him to task several times when he was physically abusive, and that in our presence. What she had to cope with when they were alone, I dare not imagine.'

Angeline's eyes were wide and she couldn't believe her ears. Mirabelle was lying, or at the very least stretching the truth to breaking point.

'He was not discreet about his other women; in fact one could say he seemed to take delight in taunting her in that regard. And what really sickened my husband and I, and persuaded us to end our friendship with him for good, was that in front of certain members of our group he would behave like a devoted husband, all the while laughing behind his hand. It was too, too distressing.'

'Thank you for that background history, Mrs Jefferson. May I ask if you and your husband were aware of the circumstances in which Mrs Golding was forcibly locked away in Earlswood Asylum?'

'Not when it first happened, no. We knew of course that Mrs Golding had sadly lost the child she was carrying, and was ill unto the point of death. A great many of her friends were praying for her at that time. Lord Gray' – Mirabelle paused for a second, to let the name sink in with Justice Cook, knowing that such an illustrious and influential connection would do Angeline no harm – 'was particularly concerned, having suspected for some time that Mr Golding was not the husband that Mrs Golding deserved. Once Mr Golding had his wife locked away, he kept up the pretence she was at home and too ill to see anyone. It was only Mrs Golding's personal maid – or ex-maid, I should say – who had married and was living in this area who discovered the truth. She came to see me in London, knowing my husband and I had been friends of the Goldings, and at that point my husband knew he had to do something about such a grave injustice. One does not like to interfere between man and wife, but we realized that by adhering to that thinking we, along with the rest of Mrs Golding's friends, had been as guilty as Pilate was in washing his hands, so to speak. Unfortunately the fire that has been spoken of today occurred, and we were too late.'

'I see. Thank you, Mrs Jefferson.'

'May I just add something more?' Mirabelle turned with queenly grandeur to Justice Cook. 'As we speak, Mr Golding has huge debts. My husband knows this for a fact. And again he's set to marry a woman who has unlimited wealth . . . '

Justice Cook hastily forbade Mirabelle from saying any more, but she had said enough. There was heated muttering between Oswald and his barrister, and after a few moments the barrister stood to his feet. Angeline, along with everyone else present probably, had been wondering if Oswald would challenge Mirabelle's description of his character. To do so could possibly dig a deeper hole for him, but not to do so would be tantamount to admitting she was telling the truth.

'Mrs Jefferson, have you ever heard the expression "Hell hath no fury like a woman scorned"?'

Mirabelle's beautiful face did not move a muscle; her eyes, staring at the barrister, did not blink. After a moment she said disdainfully, 'Of course.'

'Is it not true that you were, in fact, the mistress of Oswald Golding before his marriage to Mrs Golding and that, when you were discarded, you vowed to make him pay for his treatment of you?'

Mirabelle allowed herself a cuttingly contemptuous glance at Oswald, which was more effective than any ranting or raving. 'How utterly ridiculous and insulting that suggestion is. I have never been Mr Golding's mistress, and it shows the worth of the man that he can claim such a thing in order to discredit me and, ultimately, the truth about his poor wife. My husband and I were friends of Mr Golding, as I have explained, and our group of friends spent a great deal of time in each other's company. A "falling-out" such as you have insinuated would not have been tenable. Any number of people can confirm this.'

'Not if the "falling-out" occurred at the same time as Mrs Golding's pregnancy and miscarriage. Obviously everything changed at that point, and Mr Golding claims he has been somewhat ostracized in later years.'

'Excuse me?' Mirabelle's voice was as sharp as a scalpel. 'Are you telling me that Mr Golding claims this imaginary relationship was happening at the time he was *married* to Mrs Golding? That he was committing adultery?'

The barrister, who had clearly been unhappy at being instructed to go down this line, cleared his throat. 'Yes.'

'Let me make one thing perfectly clear.' Mirabelle's eyes were flashing, but her voice was controlled and clear. 'My husband and I are deeply in love and have been from the day we met. This ostracism by Mr Golding's group of friends, which he speaks of, might well be true, but it is due purely to the nature of the man himself. He is a womanizer, a gambler and a drunkard. It is well known that he ill-treats his servants, is violent and is possessed of a fiendish temper, but when this abusive behaviour was seen to include his wife, even his friends could not stomach it.'

Again Mirabelle paused, drawing herself up, and with her voice holding an unmistakable ring of truth she declared, 'Mr Oswald Golding is not a gentleman – not in any sense of the word. This has never been more obvious than in this courtroom. I came here today because of a great injustice, even though I was warned Mr Golding might well react like a savage dog does when it is cornered. Well, an animal might have the excuse of being led by primal instinct and not knowing any better, but a man with Mr Golding's education and breeding has no excuse whatsoever. Mr Golding is guilty of adultery, but not with me.'

'Damn you to hell, Mirabelle! You and the rest of those mealy-mouthed cretins!'

The barrister was now physically restraining Oswald as he fought to reach Mirabelle, a clerk of the court rushing to help, as the enraged man lashed out and caught the barrister with a resounding slap on the face, which echoed around the court.

Justice Cook had his work cut out to call the proceedings to order, such was the buzz of noise and excitement. And Jack, careless of Mr Havelock, leaned across and gripped Angeline's hand for a moment. 'Bless Myrtle and Albert,' he whispered. 'They took it upon themselves to go and see the Jeffersons, but the husband didn't want her to come today, worried about what might come out, I think. But she was magnificent, wasn't she?'

Yes, Mirabelle was magnificent. Angeline's gaze met Mirabelle's for a moment, and the redhead, although white-faced and showing strain for the first time, smiled at her. And so was Myrtle; dear, dear Myrtle. And there had also been Verity, and May, and other strong women whom she had met since escaping the asylum. Mrs Burns, the farmer's wife – where would she and May be right now, if she hadn't helped them? She had so many women to thank for making her into the person she was today; women who had touched her life briefly, like Verity, and others who were with her now.

She smiled back at Mirabelle, silently mouthing, 'Thank you.' Somehow Mirabelle had emerged with her reputation intact, and Angeline didn't begrudge her that, not for a moment. She didn't know what Oswald had done to make his onetime mistress hate him so fiercely, but it didn't matter. All that mattered was that there was now surely enough doubt in Justice Cook's mind to ensure that she wasn't dispatched herewith to another asylum.

Justice Cook waited for absolute silence before he spoke. Then, when you could hear a pin drop, he opened with, 'This case has deeply saddened me, but I cannot close my eyes to the fact that it is perhaps indicative of a great wrong in society that we have ignored for a long time. Greater and greater numbers of cases concerning marital violence and the maintenance of children are being dealt with each year. And, to our shame, as many as ten thousand maintenance or separation orders were called for last year. These parties could not, of course, remarry, and the women involved are often put in the most difficult situations. Whilst it is necessary to emphasize that matrimony is the most holy and noble of institutions, a case such as this one today begs the argument that a double standard of fidelity exists.'

He joined his fingers together, his stern gaze sweeping

the court and resting for a moment on Oswald, on whom it narrowed and became icy.

'The existing law supposes that a wife may condone her husband's lapses from strict marital propriety, while it imposes no such exercise of lenity or forbearance upon the husband. The reasons for this distinction abound: adultery by a wife is more serious, because she may conceive a child by her lover; a husband is humiliated if his wife yields to another man what belongs to him, whereas a wife is merely slighted in favour of a rival; and so on. An unfaithful wife's husband may sue the third party for monetary damages, but no wife can sue her husband's mistress.'

He now placed his hands palm-down on the bench, peering at the court. 'Mrs Golding will be granted a separation order, on the grounds of her husband's persistent cruelty, because I believe she attempted to report his assaults on her more than once, but this was ignored. Should Mr Golding decide to challenge this ruling, I would advise him to be very careful, in view of what we have heard today. And in view of the character of the man, which has been clearly revealed, I can only applaud Mrs Jefferson for having the courage of her convictions to do the right thing, with no thought for herself. Mr and Mrs Jefferson can leave this court with no stain on their character whatsoever. I fear the same cannot be said for Mr Golding.'

In spite of herself, Angeline's eyes were drawn to Oswald as Justice Cook spoke, and his maddened gaze met hers. She saw that Lord Argyle had his arm round his daughter, who was leaning into him and away from Oswald, and that the barrister was holding his bruised face, his back turned to his client.

Oswald's eyes sent her a message that made her stiffen, his face contorted and ugly. He didn't need to voice the threat, for the desire for vengeance was plain to read. She dragged her eyes away from his, shaken to the core.

*This was not over yet.*

# *Chapter Twenty-Nine*

Oswald had gained control of himself by the time he left the court, but as he watched Lord Argyle bundle the weeping Wilhelmina into a cab, he knew his hopes in that direction had been dealt a death-blow.

The earlier drizzle of rain had become a steady downpour, but he didn't move towards Randall and the stationary coach situated a little way down the road. He was waiting. For her. It was clear to him now that from the first time he had met Angeline she had been a blight on his life. He ground his teeth together, his barrister sweeping past him without so much as a by-your-leave.

Jumped-up little upstart! Oswald's lip curled. Eager enough to take his money, but as useless as the rest of them. And to accuse him of not revealing the full facts – whose side was he on, anyway? One thing was for sure, this so-called learned gentleman would wait till hell froze over before he got his fee. As for Angeline, his dear, dear wife . . .

He adjusted his top hat more securely on his head,

drips of rain running down his neck. She wouldn't win, not while he had breath in his body. He wouldn't rest until she was six feet under, and this time he would make sure there was no chance of her resurrecting herself. He'd see his day with her, and this time she would stay dead.

More folk left the building, and Oswald saw Randall jig the reins and bring the coach towards him. As it came closer, Angeline emerged from the courthouse in the middle of a throng of people. The Jeffersons weren't there, for they had been among the first to leave and had disappeared before Oswald had come outside, but he recognized Angeline's onetime maid, along with the nurse – Ramthorne or Ramshaw, or some such name – and Angeline's old governess. A man he took to be the maid's husband was holding the woman's arm, and the solicitor and his clerk were talking animatedly with Angeline. Everyone appeared elated. Oswald's teeth ground together again. He'd wipe the smiles off their faces. Scum, the lot of them.

He saw Angeline hesitate as she caught sight of him, but then the solicitor's clerk with whom Oswald had had the run-in, when he had gone to the offices in Newcastle, urged her on.

Oswald stepped forward, deliberately blocking their path, and as he did so Angeline stopped again, and this time so did everyone else. 'Think you've got the better of me, don't you?' He glared at Angeline, his fists bunched at his side. 'I'll make sure you rue this day, if it's the last thing I do.'

It was Jack who said, 'Get out of our way.'

'Listen, boy, I could buy and sell you a hundred times over, so don't try and tell me what to do.'

'Jack, please, leave him. Albert, go and get a court official.' Angeline caught hold of Jack's arm, seeing the fury in his face. 'Jack, he's not worth it.'

Oswald's eyes narrowed. 'Jack, is it? So that's it? Reverting to type, are you? They say water finds its own level, and scum settles with scum.'

'I'm warning you—' Jack never had time to finish what he was going to say, because with a roar Oswald sprang at him, taking him by surprise. It was pure instinct – and Jack's nimbleness – that saved him from being felled to the floor, because if the blow Oswald had launched had reached its target, it was doubtful Jack could have withstood it. Certainly his jaw would have been broken. But Jack was lighter and slimmer, added to which he had been brought up in a district where most disputes were settled with the fists from an early age. Ducking so that the blow merely glanced off his shoulder, he came back at the heavier man with a punch worthy of the boxers at the Michaelmas Fair.

Oswald staggered backwards, his feet sliding out from under him on the wet, slippery pavement, and ended up in an undignified heap sprawled in the gutter. For a moment he appeared stunned, but then, as Randall came to his aid, helping him to his feet, he let loose a tirade that would have caused a sailor to blush, shaking off his coachman's hand as he did so.

Albert and the court official came running, along with a constable who had been attracted by the commotion and the screams of the ladies. Mr Havelock was restraining Jack, and the other three were holding onto Oswald when he suddenly became quiet, muttering, 'All right, all right, take your hands off me. I was provoked, damn it! Can't you see that? Let me go, I say.'

The constable had caught the gist of what had gone on from Mr Havelock, and it was he who now said, 'I suggest you go home, Mr Golding. Straight home. Do you understand me? Otherwise I shall be forced to escort you to the station. And we don't want that, do we, sir?'

The constable and the court official escorted Oswald to his carriage, standing in front of the group on the pavement as the coach trundled off in the pouring rain. Angeline was as white as a sheet at the ugliness of the scene, and Miss Robson had needed smelling salts from Nurse Ramshaw when the fighting was over. Among the women, it was only Myrtle who appeared relatively unperturbed, and she summed up what the men were thinking when she said, 'Well, he's had that coming for a long, long time, and he couldn't have landed in a more suitable place than the gutter.'

Jack chuckled, putting his arm round Angeline's waist, careless of those present. He wasn't prepared to hide how he felt about this glorious woman at his side for one minute more. 'He's beaten, and he knows it. He did his worst in court, and it backfired beautifully. He won't dare show his face around these parts again.'

Angeline said nothing. It wasn't the moment. But she knew, as surely as night follows day, that Oswald was more dangerous now than he had ever been. And now that he had an inkling about Jack and her, it wasn't only her own safety she was concerned about. From this day forth she would never know a moment's peace. Jack and Mr Havelock could count today as a victory, but she knew she hadn't won. She shivered, the memory of Oswald's enraged eyes clear in her mind. The war would go on until one of them ceased to draw breath, or until he accomplished what he had tried to do when he had her locked away – and really sent her mad this time. Because how could she live, looking over her shoulder every moment of every day for the rest of her life, without losing her mind?

'All right, my love?' Jack had noticed her silence and now he drew her round to face him, his gaze on her face. 'What is it? You're not still worried about Golding, are you? We have the separation, and I tell you now I shall not rest until you are legally divorced from that fiend. You are not alone. You have me. Forever and ever.' He kissed her and then tucked her arm in his, and as a group they walked away from the courthouse, with the others talking amongst themselves.

Yes, she had Jack. She hugged the thought to her. And her dear friends, her job, her little home. And she wasn't the young, silly girl she had been when she met Oswald Golding. She was a woman now – a woman who had carved a new life for herself against all the odds, a good life.

A coach drove past them and immediately her eyes flashed to the window before she realized it wasn't the Golding crest on the side of the door. She sighed, the sound inaudible, at the realization that she could talk to herself till the cows came home, but the fact was that Oswald would forever be the shadow at her elbow from now on, an evil presence that would haunt her day and night. She just had to learn to live with it. She had no other choice.

Oswald found it difficult to sit in the coach, so great was his rage. The humiliation he had endured in court had been compounded by his ignominious defeat at the hands of the man he now believed to be Angeline's lover. She had dared to sit there, acting as pure as the driven snow and looking as tragic as any wronged heroine in a novel, when all the time she had been sporting with a damned clerk. At least Mirabelle had class, much as he would like to get his hands round her pretty little neck and squeeze till her eyes popped.

They were passing an inn, and now he yelled at Randall to stop the coach. Leaving the coachman outside in the pouring rain, he entered the public house and found a seat near the roaring fire, ordering a bottle of whisky from the buxom barmaid. When he left the premises over an hour later the bottle was empty and he staggered slightly as he climbed into the coach, swearing and cursing at Randall as the coachman helped him into his seat.

The rain had eased, and as they left the town the sun came out, touching the newly washed countryside with the mellow golden light that precedes the onset of dusk. They passed meadows gilded with the yellow blooms of buttercups, horse-chestnuts displaying their spiky blossom amid great fan-like leaves and creating a vivid patchwork of green and white. Overhead the skylarks soared joyously in the heavens. Inside the coach Oswald sat in drunken moroseness, muttering foul obscenities and occasionally rousing himself to shout and swear at Randall when the coach bumped over a pothole or two.

The massive gates into the estate were open when they reached it, and as the carriage bowled along the gravelled drive, Oswald sat up straighter. His anger had not abated one jot; rather it had been fuelled by the amount of alcohol he'd poured down his throat. The desire to hurt something, or someone, was so strong he could taste it. On reaching the forecourt, he flung open the carriage door and descended, glaring at Randall as the coachman made to drive off. 'Where the hell are you going?'

'To the stables, sir.' Randall recognized the signs and kept his voice even, knowing that in this mood the master would pick on the slightest inflexion to accuse him of being insubordinate.

'Get someone else to see to the horses. I'm going shooting, and you're accompanying me.'

'Me, sir?' It wasn't unusual for the master to go and

kill a few birds and rabbits, and maybe the odd deer, when he was in a temper, but normally the gamekeeper had to put up with his curses and snarling when he missed a target. 'You don't want me to inform Brodie that you need him?'

'If I wanted that, wouldn't I have said so, you fool? I'm not waiting for Brodie – it'll be dark soon, dammit. Now do as you're damned well told.'

'Shall I change, sir?' Randall glanced down at his livery.

'Not unless you want my boot up your backside.' Oswald strode into the house, shouting for Palmer to fetch his guns from the gun cabinet. Within minutes the two men were tramping the grounds of the estate, Randall in his coachman's regalia and Oswald equally unsuitably attired in the formal clothes and shoes he had worn for the court appearance.

Randall was carrying the guns and heavy canvas bags for the kill, skidding and sliding in places where the sticky mud made the ground slippery in their inappropriate footwear. Ahead of him, Oswald continued to turn the air blue with descriptions of what he would do to Angeline when he got the chance. Randall, who wasn't easily shocked, having been coachman to Oswald for years, felt defiled just listening to it. He had watched the young mistress – as he still thought of Angeline – outside the court as she had faced the master, and had seen the fear and dread in her face. And she had good reason to fear him, Randall told himself. The master was quite capable of buying the services of ne'er-do-wells to do his dirty work for him; he wouldn't think twice about having the mistress and this clerk fella done in.

Oswald lurched and then fell heavily, striking Randall's hand away when the coachman tried to assist him, and breathing fire and damnation as he hauled himself unsteadily to his feet once more. They were now some way from the back of the house, but had not made for the usual, more straightforward route to the fields and woodland where the shooting would take place. Randall had known better than to query this, however, and had simply followed his drunken master, inwardly swearing as his livery had become more and more dirty. It would take his wife hours to get the stains out, he was thinking, when suddenly the sound of breaking wood, followed by a shriek and the master disappearing from view, brought him up short.

He didn't need to think about what had happened, for the stench that hit him was answer enough. The master had fallen into one of the cesspits that this part of the grounds, at the back of the building, contained. The cesspits were specially dug holes to accept the human excreta from the house via channels that dropped away some twenty feet deep, with an access point covered with a lid of wood. A well-built cesspit, as these were, could last for more than two or three years without having to be emptied, being well lined with stone and brick. Clearly the cover of this one, however, had perished and become rotten, without anyone noticing.

Randall walked gingerly to the edge of the pit, the smell nearly choking him as he peered down into the foul depths. Oswald must have gone right under the mass of rotting, gassy excrement and urine, because his hair and face were black as he floundered and trod the obnoxious mass in an effort not to sink again, coughing and spitting as he called out, 'Get me out of here, damn you. I'm suffocating.'

Randall looked behind him and saw, buried in the grass and mud, the long wooden ladder that the scavengers used when they came to empty the cesspits – one man going down into the depths and filling a tub by immersing it in the excrement, which two of his comrades would then haul up and carry, suspended on a pole, to their cart. It was a dangerous and unpopular job. Scavengers were reported to suffer from suffocation from the gases, a wide range of illnesses and sometimes temporary blindness. Smelling the full force of the cesspit now, Randall could understand why.

He had actually bent down to pick up the ladder when he froze, a picture of his brother's mutilated face searing the screen of his mind, followed by a hundred and one other degrading, shaming incidents that he had been forced to watch, or endure himself, over the years. And he thought of this latest incident with the mistress – as kind and as bonny a lass as you could wish to meet.

Straightening slowly, he walked back to the edge of the cesspit, where the smell and gases made his eyes begin to water. Oswald was clawing at the sides of the pit, which were slimy and foul, in a vain effort to get a handhold, and Randall watched him for a moment before he said, his voice deep and throaty, 'Don't like it much down there, do you, sir?'

'What?' Oswald was choking and gasping, his voice rasping. 'Get a ladder down here, man.'

'You remember me brother, sir? Toby by name, but of course you wouldn't know his name. We're not even human beings to you, are we? But you might recall what you did to him, even if you don't remember his name, cos you took his eye out with your whip. Handsome fella he was, our Toby, and just sixteen years old when you maimed him for life. Walking out with a lass from the village, he was, but she couldn't stomach how he looked after, and upped and married someone else. Hard for the lad to take.'

'Shut up about your damned brother and help me.' Oswald was wheezing now, a note of panic in his voice.

'I don't think I will, sir, if it's all the same to you. In fact, I think you're exactly where it's fitting for you to meet your end, covered in filth and human muck. You've dished enough of the same out in your time, haven't you?'

There was a horrible gurgle as Oswald must have swallowed some of the putrid sludge, and then a mad thrashing and animal whimpering.

The smell was making Randall gag and he moved away from the edge of the pit, walking back a few yards and listening to the cries and strangled pleas and curses, as he shut his eyes and lifted up his face to the sun. After a while the sounds became weaker. And eventually there was a silence, broken only by the cooing of wood pigeons in the distance.

Randall waited for another thirty minutes because, although he did not regret what he had done, he couldn't stomach looking down into the bowels of the pit once more to make sure the master was dead. Then he slowly bent down and reached for the guns and walked back the way he had come, breaking into a run as he neared the back of the house. Bursting into the kitchen, he frightened the cook and kitchen maids witless, shouting frantically, 'Help! Get help! The master's fallen into one of the cesspits!'

The news report about the landowner, Mr Oswald Golding, who had drowned 'monstrously in the household's excrement' was talked about for weeks, until another, more worthy news item took its place in local gossip. The inquiry into the tragic accident ascertained that a number of events had led up to the incident. The deceased had been drinking heavily in the hours before the accident occurred – a local barmaid testifying that Mr Golding had consumed a whole bottle of whisky in the public house in which she worked, and had been unsteady on his feet when he left the premises. On arriving home, he had apparently insisted that his coachman – rather than his gamekeeper, who knew every inch of the estate and would most certainly have directed Mr

Golding away from the area of the cesspits – accompany him on a shooting exercise. The cesspit into which the unfortunate Mr Golding fell had a decaying wooden top through which he had dropped and, being twenty feet or so down, he had had no chance of climbing out without assistance. By the time the coachman had run to the house to fetch help, the deceased had breathed his last, suffocated by the fumes. A ladder had been hidden in overgrown grass and nettles, which the coachman had not seen, although the inquiry stressed that no blame could be attached to the man because of this. Indeed, the amount of alcohol Mr Golding had imbibed was most likely the prime cause of the accident, making him careless and unwary, and possibly more easily overcome, once he had fallen. Here the coroner had remarked in an aside that he certainly hoped this was the case anyway; the thought of a man thrashing about and slowly suffocating in such foul conditions was the stuff of which nightmares were made. Such a grisly end one wouldn't wish on one's worst enemy . . .

Angeline heard the news the day after it had happened, when the police traced her through Mr Havelock and came to the house early in the morning, accompanied by the solicitor, who had insisted that he come along, and Jack. Sickened and appalled, she had sat with Mr Havelock and Jack on either side of her and struggled to take in the horror of what she was hearing. For anyone – even Oswald – to die in such a macabre way was unthinkable.

But it had happened, and once the shock had worn off, it began to dawn on her that she was free. Free in a way she could never have been if Oswald was alive. And then she felt terribly guilty for thinking in such selfish terms.

After going through a whole sequence of emotions over a period of days, she made her peace with herself and God, and allowed herself to look to the future. A future that had been made miraculously free of the dark shadow of Oswald Golding. Not that she would have wished him to die in such a way – not even him, evil and manipulative as he was. But neither was she going to be hypocritical and pretend that she would have wished him back, if she could.

Shocking though most people would have found it, Jack proposed to her once he could see that she had worked through her feelings. He had been her rock and support since the court case, but he hadn't rushed her, knowing it was important that she came to a place where she had fully let go of the past, especially now that Oswald had met the end he had.

So it was that, on a long hot June day, with towering elms and oaks casting heavy shadows over leaf-bound lanes, they cycled out to their favourite meadow once again for a Sunday spent together, away from the rest of the world. They found the meadow without any trouble, clover and bird's-foot trefoil and forget-me-nots starring the thick green grass, and clusters of creamy-white bloom covering the dogwood and elder at the edges of their little retreat. And it was here, after a picnic lunch filled with soft murmurings and laughter and whispered words of love, that Jack took her hands in his.

Gazing into his clear green eyes, Angeline knew what he was going to say, and she trembled at the wonder of it. 'Marry me, my darling?' he asked softly. 'Be my wife, the mother of my children? Grow old with me while we love each other and make every day better than the one before it? I love you with all my heart, and I swear I will make you happier than any woman has ever been before.'

It needed no thought. 'Yes, please,' she said softly, before surprising him as she flung herself into his arms, causing them both to overbalance and fall back into the lush carpet of flowers at their feet. 'Yes, yes, yes – forever yes.'

There was no need for further words, for the language of love said it all.

## *Chapter Thirty*

The wedding took place at the tiny parish church a short walk away from Garden Street the week before Christmas. It was a very quiet occasion, with just Myrtle and Albert and their children, May and Howard and their bouncing twin baby girls, and Mr Havelock and his wife attending. The couple had wanted it that way. After the short ceremony, when everyone said how lovely Angeline looked in a dress of ivory lace, they all went back to Garden Street, where Angeline had prepared a lavish wedding breakfast.

It was a happy day, a day full of laughter and joy, and little children squealing as they played. And afterwards, once everyone had gone, Jack held her in their big, soft bed and took her to heaven and back. For the first time Angeline understood how wonderful a man's lovemaking could be, and that night healed so many wounds that she cried happy tears in Jack's arms.

Jack moved into the house in Garden Street on the day of the wedding, and they enjoyed several joy-filled weeks before Angeline received an official-looking letter from the Golding solicitors. It stated that the estate and the London property had now been sold and, after Oswald's massive debts were settled, she was entitled to several hundred pounds, as the sole beneficiary of the will that Mr Appleby had insisted be made, upon her marriage to Oswald years before.

Amazed and pleased, they decided to invest the money in a small property in the heart of Newcastle, which would serve both as a family home and an office, where Jack could at long last set up as a solicitor among the people he had always dreamed of helping. They would work together, with Angeline employing her shorthand and typing skills and Jack his law degree, taking enough cases on behalf of clients who could afford to pay for their services to finance those who hadn't two farthings to rub together, but who desperately needed their help.

They didn't expect to become rich, but neither of them desired that. It was enough to be together, joined in heart and purpose among the rough, salt-of-the-earth folk they admired and respected. There were so many women and children ill-used by the system and by their menfolk – the silent ones who were at their wits' end: wives who were regularly used as punch-bags, whose youth and looks had fled before they were thirty; children who were prostituted or made to work in the factories or rope works, and other such places, when they should have been at school; men who received a pittance for the long, hard work they did and were treated no better than dogs by their employers. The list was endless, and Jack and Angeline knew they couldn't help them all, but in their small corner of the world they might be able to make a difference. If nothing else, they had to try.

Mr Havelock, purely with their best interests at heart, told them they were setting themselves up for disappointment and heartache. He was right about the heartache. To see folk struggling with the unending cycle of poverty was both humbling and depressing for Angeline. The stillbirths and attempts at back-street abortions; the suicides that were never reported because no one cared enough; the unemployment and total monopoly of power by those in any kind of authority – these were real and harsh. And the fear, not so much of death, but of the stigma of the workhouse. Originally intended as a deterrent, the workhouses had been only too successful in that role. Working people would accept almost any privation rather than enter that dreaded place. This made them vulnerable to exploitation, and the mine and factory owners, the landed gentry and the wealthy and influential made full use of the fact.

Angeline's eyes were opened to much in the first year of working with Jack in their new home and, but for his reassurance that the processes of change were happening, albeit slowly, she might well have lost heart. But she didn't. Instead she developed a passion for the folk around them that was every bit as fierce as her husband's. While the Boer War raged and Britain, the Western European states, the United States of America and even Japan divided up a large part of the world between themselves as colonies, Angeline and Jack fought their own war against blind acceptance of injustice and pauperism.

Jack began to win most of his cases for the underdog, and Angeline pioneered a scheme whereby a large group of women in the surrounding area, whose husbands were in prison, unemployed, too ill to work or had simply deserted their families, nominated one of their members to stay at home and take care of everyone's children, while the rest of them worked, free of worry about their offspring. This took a while to put into action, partly because of the widely held view that a woman's place was in the home and her duty was to look after her own children – even if it meant the family starving – and because many of the women had no confidence or belief in their own worth. But at the end of their first year of marriage, both Angeline and Jack had had it confirmed in a hundred different ways that they were exactly where they should be, doing exactly what they should be doing.

On the evening of their anniversary Angeline cooked a special meal for the two of them in her little kitchen, and Jack closed the office – which was the front room of the house – early. He was in a buoyant mood as he came through to the back of the house and saw Angeline stirring something at the range. He looked at her, so beautiful and warm and sweet, and then his gaze moved around his home. Everything looked shining and mellow in the light from the oil lamps and the glow from the range. Angeline had sewn bright yellow-and-blue curtains for the window, full and generous, and they matched the blue willow-patterned china on the oak dresser and the huge shop-bought rug that covered half of the stone slabs. Even their two comfy easy chairs set at an angle to the range blended in, Angeline having made loose covers for them with the same material she had used for the curtains. He loved this room, and he loved his wife. His smile widened as she turned and noticed him, giving a little start as she scolded, 'You made me jump – creeping up like that.'

'Sorry.' He crossed the room and lifted her off the floor with his hug, kissing her until she was breathless and laughing. 'What's for dinner, wench? Something smells good.'

'Stuffed roast breast of lamb, and Durham pudding with cream to follow,' Angeline said, extricating herself from his arms, 'and this gravy will burn, if I don't stir it.'

'Blow the gravy!' He whisked the pan off the stove and put it on the steel shelf at the side of the range to keep warm, ignoring her protests. 'Come and sit down a minute, I've got some good news on our anniversary.'

Her eyes bright, Angeline sat down at the kitchen table, which was already set for their evening meal, the blue-bordered cloth and plump red earthenware pot holding four hyacinths, which were just coming into bloom, satisfying her home-making instincts. She didn't think she had ever felt as happy as she did this night. So happy that she could burst with the joy of it.

Jack sat down on a chair beside her, taking her hands in his. 'I've done the accounts for the last little while, Mrs Connor,' he said, a lilt in his voice, 'and you know how we said we'd be thrilled if we even broke even, in the beginning?'

Angeline nodded. They had kept a little money by, after buying the house and setting up the business, knowing that it would take a while for Jack to build up his reputation and recognizing that, with their desire to take as many non-paying clients as paying ones, money would be tight.

'Well, my love, we've made a profit. A small one, admittedly, and it wouldn't have been enough to live on, but the good news is that the profit's all been made in the last three months, which means we're on the up and up. I've a big case for Foster's, the butchers, in January, and that will mean a very nice deposit into our bank account to start the new year. What do you think of that? I never expected things to be this good so early on. We're going to make a go of this, my sweet; the writing's on the wall – or in black-and-white in the accounts, which is even better. You're looking at a successful solicitor.'

'I'm looking at more than that.' Angeline had some news of her own, which she had known for some days, but had wanted to keep for their anniversary.

Jack smiled at the excitement in her voice, but his eyes were puzzled. 'Come again?'

'I'm looking at a father.' And when he stared at her

blankly, she giggled. 'I'm expecting a baby. You're going to be a fa—'

She didn't get any further. Jack gave a whoop of elation, whisking her up and dancing her round the kitchen until she was giddy and begging him to stop. Then he pulled her close, smothering her face in kisses as he murmured over and over again, 'A bairn. Oh, lass, lass – a bairn. Just when I thought life couldn't get any better. I'm going to be a da. A *da*. Can you believe that?'

Angeline smiled, her face alight at his reaction. It was everything she had dreamed of and more. She reached up and cradled his dear face in her hands. 'Yes, I can believe it, Jack Connor,' she whispered tenderly. 'And you're going to be the best da in the world.'

'I love you, lass.'

'And I love you, so very much.'

The veil of tears that had shrouded her for so long had been ripped in two, and beyond it lay a bright future filled with love. It was a new beginning.